Developing the imagination one might expect of a fantasy author, Guernsey writer N.K. Harrison has always loved creating stories. Studying business, media and film at A Level but finding her ideal career in the travel industry, alongside writing novels, Nicki runs her own business as a travel counsellor.

Her travels and experiences strengthened her love for creating immersive characters and unique worlds, hoping to take readers on the only type of journey she cannot create in her day job. Supported by husband, Shaun, family and friends (and of course the dogs), Nicki hopes that her writing will provide a fresh escapism for every fantasy lover.

For my 'beta' readers

Thank you for all your support when turning this world from pure imagination to a real creation.

THE ENCIA TRILOGY

N.K. Harrison

THE WITHERING

BOOK 1

Enjoy the escapism

Harrison

AUSTIN MACAULEY PUBLISHERS™

LONDON * CAMBRIDGE * NEW YORK * SHARJAH

A CIP catalogue record for this title is available from the British Library.

ISBN 9781398489424 (Paperback)
ISBN 9781398489431 (ePub e-book)

www.austinmacauley.com

First Published 2023
Austin Macauley Publishers Ltd®
1 Canada Square
Canary Wharf
London
E14 5AA

For putting up with my endless hours of typing, editing, reading aloud, myriad of questions and reading this story more than anyone else, my deepest thanks goes to my husband, Shaun. Thank you for encouraging me at every step on this journey to become a published author. I also give my heartfelt thanks to my parents for their unabated support throughout.

To my friends Kerrie and Becky, the dedication hopefully says it all but honestly, your support really gave me the confidence to get this story from the realms of my mind to the page and then from the page to the publisher. I also wish to thank Danielle and Brittany whose early feedback sparked my desire to continue improving the story until reaching this final version.

When thinking about what inspired me to create this story, there are too many authors, creators and writers to name, but I must mention one. Since my early teenage years, I have grown up with and loved several of the *Final Fantasy* series, created by Tetsuya Nomura and developed by Square Enix. If there was ever a franchise that made me treasure escapism into fantasy and want to create my own, it is those stories.

Lastly, but by no means least, I want to thank my colleague and fellow author, James Angell. Thank you for introducing me to the team at Austin Macauley who have offered me this wonderful opportunity.

Table of Contents

Prologue

As he knelt in the water, cradling her body, Harrison Stone's mind reeled. How had it all gone so wrong? The water beneath him, purified of toxic Encia, was instead darkened by blood. He battled against the memories, training at the academy, studying world history and the recent horrors humanity had both caused and endured; but at just twenty years old, nothing, not even the adversity he'd faced from his father could've prepared him for this.

Twenty-five years ago, a war known as the Uprising ravaged the world, creating soldiers and ruthless leaders like his father, as well as no shortage of rumour and deceit. The Uprising had begun out of pure envy and caused the near extinction of an entire race, the Ar'encal. Once a wise and gifted race, they were now little more than slaves and a cautionary tale to anyone that attempted to support them.

Several years before the war, it was discovered that not only were the Ar'encal immune to Encia, which if consumed by an average person would lead them to suffer a fatal illness known as 'the withering' but they also developed magical abilities. Human scholars, naturally curious, soon flocked to their lands, in hopes of discerning how something harmful to the other races could empower one.

While the scholars were invited in by the Ar'encal, the human leaders established a collaboration with the deep-dwelling Terrans, a race of stout, stubborn people, and gifted engineers. Choosing to live beneath the mountains, the Terrans were often nicknamed the 'Stone-folk'. Over time, their partnership successfully manufactured a device to purify the water and this outcome led to a long-standing peace between the races.

In the meantime, the Ar'encal and the scholars that joined them became reclusive, living isolated lives in the deep forests scattered across the world. It wasn't long before intimate bonds were formed, resulting in cross-race children. Had the story ended there, Harrison would've been proud of humanity, but it didn't.

These children, like the Ar'encal, proved resistant to Encia but otherwise appeared entirely human, and initially possessed no magical abilities. It was discovered it took a stressor for the children to wield magic, and the power they could harness was linked to that stressor. Those who did trigger abilities were labelled mages.

Divided into two distinct dominions, humanity became more fractured as time went on. In the Eastern Kingdom of Carlisse, the ruling monarchy focused on aiding the mage scholars while to the West, the Siranor Imperium, led by an elected Imperator focused on scientific discoveries. Before long, the goal of both dominions veered away from the quest for enhanced human preservation, to one of power. The situation became volatile under the last Imperator, Joseph Rainer when his brother and head-scholar, Dr Elias Rainer became obsessed with wielding magic. He caused several arguments with the Ar'encal leaders and uncertainty soon spread. It wasn't long before they asked him and his supporters to leave their lands.

Insinuating they were concealing the true nature of their abilities, Dr Rainer encouraged his brother to join forces with the Carlisse Kingdom, becoming a dominant military force and threaten the Ar'encal, who were by no means prepared for conflict. With magic at their disposal, the Ar'encal were able to withstand; until Imperator Rainer enlisted the aid of their Terran allies.

Learning about the atrocities of the war solidified Harrison's opinion; it was a sad time in history when their combined might decimated the Ar'encal in just under a year. After the war, the Terrans returned to their sprawling cities deep within the mountains, leaving the land above to the rulers of Carlisse and Siranor.

While Carlisse focused on devaluing the Ar'encal and their mage offspring, living in a defined societal hierarchy where the royal family had supreme governance, Siranor became technologically advanced and encouraged mage hatred. Looking the same as humans, mages proved difficult to identify, those with powers doing all they could to conceal them and avoid persecution. Their efforts led to the Imperator introducing 'mage hunts' aimed at seeking them out, and these ruthless hunts persist to the present day, even after the death of Imperator Rainer.

Harrison hated the thought of hunting innocent people but against his better judgement accepted that with no reliable knowledge of the magical abilities they could trigger, mages could be a threat. None of that mattered now though. He was a warden. He was meant to guard people, to protect them from harm. He'd failed. Where had it all gone wrong?

Chapter One
Warden Academy

The Warden Academy could be a cold and dreary place, but what could you expect from a converted fortress that was a stronghold during the war? Despite the never-ending dull granite hallways and creaky wooden floorboards, Harrison felt at home within the hulking edifice. The halls were mostly dark, apart from the windowed alcoves that let in natural light. Sitting in those alcoves could be rather pleasant, especially on summer days, or at least Harrison thought so. Today was his rest day and he had a simple goal, to find a spot and lose himself in a good book.

Located on the outskirts of Tivani, his hometown, the Warden Academy was the largest of the four training facilities on the Western Continent. Students enrolled to become wardens undertook four years of intense training to graduate. Now in his third year, Harrison should've used his free time to head into town and visit his friends and family, but with the year-end assessments looming, his training regime had become more intense and the thought of walking forty-five minutes there and back did not appeal. He'd need an excuse to tell his mother, she'd miss him the most, but he'd think of something.

After completing the third year of training, warden students could get transferred to one of the speciality facilities by the tutors, if they showed particular promise. Harrison hoped to stay at the Tivani academy however and knew he could make up the lack of visits to his mother if he did. At seventeen, Harrison and his twin sister Siljanna both enrolled at the warden academy in an attempt to impress their father. It was hard to believe three years had passed since they began training and he'd first walked over those creaky floorboards.

Unlike the floors, Harrison had changed a lot over the years. When he'd begun training, he was an awkward teenager with floppy brown hair, the hints of auburn matching his warm brown eyes and lightly tanned skin. Back then, his hair was always just a little too long, curling at the base of his neck and he was slightly overweight. Once he committed to training however, he lost all the excess weight, replacing it with a solid, muscular build and grew a few inches, leaving him at just over six-feet-tall now. He made sure to cut his hair regularly, choosing a tapered style that was cropped on the sides but left signs of his natural curl on top, the main trait he'd inherited from his mother. It was a simple style but it suited his angular facial features and was complemented by his neat stubble beard.

Just as Harrison found the ideal perch and got stuck into the next chapter of his book, Morgan, his roommate, appeared from around the corner and headed towards him.

"Iley Harrison, avoiding the family again? One day, your mum's not going to buy whatever excuse you come up with, you know. But don't worry, when that day comes, I'll be sure to comfort her!" Morgan mocked, flashing a perfect grin and winking as Harrison grunted theatrically.

Morgan and Harrison had become quick friends when they met on the first day of training. With an athletic build, copper skin and cropped black hair, Morgan was a good-looking guy and slightly taller than Harrison. Most of the girls swooned over him, affectionately giving him a variety of nicknames. Although their comments inflated his ego, he always turned them down, saying his heart belonged to a *vision of beauty* 'namely, Harrison's mother, Anora.

Morgan had only gotten to know her because his own family lived in the small country town of Niyati, to the far south and he couldn't visit easily, so often spent his free time with Harrison's friends and family instead. Morgan would spend hours dreaming of Anora's silky auburn hair and rich brown eyes while enduring Harrison's ridicule. Despite his bravado and odd crush, Morgan was a down-to-earth, decent guy that Harrison had a lot of time for.

"Morgan, it hurts you think I'd do such a thing... and good luck getting past my father should you ever act upon your little crush. He's not well known for sharing," Harrison chuckled, just thinking of Morgan trying to confront his father. "Anyway, what's up? Shouldn't you be in combat training? We both know you need it!" Harrison continued, returning his friend's cheeky grin and receiving a punch to the arm as a result.

"Yeah, yeah whatever, I'll show you how much training I need the next time we spar. I'm only here to pass on a message, tormenting you is a bonus," Morgan jested. "Tutor Anderson wants to see you in his office as soon as possible; so get moving, you know how he can be!"

"Okay, will do," Harrison said lowering his book reluctantly.

"See you later mate, and don't forget to mark your page," Morgan suggested, pointing at the book. "I don't think you'll be getting any more reading done today."

As Morgan jogged off down the hall, Harrison looked at his book, sighed, and marked the page before heading to Anderson's office. He should've known it was too good to be true, having the afternoon off with nothing to do. Tutor Anderson was one of the toughest at the academy but was also Harrison's favourite. A no-nonsense guy, he wouldn't beat around the bush so if he needed to see Harrison on his rest day, it was likely something important.

To get to the tutor offices from the halls of the dormitory, he made his way down a winding staircase and passed the quad; a large, open-air social space filled with plants and shrubs. The quad connected the training centre, dormitory, library and tutor offices to the main fortress gate. Beyond the fortress were several vast fields and dense woodlands with logging cabins that were used mainly for storage.

The shrubs and trees in the quad were all in full bloom but at the epicentre was a large magnolia tree. It had become tradition for students to hang a small glass bottle on one of the branches after they graduated but it was only when he studied the tree, Harrison realised how few trainees had come through the academy and actually graduated. He didn't count them but in just a year's time, he was determined to increase the number of bottles adorning those branches.

Although he'd joined the warden academy in an attempt to please his father, he'd stayed because becoming a warden was to dedicate your life to protecting people, something he genuinely wanted to do. As he turned for the tutor offices, the hallways became dark again. It would be almost impossible to see if there weren't oil lamps on the walls, guiding through the maze of hallways. After a few wrong turns which he still made after all this time, he was in front of a large wooden door with 'Tutor Anderson' carved into it at eye-level. He knocked before entering.

"Sir, you requested to see me?" He asked, pushing past the heavy door and letting it shut behind him.

Tutor Anderson stood behind a large maple desk facing the bookshelves that lined the back wall. He was dressed in thick leather armour, his favoured compound bow resting on the far side of the desk. He held a letter, one he'd clearly read more than once.

"Harrison, thank you for coming so swiftly. I received word this morning that your father, Commander Stone has requested a formal visit to the academy. He wishes to be involved in the assessments of all third-year students. Did you know about this?" He asked, trying to make his voice sound curious rather than agitated.

"No sir, but perhaps he's creating an opportunity to assess Siljanna. He's always been highly invested in my sister's development," Harrison replied, then silently reprimanded himself for speaking freely with his superior.

Despite being his twin, Siljanna couldn't have been more different to Harrison. She had their father's ash-blonde hair, mossy green eyes and a pale complexion. She was tall like both of the boys in the family but otherwise mirrored their mother's petite build and was absolutely the apple of her father's eye.

"I thought you might say that. Siljanna is a remarkable student but shouldn't receive favouritism from the warden commander," Anderson replied and paused, making direct eye-contact with Harrison, revealing a frustration he rarely showed. "I don't like it… but there is little I can do." Anderson concluded as his brow furrowed while his gaze returned to the letter.

Harrison never thought any of the tutors, least of all Anderson noticed the way his father showed favouritism towards Siljanna but was secretly grateful for the acknowledgement.

"Is that why you wished to see me, sir? To ask about my father, or is there something else I can do?" Harrison enquired.

"Commander Stone expects all third-year students to take part in a series of trials and has asked me to recommend three of my most promising students to devise them. I assume he is expecting Siljanna to be selected," Anderson replied, hesitating.

It was a fair assumption. Despite already being Commander Stone's favoured child and trainee, Siljanna was incredibly bright, picking up the academic and physical elements of training easily and displayed a natural talent for tactics. Although several girls had come through the academy, it was often noted that none had Siljanna's prowess. She was the last female candidate in their training year too, making her stand out even more.

"That's understandable, sir," Harrison commented.

"But I'm not. I'm selecting Charlie, Dylan and you," Anderson announced, analysing Harrison's reaction.

"Sir, thank you," Harrison said, stumbling over his words, barely able to mask his surprise. "What are the requirements for the trials?"

"They can be team or individual based, of a physical or mental nature and you must be able to fairly participate in your own trial. Are you up to the challenge?" Anderson asked, his question sounding more like encouragement than doubt.

"Of course, sir. When do the details have to be prepared for?" Harrison replied, responding more eloquently.

Anderson looked up at him and grinned. He was a stocky, relatively short man, but what he lacked in height, he more than made up for in muscle mass. His smile was wonky but in itself was an endearing quality that made him all the more likeable.

"Commander Stone will be here in five days so please begin preparing and advise me of anything you require the tutors to arrange at least the day before. There is one final rule, you may not reveal any of the details to the other students. If you have no questions, you are dismissed."

Harrison nodded and headed out of the office towards the training centre. The meeting was much quicker than he expected but with this new challenge on his mind, he wanted to start planning straight away. He wondered how Siljanna would take the news that she hadn't been selected, then settled on *'not well'*. They were both intelligent and competitive but it was much more prominent in Siljanna. The only thing she hated more than losing was when people mispronounced her name, enunciating the 'j' in Siljanna rather than pronouncing it correctly as a 'y'.

Even with her fiery temperament and their competitive natures, Harrison and Siljanna had a better relationship than most siblings living in such close quarters. Despite winding each other up in training, it was clear they cared for one another, and they'd learnt to read each other in ways others couldn't, making them a dominant force in team-working sessions.

As Harrison approached the quad again, this time he noticed a few people picking herbs and flowers. One of the girls waved, calling him over. On his second glance, he realised it was his close friend Rylie Auren. Rylie and her family also lived in town and her parents owned the Hawk Eye tavern. It was a popular meeting place for many of the locals and Harrison and Siljanna had both befriended Rylie over the years. She was only a year younger than them and was training in medicine. The apothecary taught mostly from the school in Tivani so although they came to the academy for a few hours a week, she didn't live on-site like Harrison and the other warden trainees.

Heading towards her, Harrison noticed the other members of her group too. There were eight of them all together but he only recognised two others; Juliette and Ava, his ex-girlfriend. He'd dated Ava at sixteen for a rather intense three weeks until they both realised they weren't meant to be. She had an ardent quality that people often found arresting but had been a little too hot-headed for their relationship to last, and it resulted in them becoming awkward acquaintances. Juliette, as Ava's best friend, became cold, bullying anyone who liked him, but her tactics didn't work on Rylie.

The medical students had to wear hideous mint green jumpsuits that looked like potato sacks, but unlike the others, Rylie, who was average in height and had a curvy figure, managed to look good. Her long brown hair was tied back in her signature half-plaited ponytail, but if let loose would fall between her shoulder blades. Some of the lightly curled strands draped down the side of her face and her fringe was angled to one side, resting over her right eyebrow. Smiling in her usual, happy-go-lucky manner as he approached, Harrison had begun to notice Rylie in a different light but hadn't found the right way to tell her of his affections. While she remained unaware, they continued to be close friends.

"Ladies, to what do I owe the pleasure?" He greeted, his tone pleasant although avoiding eye-contact with Ava and Juliette. One of the girls he didn't know waved shyly before crouching down and rigorously checking the shrubs for something, while Juliette huddled the other girls, encouraging them to whisper and giggle at him. Rylie just rolled her eyes and laughed.

"We're supposed to be focusing on herbalism at the moment, finding natural sources to concoct tinctures and remedies. I suggested the quad would be a good place to find ingredients and the others were keen to come along, but now I realise it wasn't because of the herbs. Morgan and Dylan passed by earlier and that was the beginning of the end really," she teased, throwing a glance over at the huddled girls who only peered up when they thought Harrison wasn't looking.

"Any new nicknames for Morgan yet? The last one, *'black diamond'* was actually pretty good," he asked playfully.

"Don't encourage them!" She replied in jest. "Despite not fitting in with the popular girls, I like studying herbalism. Maybe one day I'll find a cure for Evie's headaches."

Rylie's little sister Evie had just turned twelve and was a lovely kid, but from a young age had suffered from nightmares, severe headaches and although rare, also endured seizures. Due to her condition, her parents Nate and Paige decided to home-school her, which had turned Evie into an introverted girl with few friends her own age. She never seemed to mind though and spent as much time as she could with her big sister, who she idolised, and Rylie adored her in return. She would do anything to make her little sister smile.

The whole Auren family were close, but at the same time, always left their door open to anyone in the community. Having an arduous relationship with his father, Harrison had called on them several times in the past and grown close to the family as a result. Rylie's father Nate in particular was liked by pretty much everyone in town, and it was only partly because he owned the best bar within fifty miles, while her mother Paige had become good friends with his mum Anora. Harrison could recall many evenings when his father was out of town, called to the capital as a *'military consultant,'* while he, Siljanna and their mum would stay for dinner with the Auren's, spending hours socialising, laughing and just being what he presumed a normal family felt like.

Smiling kindly at her, Harrison looked down and spotted Rylie had some peppermint, sage and valerian, among other things tucked in the various pockets of her apron. He assumed these would all be part of her next wave of remedies.

"I bet Evie would love that. I don't want to imagine how painful those headaches are. Tell her and your folks I said hello, and I'm sorry I haven't been back to town recently," he said.

"Of course, I will. Mum and dad are both fine, but Evie definitely misses you. She's had a good reprieve recently with no nightmares or headaches for a couple of weeks but I can't assume it's going to last; hence the herbs," she explained, looking down at her apron, formulating a plan of how to brew them.

"I miss her too. I promise to visit soon," Harrison replied, holding his hand up as if making a solemn swear.

"Hey isn't it your rest day today? What's the excuse for not going home this time?" She asked, trying to pull a judgemental face, but her tone gave away the fact she was just teasing him.

"Actually, the stringent Commander Stone is making a formal visit to the academy in a few days, and I've been selected to create one of three trials that all the third-year warden students will be assessed on. That's a compelling reason for not going home don't you think?" He replied playfully, sticking out his tongue.

"Wow, a good reason for a change!" She remarked with a chuckle. "So are you organising your own year-end assessment? I wish I could've been that lucky! We took our exams yesterday and I have no idea how mine went."

"I don't think it's giving me an edge if I'm honest," Harrison confessed with uncertainty. "If the trial is too easy, he'll mark me down. He'll probably do the same if it's too difficult and if I don't perform well enough. So, I've got to participate and clear all the trials but also make mine intricate, challenging yet achievable."

"That's no small feat, but Tutor Anderson is a tough nut to crack and he's picked you, Harrison," she reassured, placing a gentle hand on his shoulder.

"But you know nothing I ever do meets up to my father's lofty expectations. I guess you could say I'm already at a disadvantage because of our strenuous relationship," Harrison replied, doubting himself further.

"Try not to think like that. I've heard from Morgan how incredible you are in training. When your father assesses your trial, even he'll have to admit the wardens will be lucky to have you. Is there anything I can do to help?" She enquired, fidgeting with the herbs in her apron, making room for some camomile from a nearby planter. She gave the flower a quick sniff before placing it with the rest.

"You know, I think you've just given me an idea," he replied with a smile.

"What? How... what did I do?" She asked curiously.

"That's for me to know," he teased lightly.

"Fine Mr Cryptic! I'm glad I could help," she replied, her playful tone back again. Before re-joining the other medical students, she stopped and looked back at him. "Hey Harrison, I'm not going to forget that promise, you will visit soon, right? We'd all love to see you."

"Of course, and thanks for the idea Rylie," he replied, winding her up again. She was just about to retort, but instead rolled her eyes, gave him a smile and returned to the group.

Freshly inspired, Harrison made an about-face, heading to the library to iron out his plan and wondered if it would finally garner him some approval from his father. As a highly regarded man both locally and in the Imperial court, it was often debated by the academy trainees, who knew one day they could be reporting to Commander Sampson Stone, whether that regard came from his prominent military career, current position, or just his formidable, stoic nature.

During the Uprising, Sampson Stone was one of the most unrelenting fighters in the Imperial military. It was well-known his career only halted after he took a blow to the shoulder which never fully healed. His injury only prevented him from battling however and he quickly demonstrated a talent for tactics, dedicating his time to supporting the war effort with strategic advancements. This led to many within the Imperator's council to believe it was Sampson's efficient and ruthless strategies that enabled the Siranor armies to advance so quickly during the final stages of the conflict with the Ar'encal.

After the war, he committed to the mage hunt effort until requesting a role closer to home, to support his pregnant wife. That led to him becoming Warden Commander, the highest-ranking position they could offer outside of the military. Sampson took advantage of the opportunity and excelled, efficiently leading the wardens ever since. In fact, there wasn't anything Sampson didn't excel at when he set his mind to it, and he expected the same, if not more from his children.

Although Harrison had achieved much during training, proving he was particularly well versed in sword combat and leadership, his father always expected better. On the flip side, anything that Siljanna accomplished was exemplary in his estimation. This led to a case of hero-worship from Siljanna, who wanted nothing more than to follow in their father's footsteps, and resentment from Harrison, who quickly learnt he'd never be good enough. At times, this caused tension between the siblings but Harrison would always be the first to walk away, leaving Siljanna shouting after him, wanting to force him to agree with her opinion of their father. Luckily, it had been a while since they'd had such a confrontation and he hoped these trials wouldn't spark anything new.

The days passed quickly and soon it was just half a day before his father was due to arrive at the academy for the trials. Harrison was in the library, having given the detailed requirements for his trial to Tutor Anderson. He, Morgan, Charlie and Siljanna had decided to finish up the additional reading material for their final written exam, which would take place the day after the trials. Since she'd found out they were selected, Siljanna had spent all her free time with Harrison and Charlie, desperately trying to get hints about their trials. She'd never crack her brother but Charlie was a different story. He had a soft spot for Siljanna but knew his affection was unrequited.

Currently, Charlie's head was buried in the pages of his book, while Morgan appeared to have nodded off. After a carefully placed nudge to the table leg from Harrison, Morgan's arm propping his snoozing head slipped, jerking him back into consciousness. Siljanna and Harrison both laughed as he grunted but she quickly returned her attention to Charlie.

"So Charlie, any plans for the year-end break? Are you going to visit your family in Siranor?" She asked.

"Yes, I've got tickets booked on the train after the written exam. I'm looking forward to seeing my brother. He and his wife have just had a baby so I get to meet my new nephew too! How about you Sil, are you and Harrison going home for the holidays?" Charlie replied, returning her question.

"Absolutely, although it feels like the holidays are coming early with dad assessing the trials tomorrow," Siljanna admitted, unable to conceal her childish joy. "I'm so excited but just wish I had the opportunity to show off my skills by creating a trial like you guys."

"Oh don't worry, he knows all about your skills, Sil. Plus, in my trial you'll—" but before Charlie could finish, Harrison threw some scrap paper in his face and the now awake Morgan tipped his chair back, causing Charlie to tumble to the floor. With a heavy thump, Charlie grumbled a few curse words before pulling himself back up into his seat. Morgan, with his eyes resting again, chuckled.

"You're not supposed to reveal trial details Charlie, remember? We all know you have a crush on Sil, but the Commander already favours her, so the last thing she needs is clues from you to give her an advantage," Morgan teased.

"What are you talking about Morgan? Just because he's my dad, doesn't mean he'll favour me in the trials. He's Harrison's father too, pick on him!" Siljanna whined.

With that Morgan slowly opened his eyes again, gave Harrison a quick glance and just smiled, knowing exactly why he wasn't getting targeted with such comments. Morgan roused himself until he was sitting up properly and looked back at Siljanna.

"Come on Sil, everybody knows that you're the favourite twin! If anything, it would've been too easy for you to impress if you'd created one of the trials. What I'm more curious to find out is if any of us are going to be recommended for the *speciality* facilities," he said, saying the word speciality with a hint of sarcasm.

"That's a good point, and likely the main reason the Commander is assessing us tomorrow," Charlie added.

"I hope I'm not moved! The training centre here is the best on the continent. They are going to have to physically kick me outta here!" Morgan protested.

"But if you were based at the naval facility in Yasras you'd be a day's travel closer to your family, wouldn't that be good?" Siljanna asked curiously.

"I'd love to be closer to home but my parents know I want to be the best warden I can and to do that I need to be here. Besides, how could I leave Tivani and all my dear friends? You'd miss me too much!" Morgan teased.

"And if you speak *'Morgan,'* what he actually just said is that if he left, he wouldn't be able to drool over mum anymore and he'd never sacrifice that," Harrison jested.

"Urgh, not this again! You know being our mother makes her old enough to be your mother, right?" Siljanna moaned. She knew of his infatuation but rather than finding it funny like Harrison, she found the whole notion annoying. "When are you going to drop this childish fantasy? I mean, what possible reason could persuade her to leave our dad for a guy like you? She has far too much sense," Siljanna quipped, pulling a disgusted face at just the thought of it.

"Ouch, low blow! And I thought we were friends," Morgan replied, feigning a strike and doubling over as if in pain. When Siljanna crossed her arms and glared, he pulled an *'I'm in trouble'* face, chucked his books carelessly into his bag and stood up. "Well, on that note I'm gonna hit the showers and get some sleep; big day tomorrow."

As Morgan left the room, Siljanna rolled her eyes with a smile, feeling like she'd won the discussion and Harrison gave an informal salute to his friend. Shortly afterwards, Harrison began to pack up his own books too, but with much more care.

"I better head back as well, see you guys in the morning," he said before pausing and turning back to his sister. Usually, as twins, he could get a sense of how she was feeling, but lately, their connection had faded. "Hey Sil, I need to ask; are you mad Tutor Anderson picked me as the final candidate for the trials?"

He was trying to get her to make eye-contact with him, she could never lie directly to his face. After a moment she looked up at him, her green eyes bright and filled with honesty.

"I can't say I'm not disappointed, but I don't blame you, Harrison. You're a great student, it must've been a tough choice for Tutor Anderson. I'll just have to work even harder to get dad's attention during the trials, right?" She asserted, giving him a thumbs up.

It was obviously a rhetorical question as she quickly began packing up her things and turned her attention to Charlie for the third time. He was engrossed in his book yet again, at least he was until she dropped her book bag over his shoulder and the sudden weight snapped his attention back to the real world.

"Fancy walking me back to my dorm, Charlie? These books sure are heavy," Siljanna asked, rubbing the back of her neck, pretending it ached. Harrison and Charlie both knew Siljanna was more than capable of carrying her own bag, but only Harrison seemed to acknowledge her flirting was purely an attempt to learn more about his trial.

"Sure thing," Charlie agreed as he slung his bag over the other shoulder. His blonde hair was tousled and scruffy but otherwise, Charlie was smartly dressed. Compared to the rest of them in casual wear, he looked a little out of place. He was more slender than Morgan and Harrison and a true nerd at heart, but despite his appearance, he was strong, taking the weight of both bags easily. With his thin glasses perched on the end of his nose and slight frame, it was easy to forget he'd completed the same training they had over the years. You were more likely to see him with a book in hand rather than a weight or weapon but if push came to shove, he could hold his own.

"Remember Charlie, no clues!" Harrison insisted, tapping his temple and pointing at his friend before they all left the library.

Charlie and Siljanna took the first stairwell towards the female dorm rooms and Harrison just about overheard Charlie say he hoped to be recommended for the science facility in Siranor before the pair were out of range. He continued down the hall reaching his and Morgan's room a few minutes later. Morgan was right about one thing, it was going to be a big day tomorrow, so once he'd prepared his gear, Harrison settled in for the night.

Chapter Two
The Trials

The light creeping in through the window told Harrison it was dawn, and he couldn't wait to get up. His skin tingled as energy resonated through his body. It could've been nerves or excitement but either way, he was eager to get going. He got dressed in his training gear; light and flexible leather armour with a complex utility belt for holding weapons. Given the choice, Harrison liked the broadsword but as he didn't know what they might require for the trials, he ensured his gear could adjust for anything. He strapped on his boots and gave Morgan's bed a kick to ensure his friend was awake. Morgan tumbled out with a gratifying thud, making Harrison laugh as he walked out the door.

As he arrived at the training centre, most of the other third-year students were present. There were only twelve of them left now, but their numbers could decrease again after the trials. The trainees assembled as Tutor Anderson and two others; Tutors Matthews and Taylor arrived in the courtyard. Harrison spotted Morgan slip in as they all lined up and saluted. Shortly afterwards, Commander Stone appeared from inside the training centre.

As usual, his father looked immaculate. His white leather armour with black and gold trim, the colouring of the wardens, was pristine and his shoulder-length blonde hair was tied back, neatly falling within his tall collar. There was an uncomfortable silence as he walked the line, examining each student intently for the slightest flaw in their gear. He paused as he came to Siljanna and smiled. She was in her favourite black training armour and it was spotless. Harrison didn't expect any less of her, especially today. No one could argue that she'd put in the effort to get noticed for all the right reasons. After finishing his inspection, Commander Stone stood behind the lectern and they knew, the trials were about to begin.

"Third-year candidates; today you will be participating in your critical year-end assessments. Some of you may believe your result will be equally split between today's trials and your final examination, but I have decided that a written exam will not be conducted this year. Your future at the academy will be based purely on your performance today," Commander Stone announced with authority. He obviously hadn't told the tutors about cancelling the written exam but they didn't argue. "You will each undergo three trials crafted by a student Tutor Anderson believes has displayed the most promise over this last year. Anderson, please call forward your selected students."

As Sampson turned to face him, Tutor Anderson's nerves were palpable. Harrison wondered if now more than ever, he was regretting not selecting Siljanna to create one of the trials. After a second's hesitation, Anderson cleared his throat and spoke.

"Dylan Rose, Harrison Stone and Charlie Blake, please step forward," he announced and the boys did as instructed. Harrison glanced over at his father and noticed the disapproving look he shot Tutor Anderson but quickly returned to his stoic stance.

"Very well. Charlie, your trial will be first. Please address the group and explain the rules," Commander Stone said, inviting Charlie to approach the lectern.

"Good morning everyone, for the first trial we will be working in two teams in what is essentially a capture the flag scenario. The flag is located in a locked chest at the top of the large oak tree in the western field. There are two copies of the key and we will be provided with a series of clues in order to locate them. Once in possession of a key, each team must find a way to scale the tree and retrieve the flag,"

Charlie explained. "I have given the tutors examples of the type of clues but they have selected the final material so that I may fairly compete in the challenge. Commander Stone, please select the teams."

Charlie and the whole group turned to the Commander as he looked over the group and selected Charlie and another boy called Aiden to lead the teams and allowed them to select their own members. Taking it in turns, Charlie couldn't have been happier to get Siljanna, Harrison and Morgan in his team with two other guys, Carter and Reece, completing his group.

With the two teams formed, Tutor Matthews approached the opposing team while Tutor Taylor came their way. Tutor Taylor was the only female instructor but like Siljanna, she was not a woman to be underestimated. As a master archer and incredibly well versed in dual-wield weaponry, she was admired among her peers and students. Her short brown hair was practical and when not in combat, she wore glasses that framed her slender face and blue eyes. She approached holding a small pouch and gave it to Charlie.

"Good luck team one, I'm rooting for you!" She announced with a friendly wink.

As she walked away, Charlie noticed Carter leer, love-struck before returning his attention to the task at hand. He opened the satchel and found three scraps of paper. The first one displayed three numbers, '7', '132' and '265'. The second had the word 'Rainer' and the third had 'F. Theory' written on it. Charlie shared each clue with the team as they discussed what they could mean.

Quickly agreeing they were looking for a book, the team ruled out anything to do with the current Imperator, Harlyn Rainer as she didn't have any published works and it made little sense to be a book about her father, Imperator Joseph Rainer as most books on him focused on his military achievements, nothing theoretical. Siljanna kept focussing on the third paper stating 'F. Theory' and was convinced that was the main clue they needed to solve.

A moment later, Charlie recalled in their second year, they spent time studying the works of Dr Elias Rainer, the late Imperator's brother. Prior to Dr Rainer's disappearance, he was the leading Imperial scientist, whose work mainly focused on Encia and the theoretical ability to use it to enhance armour and weaponry. The team decided that was too much of a coincidence so headed to the library to search for books written by Dr Rainer.

As they set off, they noticed the other team heading in the same direction but as they arrived at the library, team two veered off down a different hall. Inside the library, they found a small round table next to the main shelves, and on it, among a few other random books, was a text written by Dr Rainer. Siljanna picked up the book, hoping it might contain the key they needed but had no such luck. She quickly flicked through the pages while Morgan peered over her shoulder. As she did, Morgan spotted something and asked her to go back, until landing on a page entitled 'Fusion Theory' written boldly as the chapter title. They smiled, two clues down. Now they just had to uncover the meaning of the numbers. It was Harrison who came up with a suggestion.

"What about a word count? What are the seventh, one-hundred and thirty-second and two-hundred and sixty-fifth words in this chapter?" He asked.

Being the quickest reader, they handed the book to Harrison who announced each word in order, 'Elite', 'Sword' and 'Crafting'. The group dashed over to the library index on the main desk and searched for a book titled 'Elite Sword Crafting'. Identifying it was in the metalwork section, the team headed up to the second floor to find it. The bookshelf they needed was close to the balcony on the western side of the room and it didn't take long for Charlie to find the correct book. Opening it, he revealed a small silver key neatly tucked inside the front cover.

"Got it! Let's get out to the western field," he said pumped, until Siljanna stopped him. She was staring out the window and drew her teammates closer to take in the depressing sight.

Team two were already out on the western field heading straight towards the oak tree. How could they've gotten such a lead on them? As the team watched, horrified, they realised the other group were unravelling a rope. The oak tree was incredibly tall with the first of the branches at least nine feet above the ground. The other team had obviously grabbed the rope after finding their key and were in the process of securing it to the tree trunk. Commander Stone and the other tutors were also out in the field, overseeing team two's progress and looking particularly impressed with their dominant lead.

"We don't stand a chance at catching up now!" Carter groaned, sounding defeated. "They've got their key and are already out there with the equipment they need."

"I don't think we need to worry quite yet," Harrison announced, sounding more confident than anyone expected.

As they turned to look at him, they realised while the rest of them had been watching the other team below, he'd retrieved a crossbow and zip-line kit from a display case nearby. Holding it triumphantly, he made it clear they were not only still in the race but could win. Running to the library balcony which had a clear view over to the oak tree, Harrison glanced around his teammates and then handed the crossbow to Charlie.

"You're the best shot Charlie and we've only got one rope dart for the zip-line, don't miss!" Harrison recommended with confidence. Charlie nodded, taking the crossbow from him.

"Sil, you're the lightest between us, and quick, you should traverse the line and claim the flag," Charlie instructed, handing her the key as she nodded, agreeing to the plan. "Morgan, you and Harrison secure the line. Carter, Reece; get down to the field and slow team two down."

Each with their individual tasks the group dispersed, fuelled with a fresh determination. Charlie aimed at the thick trunk of the oak tree, just above the sturdiest looking branch and fired. His shot was perfect and the dart took a firm hold in the tree trunk. The impact made Commander Stone look towards the balcony, and he quickly realised what their team were planning. Morgan hooked the rope to an iron fixture on the wall to give Siljanna a sharper trajectory and then looped it around the stone balustrade while Harrison fixed a pulley with handles onto the rope to enhance her descent. Once everything was set, they agreed that Morgan and Charlie should head down and help Carter and Reece who'd made it to the field and were distracting their opponents. As they left, Harrison looked over at his twin.

"I'm going to stay and make sure the line remains secure. If you fall from this height, it's safe to assume you'll be in the infirmary for a few weeks and I do not want to go home for the year-end break without you," Harrison admitted, winking at his twin and gripping the remaining rope around his arm, grounding himself as best he could.

"See, I knew you loved me," she said, giving him a quick kiss on the cheek. Before he could retort she was up on the balustrade, grabbed the handles of the pulley and leapt.

Soaring through the air, her long-braided hair whipped behind her while the shorter strands of her fringe blew wildly in every direction. She couldn't help but squeal an elated cry as she hurtled towards the tree. Hearing her, the members of team two looked up and once they realised what was happening, were left in complete shock. They clearly thought they had this challenge in the bag and that made Siljanna feel even more exhilarated.

As she got closer to the tree, she tucked her legs and landed gracefully on the thick branch, just as her team had undoubtedly expected. She glanced back at the balcony and saw Harrison grasping onto the balustrade and looking rather exasperated. She gave him a quick thumbs up and told herself to thank him later but right now, her mind was set on finding that flag chest.

After a quick search, she spotted it, a small silver chest marked with intricate carvings that was slightly out of reach. Climbing to the branch above her, she noticed Dylan had begun scaling the rope from the ground below. With a new sense of urgency, Siljanna found a sturdy foothold and propelled herself upward, stretching as far as she could to reach the little chest. She missed but quickly tried again and was able to grab it. Pulling the key from her pocket she unlocked the chest, revealing a small flag marked with the Warden emblem. She dropped to the lower branch as Dylan was just hauling himself up and revealed the flag to both teams, the tutors and most importantly, her father. The trial was over and she'd won it for her team.

As she and Dylan both descended, the teams gathered before the tutors and Commander Stone to receive his review of their performances.

"Good work team one," Commander Stone announced. "You successfully deciphered all the clues and used the equipment available to defeat the opposing team, even when it looked like the odds were against you. Siljanna, your agility at traversing to and scaling the tree was extremely impressive, you were a true asset to your team."

Everyone in team one smiled and congratulated each other while Siljanna beamed with delight at her father's comments.

"Well done everyone!" Charlie said, smiling proudly at his teammates.

"Team two, good effort. You worked well and solved your clues incredibly quickly. Dylan, you didn't lose sight of your goal and displayed great determination scaling the tree, despite your team being distracted. Had your opponents not delayed your efforts, you likely would have been the one releasing that flag and winning this challenge. Overall, a good display from both teams with notable performances from Siljanna and Dylan."

All the members of team two sighed with relief after hearing the Commander's comments. Although they knew losing wasn't going to help their final assessment, they hadn't been reprimanded by Commander Stone and took that small consolation eagerly.

Returning to the training centre, the students waited anxiously for the next trial to begin. A short time later, Tutor Anderson called Harrison forward. He noticed his father glaring at him as he did, obviously still bitter that Anderson had picked him over Siljanna. Remembering Rylie's words of encouragement, he pushed any anxiety to the back of his mind and addressed the other trainees.

"I hope everyone is ready for the second trial. In this challenge, we will face off in pairs and rely on our instincts and physical prowess to succeed. Beginning in separate rooms, the opponents will use their key senses; sight, sound, taste, touch and smell to find a way to enter a duelling arena. Once there, the opponents must locate melee weapons and duel until one person is disarmed," Harrison explained. "If progress from the initial room isn't completed within fifteen minutes or the melee weapon not obtained, that participant will be disqualified."

As he finished detailing the rules, Harrison wished everyone luck and moved back into line so his father could select the pairings. Harrison was to be against Morgan while Siljanna was against a trainee called Samuel Fischer.

Three of the other pairings completed their trials before Harrison and Morgan were called to begin. They were led down to the training centre basement and then on to different rooms. Commander Stone escorted Morgan while Harrison followed Tutor Anderson until they were standing in front of a solid metal door.

"Are you ready to begin Harrison?" Anderson asked.

"Yes sir; I just hope I'm not beaten by my own idea," Harrison said, taking a deep breath to relax. Tutor Anderson held him reassuringly on the shoulder before covering his eyes with a blindfold and loosely cuffing his hands to his utility belt. As they entered the first trial room, even blindfolded Harrison could tell it was much darker than the corridor he'd been in a moment ago. He was made to sit in a chair before Anderson spoke again.

"Okay Harrison, your trial will begin in just a moment. As you know, you need to trust your instincts and follow your senses to complete this part of the trial. Once you hear the door close, you may begin."

Harrison closed his eyes, even though he couldn't see anything, and focused on his breathing until he heard the metal door close with a loud clunk. He couldn't help but wonder, was that the use of hearing? He decided it probably wasn't and set his mind to the task at hand.

Sitting in the chair with his hands bound he tried to focus on the senses that hadn't been restricted; sound and smell. He took another deep breath and that's when a scent caught his attention. It was faint at first but the more he concentrated, the more he was sure. It was burning sage. He stood up from the chair and headed towards the smell, stretching his arms out as far as he could, hoping to find something for guidance. His hands connected with the cold surface of the wall, causing him to shiver, but it helped him balance as he moved towards the smell.

Soon, the scent was undeniably strong and as he moved his hands down, he could feel the warmth of the gently burning sage stick. It was in an incense burner on what felt like a small wooden table. He brushed his hands over the table, and that's when his fingers found something soft. He turned the object in his hand, giving it a gentle squeeze and although he couldn't be entirely sure, it felt like bread.

Knowing that the trial required the use of all his senses, he decided to literally take the bait, leant over picking up the object in his mouth and took a bite. He tasted a natural sweetness, telling him it was a kind of brioche and then, something much sharper, more metallic. A key! He spat it out carefully onto the table, collected it and fumbled slightly as he found and released the lock on the restraint binding his hands to his utility belt. With his hands free, he was also able to remove the blindfold.

It was still dark in the room but he was able to see the outline of the door that he'd entered through and the chair he had been made to sit on. He headed towards the door and tried the handle, but of course, it was locked. That would have been too easy. He felt around the doorframe, found a switch and flipped it, causing a single light to come on overhead. At first, the light was blinding but his vision quickly adjusted and he could take in his surroundings. As well as the wooden table he'd found, he spotted that the far wall was painted a slightly different colour so decided to check it.

Initially, it seemed like a perfectly normal wall, but Harrison knew it had to be different for a reason. He started tapping the wall and after a few strikes, heard a hollow sound. He kicked the wall with enough force that a wooden panel snapped under his boot. After a few more decisive strikes and pulling away the remaining debris, he discovered a small chest. He was expecting it to be locked but upon further examination found two pressure latches which, when squeezed made the box click open and reveal a screwdriver.

Raising an eyebrow in confusion, he took the tool and searched the room for any way it might be useful. At first, he didn't see anything until he looked above the chair and spotted an air duct with a grate screwed in place. He stood on the chair and unscrewed the grate, dropping it to the floor and hauled himself inside the vent. It was cramped but he managed to pull his way through the crawl space and drop down into the next room.

As he landed, he glanced across and saw the duelling platform hung over a vast drop in the centre of the room, and Morgan on the opposite side. He could see the glint of weapons on the platform too but no obvious way to get there. Morgan looked over to him and shrugged, clearly also unsure how to reach the platform. Searching for another minute, Harrison felt a floor tile beneath him depress. It was a pressure plate and once activated, some bars overhead were revealed but the floor beneath him began to tremble. His instincts kicked in and he jumped, grabbing hold of the bars. The drop to the actual floor must've been twelve feet, but instead of worrying about that, he focused on manoeuvring to the elevated duelling platform.

As Morgan also made his way to the platform, the two friends found themselves facing each other. Just in front of Harrison was a katana and before Morgan, a broadsword. Looking at the weapons, they both smiled, acknowledging them as each other's favourites and threw the blades across to one another. The grip of the broadsword seemed to meld into Harrison's hand and despite its size, it felt weightless to him, like a natural extension of his arm. He turned his attention back to Morgan, who emanated confidence with his favoured long, thin katana in hand.

"Let's give 'em a good show, ready bud?" Morgan said, charismatic as usual while taking his battle stance.

"Show me what you've got," Harrison replied, mirroring his friend's charm. He knew Morgan wasn't going to hold back so he had to bring his all too.

Within a split second, the pleasantries were over and Morgan lunged forward. As their blades collided, the two of them shifted and struck out with grace and determination, each trying to create an opening. Morgan quickly grew impatient with the stalemate and made a flurry of strikes that Harrison deflected. Following up with a leg sweep, he knocked Morgan to the ground.

As Harrison pivoted, he saw Morgan roll and return to his feet. He hadn't dropped his weapon so the duel wasn't over. Harrison focused on his friend, noticing that he looked frustrated. He adopted a defensive stance as Morgan charged again with another series of ferocious blows. He clearly hadn't taken kindly to being knocked down, but Harrison knew he could use his friend's impulsiveness to his advantage.

He defended against more blows until he felt Morgan put additional weight into the attack, then Harrison used his friend's own momentum against him. He twisted his broadsword, feeling the steel run down the blade of the katana until it made contact with the hilt. One more sharp twist and the katana was sent flying out of Morgan's grip and crashing to the ground. Morgan stumbled forward, and when he turned back, found Harrison's blade raised to his chest. He lifted his hands in defeat and the duel was over.

"Looks like I need more training after all," Morgan admitted, his smile returning, "good duel, I'll be counting on a rematch!"

"Anytime!" Harrison promised, holstering his blade with a smile as they shook hands.

Shortly afterwards, they heard a side door open and Commander Stone and Tutor Anderson were there. They slid a metal walkway across to the platform to allow both of them to cross over. As they walked towards him, Commander Stone stood with his arms folded and an unreadable expression. The boys glanced at each other, fairly certain they'd performed well, but Commander Stone's expression gave them no reason to feel confident. They stood before him and saluted as he delivered his evaluation.

"Morgan, your time to complete the 'senses room' is so far the time to beat but you failed to disarm your opponent in the duel. That being said, you displayed an impressive level of agility and tenacity in your attacks and recovered quickly from your opponent's initial attempt to disarm you; there is room for improvement, but well done," Commander Stone advised, to which Morgan nodded gratefully. Then the commander turned to Harrison, his expression grave. "Harrison, you were slower than your opponent right up to the commencement of the duel and as for the duel itself, you took a repetitively defensive stance, failing at the first opportunity to disarm your opponent. I expect better," Commander Stone said, his words harsh, almost cruel.

They were dismissed and returned to the others while they waited for the final pairings to complete their trials. Last up were Siljanna and Samuel. As her father expected, Siljanna was incredibly quick to solve the clues in the senses room, reaching the duelling arena in record time. As she examined the second room, the first thing she noticed was that her opponent was nowhere to be seen. She even found the pressure plate and traversed to the elevated platform before Samuel crashed through the vent and landed in the second room. He was panting heavily and looked rather distressed. *Is he nervous?* She asked herself.

Feeling no pressure, Siljanna found a pair of hand axes on the platform in front of her. Collecting them, she familiarised herself with the weight and feel of them before looking back over to Samuel. She watched as he fumbled around, eventually finding the pressure plate in the floor and swung towards the platform. As he propelled himself from the final bar, he missed the edge, barely grabbing on so as to not fall to the floor below. Growing tired of his inadequacy, Siljanna walked towards him, axes in hand. Just as he raised his upper body onto the platform, she thrust the blade forward, preventing him from recovering.

"Siljanna, what are you doing?" He cried, shocked that she was preventing him from climbing up.

Before she could speak, they heard a loud whistle blow, and both assumed it indicated Samuel had failed the trial. Smiling, Siljanna lowered the axes so that Samuel could clamber up and watched as her father emerged from a room on the far side, sliding a metal walkway across to them. They crossed and stood to attention before him, Samuel looking particularly pale.

"Congratulations Siljanna, you cleared the senses challenge and recovered your melee weapon in excellent time and outwitted your opponent in the process; an efficient and admirable performance," he said, beaming with pride. "Please, return to the group and await further instruction."

"Thank you, sir," Siljanna replied, saluting as she headed off with a spring in her step. Commander Stone then turned his attention to Samuel, a terrifying look in his dark green eyes.

"Samuel, you categorically failed this trial. I find myself wondering how you've even made it to become a third-year student at this prestigious academy based on that performance," he hissed, dismissing him with a sharp hand motion.

As Samuel returned to the group, Siljanna was still smiling until she noticed the look on his face. He was livid. She went towards him but he abruptly cut her off.

"Don't even bother Siljanna, I need to prepare for the final trial," he grumbled, storming off and leaving her speechless. Noticing her gaping expression, Harrison headed over.

"What was that about?" He asked quizzically.

"I may have taken advantage of his nerves to defeat him in the trial. I didn't expect him to take it so hard though. We've always been a competitive group, and I just wanted to win," Siljanna answered, still looking towards Samuel who was clearly expressing his annoyance to anyone that would listen.

"He's only got himself to blame. We are all meant to be at the top of our game for these trials and whatever happened in there will teach him to step it up or risk getting kicked out. He may not thank you, but he'll learn from this," Harrison replied, putting his arm around his sister's shoulders.

They'd been given a short break after the second trial, so as the trainees disbanded, Harrison and Siljanna went off together to grab some water. During the break Tutor Matthews approached Dylan.

"Mr Rose, please come with me before the final trial," he asked and Dylan went as instructed.

Chapter Three

Tension

Twenty minutes later Dylan emerged with the tutors and Commander Stone. The students gathered again as Dylan stood ready to detail the final trial.

"Welcome back everyone, I hope you're all refreshed and ready to begin. For the final trial, we'll again be working in teams but with a slight twist. Team one will consist of seven participants and be taken to a secret location that you will be locked within. Your goal is simple, to escape. Team two, consisting of the remaining five participants will begin in the training centre. You will have a series of clues to solve and must try to discover the location of team one before they are able to escape," Dylan explained. "Now for the twist, one member of team one will be a double agent. This person will have chances to feed vital information to team two in order to assist them. Credit should be awarded to team one if you uncover the traitor or to team two if they remain undetected. On the table beside me, you will find twelve pouches, each containing a team name or the word *double agent*. Any questions?"

Commander Stone looked around the candidates as if daring them to hold up the commencement of the trial and when there were no questions, he instructed them to select a pouch and assemble in their respective teams. Team one was Siljanna, Charlie, Morgan, Dylan, Aiden, Samuel and Reece; leaving Harrison, Carter and the other boys, Joshua, Kyle and Mark forming team two. Team two were instructed to head inside the training centre and wait while team one were relocated.

After they'd left the training centre, all the members of team one were blindfolded and escorted by Tutor Matthews and Commander Stone out of the courtyard. Getting in a truck, they were driven on a short but winding journey until the truck finally pulled over. As they got out, still blindfolded, they walked up a few steps and heard a large door open.

Thanks to the various turns, Siljanna had completely lost her bearings but assumed that was part of the challenge. They were shuffled inside and told to remove their blindfolds. The room was mainly wooden, with the windows obstructed by heavy iron bars and very little inside. It looked a bit like one of the woodland cabins but Siljanna couldn't be sure. Tutor Matthews departed with an encouraging nod, leaving Commander Stone alone before them, blocking the only clear exit.

"Welcome to your prison team one. Within these walls, you won't find much, but equally, all the clues you need to escape. If any of you have weapons equipped, hand them over now, you will not need them," he instructed, pausing to collect any weapons they had. "Once I leave, the door behind me will be double-bolted from the outside. Breaking it down is not the correct escape route and doing so will lead to your team being disqualified. Although you won't see us, know we will be monitoring you carefully throughout the trial," he announced, looking at each of them intently but giving his daughter a discreet smile.

As Commander Stone left, they heard the bolts he'd mentioned scrape across, sealing the door behind him. As he'd literally told them the main door was not the way to escape, team one focused on finding something that would lead them to the true means of victory.

It had been about fifteen minutes for team two before Commander Stone re-entered the training centre. He glanced at each of them, assessing their demeanours before placing a small box on the table in front of them.

"Team two, let the hunt begin," he said, raising an eyebrow and encouraging them to open the box. As Harrison opened it, he pulled out a note and read it aloud.

"*To find what you seek, head to high ground and locate the watchful eye*. Well, that's not at all ambiguous!" He said sarcastically.

All the guys looked at each other but nobody spoke. Harrison sighed, scanning the letter again in hopes a second read-through might help.

"Any ideas?" Carter asked nervously.

"It could be too obvious but how about we head to the watchtower by the main gate? It's the best vantage point in the academy so could be the *'high ground'* we need," Harrison suggested.

Everyone seemed happy to start there so they all headed towards the watchtower. From the base of the tower, the team reached a spiral stairwell that ascended to the scouting platform. Harrison led the way and once he reached the top, found a ladder and hatch that would grant them access to the upper level. They came up one by one and joined Harrison who was reading the note again. He was trying to decipher what the *'watchful eye'* could be. A few moments later, Carter tapped him on the shoulder and pointed to a spyglass.

"Could that be the watchful eye?" He asked.

"Great idea; let's take a look," Harrison replied positively.

"But if that's the watchful eye, what exactly are we looking for?" Kyle countered, sounding despondent.

"Anything unusual I guess," Harrison replied, hoping that by using the spyglass they would find the next clue.

After several minutes, team one had made no progress. They quickly realised that when Commander Stone had said there was little in the room, he wasn't bluffing. All they could see was a workstation with a sink that didn't work, some leather straps pinned to the adjacent wall and across the room, a large pile of neatly stacked logs. Finally, by the door Commander Stone had departed from, there was a solitary chair bolted to the floor. Siljanna couldn't help wondering why bolt the chair down in a sealed room? The thick bars over the windows were nailed into the frames so there was no way they could've used the chair to break through. With no other choice, Siljanna turned to Dylan, the mastermind of the trial.

"Okay Dylan, what's the deal? Do we get any kind of clue to get started?" She asked, trying not to get agitated.

"I may have come up with the concept but the tutors selected this location and organised the clues so that I could fairly compete, remember? All I can say is that there should be a series of puzzles to solve in order to find the way out," Dylan replied defensively.

Disappointed that he couldn't give any more insight, Siljanna flopped down onto the chair. As soon as she did, she felt it sink slightly and realised that it wasn't bolted to the floor at all but on another pressure plate. In the same instant, a panel in the ceiling cracked open revealing what looked like a narrow crawl space. Dylan volunteered to check it out and vaulted himself into the area above.

"What can you see up there?" Siljanna shouted.

"Not a lot to be honest. There are two passages, one has some kind of safe at the end while the other has another panel like the one we just opened. It could drop us into an adjacent room," Dylan replied. "There's a small square indentation on the panel, maybe it needs some kind of key."

"Okay, let's search the room again," Siljanna suggested, without looking to see if anyone questioned her authority. As the team searched, Siljanna noticed Charlie staring at the leather straps on the wall. "Can you see something?" She asked, touching his shoulder to get his attention.

"I'm not sure, but the placement of these straps seems odd. Notice how they are different lengths and the pins don't line up? I think if we arrange them correctly, it could be a clue," he replied.

Siljanna trusted Charlie's analytical abilities and the pair began working on rearranging the straps. They were all pinned in place at one end but could be rotated and clipped onto a vacant pin elsewhere on the wall. After a few moments, Siljanna took a step back and could see a pattern emerging. Once arranged correctly, the leather straps formed the numbers four and seven.

"Charlie, can you see those numbers too?" Siljanna asked, tilting her head, not that it helped.

"Yeah, what do you think it means?" Charlie asked, sounding proud of their discovery, even though he wasn't sure of its meaning. Noticing their discovery, Morgan shouted up to Dylan.

"Hey Dylan, that safe, does it need a combination?"

"Yeah, a three-digit code! Have you found anything down there?" Dylan called back.

"Only two numbers so far, four and seven. We'll keep looking," Siljanna replied as she turned back to the wall with the leather straps.

A few moments later, she heard a loud screech and looked over her shoulder to see Samuel, Aiden and Reece huddled around the sink. Aiden stepped away from the others and strutted towards them, holding what looked like the broken head of the tap. It wasn't until he came closer she noticed a small object inside.

"Check it out! The tap was hollow and concealing this square key, just like Dylan said he needed," Aiden announced and headed towards the overhead panel, calling out to Dylan who dangled back into the room to collect the object from his friend.

They heard Dylan shuffle back through the crawl space, inserting the key into the panel. Something clicked but the panel didn't open. He tried again but it wouldn't budge.

"Sorry guys, no such luck, I still can't open the second panel," he said, as he dropped down into the main room again. "It's pretty cramped up there so I vote someone smaller stays in the crawl space until we can open the damn thing."

"Okay, okay, I'll go," Charlie offered, his thin but lean frame considerably smaller than Dylan's. While he pulled himself up, Siljanna turned her attention back to the leather straps and after a moment noticed all of the straps could move apart from the one on the far left, which was pinned at both ends. As she looked again, she wondered if it was meant to be the number one.

"Hey Charlie, head back to the safe and try entering one-four-seven. I think that might be the combination!" She exclaimed.

Time stood still as they waited for him to reply. Before he said anything, they heard a whirring noise and the panel on their side of the room began to close.

"Crap! Charlie the panel this side is closing!" Morgan cried.

"What?" He shouted back, sounding worried.

"It's closing! Charlie get out—," but before he could react, the panel closed.

Siljanna dashed back over to the chair switch, sitting on it again but this time nothing happened. Morgan called over to Aiden, telling him to get on his shoulders and pry the panel open but it was no use. It wasn't until they heard shuffling again and a thud on the other side of the wall that they stopped and began calling Charlie's name. When he didn't reply, Samuel marched over and grabbed Siljanna.

"It's her, she's the double agent! She gave Charlie the wrong code," he growled.

"Woah, wait a minute! She and Charlie worked together to find that code, you can't just accuse Siljanna," Morgan said, coming to her defence.

"Don't trust her Morgan, she's devious. I'm telling you, she's trying to sabotage us!" Samuel spat, glaring at Siljanna.

She couldn't believe how angry he'd become, just because of what happened in the last trial. She pushed Samuel away and quietly thanked Morgan who seemed to be keeping a close eye on him.

"I swear, I'm not the double agent," she began.

"That's what a traitor would say," Samuel protested.

"I'm just worried about Charlie, not that you'll believe me. Can we just focus on helping him first, then you can get back to blaming me for everything, okay?" Siljanna asked sarcastically, focussing her gaze on Samuel.

He grunted but just as they were about to return to the panel, there was a crackling noise coming from behind the wooden logs. They started tossing them aside until they found an old-fashioned walkie-talkie. Morgan grabbed it first and started turning the dials until the crackling cleared.

"Guys, are you there? It's Charlie, can you hear me?"

With a collected sigh of relief, the rest of the group huddled around the walkie-talkie.

"Charlie, we hear you! Are you all right?" Morgan replied.

"Yeah, I'm fine. As I opened the safe, there was a button that opened the second panel. Luckily Dylan had already used the key as I don't think it would've opened otherwise," he replied, sounding grateful. "This room is small. There's a desk in here and a file filled with schematics, but the page it was open on shows a false panel in the wall between us. Twisting the coat hook by the main entrance should open it."

Dylan rushed to the coat hook and twisted it sharply, revealing the way through for the rest of the team. As they entered the second room, Charlie was looking at them with a smug expression.

"What took you so long?" He asked with a wicked grin.

Most of the group chuckled and then took a moment to assess their new surroundings. The room was smaller than the first but otherwise looked like a normal bedroom. There was an old-fashioned phone and the radio Charlie had used on the desk next to the large schematics file he mentioned, a bed and a small closet. Siljanna looked the most relieved to see Charlie and gave him a quick hug as her gaze landed on the schematics.

"Have you gone through the rest of the files? Is there anything to indicate a way out?" She asked.

"Honestly, I didn't look. When I got in here, I spotted the file but focused on the open page and getting you guys through the fake wall. That's when I used the radio to contact you," Charlie replied, grinning widely as she released him from her embrace. Siljanna didn't say anything, knowing it was her concern that prompted his expression. "Why don't we take a look at the files, and check for another use for that radio?"

Siljanna nodded and began examining the radio, flicking between bandwidths while Charlie scanned the files. She tuned into one bandwidth that simply repeated the numbers one-four-seven.

"Hey Charlie, listen to this," she announced.

"What is it?" He asked as Dylan joined them.

"It's repeating the numbers of the earlier clue, for the safe in the crawl space," she said, confused by the discovery.

"Maybe there was a radio in the other room and we missed it," Dylan suggested.

"Maybe," she replied, clearly unconvinced.

Sensing the mysterious radio broadcast was annoying her, Charlie flicked the volume off and offered for Siljanna to examine the schematics file with him while Dylan took another look at the radio.

High atop the watchtower with spyglass in hand, Harrison scanned the horizon, still unsure what he was looking for. From their current position, he could see much of the surrounding area and even Tivani in the far distance. He convinced himself they must be looking for something closer though. After all, Commander Stone had escorted team one to their location and gotten back fairly quickly so wherever team one was, it was likely to be within the academy grounds. He looked to his team but it was clear they were relying on him to solve this clue.

As he focused on the surrounding area and woodlands, he spotted a wooden cabin with an eye painted on the side. He grabbed Carter and asked him to check as well, just to make sure he wasn't seeing things. Carter agreed it definitely looked like a *'watchful eye'* so the team dashed down the tower as quickly as they could and ran to the cabin at the edge of the woods.

It took them ten minutes at sprinting speed to reach the cabin but when they arrived, they could see the large door bolted with two steel bars. Kyle tried to move the first bar until he realised there was a chain and heavy padlock preventing either from moving enough to open the door.

"Argh, we're so close," he growled, striking the door in frustration.

"Well done for announcing our presence, moron!" Carter chided, clearly annoyed at his teammate's outburst.

After giving up on the door, Kyle leant against the wall sulking while the others started to search. It wasn't long before Harrison found something.

"Guys, look, there's a loose panel here, and a radio," he announced, revealing the small device. Turning it on, they were all surprised to hear three numbers; one, four and seven being repeated on a loop. It was a lifeless voice, but distinctly female.

"Could that be Siljanna? Maybe she's sending us a clue," Kyle suggested, his interest quickly revitalised. After a moment, the clue made sense to him, and he dashed back to the door. "The padlock holding the bolts in place, it needs a three-digit combination!"

Team one were still diligently searching the second room while Siljanna looked through the schematics file. She studied the documents as quickly and thoroughly as she could but it seemed like nothing was going to be useful. There was a chance the files were just a distraction, but she refused to be responsible for missing a vital clue. That's when a page detailing a basement hatch caught her attention. About to focus on the page more intently, the group heard a loud bang on the main door and muffled voices outside. Quickly deducing it must be team two, they realised time was running out.

Before Siljanna had a chance to return her attention to the files, she was yanked from the desk and pushed face-first against the wall by Samuel. He twisted one of her arms back in a hammerlock, applying pressure until it ached.

"Now I know it's you! You sent them some kind of message through the radio, didn't you?" He snarled. She could feel his intense glare like a heat burning the back of her neck.

"I didn't, I swear! But I might've found the way out if you'll just—" she began but Samuel cut her off, taking her by the shoulders and slamming her against the wall again.

"Shut up! I refuse to believe anything you have to say!" He growled.

Seeing their altercation, Morgan rushed over and struck Samuel in the back of the head. The blow was hard enough to stun him, and his grip on Siljanna lessened enough that she could break free. With some distance between them, Morgan stood in Samuel's path and spoke with an authority Siljanna rarely heard from him.

"Back off Sam. You have no proof Siljanna is the double agent and even if she is, it's just a role. She's not an actual traitor so you have no right to treat her this way," Morgan said firmly, meeting Samuel's unrelenting glare without flinching.

"Don't be so naive, Morgan. She sent the other team a message. I refuse to fail another trial because of her!" Samuel said pointing viciously, argued, pointing viciously at Siljanna, his voice dripping with hatred. It was clear there was nothing Siljanna could say to prove her innocence, so she didn't try, but Morgan continued to support her.

"Yes, she was by the radio for a few minutes, but only Charlie and Dylan went into the crawl space and both of them spent time with the radio too. Any one of them could be the double agent. I won't tell you again Sam; back off," Morgan replied sternly. As the tension grew between the three of them, Charlie quickly interceded.

"All of you need to calm down. Team two are breathing down our necks, so we need to work together if we intend to get out of here before they get in," Charlie instructed, hoping the urgency of the situation would give them clarity. "Samuel, you and Dylan find a way to secure that panel; make sure team two can't find us before we find a way out. Morgan, Sil, let's go back over those schematics."

Focussing on the page Siljanna had found, the trio analysed the drawings of the current room and discovered the basement door was concealed by the bed. Siljanna rushed over to push the bed aside, finding the door but it was too late. At that moment team two came blazing into the main room and spotted Dylan and Samuel trying to close the false wall. Harrison and Carter shoved their way through, catching team one, meaning they'd successfully completed their task and won the trial.

"No!" Screamed Samuel as he lunged towards Siljanna again. Without knowing what was going on, Harrison intercepted the blow, getting knocked off his feet and sent crashing to the ground.

That gave Siljanna the opportunity and motivation she needed, launching her own attack back at Samuel. Throwing a series of quick jabs that he managed to deflect, Siljanna turned sharply, thrusting her elbow into his jaw and knocking him down, just as Harrison pulled himself up. Still agitated, Siljanna exhaled a deep breath while hovering her boot over Samuel's throat.

"Don't ever strike my brother or come after me again Samuel. I get it, you're pissed at the way I beat you in the last trial but don't pretend you wouldn't have done the same thing given the chance," Siljanna hissed.

Harrison couldn't help but hear their father in the way she spoke and just like Commander Stone could, Siljanna's tone left Samuel speechless. He turned his face away from her and remained motionless on the floor until she lifted her boot and walked away. Once they'd all returned to the main room, they were greeted by the sight of the ever-intimidating Commander Stone who was once again in front of the main entrance to the cabin, his arms folded and a scowl on his face.

"Well done team two. Thanks to the successful feeding of the vital clue to you by the double agent, you have won this trial," Sampson announced unenthusiastically. "Now will the student who acted as the double agent please step forward?"

There was a pause while each of the members of team one looked towards one another, apart from Samuel who kept his gaze fixed on Siljanna. A minute later, Charlie stepped forward, revealing it was him all along. Commander Stone grunted and shot a disapproving look at Samuel.

"Charlie, it was you?" Siljanna asked, clearly shocked as Charlie nodded coyly.

"There you have it team one, not only did you fail to escape the room, you also failed to correctly identify the double agent," Commander Stone scolded, clearly disappointed. "Samuel, if you'd put your pride to one side as Morgan suggested and trusted Siljanna, she would have identified the escape route sooner, possibly securing your victory."

Samuel looked like he was going to argue his case but on the receiving end of Commander Stone's most ferocious glare made the wise decision to remain silent.

"Typical, the most honest guy I know was the double agent," Aiden remarked, still stunned at the last revelation while Commander Stone continued to address them.

"Siljanna, despite being accused of being the double agent multiple times, your ability to deal with the situation was admirable, as was your reaction, Morgan. Defending a comrade in a hostile situation outside of these training walls is what makes the warden force respected. Wardens must be seen to trust and defend one another, regardless of personal feelings," Sampson concluded, his speech doubling up as a reprimand and reminder that this trial was much more than just a training exercise.

Moving out of the doorway, he signalled for all of them to leave. Tutors Anderson and Matthews were outside, waiting to take them back to the training centre. Before Samuel could reach the door, Commander Stone grabbed him by the shoulder, pulling the young man aside. In a hushed but sinister tone, he spoke to Samuel.

"If my daughter hadn't dealt with you so masterfully, you would've been answering for your actions directly to me," he snarled. Samuel looked at Commander Stone, both shocked and terrified as his superior's grip tightened on his shoulder. "Your time at the academy and career as a warden are over, do you understand? I expect you to be gone by sun-down," Sampson ordered, reluctantly releasing the pressure on the young man's shoulder.

Swallowing his nerves, Samuel nodded, walking out of the room as quickly as he could.

It was mid-afternoon by the time they reached the Academy training centre and Tutor Anderson released them for a break. Samuel left the group without a word, his brother Mark following closely behind, clearly concerned. The others headed to the kitchen to grab some food and Harrison collected a bag of ice for his cheek, which was still sore from Samuel's blow, the one aimed at Siljanna.

Despite everything that happened in the last trial, the remaining ten students chatted normally, relaxed in each other's company.

"So Harrison, we've finally found your weakness! You can't dodge for sh—" Morgan began teasing.

"Hey! Where's the sympathy for the collateral damage victim?" Harrison protested, gently applying the ice.

They all began to laugh and for a moment, it almost felt like a normal day when they would chat and tease each other between training drills. When Tutor Anderson entered, they all hushed to give him their full attention.

"I am here to announce that Samuel has been removed from the warden programme at Commander Stone's behest, and Mark has decided to drop out too. Both of them are in the dormitory packing their belongings, so take the chance to say goodbye if you wish. You have free time now until Commander Stone delivers the final results," he advised.

"Thank you, sir," the group collectively replied as Tutor Anderson departed.

Despite the issues during the last trial, Morgan decided to say goodbye to Samuel and Mark while Charlie and Siljanna headed to the library for a bit of escapism.

Harrison was tempted to join them but ended up leisurely walking the grounds. He stopped in the quad, stretching to release the tension in his muscles when he noticed Rylie sitting under the magnolia tree. She looked dejected but noticeably perked up when she saw him.

"Hey Harrison! I just saw Morgan heading to the dorms, he said you'd finished the trials. How'd it go... and what happened to your face?" She asked, her curiosity taking over.

Her eyes were a captivating shade of blue-grey, like a cool winter sky. There was something about them Harrison had always found approachable, but right now, she was trying to conceal her own feelings. He sat next to her, letting the bench take his weight as he relaxed, realising just how physically tired he felt.

"Oh this, it's nothing. I got caught by some friendly fire. The trials were tough though, but I'd take this kind of assessment over a written exam any day! And that's the best part, they've cancelled our exam, so after today we're home-free!" He revealed, closing his eyes and letting the warmth of the sun recharge him.

"That's great!" She replied happily.

"We don't know the final results yet, but I did the best I could. My father didn't acknowledge my achievements but I'm proud of myself," he said, eyes still closed.

Rylie was one of the few people Harrison had openly spoken to about the issues with his father. She'd seen the way Sampson could be and understood Harrison's situation like few others.

"You've never needed his approval Harrison, but if it means anything, you've got mine," she commented, lacing her fingers through his and giving his hand a squeeze.

"Thanks Rylie. Let's just hope I've done enough to pass and become a fourth-year student," he replied softly, returning her gesture gratefully.

"It will be enough Harrison. The tutors know you are one of the best warden students here, just don't tell Sil I said that!" She said, whispering the latter part. They both laughed just thinking of Siljanna's reaction until Harrison remembered the apothecary students weren't meant to be at the academy that afternoon.

"Anyway, what are you doing here Rylie? I thought the medical students finished your courses yesterday."

"We did, but I came back to have a word with my tutor," she explained. "Do you remember the other day, I said Evie's been doing well?" She asked, checking he recalled their conversation.

"Yeah, no headaches or nightmares for what, a couple of weeks now?" He replied, a twinge of nerves furrowing his brow as he allowed her to continue.

"It was over two weeks, but last night she had a terrible seizure. Honestly Harrison, I've never been so scared. The way her body shook still makes me shiver," she admitted, trembling slightly, "and her eyes, they rolled right back until all we could see was white. For a moment I thought she was going to die."

Recalling the memory was clearly traumatic and Harrison couldn't resist pulling her into his arms.

"That's awful, is she okay now?" He asked, hesitantly releasing her.

"She's fine now," Rylie answered, taking a deep breath, "but I've decided to drop out of the medical training programme to help run the tavern. It'll free up time for my parents to look after Evie."

"Oh Rylie, I'm sorry. I know how much you were enjoying the course. Are your parents going to take Evie to Siranor? Maybe one of the doctors there could help," Harrison suggested.

"I asked dad about it and he said they've spoken to a specialist before. They called again but apparently there isn't anything the doctors can do." Although clearly frustrated, she managed to force a smile. "Anyway, I'm glad I got to tell you before I leave. Oh, and you better start planning to visit us on your rest days. I definitely won't believe any excuse you come up with!" He laughed again which in turn, raised her spirits and made her look more like her usual, happy self.

"When you put it like that, I wouldn't dare," he said, giving her a friendly nudge. She playfully pushed back and then they continued to chat aimlessly until Morgan, Siljanna and Charlie arrived.

"Hey Rylie!" Morgan greeted with a wave as he and the others approached.

"We thought we'd find Harrison here but had bet on him tucked away in a corner reading," Charlie added.

"We'd have come sooner if we knew you were here," Siljanna began as Rylie got up and gave her a hug. "I'm sorry, we can't stay and chat though. Harrison, dad's called us back for our final marks!" Siljanna added, breaking away from Rylie and bouncing on the spot, the anticipation literally bubbling out of her.

"Go, before Siljanna explodes!" Rylie giggled.

At that, Siljanna charged off, yanking Charlie by the arm, ensuring he was with her. Morgan and Harrison laughed, saying their goodbyes to Rylie and then heading to the training centre.

Arriving in the courtyard, they spotted the other students huddled around Commander Stone who was writing on a blackboard. As they looked closer, they could see each of their names in numerical order next to a location. After a few minutes, Commander Stone was standing at the lectern again and they amassed before him for the last time.

"Congratulations, third-year students; for those of you that remain, know you have performed well enough to become fourth-year warden students," Commander Stone announced. "On the board beside me, you will find your ranking and my recommendations for your fourth-year placements. You are all free to depart at leisure and enjoy your leave. Dismissed."

As soon as he finished speaking, all the students turned their attention to the blackboard.

1. Charlie—Siranor science institute
2. Siljanna—Tivani academy
3. Dylan—Covert-ops
4. Morgan—Tivani academy
5. Harrison—Tivani academy

The list went on, but Harrison's eyes stopped after spotting each of their names and recognising that Charlie had made the top spot. He was proud of his friend but also sad at the realisation he'd been recommended for the science facility in Siranor. That meant he wouldn't be returning to the academy next year.

"Congratulations Charlie! You get to go to the science facility as you hoped!" Siljanna said, openly delighted for him. Morgan and Harrison also congratulated their friend with a fist bump and ruffle to his already scruffy hair. It was, and always should be the only part of him not well-groomed.

"Thanks guys, I'm really pleased, although, it's going to be weird not training with you lot next year," he admitted while playfully swatting Morgan and Harrison away. "I promise, I'll come back for graduation. Just because I won't be staying here anymore, doesn't mean you can forget me."

"How could we ever forget you mate? I mean seriously, I've tried but you just don't go away!" Morgan replied in such a goofy manner that Charlie burst out laughing.

Then just like that, it was over. Harrison was far from surprised that Siljanna had been ranked second in their group but was genuinely happy for her. Fourth and fifth for himself and Morgan was good too, and he was pleased they'd both be staying at the Tivani academy.

As it was likely their last day together, all ten of the remaining trainees sat and chatted for a while. They discussed their plans for the upcoming break and for those moving on, what they hoped the new training facilities and tutors would be like. Carter vocalised his devastation at being assigned to the Yasras naval facility, but they all knew his true issue was leaving Tutor Taylor. He cheered up immeasurably though when, despite Siljanna's grumblings, they started discussing the possibility of female naval instructors. As the hours passed, the group slowly disbanded, preparing for their varying trips home.

Chapter Four

Trust

Harrison rarely found the year-end break went quickly, but this time had been different. He'd mostly enjoyed being home, despite not spending much time at his actual home. When he and Siljanna arrived, their mother, Anora was ecstatic, greeting them in her usual warm manner. Being the children of a baker meant they were spoiled with home-cooked delicacies and this visit was no different.

It always made Harrison smile to enter their kitchen and see his mum, her fiery auburn hair covered in flour because she was baking something special for her beloved children. His father on the other hand spent every possible moment praising Siljanna while diligently ignoring any mention of Harrison, but that came as no surprise. Rather than letting it get to him, Harrison often removed himself to the Hawk Eye tavern and spent quality time with Rylie and her family.

On his first visit, he was comforted to see that nothing had changed. The tavern was a wide, L-shaped building, located in the heart of town, with the public bar overlooking the main square and its iconic water fountain. The Auren family home connected to the rear and was spread over two floors, the upper level also having rooms they rented out to travellers. All the houses and shops in Tivani had a rustic look but the tavern even more so, with its thatched roof and bold wooden framework. Walking inside the main bar, visitors were faced with an impressive wall of varying beverages and alcohols, beautifully exposed wooden beams and a large seating area filled with comfortable sofas and chairs. Tucked in the corner was Paige's prized piano and adjacent to it, a beautiful hand-made stone fireplace. When lit, it was the heart and soul of the tavern.

Heartier though was the welcome. When he arrived, Evie had been drawing in her sketchbook until Rylie hinted for her to look up.

"Harrison?!" Evie exclaimed, launching herself into his arms.

"Hey kiddo!" He called, receiving the biggest hug he could imagine. She was due a growth spurt but it hadn't come quite yet so Harrison easily lifted her feet off the ground, spinning her as she squealed with delight.

"You finally came! How long can you stay?" Evie asked excitedly. He looked over at Rylie who was smiling widely then spotted Nate behind the bar, who gave him a friendly nod while cleaning glasses.

"Today, I can stay as long as you like," he replied.

"Dad, can Harrison stay for dinner?" Evie pleaded, giving her dad a big doughy-eyed look.

"Your mother is cooking tonight, you better ask her," Nate replied, laughing softly as Evie charged off into the kitchen to find her mother.

"You've got no choice but to stay now," Rylie said smiling.

"That was my devious plan all along," Harrison replied, giving her a cheeky wink.

"You kids never change," Nate commented, still laughing.

Harrison spent a lot of time with the Auren family during the academy break, partly to avoid his father but mostly because he enjoyed their company. He even enjoyed helping out around the tavern and was more than willing to volunteer whenever Nate or Rylie asked.

Once the five-week break was over, Harrison and Siljanna returned to the academy for their final year. Morgan was already in the dorm when Harrison walked through the door. He'd arrived the day before, after spending the break back in Niyati with his family. They shared stories of their time off as they settled in but agreed that this year would be strange. With only four of them left training in the

Tivani academy and Rylie also not authorised to visit, although that didn't stop her trying, the place felt devoid of its usual buzz. Another of the medical students, Juliette also seemed to have left but they didn't miss her at all. Realistically, Harrison and Morgan didn't need to share a room anymore, but they both decided they wanted to.

Despite the strange emptiness, they all got back into training quickly and during the course of the year, each developed new specialities. Harrison's interest and skill in smithing greatly increased and he was really excited when the local blacksmith, Elijah Ashby introduced a side course in weapon and armour crafting. He quickly impressed Elijah too, so much so that he sold a piece of Harrison's work, giving him a sizeable cut of the profit. While Harrison focused much more of his academic time on smithing, Siljanna honed her tactical abilities and Morgan started taking psychology classes with Tutor Matthews. The fourth student that remained at the academy with them, Aiden, decided to spend his time learning about the mountain cities crafted and occupied by the Terrans, as well as their cultural differences to humanity.

Although each of them had newfound interests, each of the students also kept up with their combat training, knowing that every senior who came through the Tivani academy had to complete an ultimate trial to graduate, one that had become Tutor Taylor's living legacy. Somehow, despite its reputation, no student ever learned the details prior to the trial, it was probably the best-kept secret at the academy.

When the year was almost over, Harrison, Morgan, Siljanna and Aiden were eager to take on the final challenge. The morning started like any other, the four of them doing training drills and enjoying a sparring session.

"Not this time," Morgan called out, deflecting Harrison's attempt, then striking back with lightning precision. Harrison lost his balance and dropped his blade. "Finally!" Morgan yelled triumphantly.

"I had to let you win, at least once, didn't I?" Harrison quipped, collecting his sword with a wicked grin.

"Oh no… you are not taking this victory from me," Morgan insisted, refusing to rise to the bait. He sauntered around the courtyard, flexing his muscles while Harrison shook his head, making Siljanna laugh.

They'd taken their final written exam the week before and knew all that remained was Taylor's trial. It was midday before Tutor Taylor found them in the quad.

"Good afternoon everyone, your graduation trial is about to commence. Are you ready?" She asked energetically.

"Yes ma'am," Siljanna replied eagerly as the others recited similar acknowledgements.

"Good, please change into light armour and collect a melee weapon of choice. Make sure to equip comfortable boots and sturdy gloves too. You have thirty minutes then report to the main gate," Tutor Taylor instructed before dismissing them.

Siljanna's room and the female dorm was in the other direction to the boys so they each gave her a wave as she darted towards her room. As the only girl left for the last two years in their group, the female dorm was filled with younger recruits, with whom Siljanna didn't have any close friendships. The eldest were the second-year students and although just two years younger than Siljanna, she saw them as little more than immature children.

As she arrived, there was a group of girls chatting and filing their nails in the common area. She couldn't help but look down at her own unpainted, misshaped nails and thought, *really? How do they have time for such frivolous interests?*

Giving them a courteous smile, she quickly headed to her room to change. Her favourite training armour was completely made of black leather, but so breathable, wearing it felt like putting on a second layer of skin. She'd intended to enhance it with a breastplate Harrison had made but she hadn't gotten around to it yet. She pulled on shin-high boots, the thick tread having plenty of grip for whatever they may face in the trial, buckled up the straps and found a pair of matching gloves.

She turned to look at herself in the mirror, admitting she looked skinnier than usual, but the sleek muscles on her arms showed that she was in good shape. Her ash-blonde hair was in a mess from the sparring session so she untied it, letting the hair fall down her back. It had grown too long now and she made a mental note to cut it, soon. Taking a brush through it quickly, she pulled her hair back and braided it, liking to keep it away from her eyes but always left two prominent strands loose on either side of her face. Without them, she looked too masculine.

As she looked at her reflection again, she couldn't help but wonder if she should do something different with her hair, something unique, but then shook the thought away. She had a much more important focus right now. Finally, she grabbed her utility belt and made her way to the weapons room in the training centre. Over the last four years, she'd never had a *'melee weapon of choice'* preferring firearms, mostly pistols although she also had an affinity with rifles. She'd trained with pretty much everything so really wasn't sure what her favourite was.

When she arrived at the weapons room, she walked down the corridor and spotted an old photo on the wall of her father and presumably the first academy students he'd assessed on their graduation. She'd passed it so often during the last four years but it wasn't until that moment something in the photo caught her eye. Strapped to her father's back was a large, imposing axe which had been his weapon of choice during his military days. Seeing him with it made her recall Harrison's third-year trial when she used one-handed axes to successfully defeat Samuel. She smiled to herself and thanked her dad for inspiring her yet again, now confident what weapon to take.

When she arrived at the main gate, axes neatly crossed on her back, she noticed the guys were already there. Like her, Harrison was in his favourite leather armour too, but unlike Siljanna who treated hers after every use, ensuring the leather was smooth and supple, Harrison's looked comfortable but well-worn. There were slight cracks all over but he insisted that the armour was still his best. He also had his beloved broadsword but unlike his armour, the sword was pristine. If she hadn't seen how many times he'd used it, she would've thought it brand new.

He'd modified it slightly since growing an interest in smithing, but overall, the weapon looked as it always had and sat comfortably on his back. The blade was long, reaching below his knees while the handle protruded past his shoulder. She reckoned it must've been at least five feet long, eighteen inches wide and unimaginably sharp.

Morgan had decided to go for slightly heavier armour but with his strength, the weight wasn't an issue. And, as expected he had his trusty katana. Lastly, Aiden had gone for light leather armour that was pale, even in comparison to Harrison's and in his belt hung a pair of nun chucks. As they greeted each other, Harrison passed her a flask of water. She took a swig and then strapped it to her belt. He was always prepared with the *little things* she often forgot, like food and water.

It wasn't long before they heard a truck pull up outside the gate and Tutor Taylor strode in.

"Hop in everyone, we've got a bit of a journey to get to the trial site," she announced.

They made haste, jumping into the cargo bed of the truck which had been fitted with metal benches for them to sit on. The truck was an old army vehicle but like many things at the academy, it was reliable. All the tutors used it if they had the choice.

As they drove out of the academy, Siljanna took a moment to look back at the mighty fortress she'd called home for the last four years. Although she loved the fact she could be with her family easily, the walk back into town taking less than an hour; that giant stone structure would always be a place of good memories for her. The thought of her next return to the academy was even more exciting though, for when she did, she was confident she'd have passed the trial; finally able to call herself a true warden.

As the journey continued, she thought of all the friends she'd made along the way, especially the ones she missed, like Charlie and Dylan. She silently hoped that they were happy at their respective new facilities and succeeding in their final trials too. She also wondered if Charlie still had a crush on her, or if the year's absence had allowed him to move on and settle with a new girl. Then she imagined him turning up to a date with a book in hand and talking scientific theories all night and laughed to herself.

When they hit a few bumps in the road, Siljanna's attention was brought back to the present and she noticed them veer off the main road onto a mountain path. The scenery dramatically changed as they drove deeper into the mountains. The sheer rock faces were hard and unrelenting, yet there were patches of greenery poking through, proving that even in the harshest environments, nature found a way to thrive.

Finally, the truck stopped and they found themselves on the edge of an enclosed canyon. The escarpment before them contained a series of rope bridges connecting several protruding stacks of rock that had broken away over years of erosion. The stacks all varied in size, a few of them with sprawling trees and roots hanging down as did many of the overhanging ledges. Far below, a river wound gently between the stone pillars. To fall from their current height was not something any of them would want to endure, mainly because if the impact didn't kill them, the exposure to Encia in the river surely would. Despite the obvious dangers, the area was strikingly beautiful. At the summit, they could just about make out an old stone temple. As Tutor Taylor turned off the ignition, she gave them a moment to take in their surroundings before calling them to attention.

"Welcome to Wutel Canyon. This part of the canyon has been a well-kept secret of mine for many years. When I became a tutor, it felt like the perfect location to challenge aspiring students, like the four of you," she began, looking at each of them with pride. "May I first say that you have each impressed all the tutors over the years, and I am confident each of you are more than capable of passing this final test."

"Thank you ma'am," Morgan replied courteously.

"So now for your final challenge; there are two paths before you and each split halfway down. Siljanna and Morgan, please take the path to the left; Harrison and Aiden, the path to the right. Once you find the forks, please choose your own paths until you reach the end of the trail. All of them lead back to the area you see before you. To pass this trial, you must all make it from your starting points to the abandoned stone temple at the summit. Your challenge is to retrieve the graduation symbols within and return them to me. Doing so will mean you've earned the right to graduate and call yourselves wardens," she explained and noticed how the statement made each of them smile, especially Siljanna. "Once you are all in position, I will signal with this flag that the trial has begun."

They took a moment before leaving, wishing each other luck and preparing themselves for what they were about to face. As Siljanna and Morgan took the path to the left as instructed, Harrison and Aiden headed right. The path was dusty and after a few turns became steep. As they pushed forward, they found the split in the road. One seemed to keep climbing while the other dropped back down.

"Flip you for the lower path?" Aiden joked.

"You go ahead. Who knows, maybe my kindness will be rewarded with an easier path during the trial," Harrison jested.

"Well, when you put it that way, I want that route!" Aiden said, before looking again at the steep path. "Oh, who am I kidding? I don't want that route, see you at the top."

The two boys bumped fists and then Aiden dropped down onto the lower path, leaving Harrison to continue upward. The trail soon became so steep, it was more like climbing than walking. When he finally reached the end of the track, he found himself at a dead end overlooking the area where they first arrived. From where he stood, the view was even more spectacular. The only downside was that he couldn't see a way of getting to the top of the canyon or even progressing forward from his position. What he could see, however, was Aiden below him, Siljanna on the lower path across the way and Morgan above her, but not as high up as him.

As they all realised they were in position, they looked towards Tutor Taylor and she released the flag signalling they could start. Siljanna struck off first, but she also had the easiest starting place, having a rope bridge directly in front of her. As for Morgan, the only way he could go was down, so he started traversing the rock edge using a thick tree root until he reached a lower level and entered a cave. Looking down, Harrison realised Aiden was out of sight too so focused on what he could do.

There was no bridge or any outstanding trees that could help him to move forward or down so instead, he checked the surrounding rocks. He noticed a traversable outcropping, took a firm hold and swung himself off the track and onto the ledge. Rocks crumbled beneath his feet but he had enough grip to continue moving towards what looked like a small alcove. When his feet found solid ground, he couldn't help but breathe a sigh of relief. The only thing in the alcove was a rope, securely tied to a deep-set wooden pole. Harrison grabbed the rope and leant cautiously over the edge, checking it would take his weight before beginning to rappel down.

After descending several feet, he realised that the rock below had eroded, meaning if he went much further, he would literally be dangling over the canyon. Despite the reservations ringing through his mind, Harrison wrapped his legs around the rope and let himself slide down until he was completely hanging off the side of the cliff. His feet connected with a large knot near the base of the rope, thankfully giving him something to cling to.

Moments later, he caught sight of Siljanna. The rope bridge she'd dashed across had led to a series of rock stacks but now, she was unable to progress further. She was just above his current location and called out when she noticed him.

"Harrison! Who said you could just hang about like that? We've got a trial to complete," she teased. It was a hollow gesture though as she was clearly frustrated that there was no clear route forward. "Can you see anywhere I could reach from your angle?"

He adjusted his weight trying to evenly distribute himself so he could look around. Beneath Siljanna was a thin ledge that spiralled the pillar and would lead her to another bridge but reaching it would be tricky.

"There's a ledge underneath you but getting to it is going to take some effort. Do you trust me?" Harrison asked.

"With my life!" She replied without hesitation, filling him with pride. He began to rock back and forth and as he gained momentum, he called back to Siljanna.

"When I give the word, jump towards me," he encouraged, his voice and body carried by his determination.

"Shit! Seriously?" She asked but didn't wait for a reply. She took in a deep breath, switching her gaze momentarily from Harrison to the sheer drop below. "Don't make me regret this!"

Edging back as far as she could, Siljanna readied herself until Harrison's swing reached the top of its arc.

"Now!" He called, and as the word left his mouth, she bolted forward. After a few energetic strides, she leapt, her arms outstretched as Harrison's swing propelled him towards her. Perfectly timed, he caught her and pulled her close. The impact obviously hurt, but Siljanna didn't complain. Grabbing his belt with her other hand, she steadied herself while his momentum carried them backwards first, then towards the pillar again.

When they were as close to the lower edge as possible, Harrison flung his sister towards it. She connected with the rock face and scrambled to grab the ledge. As his swing took Harrison away, he did all he could to look over his shoulder to make sure Siljanna was all right. He was relieved to see her quickly traversing around the pillar and then drop to the lower area.

With his sister out of sight again, he returned his attention to his own predicament. He couldn't create enough momentum to propel himself to the same ledge and otherwise, seemed to have nowhere to go, again. So much for having the easier path he thought to himself until hearing Morgan's familiar voice.

"At the end of your tether there bud?" He called out, clearly mocking him.

"Yeah, yeah all right! Can we save the jokes for when I'm not hanging precariously off the edge of a cliff?" He asked, his hands sweating.

"Why don't you just let go? You'll find something to grab onto!" Morgan replied, his voice echoing around the canyon.

Harrison looked below him and couldn't see anything that would be within his reach but Morgan's tone was no longer mocking. He rotated but couldn't see his best friend, but like Siljanna had trusted him just a moment ago, Harrison knew he had to trust Morgan now. He took several deep breaths and tried to release his grip. Despite believing in Morgan and the ache in his hands, when he needed to, he couldn't seem to let go. It was like his mind had to convince his body he wasn't about to plummet to his death. He closed his eyes tightly and eventually, was able to release his grip.

As he began to fall, adrenaline kicked in and his eyes flew open just in time to see a rope ladder thrown in his direction. Harrison grabbed it, clinging on with all his might. The ladder went taught and slung Harrison towards a new ledge. That was when he spotted Morgan grasping onto the other end. He collided hard with the canyon edge and it was only by turning in mid-air, so his back took the brunt of the impact, that Harrison was able to maintain his grip.

"Not to sound ungrateful but you could've given me a heads up," he shouted up to his friend.

"Come on, don't be such a baby and get your ass up here," Morgan replied, the mocking tone returning.

Climbing up the ladder, Morgan offered his friend a helping hand onto the ledge. Harrison rolled onto the path and laid on his back for a moment. He didn't want to stop, knowing if he did, his adrenaline would fade, making the aches in his body more prominent. Knowing this about his friend, Morgan pulled Harrison to his feet. Then he pointed out a ledge above the cave he'd come through. It would've been out of reach for one person but by working together they could scale it. Morgan gave Harrison a boost and once on the upper level, Harrison reached down and pulled his friend up and over. On the higher ledge, they were in line with the rock stack Siljanna had been on to begin with and found another bridge. It took them across the canyon and significantly closer to the temple.

As they crossed, the path in front of them ended but above them, they could see the top of the cliff and another rope ladder, but it was tied out of reach. Before they could even look for a way to release it, their attention was drawn to Siljanna, who was climbing up a series of smaller ledges a few yards away. The ledges would lead her to the top of the canyon and she was powering up them like a woman possessed. Their joy for her imminent success was cut short however when they heard Aiden desperately trying to get her attention.

"Siljanna, wait! Can you see that rope? It's out of my reach but you should be able to release it if you just head back down a bit. I need it to swing across this gap," Aiden called out.

Both Harrison and Morgan saw Siljanna look across and acknowledge the rope, but to reach it she'd have to climb away from the summit. They both knew with her competitive nature, although it wasn't stated as part of the challenge, Siljanna wanted to reach the top first. After a moment, the temptation proved too great and she continued climbing up, away from the rope that Aiden needed.

"Come on Aiden, this is the ultimate trial to prove our worth. You can make it, just jump!" She called, trying to encourage him but clearly succumbing to her own ambition.

Aiden groaned loudly so that she would hear his annoyance. With everything they'd experienced so far, it was becoming clear to Harrison and Morgan at least, the true nature of this trial was about trusting in each other and working as a team. It was hard not to wonder if by leaving Aiden to fend for himself, Siljanna had just failed a vital part of the trial. As Siljanna rapidly travelled to the summit, Harrison and Morgan looked for a way to help Aiden. After a moment, they spotted a long pole on the floor. With no obvious use for it in their current situation, Morgan checked with Harrison who nodded in agreement.

"Aiden, we've got something! You should be able to use this to pole vault the gap. Get ready to catch in three, two, one," Morgan shouted, taking a step back and launching the pole like a javelin. Aiden caught it easily and held it up, showing Morgan and Harrison he'd done so.

"Thanks guys, this will do nicely. It looks like there's a ladder on the other side. It'll take me straight to the top," Aiden announced as he vaulted across the gap.

With Aiden's predicament sorted, Morgan and Harrison continued looking for a way to release their ladder, so they could join Siljanna and Aiden at the top. It was beginning to look futile when all of a sudden, the ladder uncoiled and was within their grasp. They looked up and saw Siljanna, hands on her hips and a smile from ear to ear. Both boys quickly manoeuvred up the ladder, rapidly reaching the top to join her.

"What would you do without me?" Siljanna jested just as Aiden reached the top of his ladder. Hearing her comment, he rolled his eyes, obviously still sore she hadn't assisted him.

With the four of them together at the summit, they headed as a unit towards the stone temple. The doorway to the temple was at the top of a wide stone stairway and to their surprise, was guarded by a group of soldiers; and not just any soldiers but twelve Siranor military trainees. As Harrison and the others approached, they stopped just before the steps and three of the militants walked towards them. The leader was a young man with olive skin and jet black hair.

"Am I safe to assume you are the four warden academy students?" The young man asked, polite but formal. As Harrison and the others looked at each other, mildly confused, Siljanna stepped forward to respond to the young recruit.

"We are, and your team are standing between us and our graduation. Will you be kindly stepping aside?" She enquired, her words dripping with sarcasm, clearly not asking with any sincerity.

"That's not exactly the plan," he replied, picking up on her attitude. "We are the final part of your trial."

He paused, looking at each of them, assuming their capabilities and seemed to accept that each of the boys were a moderate threat but clearly underestimated Siljanna.

"You're part of our trial?" Morgan asked, taking note of the soldiers behind the three that approached them.

"You and your team are part of our training exercise as well. What better way to train the future Imperial military than by defeating its own elite guardians?" The young man said, his tone cocky as he drew his sword.

Siljanna glanced at the other recruits on the stairwell, each of them also drawing their weapons and her mind went straight into tactical mode. The army recruits had the high ground and some were equipped with firearms, so the first thing she and her team needed was cover.

Harrison, reading her mind like he often could in battle scenarios, drew his broadsword and pulled Siljanna behind him. In his defensive stance, the sword provided a decent amount of cover. Realising that neither he nor Siljanna were retreating, but pressing forward, the olive-skinned leader ordered the four shooters in his team to fire. The wave of bullets struck his blade but after deflecting the shots, Harrison charged at the leader and the two soldiers beside him.

While the four ranged soldiers were distracted, Morgan and Aiden had flanked them, leaving Siljanna open to strike the unorganised bulk of the force. It was five-on-one, but they were in disarray. She drew her axes and sprinted in their direction, emanating confidence. As she neared, she quickly looked over to see Morgan and Aiden reach the shooters, forcing them to draw melee weapons in order to defend themselves, and Harrison comfortably contending with the three recruits before him.

Siljanna whipped past her brother and propelled herself towards the remaining fighters. With a ferocious flurry of strikes, Siljanna overpowered the first two recruits in her way until they dropped their weapons and surrendered. The third fighter charged down the stairs, but instead of using the high ground to his advantage, he lost his footing and she struck him in the sternum. Then throwing him over her shoulder, he went crashing into the steps below. She couldn't help but smirk at the crunching sound of the soldier's impact, that was going to hurt in the morning!

She took a second glance at the others, making sure her team weren't in trouble. Harrison had made quick work of the two subordinates but was still fighting the olive-skinned leader while Morgan and Aiden still battled the recruits that initially fired at her and Harrison; one of which was now unconscious. They stood back-to-back taunting the remaining military trainees and their tactic worked. Their opponents charged recklessly at them and Siljanna knew those fighters didn't stand a chance against the combined force of Morgan and Aiden.

She returned her focus to the last of her own targets and decided to change her approach. Holding her axes more defensively, she strode up the stairs and attempted to circle the soldiers. High ground had been their only advantage and she reckoned she could strip them of it. Striding carefully, she kept her gaze on the clueless army grunts. They'd completely lost focus, their eyes flicking from her to their floored friends and then to their leader, who was clearly struggling to defend against Harrison's attacks.

With their confidence diminished, Siljanna took her chance, manoeuvring above them on the steps, feigned a couple of strikes and then dashed towards the temple doorway. She could hear them pursue her but once sure they'd let their guard down, she turned sharply, striking out with a series of kicks. She caught one of them in the chest, winding him and as her kick landed, she used the contact to spin in mid-air and strike the last fighter. Her heel connected with his jaw and he too went crashing to the floor. With all five of the soldiers she'd set her sights on down, she took a moment to enjoy her victory before checking on the rest of her team one final time. Morgan and Aiden had all of the former shooters on the floor, disarmed. Then turning to her brother, Siljanna saw Harrison use a strong, thrusting blow to knock the olive-skinned leader's weapon away.

With no way to defend himself, the leader's knees gave out and he crumpled to the floor. He raised his hands in surrender, realising his whole team had been defeated. Harrison holstered his weapon and offered the leader a hand. The young man took it hesitantly but once back on his feet, dusted himself off and looked rather sheepish.

"How? There are four of you, against twelve of us. We had the high ground and ranged weapons but you defeated us. That girl took out five of my guys!" The young leader exclaimed, his voice breaking as the shocking turn of events stumped him.

"We've been intensively training for four years, and you're what? First, maybe second-year recruits? Don't berate yourself too much," Harrison explained. "Your biggest mistake was assuming the number of people in your team meant this would be an easy fight for you, and for under-estimating my sister. She's easily worth ten untrained men."

Harrison smirked as he turned away and headed up the stone stairs to re-join the others. As they reached the top, the four of them smiled at one another and proceeded through the temple doorway. In front of them was a table with four small glass bottles standing proudly upon it and they knew instantly those were the graduation symbols they had to collect. They were the same bottles each of them would hang on the magnolia tree at their graduation ceremony. Once each of them had collected a bottle, they headed back out of the temple and were greeted by Tutor Taylor.

"Well done graduates! It was close, but you've all passed the final trial. Please head down the path behind the temple, you'll find the truck waiting. Once you are all in and ready, we'll head back to the academy."

Chapter Five
Graduation

The return journey felt much shorter to all of them, but that was probably because they were all significantly more relaxed. As they pulled up before the main gates, the four of them were thrilled to walk in and see Charlie and Carter standing in the quad waiting for them. It was like a partial family reunion! They embraced one another in a variety of friendly manners and Siljanna couldn't resist giving Charlie a kiss on the cheek, making him blush. When Tutor Taylor arrived in the courtyard, she was joined by Tutors Anderson and Matthews.

"Welcome back to both Charlie and Carter. It's been strange without you, but your new tutors inform me you have both performed admirably and passed your final examinations with honours," Tutor Matthews confirmed, making both of them smile gladly.

"Congratulations and thank you for making the journey back to join us for the graduation ceremony," Tutor Anderson said, beaming with pride. "Each one of you is an asset to this training program and I know you are all capable of doing incredible things. I am also pleased to inform you that Dylan Rose has passed his training but due to the nature of his new assignment, he can't join us tonight. We have a glass bottle that will be hung in his honour."

"You each have free time until dusk to freshen up for the ceremony. If there is anyone you'd like in attendance, please contact them at your earliest convenience. They only have a couple of hours to get here," Tutor Taylor advised and as soon as she did, Siljanna dashed over to the phone and started to dial.

Harrison didn't even need to guess, he knew she'd be calling their father. He was waiting to hear her elated tones but instead, what he heard was the sound of disappointment. He caught her say, *'of course I understand'* as she hung up the phone. Harrison headed over and put a hand on her shoulder.

"He's not coming, is he?" Harrison asked.

"No; he wishes he could, but he's been called to the capital on business," she replied sadly.

"I'm sure it's important. He would've been here for you if there was any chance Sil. Is mum coming?" He enquired.

"She wants to but isn't sure about coming alone. She hasn't been here before and it'll be dark by the time the ceremony ends," Siljanna sighed, clearly disappointed. It was obviously affecting her that neither of their parents would be coming to celebrate their achievement.

"Let me call Rylie. I'm sure she'll bring mum here," he said, giving her hope. She smiled and stepped away from the phone, allowing him to make the call.

"Good afternoon, Hawk Eye tavern," Nate answered.

"Nate, it's Harrison," he replied.

"Hey Harrison, is everything okay?" Nate asked.

"Absolutely, we just passed our final trial! We'll be graduating as wardens tonight," he explained.

"Harrison that's incredible, not that we had any doubt. I'm so proud of you, and the others of course," Nate replied, his reaction pure joy. It took a few minutes of listening to words of praise before Harrison was able to explain the situation.

"Thanks Nate, that means a lot. Listen, I was wondering if Rylie could do me a favour. My father cannot make the celebration and mum's nervous to travel here alone. Could Rylie bring her?" Harrison asked.

"Of course! I'll tell her to get ready. In fact, if you'll have us, I'll close the tavern and we'll all come," Nate added.

"Really? That would mean the world to us, Nate!" Harrison said, truly touched.

"Of course, we'll spread the word too, in case anyone else wants to join us," Nate replied, his voice still elated.

Shortly afterwards, the plan was set and Harrison told Siljanna they were all coming. Although obviously gutted their father wouldn't be there, the fact everyone else was coming lifted her spirits. Not as much as Morgan's though, for as soon as he heard that Anora was attending, he rushed to the showers to freshen up.

As dusk fell, all the graduates had the chance to clean and catch up before the ceremony started. Getting all the dust and grime off his skin was such a relief and even though he felt more comfortable in his training armour, Harrison decided to wear dark jeans, ankle boots and a white shirt for the evening's celebration. He also trimmed his beard and hair so he looked at his best, even though he ached from head to toe. The shirt didn't quite cover the large bruise on his back that now spread to the base of his neck from when he'd collided with the cliff, so he also grabbed his favourite leather jacket and slung it on. It was going to be a warm evening but his mum had never seen the bumps and bruises that came with training, and he didn't want her to start now.

Knocking on the bathroom door, Morgan called back to him so that Harrison knew he was nearly ready. When he emerged, Harrison was stunned to see Morgan, who over the last four years had mainly worn training gear or armour, was wearing a black shirt, grey trousers and smart shoes. He was also fairly sure his best friend was wearing cologne. He'd shaved his head, leaving a distinct hairline against his dark skin and removed any sign of facial hair. Harrison would never admit it aloud, but he looked pretty damn good.

As the two boys headed down the stairs, they bumped into Charlie who was looking as smart as ever, even his hair looked combed for a change, and Aiden and Carter, who were both dressed a bit more casually. As the five of them headed down the hallway, taking in each and every creaky floorboard, knowing it could be the last time; they found themselves joking about all the memories they'd made over the last four years.

Reaching the stairs to the female dorms, they stopped to wait for Siljanna. As she came down, Harrison could've sworn he heard Charlie's heart thudding. Siljanna had styled her hair in a way they'd never seen before, shaving the left-hand side just above her ear and framing it with a neat braid, clipping it in place under the layers at the back. She'd also cut the length and crimped it so her prominent strand, now focused on the right-hand side, fell longer at the front and bounced gently as she walked. She was dressed in skin-tight leather trousers, knee-high boots and a red, bodice-style top. Harrison had never thought of his sister as attractive, but this was not a side of his sister any of them had ever seen. Charlie extended his hand as she reached the bottom of the stairs and linked her arm with his.

"You look absolutely stunning, Sil," he said almost gawking. She blushed, the compliment obviously surprising her.

"Thank you Charlie, you guys look great too. Shall we go? We shouldn't be late for our own graduation," she replied ducking her head to avoid their stares, a little self-conscious by their reaction to her transformation. With all six graduates together, they made their way to the quad.

When they arrived, the area looked incredible. The sun had almost set but the quad was alight with candles in glass jars and lanterns dangling lazily in the trees. The magnolia tree at the centre was in full bloom, with dusty pink flowers cascading down each of the branches. They followed the stone path towards the tree and saw all of the tutors, the Auren family and Anora standing next to a table filled with champagne glasses, all poured and ready to enjoy. Elijah Ashby and a few of their other friends from town had also come for the celebration.

Rylie spotted them first and came charging up to give Harrison a hug. After congratulating him, she embraced the others and spent at least two minutes obsessing over how drop-dead gorgeous Siljanna looked. Nate, Paige and Evie all waved with huge smiles on their faces as Harrison went over to hug his mum. She embraced him tightly before taking a good look at him.

"Look at you, my wonderful boy. All grown up and becoming a warden. I've never been prouder of you and your sister than I am right now!" She exclaimed, her chocolate brown eyes twinkling with pride, or possibly the side effect of the champagne.

"Thanks mum, I'm so glad you came," he said, smiling. He realised then how genuinely pleased he was to have her there. He hadn't given the graduation ceremony much thought, focussing entirely on earning the right to be there but now he'd done it, he couldn't imagine celebrating without his mum, sister and friends by his side.

Next, he went over and shook Nate's hand but was pulled in by him for a hug. Harrison tried his best to swallow the pain of being struck on his bruise during Nate's embrace and luckily no one noticed his grimace. If it wasn't for the fact Nate had light brown hair with streaks of blonde, people could've mistaken them as being related.

Like Harrison, Nate had brown eyes, strong facial features and a defined jawline framed by a light stubble beard but it didn't quite conceal the faint scar on his upper lip. Nate had come to the celebration in dark corduroy trousers, a green shirt, brown boots and a matching jacket. All his earthy tones made his wife's attire stand out even more than usual. Paige was wearing a summery blue dress and white jacket which contrasted her sleek, dark-brown hair. Rylie had certainly inherited her feminine features from Paige.

After hugging both Paige and Evie too, who were thankfully much more gentle with their embraces, Harrison noticed Evie's growth spurt had finally kicked in. She was going to be one of those girls that was always rather short, but the difference in her height now was noticeable, at least to him. Her light brown hair had strands of blonde just like her father's but was incredibly long, falling almost to her waist and lightly crimped all the way down. It looked like she'd had it in a tight plait all day. She was wearing a sweet green blouse, frayed white shorts and little slip-on shoes.

With the greetings done, Harrison moved over to the champagne table to grab a glass and spotted Morgan awkwardly talking with his mother. It was hilarious seeing him fret over her, but he seemed to be handling himself better than usual. Siljanna was with them, rolling her eyes, still with her arm linked through Charlie's. Harrison was certain Charlie had no intention of letting her go for the entire evening.

A light clinking of glass drew everyone's attention to the tutors standing in front of the magnolia tree.

"Good evening everybody and welcome to the Tivani Academy. For those of you who don't know me, I'm Tutor Anderson and it has been my pleasure to be the head instructor for the warden graduates before you," he explained.

Anderson had a thin glass of champagne in his stocky hand and frankly, it looked odd. He needed some kind of pint glass or even a pitcher to look more natural, but that was bound to happen later.

"Speech, speech! Don't make a speech!" A joking voice called out. With a smile, Anderson continued anyway.

"It is our pleasure to announce that Harrison and Siljanna Stone, Morgan Foster, Charlie Blake, Aiden Moore, Carter Henley and although not with us tonight, Dylan Rose are this year's successful graduates. Effective immediately they are fully-fledged wardens!" He began, and there was a round of applause from everyone present. "Whilst Charlie will be returning to his duties in Siranor and Carter to Yasras in the morning; Harrison, Siljanna, Morgan and Aiden, you have the choice of placement between any of the Imperial towns or a place in Siranor. We do hope you will choose to stay with us in Tivani but there is no need to decide now. Tonight we are here to honour your fantastic achievement by placing your names on our iconic magnolia tree, and of course, to drink!" Anderson exclaimed, finishing his toast and making everyone laugh, most of them not expecting him to be so entertaining.

"As I call your name, please come forward and place your keepsakes on the tree," Tutor Taylor said, standing beside her colleagues. She called them forward one at a time, allowing each of them to tie their bottles to a branch. As the sun set, the bottles gleamed in the fading light. Tutor Matthews then took the bottle they'd prepared for Dylan and placed it next to the others.

After the ceremony was over, the drinking did indeed begin, but Harrison was not in any hurry to get drunk. He wanted to take in every moment as he'd worked so hard over the last four years to get here. Standing to the side watching his friends and family merrily chatting with one another, he didn't notice when Rylie came up behind him and linked her arm through his.

"Congratulations Harrison, you did it!" She said, the purity of her smile illuminating her eyes. They looked more silver than grey in the lantern light, like a precious stone.

"Thank you Rylie. It means so much that you and your family came tonight, and brought our mum along too," he replied, blinking to prevent himself from staring at her.

"Are you kidding, wild horses couldn't have kept us away. I mean, the sight of Morgan drooling over your mum alone was worth the walk!" She giggled.

They glanced back towards Morgan as she made the comment. Somehow, he had made Anora laugh so much she almost coughed up her champagne. Even Charlie and Siljanna were laughing at whatever he'd said.

"So, I put a little keepsake in my graduation bottle, did you see it?" Harrison asked, encouraging Rylie to look back at him.

"No, what was it, something special?" She enquired in her playful yet curious way. She was definitely getting drunk and the thought made him laugh softly.

"It was a small stick of sage," he replied. As Rylie tilted her head, clearly puzzled by the announcement, he explained. "Do you remember at the end of last year, I said you'd given me an idea? It was smelling those herbs in your apron. They inspired me to use the senses for my trial. It was one of my most defining moments at the academy and I only had the idea thanks to you."

As he spoke, he focused his gaze on his graduation bottle and the keepsake within. After a moment, when Rylie hadn't replied, he looked towards her and realised she was quite possibly speechless, a state he'd never seen her in before.

She shied away momentarily but as she did, Harrison noticed just how beautiful she looked. Her long hair was loose, its natural curl flicking out where the layers ended and her angled fringe framed her face. She was wearing navy jeans that highlighted the gentle curve of her hips and an off-the-shoulder top. Her heeled boots made it so there was slightly less of a height difference between them and complimented her look. He gently pushed back a strand of hair that blew across her face and as his fingers brushed her cheek, she giggled and took his hand.

"Dance with me," she said, not really asking. She gave him an encouraging tug but as she'd had quite a few more drinks than him at that point, he could easily resist her.

"I'm not dancing," he replied with a laugh.

"Why not? I'm sure you can!" She insisted, trying to give him another tug but instead, he adjusted her grip so she twirled on the spot and lost her balance, falling into him. He cushioned her fall with his bruised arm and winced from the pain but despite his reaction, they both started laughing.

"I can dance, but you've been drinking, and I've got enough bruises already! I don't need bruised toes too," he replied, smiling with a wicked grin. She answered his comment with a friendly shove and feigned treading on his toes anyway before they re-joined the others.

The rest of the party went in a bit of a haze. There was music and laughter, story-telling and dancing. With a considerable number of drinks behind them, one of the most memorable parts of the night was watching Anora and Paige sing while Nate and Rylie danced around the quad. Nate was a talented dancer and even tipsy, Rylie followed his lead like it was as natural as breathing. Harrison found watching them almost hypnotic. However, hands down the best moment of the night was watching Tutor Anderson fall off a bench. He'd had way too many drinks but somehow managed to save the beverage in his hand whilst crashing to the floor.

It had been dark for hours before the visitors left, starting the long walk back to town. The graduates all crashed in the quad, deciding to spend one last night at the academy instead of going straight back home. Siljanna and Charlie disappeared first while the rest of them dispersed one by one after that. Morgan and Harrison chatted for another hour whilst gazing up at the stars, finally crashing one last time in their room.

The following morning, they all stirred with varying degrees of both body and headaches but the memories of the day before were worth it. Charlie was the first to say goodbye. Siljanna seemed especially sad to see him go, wanting him to linger but as he departed for the train station, she gave him a big hug and waved him off with the others. Harrison couldn't help but wonder if something had happened between them but now wasn't the time to ask. Carter left shortly afterwards, needing to walk to Tivani to fetch his horse from Elijah's stables before returning to Yasras.

That left the final four once more. With all their belongings packed, they headed to the tutor offices to assign themselves to their chosen towns. Harrison knew that he and Siljanna planned to be posted in Tivani and Aiden had mentioned at the party he wanted to transfer to

Hale, a town in the North; but Harrison hadn't asked Morgan what he was going to do. He could choose to take a position in Niyati, to be with his family, but his hometown only consisted of about five hundred people and they already had three wardens compared to the near six thousand in Tivani with just forty wardens. Selfishly, Harrison hoped that Morgan would choose to stay in Tivani rather than returning home, but he didn't have to wait long to find out.

As they arrived at the tutor offices, Matthews, Taylor and Anderson were all waiting for them. Tutor Anderson was still nursing a hangover, so it fell to Tutor Taylor to address them. She rolled her eyes as Anderson stepped aside, overplaying the severity of his headache.

"Good morning everyone, I take it you all enjoyed your graduation ceremony? Today we perform our final duty as your tutors, to confirm your chosen locations where you will serve as wardens. Have you each decided?" She asked. Harrison looked to each of his friends and his twin with a smile.

"I would like to be stationed in Tivani please, under Commander Stone," Siljanna replied first. It was the least shocking revelation Harrison thought he'd ever hear. He decided to go next, confirming what they probably expected.

"I too would like to be based in Tivani," he announced. With a smile, Tutor Taylor marked both of them with placements at the Tivani guardhouse. Aiden then spoke up confirming he wanted to transfer to Hale, leaving just Morgan to announce his decision. He nodded as if confirming to himself before speaking.

"I've given it much thought and I would like to be based in Tivani please," he said and Harrison literally had to prevent himself from cheering. "I would also like to put in a partner request if I can, that is if Harrison is willing to continue working with me for the foreseeable future?"

Morgan chuckled as he spoke, but there was genuine uncertainty in his words. Tutor Taylor looked at Harrison, encouraging his response.

"Of course! I'm probably the only person that can put up with your crap anyway," Harrison joked, walking over and giving Morgan a friendly hug. He couldn't have been happier with the outcome.

"I can make the request," Tutor Taylor replied. "You will initially be assigned into the same guard unit, with senior warden Logan your reporting officer. He is nearing retirement so if you prove to him how well you work together, I'm sure he'll swiftly approve your partnership within the unit."

With their placement letters in hand, Harrison, Siljanna and Morgan walked Aiden to the train station and waved him off as he began his journey to Hale. Once he'd gone, they followed the winding path into town. Going through the woodlands, they passed the road to Lake Ismay and Elijah's blacksmith before reaching the northern bridge of town.

Located on the conflux of two rivers, to get in or out of Tivani, travellers had to cross one of three bridges. The northern bridge linked the town to the academy, train station and onward to Siranor; the eastern bridge to the coast and Yasras or the southern bridge towards the smaller towns of Fenian and Niyati.

They'd all made the trip several times over the years and knew the path like the backs of their hands but this time the journey had a greater impact. They were going home but once they arrived, their lives as wardens would begin. The sound of running water told them they were close and five minutes later, the northern bridge was in sight. Unable to contain her excitement, Siljanna started running towards the bridge.

"Race you!" She shouted playfully.

Neither Harrison nor Morgan were expecting it but pursued her just for fun. Running as fast as his legs would allow but still aching from the previous day, Harrison couldn't quite catch his sister before she reached her target.

The weathered granite bridge was a pleasantly familiar sight. It neatly arced over the river below and was wide enough for travelling merchants to cross with their caravans or small vehicles but was mainly used by pedestrians. Very few people outside of Siranor owned vehicles, most being kept by the military or Imperator for official duties. The only car any of them had been in was the academy truck, but Harrison did love the idea of one day owning a motorcycle. Once Harrison caught up to his sister, who was doing a victory dance on the bridge, he grabbed her around the waist and chucked her over his good shoulder. She was so light, he had no problem picking her up but she quickly wriggled out of his grasp.

"Oi stop that! I still won!" She claimed, laughing as she broke free and continued to mock him.

They carried on play-fighting until they were met by the wardens on duty. One of the more mundane warden tasks was to check any new or unknown arrivals to town as per Siranor's strict rules on arresting mages or mage sympathisers. Recognising them instantly, all three were let through by the guards without trouble, so they carried on towards the main square.

As the third-largest Imperial town, Tivani was home to just over six thousand people but several more families lived in the outskirts and would venture into town for the market, apothecary or school. Most of the houses were made from a combination of stone and wood with thatched or cedar roofs. It gave the town a rustic charm but each home still had many modern comforts, thanks to their close connections to the technologically advanced Siranor.

When they arrived in the square, the town's iconic fountain stood proudly before them. It had been built to commemorate the creation of the Encia filters, the devices that ensured the water that flowed from the fountain and into their homes was safe to drink. Created to look like a natural waterfall, the harmless water cascaded down several tiers of marble ledges to the basin below and had become the iconic focal point in town. Overlooking it was the next most notable feature of Tivani, the Hawk Eye tavern; but they couldn't stop in just yet. They had to report to the guardhouse first, which was just off the western side of the square, past the market.

The guardhouse looked smaller than they recalled but compared to the size of the academy, realistically it was going to look small. It was easy to tell that Commander Stone was out of town because the wardens on-site were all much more relaxed, socialising with each other and passers-by. The guardhouse was a tall stone building with a prison next door but it was rarely needed. Serious offenders would be transferred straight to Siranor so its main uses were to detain the odd domestic or drunken altercation and theft offenders.

Seeing the warden's demeanour reminded Siljanna that their father wasn't there and her excitement level notably decreased. The trio headed inside and met senior officer Logan, who was overseeing the guardhouse in Commander Stone's absence. He was the officer they'd be reporting to, at least until he retired. His soft grey hair and crow's feet highlighted his age but he still gave them an enthusiastic welcome.

"Ahh the fresh blood! It's good to see you all again. Are you looking forward to getting started?" Logan asked.

"Absolutely, we can't wait sir!" Morgan replied.

"That's great; the sooner you guys get settled, the sooner I can retire. But before I get ahead of myself, let's get you kitted out with your warden uniforms. Oh and Siljanna, I have a letter here from your father. I think you'll enjoy reading it," Logan hinted, handing over the letter. As she read it, Siljanna's spirits were lifted immeasurably.

"No way! Dad has arranged for me to train as his next deputy, with the view of taking over as Commander when he retires. This is amazing!" She exclaimed, squealing as she spoke.

"That's great Sil, what you always wanted," Harrison congratulated, gripping her shoulders affectionately. "If there is anyone who can fill our father's shoes in the future, it's you."

"Thanks Harrison, that really means a lot," she replied. "The letter also says he'll be home the day after tomorrow. We can have a family dinner to celebrate then!"

Harrison wasn't so keen to hear that part but it was to be expected. When Logan showed them to their lockers and handed over their uniforms, it was a humbling moment. The standard warden uniform was a grey leather armour with the iconic black and gold trim and the emblem of the guard, a golden lion on the pauldrons.

All warden armour had the same trim but the senior officer's main leather was lighter and the Commander's, white, so it was literally clear to see their rank based on the shade of their armour. Logan also confirmed that Siljanna would shadow him until her father returned while Harrison and Morgan would join their guard unit. Their first task being the southern bridge checks. It wasn't a thrilling assignment but they couldn't expect to be heroes the first day on the job. After completing their orientation, Siljanna and Harrison headed home while Morgan went to the Hawk Eye tavern. He'd arranged to rent a room until he could find an affordable place of his own.

The Stone's house was between the guardhouse and the square. The house was small but comfortable, although they had converted the attic into a third bedroom once Harrison and Siljanna had gotten too old to share. As they reached the front door, the smell of baking was once again floating through the air. Anora almost dropped her tray of brownies when they entered. She rushed up to her children and squeezed them both tightly.

"You're home! I wasn't expecting you until later," she exclaimed.

"Well, we could always leave," Harrison teased but quickly got tail whipped with a tea towel in response.

"Don't you dare! Nate and Paige have invited all of us for dinner at the tavern. That's what the brownies are for, a thank you for escorting me yesterday. It was such a wonderful evening and your friend Morgan is delightful," Anora said, looking down at the plate of treats which she knew were Paige and Evie's favourite. In the process, she missed Siljanna rolling her eyes and Harrison spurt out a laugh over the Morgan comment.

As usual, the evening at the Hawk Eye tavern was great. Several of the locals came into the bar and congratulated them on their achievement whilst sharing a drink from the impressive array behind the bar. Rylie, who'd now been working full-time at the tavern for a year had become somewhat of a pro and was mixing a variety of cocktails, while Paige played the piano by the fire. Evie's face lit up when she saw the brownies and they spent hours chatting and looking forward to the days ahead.

The first two days on the job went by like a flash but when Commander Stone returned, as expected the atmosphere changed. Siljanna went straight under his wing while the other wardens diligently attended to their duties, barely speaking unless Commander Stone wasn't within earshot. Harrison and Morgan tried not to let his presence affect them, but it helped that the southern bridge kept them pretty far from the guardhouse.

That night was the Stone family dinner, and despite Harrison's best efforts, the gathering was awkward from the moment they left the guardhouse.

"What happened to you today Harrison, you're covered in scuff marks?" Siljanna asked innocently.

"I was helping some merchants with heavy wares across the bridge. I didn't realise how filthy I was until now!" He replied.

"You should take more pride in that uniform Harrison, like your sister. You'll never see her looking so tarnished," Sampson interjected, his tone exuding disappointment.

"Apologies father, I'll take more care next time," Harrison said with remorse, judging himself more harshly while Sampson disregarded his apology.

When they arrived at their front door, they were greeted by the wafting smell of dinner. Whatever Anora was cooking smelt divine. Sampson entered first and when he found his wife, gave her a gentle kiss on the cheek.

"What delights have you prepared for us this evening my love?" He asked.

"Your favourite of course, now all of you go clean up, dinner will be ready soon," Anora replied sweetly.

Sampson laughed at the comment looking specifically at his son before heading into his bedroom to change. Over dinner, Anora asked about their day.

"So how was training with your father today Siljanna, has he moulded you into the ideal successor yet?" She asked playfully.

"No moulding required, she's already perfect," Sampson answered, making Siljanna blush.

"It was great, everything dad has taught me has been inspiring, not that I had any doubt," Siljanna replied, making Sampson's smile spread further.

"How about you Harrison, any exciting tales to tell?" Anora asked, turning to face her son with a look of genuine curiosity.

"Most of my afternoon was spent aiding merchants coming in for the market. One is a quality spice supplier, you should visit once the stall is up. I think you'd like the variety he's brought," Harrison said, smiling softly. Anora was about to comment when Sampson interrupted.

"Have you given more thought to the Imperial council Siljanna? I would like to introduce you once we've completed more of your training," he asked, completely disregarding the conversation Harrison and his mother had begun.

Resigning that his involvement in the dinner conversation was over, Harrison sat back and listened to the rest of his family converse, only speaking when asked a direct question. After two hours, Harrison excused himself and headed to his attic room. Siljanna gave him a confused look as he left, but said nothing to stop him. As usual, she hadn't noticed their father's disdain towards him and was enjoying the attention.

He could still hear their muffled voices as they chatted in the living room but distracted himself by re-reading his favourite fantasy book. In the tale, the hero was part of a cursed warrior caste that had to prove themselves in combat or die trying to regain their honour. He'd read through the story at least a dozen times and knew the book almost word for word, but reading the journey of his hero soothed him. When it came to dealing with his father, escapism really was the best cure.

Over the next two months, Logan retired and his final act was to confirm Harrison and Morgan's partnership. They had patrols covering the entire town so became familiar faces with many of the locals. They were both promoted to senior wardens too, their natural abilities quickly outshining even some of the longer-standing wardens at the guardhouse.

When a courier delivered a letter from Siranor, summoning Sampson to the capital for another consultation with the Imperator's council, Siljanna was going to face her first stint as acting commander. Sampson kept a travelling bag in his office so was prepared to leave at a moment's notice and gladly handed over the guardhouse and office keys to his daughter. He was eager to leave, but in his heart, Sampson knew it was only so that he could return and hear all about her inevitable success sooner. The letter implied that he was going to be required in the capital for a week but he prepared her for longer, just in case. She diligently listened to all of the duties she'd be responsible for and saluted as he left. He saluted back but smiled before departing.

Reaching the northern bridge, Commander Stone was asked to wait by Morgan while Harrison inspected an incoming merchant. The man was wearing a dark, hooded cloak and looked odd. His horse moved slowly as if struggling to pull the heavy load of goods, all of which were covered by a variety of sheets and a tarpaulin. Harrison signalled for the man to stop and noticed he was clearly agitated. Before he got a chance to even look under the sheets, his father called out to him.

"What's taking so long Harrison? I need to pass, now," Sampson shouted, his arms folded in frustration.

"This won't take a moment Commander, it's just standard procedure, sir," Morgan interceded, trying to let Harrison continue his search of the merchant's cart.

"Just let this man pass so I can get on my way, or you boys are coming with me to personally explain to the Imperator why I'm late for the meeting," Sampson ordered impatiently.

Hearing his father's threat, Harrison sighed, ceased his search and waved the merchant through. Once he'd cleared the bridge, Sampson was on his way without a second glance at his son. Harrison gave a sarcastic wave as his father moved out of sight, making Morgan laugh. Standing next to his partner, he couldn't help but look back at the merchant.

"Something wasn't right with that guy," Harrison said, vocalising his intuition.

"Who, your father?" Morgan asked humorously.

"Well, him too but no. I meant that merchant. He looked shady. I wish I'd had a better chance to examine him and his wares," Harrison said, shifting his weight from one foot to the other, clearly anxious.

"The guy was probably tired, could've had a long journey to get here. Try not to worry about it and focus on the positive. Your father's going to be out of town for at least a week!" Morgan commented, highlighting their commander's hasty departure.

"You always know how to cheer me up!" Harrison replied as he and Morgan continued their patrol.

The merchant looked back through his hood at the wardens. He'd gotten lucky with the impatient traveller seeking passage but believed his ruse would've held up. After all, he'd pulled off the humble book merchant well enough to convince the other town wardens over the last few years. His situation, however, had dramatically changed, and although he knew he'd never be able to return to Siranor openly, he needed to let his niece at the institute know what they'd worked on for so long *was* possible. The *power* they sought within their grasp. He had the formula and no guard or his own fleeting mortality was going to stop him.

Chapter Six
Consequences

The trader's market had been in good flow for a week with dozens of visiting traders in the main square and around the fountain. Paige and Anora were casually browsing through the stalls, chatting as they shopped. Anora was mainly searching for the spice vendor Harrison mentioned while Paige liked to look for old books. Anora knew her friend was curious about mages and magic although Paige claimed learning about it was just a teacher's habit, not a specific interest.

One of the stalls in the square they hadn't seen before was a book vendor, his stand brimming with old texts on the planet, religion, history and even the Encia studies. Anora was surprised the vendor had been let through but Paige was captivated, searching through the titles and making a pile she presumably wanted to buy. Anora flicked through a random book while she waited until suddenly the vendor came up and grabbed her wrist. The man was wearing a hooded cloak and had a vice-like grip.

"See anything you like?" He said in a creepy tone that sent shivers down her spine.

"I'm just waiting for my friend," Anora replied politely.

"Begone then! If my wares are not good enough, just go!" He spat, discarding her. Seeing the altercation, Paige abandoned the books and the two women quickly stepped away, Anora cradling her hand.

"What a creep, are you okay Anora?" Paige asked, concerned for her friend.

"Yes, I'm fine. Sorry, I have no idea what I did to offend him," she apologised, baffled at the man's reaction to her idle browsing.

"Forget it and forget him. Let's go fill that basket of yours with some delectable goodies to feast on later," Paige replied, secretly crossing her fingers for more brownies. She tried to change the subject to take Anora's mind off the odd book vendor.

"Did I mention we are hoping to visit Yasras next weekend? My parents are so keen to see the girls and Rylie can't stop talking about travelling. She's clearly her father's daughter!" She said humorously.

"That sounds lovely, it's easy to forget Nate was a traveller. He was from Carlisse, right? But travelled here and met you just before the war?" Anora checked, recalling Paige's earlier tales.

"That's right, but he'd been travelling for a few years before we met too. There's not much of the Eastern Continent he hasn't seen but luckily he wanted to stop travelling after we met. He always loved seeing the world, and Rylie is becoming more and more like him every day," Paige replied, and Anora could see the love on her friend's face as she spoke about her eldest daughter.

"Sampson and I have never even talked about travelling as a family. Then again, he's only ever interested in travelling to the capital or working, and with the issues between him and Harrison, it's probably for the best," Anora admitted, saddened at just the thought of the way things were between her husband and son.

Paige was well aware of the situation, having taken Harrison in on several evenings when he couldn't bear to stay at home. It wasn't something Anora liked talking about but Paige knew she was thankful Harrison was always welcome at the tavern. Paige gave her friend a cuddle as they carried on shopping.

Back at the tavern, Nate and Rylie were preparing for the evening rush. They'd just received a delivery of wines and spirits that Nate was lovingly adding to his display wall while Rylie focused on cleaning the tables before they opened. Evie was sketching joyfully in the corner, sticking her tongue out as she concentrated. She'd loved Harrison's graduation party so much that ever since every drawing was either of the magnolia tree lit up by the lanterns or people celebrating. One of her drawings really looked like Rylie and her father as they'd danced, and Rylie loved it so much that she framed it in her room.

Covered in chalk dust, Evie was lying on her stomach by the fire when without warning, she dropped the chalk and started shaking, her eyes rolling back into her head as a seizure took hold. Nate and Rylie both dropped everything and rushed to her side. Pulling his daughter into his lap, Nate started talking to Evie in a clear voice which he tried desperately to keep steady.

"Evie, sweetheart, can you hear me? Please… open your eyes," he pleaded while stroking her hair.

"Come back to us little sis', please," Rylie begged, taking one of Evie's hands and holding it firmly. She was almost in tears as she watched helplessly. She could hear Evie's ragged breaths as she sputtered out random words. She heard *'blood'* but everything else was too muffled to understand. Unable to bear it anymore, Rylie turned to her father, tears rushing down her face.

"Dad, we have to take her to the doctors in Siranor again. We should get a second opinion. There has to be something they can do!" She cried. Nate turned his face away, unable to look at his eldest daughter. He shut his eyes and continued whispering to Evie. "Please, listen to me!" Rylie shouted, trying to get him to face her. "We can't make her live like this. If you don't take her, I will!"

"We can't!" He cried, his voice tearing through his throat as he sharply faced her, eyes pleading.

"Why not, I don't understand?" Rylie sobbed, her voice laced with despair. *Why wouldn't he even try getting a second opinion?* After a slight hesitation, Nate's deep brown eyes connected with hers and Rylie paused, seeing tears roll down her father's face.

"Your sister isn't sick Rylie. She's a mage!" He exclaimed in a hushed tone.

His words rang in her mind as she leant back in disbelief. *How could this be?* The silence between them lingered until they noticed Evie's spasms stopped and she was lying still, cradled in Nate's lap, breathing softly. Realising she was okay, both Nate and Rylie let out a joint sigh of relief. As Nate focused on Rylie again, he could see the questions running through her mind and knew he had to explain.

"Do you recall the stories I told you about my parents? How they sadly died a few years before you were born? Well, what I haven't told you is that your grandfather was a mage, and your grandmother, an Ar'encal." The look on Rylie's face was completely dumbfounded, her eyes wide and lips gaping. "I know it's a lot to take in sweetheart, but it's true. Your mother and I only kept it from you because knowing put you at risk with these damn mage hunts," Nate revealed, wiping tears away.

He saw the look in her eyes change but continued regardless. Rylie had given up her dream to help run the family tavern and be there for Evie, so she deserved to know the truth.

"Dad I—" Rylie started but couldn't finish.

"When Evie first started getting severe headaches and nightmares, we took her to see the doctors in Siranor. Once the seizures started though, Evie told us she had another nightmare, but during a seizure and that changed everything," he explained, still incredibly worried about Evie, but now for Rylie too. Finding out this way was going to be hard for her. "Knowing my family history, your mother and I had to accept the possibility that Evie's been having premonitions, not nightmares."

"Premonitions?" Rylie asked, her tone questioning.

"It's like a vision, she sees things that are yet to come but often, cannot make sense of the images. Your mother and I agreed it was too dangerous to go back to the Siranor doctors again. We were lucky the results came back inconclusive after the first set of tests," he explained and as Nate opened up to Rylie, the words just fell out. "We told Evie and she also didn't want to go back to the doctors, so we've just been trying to help her control the side effects ever since. She says talking about the visions helps, and that she can feel us when we stroke her hands or hair during the seizures."

When he paused, Rylie looked up at her father while holding Evie's hand, stroking again. She'd never seen him so broken. Any upset or anger she'd felt at not being told sooner disappeared.

"How long have you known?" She asked quietly, her mind reeling from the information.

"A few years, I'm so sorry we didn't tell you sooner Rylie. We just wanted you to have a normal life," Nate said, dropping his gaze back to Evie again, dreading to hear how Rylie felt, but Rylie was so choked by everything that for the longest time, she couldn't speak.

"I wish I'd known earlier," she finally whispered.

"Let's put Evie to bed and then we can talk. She should sleep for a while yet," Nate explained, picking up his little girl and carrying her up the stairs to her bedroom. When she woke, Evie would want to talk about what she'd seen so the images wouldn't haunt her.

Once Nate placed Evie carefully in bed, Rylie gently touched his arm so that he turned to face her. He was expecting her to be angry but she just buried herself in his chest. Grateful for the embrace, he hugged her so tightly that he felt her body shake.

"I can't believe I didn't even think of this. It makes so much sense!" Rylie admitted, hiding her face momentarily before looking at her father again. "Thank you for trying to protect me. I love you dad, but no more secrets okay?" She continued, her voice a little shaky but she was trying to be brave. "I want to protect Evie too."

"I promise Rylie, no more secrets. I'll answer any questions you have about your grandparents too. Your mother and I have always taught you not to hate mages and it wasn't just because we don't agree with the mage hunts, but because of my heritage too," he said, looking sad as he continued. "I'm glad they never survived to see the world as it is now, with the mage hunts and the destruction of the Ar'encal, but I've always wished my parents could've met your mother and the both of you. My girls..."

"I wish I could've met them too," Rylie replied with a sympathetic smile.

"I hope that even with the burden of this knowledge, you know that no matter what, your mother and I will never let anyone harm you or your sister," Nate assured, searching her eyes, hoping that she truly believed him. She answered him with another loving embrace. He kissed her head in response and wrapped his arms around her.

"What about you dad, are you a mage?" Rylie asked.

"No, I never triggered abilities. Whether that was luck or good judgement, I don't know, but I'm glad. I may never have met your mother had I been a known mage," he replied.

It was only the sound of Evie stirring that caused them to break apart. As her eyes started to flinch, they both began speaking softly to her. She raised her hand to her forehead and quietly called to her father.

"Dad... are you there?" Evie asked, her voice timid.

"I'm here sweetheart. We're in your bedroom, Rylie's here too," Nate replied softly, caressing his little girl's hair once again.

Hearing that her sister was there made Evie open her eyes. Rylie instinctively leant in to give her little sister a hug. She whispered in her ear as they embraced.

"It's okay Evie, I know about your visions," she said affectionately. As she pulled away, she gave Evie a gentle pinch to the nose. It was a term of endearment she'd done ever since Evie was a baby. After processing what Rylie had said, Evie sat bolt upright and looked between her father and sister, as if seeking confirmation that Rylie really knew.

"It's true Evie. I've told Rylie everything. It wasn't fair to hide it from her anymore. But nothing has changed darling. Rylie still loves you," he confirmed with a smile that relaxed his entire face.

"And don't you ever think otherwise little smidge! I just wish I'd known before and been a better big sister to you. All these years I thought you were just having bad dreams and headaches!" Rylie exclaimed with a hint of remorse.

"You're already the best big sister I could ask for... but I'm so glad you know the truth now. It was hard not telling you, but mum and dad explained that anyone who knew could get in trouble," Evie confessed and hearing the excuse come from her melted Rylie's heart. She smiled, holding Evie's hand and noticed she was trembling slightly.

"It's okay, let's focus on you right now. Dad said talking about what you've seen can help. So tell us, what did you see?" Rylie asked, tightening her grip on Evie's hand, giving her what little support she could.

Nate sat beside Evie again, wrapping one arm around her shoulders. Evie took a few deep breaths and was able to stop trembling as she spoke.

"The first vision I ever saw was of death. It looked like a regal man who'd been poisoned. Then a few months later, mum heard the news that the king of Carlisse had been assassinated, poisoned, but I was too scared to believe what I'd seen was the same thing. I've seen so many scary images, but not another death until a year ago... and the vision I had just now was the same one again," Evie explained, her voice breaking as she tried to control her breathing.

"Evie, that's horrible!" Rylie exclaimed, shocked she was able to endure such terrifying images.

"It's awful! I can't see any faces but I'm sure the images are here, by the fountain in the square. There's a hooded man; I can feel his rage burning through his veins. He's shouting at someone, but I can't make out the words, I only know he's taken a woman hostage. When the vision focuses on her, it's like I am her. I can feel her fear. She's trembling and crying but unable to move."

As she recalled the vision, Evie began to cry but neither Nate nor Rylie stopped her. The images were ghastly but she had to let it out.

"Take a deep breath sweetheart," Nate suggested, still mindlessly caressing his youngest daughter, who did as he instructed.

"Then, all I can see is the knife in his hand. The hooded man starts to shake but keeps the blade pressed against the woman's throat. Finally, he slashes and I see the blade cut deep into the woman's neck, and there's blood. So much blood!" She whimpered, causing Nate to embrace her tightly.

Rylie couldn't begin to imagine how vivid the images were, let alone feeling them too. She wasn't sure if it was hearing what Evie had seen, or the knowledge she'd seen these kinds of visions since she was just seven years old that upset her the most. As Evie curled into her father's arms, Rylie continued to hold her hand and the three of them sat in silence. If there was any chance that Evie was right and what she saw happened in the town square, all they could do was hope she never had to see it again, as a vision or in real life.

Eight days as interim commander and Siljanna had become confident in charge. Although she was looking forward to her father coming back, there was something she really enjoyed about being addressed as 'Commander Stone' every day. The thought of it being her title one day was exhilarating. For the time being though, she was more than happy being under her father's tutelage. He was the most honourable and brave man she knew and was grateful for the opportunity to learn from him.

He'd sent word that he was going to be back soon, so she expected him home by nightfall or morning at the latest and wanted everything in perfect order before he returned. She was checking through the patrol reports when a warden called Téa came bursting through the office doors.

"Commander Stone, we've just received word of a hostage situation in the fountain square. Initial reports and public statements suspect the man responsible is a mage!" She cried, panting as she spoke.

Siljanna's mind snapped into focus as she processed the information. A mage of any kind was basically a fugitive but if there was a hostage involved they couldn't go in guns blazing. After a moment, she looked back towards Téa to give her the instruction that she was clearly waiting for.

"Deploy all available wardens to the area, we have to establish a perimeter… and get Morgan. He's trained for hostage situations so has the best chance of talking the perpetrator down," she instructed. Téa nodded but didn't leave, causing Siljanna to shout irately. "Now Téa! Report back as soon as possible."

Ten long minutes passed and Siljanna didn't have a single update. Striding back and forth in the office until she couldn't take the silence anymore, Siljanna grabbed her jacket and prepared to leave. As she reached the main exit, Téa cautiously approached.

"Téa, report," Siljanna demanded.

"The situation is unchanged… but I come bearing bad news. We were unable to establish a perimeter. There are too many people blocking the square who are in town for the trader's market. Morgan has been contacted and told to urgently attend the scene though," she said hastily, her eyes glued firmly to the floor.

"That's all you've got?" Siljanna barked, furious at her subordinate's incompetence.

"There is one more thing," Téa stuttered. "The offender has yet to be identified but we've had confirmation of the hostage. Ma'am, it's your mother."

Initially, Téa's words didn't sink in. Siljanna shook her head in disbelief and convinced herself the report had to be wrong. Resolving that she had to attend the scene personally to get the truth, she stormed out of the guardhouse and walked briskly towards the square.

When the call came in, Morgan had to ask the guard on the other end to repeat himself twice before he believed what he'd heard. When he'd last seen Harrison, he was overseeing a group of elderly travellers heading south to Fenian, but there was no time to search for him. Morgan instructed the warden on the radio to make sure Harrison was contacted before sprinting to reach the scene.

Moments later, Harrison received the same call. The warden on the other end made sure to emphasise the urgency of the situation. Telling him that his mother was the hostage was all it took and he dashed towards the square. Once he neared, he found himself blocked by hundreds of on-lookers. Trying desperately to move people out of his way, Harrison clawed his way forward, making it as far as the steps overlooking the fountain before the gathered crowd were impassable. All he could do was jump onto a bench to get a clearer view. The sight before him was worse than he'd imagined.

His eyes were drawn straight to the fountain. Standing upon the top ledge was a man wearing a dark cloak. The assailant's hood was down revealing an older man with long hair, pale skin and dark circles under his eyes. His prominent wrinkles were shadowed by the furrows in his brow and he was shouting down towards Morgan, who was at the base of the fountain, weapon trained on the man whilst also guarding Paige Auren. Harrison wondered briefly *what was she doing there?* until his attention was taken back to the hostage.

The woman held tightly in the man's grasp was terrified, her auburn hair soaked and ragged. She wasn't just any woman, Harrison knew that, but seeing truly is believing and there was no denying his mother's life was in immediate danger. Pressed firmly against her throat, he caught a glimpse of a dagger.

The assailant continued screaming something at Morgan but it was like Harrison's mind couldn't take in everything before him; the sights registering but not the sounds. All that filled his ears were the frantic mumbling of the crowd around him. He jumped off the bench and continued pushing his way forward while praying to himself that Morgan could somehow buy time. His mind cast back to the suspicious merchant he'd let into town. *Could it be the same man?*

Would he ever forgive himself if it was? Still struggling to pass, Harrison tried a different route, thinking he might be able to flank the man and get a clear shot, one Morgan currently didn't have. Upon reaching the northern side of the square, he saw a familiar sight, his father Commander Sampson Stone.

At first, Harrison was washed with a sense of relief. His father was at the front of the crowd, the cloaked man easily within range. He could see that Morgan had also spotted his commander and was clearly trying to keep the assailant distracted to give Sampson time to strike. But Sampson wasn't moving; his eyes were fixed on the scene before him but his firearm remained holstered.

Realising his father was frozen, the relief Harrison felt soon disappeared and he frantically continued pushing his way through the crowd. As he got closer, Harrison's hearing kicked in and he caught the sound of his mother's sobs as she whimpered, begging Sampson to help. Finally reaching the front of the crowd, Harrison drew his sword and was just about to reach his father's side when the worst happened.

His mother tore her glance away from her husband, recognising it was her son doing all he could to reach her. With tears rolling down her face, she seemed to know that despite Harrison's best efforts, it was too late. He saw her mouth form the words '*I'm sorry,* 'before the cloaked man buried the dagger deep into her throat, slashing violently and taking away her life with one swift motion.

Blood poured down her throat, staining her dress as her hands went limp and her head sagged. Harrison's eyes bulged as he saw the man release his mother's lifeless body and she crumpled into the water basin below. He dropped his sword and shoved past his father, who remained motionless. As he jumped into the basin of the fountain, he heard a gunshot. Morgan had pulled the trigger, his shot connecting with the killer's temple, causing the man to fall backwards, dead on the upper ledge of the fountain. As Harrison knelt down, blood staining the water around him, time stopped. The adrenaline gone, Harrison found himself stunned, unable to do anything but cradle his mother's body.

The gunshot was the first thing Siljanna heard as she rounded the corner. Filled with a sense of panic she marched forward as the people who'd been in the square slowly moved away, allowing her to pass until she was confronted with the horrific scene. She was completely taken aback as she tried to process everything before her. Harrison was sitting in the basin of the fountain, the water around him bloody, cradling their mother; Morgan with his gun still aimed above them at the dead figure of a man lying on the top ledge of the fountain and finally her father, on the other side of the square.

As the images smashed through her consciousness, without thinking, Siljanna ran to her father, crashing into him as reality took hold and she knew her mother was dead. Her father didn't move as she embraced him but he must've just arrived too, so it was completely understandable for even the mighty Commander Stone to be in shock. As she continued to squeeze her arms around her father's torso, he placed one hand softly on her back and Siljanna allowed herself to cry.

The people departing spoke in hushed voices but even with her face buried into her father's chest, she could hear some of them talking. She picked up things like *obsessed with power, did you see the look in his eyes?* and *something wrong with people like him.* Hearing them confirmed the rumours; Siljanna's mother had just been killed by a mage.

Hearing the commotion outside drew Rylie's attention away from her sister to the window. As she peered down and saw the fleeting crowds, she left her father caring for Evie, dashed down the stairs and out through the main bar door. With people passing left and right, she couldn't understand what was going on until Morgan approached the tavern, his arm wrapped around her mother's shoulders. She was shaking, clearly distraught. As they made it to the door, Rylie's expression begged Morgan to explain what was going on.

"Something terrible has happened Rylie. Your mother was in the market with Anora Stone when a merchant took Anora hostage," Morgan explained, his voice quaking. "I did everything I could, but it wasn't enough. Anora is dead."

As Morgan's words registered in Rylie's mind, she made a mad dash outside. After everything that had just happened with Evie and her vision, Rylie had to know. *Had Evie just seen Anora's death moments before it happened?* When she made it to the edge of the square, she saw Siljanna embracing her father on the far side, and then her vision locked on Harrison, who was alone, kneeling in the fountain, holding his mother's body.

She rushed over to him, hopped over the edge of the fountain and waded towards him. Harrison didn't say anything, his eyes fixed on his mother but as Rylie looked down, she could see that Anora's throat had been slit, just as Evie had described. The water was cold but Rylie didn't care. She knelt down, tucking her arms underneath Harrison's and curled herself into his back. As she held him, he released a deep exhalation, bowing his head and using her as an anchor, allowing tears to soak his cheeks.

They sat like that for minutes before Harrison moved, scooping up his mother's petite body and laying her gently on the edge of the fountain. He closed her eyelids and rested her hands over her chest so she looked peaceful. Another warden approached with a blanket to cover her as Rylie led Harrison away. She didn't know what to do so instinctively took him to the tavern.

Siljanna who had finally gotten Sampson to move, and was slowly leading him towards Anora's corpse, looked at Rylie and nodded, confirming they would join them in the tavern shortly. As Rylie took Harrison inside, she could see her mother and father in a tight embrace. Morgan was at the bar, drink in hand, shifting the glass between his fingers without taking a sip.

As if noticing his partner for the first time since the traumatic event, Harrison turned to Rylie, placed his hand on her cheek and looked over towards her parents, silently letting her know she could go and check on them. Rylie promised him she'd be right back as he sat on the stool next to Morgan.

"Morgan..." Harrison began, trying to speak but couldn't find the words. He wanted to tell him he didn't blame him, knew he'd done everything he could, but the words just didn't come.

"I'm sorry Harrison. Please know I would've given anything to save Anora," Morgan began, and Harrison could feel the sincerity in his words. He couldn't speak but the natural warmth of his eyes showed his gratitude. "There's something else you need to know," Morgan continued. "I don't know how, but I'm certain your father knew the killer. He was marching up to us until he saw the man's face and then he just... froze. I can't explain it but he recognised that cloaked man and did nothing to stop him from killing your mother."

Harrison was stunned as Morgan's words ran through his mind. He disliked much about his father but had never questioned the man's unconditional love for his mother, until that moment. But that wasn't the main thing bothering him. Harrison needed to know the identity of the killer, the *'cloaked man'.* With the torture visible on his face, he spoke.

"Morgan, do you think the killer was the man I let through the northern gate last week?" He asked, his entire body trembling.

"I do. But Harrison, you didn't let him through, your father made you. I'm telling you, something about this whole thing doesn't feel right," Morgan answered firmly, slugging back his entire drink in one go before sliding the glass down the bar.

Harrison recalled that day and his father's insistence the merchant be allowed to clear the bridge so he could make haste to Siranor. Despite Morgan's suspicions, Harrison believed his father hadn't taken a good look at the merchant as he left. *Sampson couldn't have known who he was, could he?*

"I can't believe this is happening," Harrison stuttered.

"There's one more thing Harrison; the man, the killer… you were right to suspect him, but he wasn't a mage. I'm confident he was suffering from the withering," Morgan said adamantly.

"How do you know?" Harrison questioned.

"All the signs were there, the black tint to his fingers and hands but otherwise pale, sickly skin; pronounced wrinkles and dark circles around his eyes. The guy was dying Harrison, but the things he said are what's really convinced me," Morgan explained, his gaze stern. "He kept saying he deserved the ability to wield '*true power,*' and that he had to '*tell her she could do it, even after he was gone*'. I think he'd taken Encia, maybe intentionally! He was obsessed with magic but definitely didn't wield any. I mean if he had magic, why use a knife?"

Harrison had never seen his friend look so sure and could tell Morgan was truly distraught about the whole situation. He knew Morgan cared greatly for his mother and clearly blamed himself for what happened. Harrison placed a hand on his friend's shoulder and without words, Morgan knew there was no hardship. Sadness still wracking his body, Morgan stood up and headed upstairs, retiring for the night. Harrison tried to speak one last time, but Morgan just smiled sympathetically. Knowing that Harrison believed him was enough.

As Morgan departed, Harrison turned back on his stool and rested on the bar. When Rylie returned, she ducked under the counter and began pouring drinks for the two of them. He didn't really want anything but knew she'd struggle to be passive company so accepted the beverage.

She'd just taken a swig when Siljanna and Sampson entered. They sat down a few seats away as Nate and Paige approached, giving their condolences and embracing both Harrison and Siljanna who gladly accepted their kindness. Paige was still clearly shaken but did everything she could to hide it, knowing how she felt couldn't compare to each member of the Stone family. Sampson did nothing to console his son, who he was seeing for the first time since the events in the square. He just ordered Rylie to pour him a drink and took a few sips before speaking.

"This was your doing, Harrison. It's your fault," Sampson accused. With Morgan, Harrison hadn't been able to find the right words but hearing what his father said literally stripped him of the ability to speak.

"What?" Rylie gasped, but Sampson didn't even look up.

"You let a murderer into our town, and your incompetence cost your mother, *my wife* her life," Sampson hissed, refusing to look up from his glass.

The tension in the room became so intense that everyone seated at the bar barely dared to breathe. As Harrison took in his father's words, he gritted his teeth but chose not to respond.

"Sampson, you can't possibly mean that," Nate interceded, trying to alleviate the tension but Sampson just thrust his hand into Nate's face, forcing him into silence.

"I mean every word," he said with cruelty. "Do you have anything to say, Harrison? Not that anything you could say will make up for what you've cost this family."

At that, Harrison couldn't control his temper anymore. He stood, taking the glass in his hand and tossed it at his father. It smashed into the wall just past Sampson's face.

"I did not cost my mother her life, you did! You had her killer flanked but just stood there! You could've saved her, but you did *nothing*! And I think I know the reason. You let her die because you knew her killer, didn't you? Who was it dad, one of your friends from the capital? Clearly whoever it was, was more important to you than mum," he shouted, redirecting the blame at his father.

Instantly, Sampson stood and viciously punched his son but Harrison took the blow without flinching. Sampson was so used to people cowering down to his authority, but despite the strike hitting him squarely in the jaw, Harrison wasn't backing down. Realising the situation was going to unravel quickly, Nate pushed his way between them.

"Not in my bar; either stay in peace or go!" He yelled.

Out of respect for Nate, Harrison stepped away first and headed towards the door. Before he left, Sampson returned to his seat and called over his shoulder to his son.

"Return your uniform and firearm to the guardhouse by morning. You are no longer a warden of Tivani, Harrison Stone. You can also find a new place to live," Sampson declared.

Harrison paused, rage coursing through him. He clenched his shaking fists and then marched out the door. He heard Siljanna beg for him to wait but knew he couldn't stay. That night Harrison slept in the park by the southern bridge, with the stars and a thin blanket as his only comfort.

Chapter Seven
Burning Bridges

Standing before his mother's memorial a year after her death was one of the hardest things Harrison had ever done. Various emotions swept over him as he read the headstone dedicated to her. Fear, urgency, and desperation; everything he'd felt when racing to the square, quickly followed by disgust, disappointment, and rage at his father's lack of action and the conversation that led to Harrison no longer being a warden.

He might not have come if Nate hadn't offered to join him. Nate, who was silently paying his respects to Anora was the father figure Harrison needed. Placing some flowers next to the headstone, Harrison spoke softly to his mother.

"I miss you," he began, struggling to say aloud how he felt, "and I still don't know what you had to be sorry about. It's me who should be sorry. I couldn't save you."

"I think she was apologising for leaving you," Nate said, thinking out loud.

"What do you mean?" Harrison asked.

"Deep down, I believe she knew your father wouldn't treat you kindly. I'm sure she never imagined he'd say and do what he did, but still," Nate explained, likely trying to imagine what thoughts would've gone through his mind in Anora's position.

"I... I never considered that," Harrison admitted, looking back at her memorial, somehow feeling even more guilty. "Thank you, Nate. I appreciate you taking the time to come with me today."

"You don't need to thank me, I'm always happy to support you, Harrison. You're like extended family after all," Nate replied smiling, as the two of them turned to leave. "How are you anyway? Still like working with Elijah?"

After his father stripped him of his warden title and kicked him out of their family home, Harrison had been lost for a while. He spent a few weeks living at the tavern with Nate and his family until Elijah Ashby, the town blacksmith, heard what happened. He knew of Harrison's natural talent for weapon and armour smithing from his final year at the academy and offered him an apprenticeship. Elijah also had a loft room above his shop which he gave to Harrison, deducting the rent from his pay, an ideal solution for them both.

Harrison had settled in quickly and really enjoyed the work. Elijah also greatly appreciated the increase in his profits once Harrison started. The fact that the blacksmith shop and his new home were a short walk from town was even better in Harrison's mind. It meant he could easily avoid further confrontations with his father. Occasionally, Harrison had been at the Hawk Eye tavern when Sampson entered, but on those days Sampson would swiftly turn and leave again. They hadn't spoken a word to one another since that fateful day and Harrison had no intention of changing that.

He still blamed Sampson for his mother's death and was disgusted at how the situation transpired. Those were wounds no amount of time would heal. He'd left his warden uniform and firearm on the table at his former home that night, purely to leave a letter for Siljanna, apologising that she would be stuck in the middle of this situation and hoping they could stay in touch. Returning his attention to Nate's question, Harrison replied.

"I really do like it at the smithy. After spending four years trying to become a warden worthy of my father's respect, it feels great to be appreciated in another job, just because of my natural talents. Elijah is a decent boss too, I owe him a lot."

"I'm glad. Tell him the next round is on me when the two of you pop in for a drink," Nate said, making a mental reminder of the gesture.

"Oh, dangerous tactic! You want both of us together at the tavern with a round on the house?" Harrison asked and couldn't help but laugh, which was the last thing he expected to do, today of all days.

As they walked through town, they purposefully went the long way around to avoid the guardhouse. Their route however still cut past the fountain. Although it symbolised the worst day of his life, it had become a tradition in town to throw a coin into the water and say a prayer for lost loved ones. They both paused beside the water feature, holding within their minds images of the parents they'd lost, tossed coins and then continued towards the northern bridge.

The woodland path on the other side of the bridge would take them to the blacksmith and Harrison's new home. They cleared the checkpoint with the wardens on duty not even attempting to stop them and started walking up the path. As it meandered through the trees, Harrison felt compelled to ask a question that had been on his mind.

"Siljanna mentioned in her letters that my father is ill; not physically but mentally. It won't change anything but, will you tell me what's become of him?" Harrison asked, telling himself he only wanted to know because he cared for his sister.

To start with, they'd exchanged regular letters to keep in touch but after a month, her letters had dwindled. Now, Harrison was lucky to get a letter every other month and assumed Siljanna's distance was because she had no time between being a warden and caring for Sampson.

"It's true, your father has been unstable for some time now. After your mother's funeral, he suffered a mental breakdown. His moods swing from severely depressed to violently aggressive and in either state, he's difficult to handle," Nate admitted. "He drinks far too much and I can't recall the number of times I've had to ask your sister to take him home after passing out in the bar. I'm not sure how she copes if I'm honest."

Siljanna hadn't gone into much detail in her letters but had mentioned that Sampson had been requested to retire by the Imperator's council and that she'd become commander, even though she'd barely finished training for the position before taking on the burden. She also hinted that caring for him was difficult because he'd become '*dependent on the bottle*'. It was hard to imagine Sampson as being anything less than the headstrong, imposing man Harrison had grown up with, but he didn't feel sorry for him, only the people around him; namely Siljanna.

As they continued walking down the path towards the blacksmith, Nate recalled some of the more dramatic evenings when Sampson had drunk too much or been particularly difficult, giving Harrison a stronger image of his father's condition and hearing the truth only made him despise the man further. When Nate mentioned an occasion he'd grabbed Rylie by the arm, Harrison's frustration rose and Nate noticed instantly.

"He didn't hurt her. I wouldn't allow that, but Rylie was definitely shaken by the situation," Nate explained.

"I'm glad I wasn't there," Harrison said, seething at just the thought. "I can't believe she didn't tell me."

"You care about her, don't you? My daughter," Nate asked with a chuckle, surprising Harrison with his forthrightness. It's not like he made a habit of concealing the truth but they'd never spoken about matters of the heart openly before. "Don't panic! It was just an observation."

"You sure know how to blindside a guy! Can we go back to the matter of those free drinks?" Harrison asked, trying to revert the conversation to something more comfortable. Nate continued to laugh but didn't change the subject.

"If you're going to win her heart, you need to work on two things. Being more open and most importantly, your moves! Rylie is a natural born dancer you know."

As he said it, he feigned a few playful blows at Harrison, making him dodge lightly on his feet.

"Hey old man, I'll show you *moves!*" Harrison replied, mischievously retaliating, and just like that the paternal bond they'd developed over the years returned. They wrestled playfully in between casual conversation the rest of the way to the smithy.

Consisting of four buildings, the blacksmith site was large. The two main buildings housed the forge and workshop but connected by a stone archway was a large, open courtyard that led to the smith shop and stables. Elijah's main source of income came from the travellers that rented stalls and paid to have their horses shod while they stayed in town or travelled onward to the capital.

Since Harrison had started working for him though, the profits from the smith shop had also greatly increased. The shop itself was like the homes in Tivani, built of wood and stone with a cedar roof. There was an iron sign fixed over the front door with the image of a sword and anvil and the word *'Ashby's'* engraved underneath. The frame of the door had horseshoes nailed all around so there was no mistaking that it was a smithy.

If they'd walked inside, they would've entered a room filled with a vast array of weapons and armour that Harrison had carefully crafted. Behind the shop was the staircase leading up to Harrison's loft, which Elijah had converted into a fully functioning apartment with a small bathroom, bedroom, living area and lockable door so that Harrison felt like the space was his own. They didn't go inside however as Nate stopped him in the courtyard, gripping his shoulder in a firm but affectionate way.

"Listen, Harrison, I know we jest but there is something I want you to know. Whether I'm right or wrong about any feelings you might have for Rylie, I know how much you care for my family, and that means the world to me. Should anything ever happen, there is no one I'd trust more to be there for my girls than you," Nate said with sincerity, and once again Harrison found himself lost for words. He shook Nate's hand as they said their goodbyes and then returned to work.

Because Siljanna had been required to take over as warden commander at such short notice, she'd never had the traditional ceremony honouring her promotion. She'd insisted given the circumstances that she didn't want one either but there was a tradition he was keen not to break. Any new commander should be presented with a personally crafted weapon, and he could do that for his sister. Their father had received an ornate two-handed axe presented to him when he took the role twenty-three years ago, and Harrison was determined to present something to Siljanna now.

He'd spent months perfecting the design and finally completed a beautiful pair of hand axes adorned with the warden emblem and engraved with their creed. When Elijah had first seen them, he was enthused at the idea of selling the blades, but his enthusiasm dissipated once he realised Harrison intended to gift them to Siljanna.

Elijah was a plump and insanely tall man, half a foot taller than Harrison, with a completely bald head and bushy beard. They'd become quick friends over the past year for Elijah really had been there for Harrison in his time of need. Harrison knew he would be eternally grateful to the man and often worked late in the evening under the peaceful guidance of the stars to make sure Elijah's shop was well stocked to show his gratitude.

When they last spoke, Elijah had ordered Harrison to take some time off because he knew the anniversary of his mother's passing was coming up. It was funny but Harrison couldn't help but think that since that day, when it looked like he'd lost everything, all the people that truly cared about him had come to his aid and made sure he landed on his feet.

His biggest supporter, however, continued to be Rylie. She'd been his confidant, an unwavering support and the best friend he could've asked for during every up and down he'd faced. He knew he was lying when he tried to convince himself that she was just a friend, *but how do you tell someone you want more without risking what you already have?* He figured one day he'd know how to answer that question and hoped that when he did, Rylie would feel the same way. There had been a brief period of time earlier in the year when she'd dated some guy called Bradley from the apothecary shop, and Harrison had to physically stop himself from cheering when they'd broken up.

Realising it was getting late and he still had work to do, Harrison tried to cast his thoughts and feelings for Rylie aside and focus. After arranging for a courier to take the axes to the guardhouse, Harrison went to help Elijah, who was currently in the stables, shodding former academy student Samuel Fischer's horse, who was being stabled with them overnight while Samuel visited the capital. Harrison needed to make sure that he was finished in the workshop soon so that he could help Elijah tend to the animals before closing up. He knew the moment he mentioned the complimentary round from Nate, that Elijah would be up for a diversion via the tavern on his way home.

Finishing up her reports for the day, Siljanna closed her eyes and let out a sigh of relief. She knew the job wasn't all about the action, but why did there have to be so much paperwork? She'd written hundreds of reports since taking over as commander but two stood out in her mind, her mother's murder and her father's retirement. After her mother died, her father stayed strong for a couple of weeks. He'd ensured the scene had been cleared and the body of Anora's killer sent to Siranor for examination. He even arranged her funeral without showing any cracks but on the actual day they buried her, he broke. The man who'd always been her rock shattered into a million pieces and Siljanna had been trying to hold them together ever since.

Most days he was depressed, refusing to leave the house and drinking himself into a stupor but sadly, that was preferable to when she took the alcohol away because then Sampson would become unimaginably aggressive. She hated to admit it but she'd needed to take advantage of his injured shoulder several times, only to subdue him when he became violent. She wished that Harrison would come back home to help her care for their father but knew it was not something she could ask of him.

She would never forget returning home that night after their father expelled Harrison from both the wardens and their family. Finding his uniform and gun neatly placed on the table, but her brother and all his things gone was heart-breaking. It was only thanks to the letter he'd left for her that she didn't lose both her mother and brother on that horrific day.

His letter had been short and sweet, telling her he was sorry she was stuck in the middle of his feud with their father but that he'd try to be there for her, even though he couldn't physically live with them anymore. She tried to write to him frequently in the early days but once Sampson's condition became severe, any free time she had, was spent tending to him.

Siljanna knew that today was going to be difficult. She wanted to visit her mother's memorial but doubted she'd get her father out of the house. Gathering her things to head home after a long day, she was delayed when Morgan knocked on the office door.

"Sil, I'm glad I caught you. There's a delivery by the entrance for you, I think you'll want to see it," he announced with a sly grin on his face.

When Siljanna took over as commander, she promoted Morgan to lieutenant. He was a great warden, but her decision was mostly because she trusted him more than any of the others. Their friendship had been rocky since Harrison was discharged, with Morgan point-blank refusing to work with another partner, spending most of his time on patrol. He preferred to deal with real people rather than the paperwork and Siljanna honoured his wishes. In return, she gained his respect.

Morgan still refused to accept the official report that her mother was killed by a rogue mage, one that Harrison had permitted through the border check into town. He insisted that the assailant was suffering from the withering but when the autopsy report from the institute in Siranor came back inconclusive, unable to confirm the man's identity and stating he was *'likely a mage'*, Siljanna had closed the case based on the official report, combined with her own experience.

"Thank you, Morgan, I'm just leaving so will collect it on my way out. Are you on the night shift?" Siljanna asked.

"I'll be on duty until first light," he confirmed, adjusting his armour until it was comfortable.

"I'm glad," she said honestly.

"I visited your mother's memorial earlier today. I can't explain why, but I need to be working tonight," Morgan replied, seeming more agitated than normal, but Siljanna presumed that like her, he was feeling the effects of the date.

Even though it had been just a stupid crush, he too had cared for her mother and witnessed her traumatic death first-hand, something Siljanna was grateful not to have seen. The aftermath was bad enough. She handed over the guardhouse keys to Morgan and said her goodbyes. As she walked towards the main exit, she saw the package he'd mentioned laying on a bench. It was a large twine bag but much lighter than she'd expected. There was a note attached.

'In honour of Commander Siljanna Stone. Love H.'

Realising who it was from, she couldn't wait to see what was inside. Pulling open the bag, she retrieved two beautifully crafted hand axes. The intricate design of the warden emblem between the blade and handle was exquisite and engraved on the edge were the words *'honour, justice and loyalty'*.

The creed of the wardens was to serve with honour, fight for justice and loyally protect the community. Harrison knew the significance of those words and what they meant to every warden. The fact he'd engraved them into each blade made the gift even more precious. She placed the axes back in the bag to take them home but told herself she must find a way to thank him.

As Siljanna left the guardhouse, she walked through the market to get home. It was much quieter than in previous years, due to the enhanced security checks she'd introduced at the town's entry bridges, which no one questioned knowing the motive. Any unfamiliar traveller or merchant had to pass a number of thorough checks before being allowed into town. If the wardens had even the slightest suspicion the person was a mage or mage sympathiser, they could be detained. It had made several of the regulars fear returning, even if they had nothing to hide. Just being suspected could ruin their reputations, but Siljanna didn't care. It was her duty to keep the people of Tivani safe from mages like her mother's killer, not to fill the merchant's pockets with coin.

When she made it to the front door of her home, it still filled her with immense sadness that the smell of baked goods no longer flowed out into the street. As she went through the front door, she was met with the same sight as usual; the windows shuttered, lights off and her father sitting slumped in his leather armchair with empty bottles scattered around his feet.

At first, she thought he was asleep so tried to creep through the house to avoid disturbing him. She tucked the beautiful axes from Harrison out of sight in the cupboard under the stairs and closed her eyes for a moment trying to conjure the strength to deal with her father. She still loved him more than anyone else, but he could be hard work.

It wasn't until she entered the living room she discovered he wasn't asleep at all, just staring into space. His green eyes were dark and devoid of emotion. It was likely he was in a numb state after drinking too much so Siljanna tried to invigorate him with the thought of food. He always used to cherish dinner time when they were still a family, and although she didn't have her mother's skills, she could still make a hearty dinner.

"I'm going to make a start on dinner dad. I thought we could honour mum tonight by cooking some of her favourites and eating together at the table like we used to. Does that sound good?" She asked, trying to hide her own sadness as she recalled how their life used to be.

"No food, just get me another drink," he replied curtly but she knew it was just the depression talking.

Trying to conceal her disappointment, Siljanna nodded and went to the liquor cupboard. Opening the door, she was mortified to see that every bottle was empty. She didn't want to work out how much that meant her father had consumed during the day, but the knowledge drained what little enthusiasm she had.

Slamming the cupboard door in frustration, Siljanna sank to the floor and hugged her knees. She needed a moment but sadly her father's shouting prevented her from it.

"Where's my drink?" He demanded.

"We don't have any left in the house. Why don't you head over to the tavern? I'll pop to the market and collect some supplies," she quavered, holding back the tears, something she'd learned to do after countless times in this situation. He grumbled but headed towards the front door. "I'll come and get you once I've re-stocked the kitchen."

As she watched her father leave, bashing the front door closed behind him, she released a sigh, grateful for the respite.

Sampson was wearing jeans and a flannel shirt which were both stained and dishevelled, not attire for going out at all. Siljanna had roughly cut his pale blonde hair when he'd refused to, so it hung flatly down to his chin but his previously clean-shaven face was now covered with rough stubble. He didn't care how he looked anymore, or what anyone thought about him. All he cared about was the next drink. Nothing was going to stop him from numbing the pain of what the day represented; his single, greatest failure in life.

He staggered through the cobbled streets until he made it to the tavern. Pushing through the main door, he marched up to the bar and flopped onto one of the stools. Nate was stacking logs by the freshly lit fire while Rylie was serving. He grunted, pointing his finger to the whiskey and then made a looping motion indicating he wanted a glass. Raising her eyebrow at the gesture, Rylie finished serving another patron and then made her way over, glass and bottle in hand.

"Hello Mr Stone, it's nice to see you. How are you feeling this evening?" She enquired with compassion.

"Shut up and pour the damn drink," he said bluntly, slapping his money on the counter. "In fact, just leave the bottle."

Irritated but unsurprised, Rylie took the payment, placing it in a small safe under the bar and returned only to give Sampson his drink. She was about to try more pleasantries but he took the bottle and walked away, slumping into one of the armchairs in the corner of the room. In no time at all, he'd consumed the entire bottle and stumbled back to the bar, knocking over a stool that got in his way.

"Get me another," he demanded, roughly pointing at another whiskey bottle but unable to keep his hand steady. Rylie took a step back and quickly decided not to serve him.

"No sir, I'm afraid you've had enough," Rylie replied firmly, even though Sampson made her nervous. She attempted to take away his glass but the motion allowed him to grab her wrist, pinning her to the bar.

"I said, *get me another drink*. It wasn't a question, so do your damn job!" He insisted, his tone venomous.

"And I told you no! You've had enough Mr Stone. Now please, let go of my wrist," she persisted, trying not to reveal how painful his grip was, or how much she feared him.

Hearing her raised voice caught Nate's attention and he rushed over to the bar. He knew of Sampson's old shoulder injury and applied a firm grip where he knew the other man was vulnerable, forcing him to release Rylie. She retreated from the edge of the bar and held her wrist, rubbing the spot where it was most painful. Realising that Sampson could have hurt his daughter, Nate lost his temper.

"Get out of here Sampson, *now*! You are not welcome in my bar anymore," he shouted.

"I'm not leaving until I get a drink. It's her job to serve me, so get me the *damned drink*!" Sampson spat, still staggering.

"If you don't leave right now, I'll make you," Nate replied with fervour.

As Sampson registered the threat, he removed Nate's hand from his wounded shoulder and pushed him away, causing him to trip on the stool that'd been knocked over earlier. Nate didn't fall, catching himself on the bar but the action infuriated him. He regained his footing, kicking the downed stool out of the way and strode towards Sampson, grabbing him by the shirt, just as Harrison and Elijah entered.

They'd been chatting casually on the walk down, so were shocked to enter the Hawk Eye tavern and be faced with the confrontation between Nate and Sampson. Nate rarely lost his temper with anyone so the fact that he had, told both of them that it was for a good reason.

"What's going on here?" Elijah asked, his deep voice and imposing stature making him look more threatening than he was.

Sampson didn't even acknowledge the question or Elijah and Harrison's arrival. Instead, he looked down at Nate's hand on his shirt and responded with a wild haymaker. Nate ducked, avoiding the blow and responded by shoving Sampson into the base of the bar. Being so intoxicated, Sampson did nothing to soften the impact and crashed to the floor.

Stepping back, Nate turned to Elijah and Harrison, his eyes wild but his expression soon turned apologetic.

"I'm sorry, you shouldn't have had to see that. I already promised one drink on the house, can I make it two?" He asked awkwardly.

"Don't worry about it Nate, but I'll claim those drinks later. For now, I'll fetch one of the wardens to make sure Sampson is escorted home," Elijah said as he headed towards the door.

"I'm fairly sure Morgan is on duty. Ask him to come, or even better, fetch Siljanna. Between them, they'll get Sampson home. I'll stay and keep an eye on him in the meantime," Harrison offered, smiling at Nate who looked grateful for the assistance.

As Elijah went in search of Morgan, Harrison headed over to Nate and Rylie. She was still cradling her arm while Nate fetched some ice. As Harrison neared, he could see a red mark around her wrist and in a wave of concern, pushed through the swinging bar door to gently take her hand.

"What happened? Did my father do this?" Harrison asked, sounding horrified. His expression proved he was desperately hoping to be wrong.

"I'm fine, honestly. He's just had a bit too much to drink. I don't think he meant to hurt me," Rylie replied, trying to make light of the situation, but Harrison could tell she was rattled.

With no one paying attention to him, Sampson got back to his feet and turned to face the three of them. He grabbed the glass on the counter and launched it towards them. It collided into the grand beverage display, breaking another bottle and knocking over several more which in turn smashed when they hit the bar, causing the alcohol to leak all over the counter and floor. Rylie screamed, ducking as the bottles behind her broke, glass shattering all around her.

Nate quickly drew her away towards the door connecting the public bar to their house but the noise caught Evie's attention and when she came through the door, she didn't notice the look on Sampson's face until it was too late. Once she did, she quickly cowered behind her father who used his arms to shield both of his girls from the enraged former commander.

By this point, Harrison had seen enough. All the pent-up anger he felt towards his father exploded within him. He burst through the bar door and lashed out with a series of lightning-fast blows, catching Sampson completely off guard. Each blow was stronger than the last with the final shot sending Sampson crashing into the solid stone hearth of the fireplace on the other side of the room. Something cracked as he landed but whether it was one of the stones or a broken bone was unclear. Sampson crumpled against the fireplace and sitting like a rag doll, sputtered a laugh while spitting up blood. Harrison glared at his father for a moment but turned away, more concerned about the well-being of the Auren's.

With his son's back turned, Sampson reached out and took one of the logs Nate had neatly stacked and turned it in the fire. With the end ablaze Sampson looked towards his son and threw the log. It clattered onto the bar which was still drenched with various alcohols and erupted into flames. The fire spread to wherever there was spilt alcohol and soon, the curtains and fixtures were on fire and smoke began to fill the room.

Distressed, Nate begged Harrison to get the girls outside as he dashed through the back door to find Paige. Sampson remained slumped on the floor laughing. He called out '*I'm coming!*' but didn't move as the fire spread around the room. Harrison convinced himself Sampson had lost his mind but had little time to worry about that and chose to focus on getting Rylie and Evie to safety. They both instinctively wanted to run after their father, but Harrison managed to pull them outside. Once he had them away from the building, Harrison made Rylie and Evie look at him as he spoke.

"I'm going back in for your parents and Sampson too. Please stay here; promise me," he asked, unsure if it sounded like a command or a plea but either way both girls nodded.

Evie started to weep so Harrison cupped his hand gently around her neck and smiled. She could see the concern on his face but his gentle, reaffirming touch made her wipe away the tears and try to be strong.

As Harrison turned back and ran towards the main door, there was a large burst of flames. It shattered the glass windows in front of him, allowing the fire to expand to the thatched roof above. Within seconds the whole building was burning. He took a step back, shocked at the sight before him and then heard Rylie scream. The sound tore through him and the last thing he saw was her sprinting off to the side door. He was just about to follow when he looked back at Evie. She was standing but her head was thrown back and she was trembling. He rushed to her side, gripping her shoulders and tried to gently shake her as the thought crossed his mind, *was she having a seizure?*

"Evie, what's happening? Evie, can you hear me?" He begged.

Rylie had told him a few stories about her seizures but he'd never actually seen one. The fear was paralysing and despite knowing her home was burning behind him, and there were people inside, Harrison couldn't bring himself to leave Evie.

"Burning, burning... her skin is burning," she wailed before passing out onto the cobbled floor. Just then, Morgan came running up the steps towards the tavern, skidding to a halt beside them.

"What happened?!" Morgan cried, having absolutely no idea what was going on and trying not to be completely overwhelmed by the raging fire and unconscious teenager next to his friend.

"Morgan, can you take Evie to my loft? Nate, Paige and Sampson are still inside and I think Rylie has gone after them!" Harrison pleaded, his voice skittish. He didn't have time to explain but knew he needed to do something, anything to help.

"Yes, of course, leave Evie with me and I'll make sure she's safe. Siljanna should be on her way. When Elijah told me about Sampson, he offered to go and find her too," Morgan explained as he collected Evie and headed off in the direction of the northern bridge.

Morgan hadn't been kidding when he said Siljanna would be there quickly for just as he rounded the corner, she appeared. She made an exasperated sound at the sight of the tavern fire and dropped her shopping bag as she reached Harrison.

"What happened?" She cried. "Where's dad?"

"There was a fight in the bar. Nate, Paige and Sampson are still inside. We have to get them out!" Harrison replied urgently.

"Dad's in there?" Siljanna shouted, her tone going up several octaves as she grabbed her brother's arm and forced him to look at her as if he could confirm the situation with just a look. As their eyes met, Siljanna had her answer.

"Rylie rushed around to the side door, will you please follow her Sil? She might've found a way in. I'll try the back door just in case," he requested, speaking almost as fast as the concerns running through his mind.

Siljanna nodded as they split in different directions and rushed to their respective goals.

When Rylie made it to the side door, she gripped the handle and jerked it several times. Her mind was racing, desperate to reach her parents so she didn't give it a second thought when the burning hot door didn't scorch her skin. All she knew was that it wouldn't budge. Looking through the nearby window, she saw what she feared most.

The room was filled with smoke and flames but she could make out her father trying to carry her mother to safety. Then one of the heavy wooden beams collapsed, blocking their escape. Realising they were trapped, she felt herself scream but the noise was drowned out by the crackling fire around her. She rushed back to the side door, wrenching the handle with all her might.

Siljanna had just made it around to the side door when she was stopped in her tracks by the image before her. Rylie was grasping onto the door of her house, her hands completely ablaze. Instead of rushing to help the other girl, Siljanna felt her blood boil. *Rylie was a mage!* Her mind fought against what her eyes were seeing. She shook her head, not wanting to believe all their years of friendship had been based on a lie; but no matter what she did, the sight before her didn't change.

Rylie's hands, like the rest of her home, were engulfed in flames. She was using magic to burn down the tavern, the building with her parents and Siljanna's father trapped inside! Siljanna launched herself at Rylie, screaming. She pulled her away from the door, throwing her to the ground. *Why would she do this? Why burn down her home?* It made no sense but there was no denying what was happening. Rylie tumbled across the floor clearly shocked by the assault.

Pulling herself onto her knees, Rylie made eye contact with Siljanna and could see the other girl was furious. She raised her hands in submission and noticed for the first time, they were on fire. The shock was so intense, she couldn't speak.

"Mage! You are under arrest for arson and attempted murder; don't move!" Siljanna shouted, reaching for her handcuffs as she strode towards Rylie with determination. She'd barely taken two steps when Harrison came from around the other corner and crashed into her.

"Sorry, I didn't see you!" He said, his attention still on the burning tavern and people trapped inside. "Did either of you find a way in?"

He hadn't noticed Rylie on her hands and knees and although it was an accidental collision, Rylie took the chance to run. She was terrified by Siljanna's accusation.

Catching her run off in the corner of his eye, Harrison called after her and then turned to his sister only to be slapped.

"You idiot, you let her get away!" Siljanna screamed.

"What are you talking about Siljanna? Why did Rylie run away like that?" Harrison asked frowning, his look questioning his sister while pressing a hand to the cheek she'd struck.

"Rylie is a *mage* Harrison, *she* caused the fire! I saw it with my own eyes," Siljanna spat, saying the word mage with disgust.

Harrison hadn't realised how much her hatred of mages had grown over the last year but that moment made it very clear. Siljanna believed their mother's killer was a mage, while Harrison agreed with Morgan's version of events; believing it was a man suffering from the withering, no matter what the official report from Siranor said. He had no ill will towards mages, knowing most of them were just scared but honest people.

"Siljanna, that's crazy! Rylie didn't start the fire, our father did! He hurt Rylie and started a fight with Nate, I saw everything! He was out of control and I... lost my temper," Harrison admitted, feeling no guilt at having struck Sampson.

"What do you mean, you lost your temper?" Siljanna spat.

"I subdued him, but even my efforts didn't stop him from lobbing a burning log at the alcohol display. *That* started the fire!" Harrison shouted, gripping Siljanna's hands, trying to will her to believe him.

"No! That's a lie, you're lying! Dad has problems but he'd never put his or innocent people's lives in danger," she screamed, pulling her hands free of his grasp. Her reaction stunned him but still agitated from his earlier confrontation with Sampson, Harrison couldn't hold his tongue.

"Are you kidding? You're saying our father, the former military veteran that killed dozens, if not hundreds of people in the war; the man that continued to aid the Imperial military with some of the most ruthless tactics on record is *incapable* of hurting people. You seriously believe that?" Harrison cried.

"No, he wouldn't... I don't believe it," Siljanna protested, but once he started, Harrison couldn't stop his verbal assault.

"Don't be so naive Siljanna! Our father did this, not Rylie. He is cruel, ruthless and ever since mum died, he's been a danger to everyone around him. But surely blame doesn't matter right now, we need to get them out of there!" Harrison shouted, desperate for her to see sense. How could her hatred blind her to the more vital task of saving their lives?

"I am not naive Harrison, and you're wrong about our father! Your hatred for him is completely unjustified, but it doesn't matter now. We can't save them from that," she screamed, pointing at the blazing building, "and you just let the one responsible escape!"

"Listen to yourself Siljanna!" Harrison begged.

"Either get out of my way or I'll arrest you for obstructing justice," Siljanna demanded, her green eyes burning with an intensity he'd never seen.

Her hair, longer again but still styled in the partly shaved way she'd done for their graduation, was sticking to her forehead from the heat. She tried to push past him in pursuit of Rylie when instinct took over. Harrison grabbed her arm and restrained her, reaching for the cuffs that were linked to her utility belt. The cuffs clicked into place around her wrist and he attached the empty cuff to a nearby wrought-iron railing.

As she realised what he'd done, she became even more enraged. Tugging against the restraint, Harrison used the distraction to take her radio and called for warden assistance, making sure to emphasise innocent people were still inside the burning tavern. He dropped the radio and turned, running in the direction Rylie had gone.

"You will regret this Harrison! I'll never stop hunting you, either of you!" Siljanna screamed, but he refused to look back. She'd made her choice and so had he.

Taking to the back streets, Harrison tried calling out to Rylie but if she heard him, she didn't respond. When fleeing, she looked terrified but he knew she wouldn't go far. If nothing else, she'd want to find Evie who would need her sister after that seizure, so Harrison had to find her, and quickly. He headed north, over the bridge and towards the woodlands. After making the radio call about the fire, all of the wardens on duty had rushed to the tavern so the usual presence at the checkpoint was gone, meaning he could cross unnoticed.

With the way he'd left Siljanna, he had to keep a low profile and get Rylie and Evie out of town. Before Tivani was out of sight, he couldn't resist looking back. The flames were still flickering from the tavern, but they had died down, so the wardens were obviously doing all they could to contain it. After that final glance towards his hometown, Harrison strode off to his loft.

Further down the road, he heard a faint sobbing from the tree line and was relieved to find Rylie. She was huddled in the thicket, but her pale skin stood out against the leaves.

"Rylie? It's okay, it's me," Harrison announced.

"Don't come any closer, I don't want to hurt you!" She cried. Harrison walked cautiously towards her, hesitating when she scrambled away from him.

"You don't need to be afraid of me, I want to help," he explained, as sympathetically as he could.

"Harrison please I mean it! Something has happened to me, and I don't want to hurt you... my hands were on fire!" She exclaimed, her voice cracking as she tried desperately to hide.

She was terrified and the sound of her voice broke his heart but her words confirmed part of Siljanna's story, Rylie was a mage, but Harrison knew she didn't start the fire so it didn't change how he felt.

He recalled his first-year studies with Tutor Anderson and learning about mages. If a person was an Ar'encal descendant, they could become a mage but had to experience a stressful event to trigger magical abilities. It was also believed that the power was linked to the stressor and the person's emotional state. Watching her home burn with her parents trapped inside easily qualified as a stressful event in Harrison's estimation, so he believed that whatever abilities she now had literally only just triggered.

Over the years, Rylie had always been there for him, often at times when he felt lost or alone, and now he had the chance to return her kindness.

"Whatever is going on Rylie, we can solve it together. Please, just let me help you," he pleaded, watching as she tried to stop herself from crying. The tears that ran down her cheek solidified, becoming droplets of ice.

"I'm so scared Harrison, what if I burn you? What if I can never touch anyone or anything again?" She whimpered, dropping her head into her knees as her own words sunk in.

While her head was down, he got close enough to reach out and placed his hand on her arm. She shied away but he mirrored her movement to keep hold of her.

"Rylie look, you're not burning me," he promised, imploring her to look up. "In fact, you're freezing."

She looked at his hand and then his face which showed no pain. Cautiously, Rylie stood and they emerged from the thicket. She hugged herself tightly as if to close herself off from him. It was a strange sight as she was usually so approachable but now even the slightest gesture made her flinch. She was so cold but didn't seem to care, so he just threw his jacket around her and tried to put his concerns to the back of his mind.

"Come on, let's get to my loft. Evie had a seizure just after you ran off and passed out. I asked Morgan to take her there so she'd be safe but we should join them as quickly as we can," Harrison advised.

"Morgan?!" She repeated frightened, mumbling words of panic about '*what was going to happen*' and '*how would Morgan react if he found out?*'

"Don't worry, I trust Morgan. No matter what's going on, he'll help us," Harrison said calmly, placing his hand on Rylie's arm. This time she didn't shy away. He hoped that was a good sign as they went back to the path and onwards to his loft.

When the blacksmith came into view, they entered and headed up the stairs to his room. Harrison was relieved to see that Morgan had waited with Evie, who was asleep. He'd likely heard through the radio what was going on at the tavern and was risking his neck to stay. Rylie was shifting nervously with Morgan in the room, and he noticed straight away.

"Rylie it's okay. Siljanna's been raving over the radio that you're a mage and caused the fire, but I don't believe it. You do not need to fear me," he announced, his blue eyes steady as he made direct eye contact with her. Rylie relaxed a little as she nodded and slowly passed him to sit beside her sister.

"But the problem is—" Rylie began but then her voice caught in her throat.

"Rylie is a mage," Harrison finished the sentence for her. "But she didn't start the fire. It was my father. He'd started a fight in the bar. I finished it. I know I shouldn't have gotten involved, but I did," Harrison explained, his tone quiet, despite feeling no guilt.

"What happened?" Morgan asked urgently.

"I thought I'd subdued him, but he threw a burning log into the alcohol. That caused the fire. He was drunk Morgan, and completely out of control!" Harrison answered.

As Morgan listened to his best friend, Evie began to stir and they all turned their attention to her.

"Evie! It's me, are you okay?" Rylie whispered, her voice filled with concern. Evie rolled over on the bed at the sound of her big sister's voice. When she saw her, Evie's eyes flew wide open as she wrapped her arms around Rylie's neck.

"Rylie, you're okay! I saw you burning and I thought you were trapped in the house. Where's mum and dad, are they here?" She asked, releasing her sister from her tight embrace but after a brief moment of scanning the unfamiliar room, continued her flurry of questions. "Where are we?"

"You're in my loft, Evie," Harrison said, making sure she was aware of his presence.

"I brought you here after you passed out. We were all worried about you kiddo," Morgan followed up. Evie knew Morgan but was notably more nervous once she registered he was there.

"It's all right Evie, we're safe," Rylie added, drawing her sister's attention back to her. "Harrison and Morgan are going to protect us. I don't know what happened to mum and dad, but they were trapped—" Rylie began, choking on her words but forcing them out. "The wardens blame me for the fire."

As soon as the words left her mouth, she regretted them. She didn't want to accuse Siljanna in front of Harrison, even though he knew the truth, but didn't expect Evie to leap up from the bed, dash over to Morgan and start hitting him.

"No, you're wrong! Rylie didn't do anything, it was Mr Stone! He was angry, he caused the fire! It's him you need to arrest, leave my sister alone!" She wailed.

Evie was so little compared to Morgan that none of her strikes hurt. He just let her hit him over and over until she was too tired to lash out anymore. When she stopped, he put his hand under her chin and softly raised her face so she was looking at him.

"Mhmm, okay I believe you," he replied, his tone kind and a little playful, but Evie didn't register it.

"You're not going to take my sister away?" She asked, her voice sceptical. As she stared at Morgan, waiting for his reply, her lips began to tremble.

"No, I'm not. But the other wardens may not believe us, so will you do me a favour? Lay low for a while, okay," he instructed, shifting his gaze from Evie to Harrison, knowing that he'd already chosen to protect them, whatever the cost. "I'll try to buy you some time. Gather what you can and get out of here. Go anywhere but north, got it?"

"Thank you, Morgan... now go. You'll have been expected at the scene ages ago," Harrison insisted, giving his friend a quick hug as he left.

"Oh, don't worry! The families around the market saw the flames and were panicking," he said, formulating the lie he would tell Siljanna and the others. "I was helping calm them, knowing other wardens were already at the scene."

He winked as he exited the loft, obviously learning how to come up with on-the-spot excuses after all those years as Harrison's roommate and hearing his tall tales. With Morgan gone, Harrison locked the door and turned back to Rylie and Evie.

"Please, talk to me. Once I know what's going on, I'll keep you safe. I promise," he implored, his warm eyes glistening, hoping desperately that they would believe him.

Rylie quickly decided to trust him and explained everything. About Evie and how her seizures were actually visions, about their family connection to the Ar'encal through their grandparents and that although their dad never triggered abilities, he and their mum had been trying to help Evie to conceal her power ever since they realised what it was.

Evie tagged in and explained how their parents had done plenty of reading and managed to find one article that called her ability *'precognition,'* meaning she saw events before they happened. Sometimes it was months before, other times it was mere moments, but Evie had no control over what she saw and when the visions would come. If they came while she slept, it was like a terrible nightmare, but if she was awake, she'd have a seizure.

Once her little sister had finished, Rylie went on to explain what happened at the tavern after Evie passed out; including how she saw their parents trapped by the collapsed beam while the room around them burned, and that she hadn't noticed her hands on fire until Siljanna threw her to the ground. She was about to say she had no idea what the power was when Evie spoke again.

"It's called *elemental magic.* I read about it in one of mum's books. It didn't say much but was listed as one of the more dangerous powers. If you learn to control it, an Elemental can create and command the elements but otherwise, they'll just react to your emotions."

"At the moment I'm not in control of anything!" Rylie replied, shocked but grateful at her little sister's insight.

"There isn't much we can do about it here," Harrison cut in. "We need to get somewhere safe, away from town, the wardens and especially Siljanna."

Knowing both of them were mages made their need to escape even more pressing. Harrison took a moment to strap on his favourite leather armour and grabbed warm cloaks for all three of them. He also collected his broadsword and a bow, slinging both onto his back and collected two knapsacks, filling them with food, water and what little money he had.

"This should keep us going for a while, but if we run out of food, I can hunt for us. We have to find somewhere to hide until we can come up with a better plan," he said urgently. It was getting dark outside, and he wanted to hit the road before they lost all natural light.

"What about Yasras? Our grandparents own the inn. Siljanna may not remember that so might not think to search for us there," Rylie suggested, adjusting the knapsack he'd given her.

Luckily, because she'd been working, Rylie was in thick black leggings, flat brown boots and a long-sleeved top, covered by a corset-style waistcoat, all ideal for travelling. Evie, however, was not so favourably dressed, wearing cropped trousers and a thin, purple strappy top; but at least she had what looked like comfortable pumps on.

It would take them a full day to reach Yasras on foot, especially taking the woodland trail but Harrison was grateful to have a place to start. He locked the door as they left and tossed the key in the shop safe downstairs. For a brief moment, he wanted to take the horses stabled outside but decided against it. They were trying not to draw unnecessary attention to themselves and stealing Samuel's and the other horses would not help.

The horses whinnied softly as the three of them headed towards the woodland path. Instinctively, Harrison threw out some food just to keep them content until Elijah returned. He silently hoped that

Elijah wouldn't get into any trouble because of him and that Morgan could buy them enough time to get a decent head-start.

Chapter Eight
Hunted

The wardens worked tirelessly to control the blaze that engulfed the Hawk Eye tavern. It had taken most of them just three minutes to respond to Harrison's radio call, and when they had, they immediately set to finding an entry point to search for survivors. Still bound to the railing until Téa released her, Siljanna was livid. On the anniversary of her mother's death, her brother had betrayed her and chosen to protect a mage, which had likely cost her father his life.

She questioned over and over again, *why? Why would Rylie do this?* With no plausible explanation, Siljanna found not knowing made her even more furious. Their entire friendship had been based on a lie, one she could never forgive. Even if her powers were new, surely she knew of her heritage and therefore knew she was a danger. Rylie should've turned herself in!

Next, her mind recalled everything that happened between her and Harrison. He was helping at first but then *accused her father of starting the fire,* something he blatantly wouldn't do, and *defended the mage she witnessed causing the blaze.* Replaying the scene in her mind she couldn't deny the truth. Every fibre of her being wanted to hunt down both Harrison and Rylie, even if it meant tearing apart the town brick by brick but she couldn't, not until she discovered her father's fate.

Fifteen minutes later, Morgan arrived and his tardiness only added to her frustration.

"Where have you been?" She spat.

"I'm sorry Siljanna, the people are panicking. I was trying to provide reassurance. This was the fastest I could get here," Morgan replied defensively.

"Your job is to protect people, not to coddle them," Siljanna countered. "Go, help Téa find a way inside."

As soon as she finished speaking, Siljanna turned her back on Morgan and began pacing restlessly. When the other wardens finally called her over, having found an access point, the sight before her confirmed her dreaded fear.

Slumped next to the stone fireplace that had once been the soul of the tavern, laid her father and for a moment she couldn't breathe. She watched, unable to move as the warden's inside checked for vital signs. Dropping his head, the warden glanced towards Siljanna, looking truly remorseful. As the realisation set in, Téa approached and placed a hand on her shoulder.

"I'm so sorry Commander," Téa offered heavy-heartedly.

"Don't! Being sorry won't change anything. Just get my father out of there and continue searching for Nate and Paige," she ordered but her eyes were still firmly locked on her father's corpse. All she'd ever wanted was to make him proud but now, he was gone. Her father was dead.

"What can I do?" Morgan asked, speaking plainly. He knew she wouldn't want sympathy, only justice.

"Find them, find Harrison and that murderous mage Rylie Auren and bring them to me," she replied, still not able to tear her eyes away from the wardens carefully carrying her father's body out of the tavern.

"I'll lead a search party. We'll start at Harrison's loft and if they aren't there, will move on to the academy. It's familiar ground for both of them so they might think they can hide there," Morgan advised, his response more authoritative than Siljanna expected, and for a moment, his assertiveness made her doubt.

"You'd turn your back on him?" She asked. "Just like that?"

"Honour. Justice. Loyalty. Those are the words of the warden oath. If what you say is true, Harrison has betrayed that oath, and I need the truth," Morgan began turning towards her, realising he'd drawn her attention away from the sight of her father. "I want to do the right thing. I failed a year ago, and I refuse to fail again," he answered, and that Siljanna believed.

"I'm glad to have you on my side Morgan, but we are going to need support from a much higher authority too," she said, her mind clearly coming up with a plan. "Ensure that Téa and the remaining wardens continue working to extinguish the blaze before you leave."

"Where are you going?" He asked.

"You'll find out soon enough," she replied as she marched off with renewed determination.

As he watched Siljanna walk away, Morgan said a silent prayer, hoping that by the time he and the retinue of wardens going with him arrived at Harrison's loft; that he, Rylie and Evie would be gone. As long as they had, diverting to the academy should give them enough time to get some distance. He felt saddened by the realisation it would be a long time before he saw his closest friend again but knew the best thing he could do was provide him with the opportunity to escape. He couldn't help but be concerned about Siljanna's plan, but without knowing her intentions, there was little he could do.

When Siljanna arrived at her home, she forcefully pushed through the front door and went straight to her father's old office. She needed his contact book. All the more recent times he'd been summoned to the capital for *consultations,* he liaised directly with the Imperator's right-hand, Cameron Weiss, and if she could get his assistance, there was no doubt she'd catch Harrison and Rylie. Rummaging through the desk draws, she found it; a small black book with dozens of names and numbers. She grabbed the receiver of the old desk phone and began to dial. After a few rings, the call connected.

"Weiss," asserted the confident voice of the Imperator's right hand, answering the call.

"Sir, this is Commander Siljanna Stone of Tivani," she said directly, hoping he'd know of her.

"Ah yes, Sampson's prodigal daughter; what can I do for you, Commander Stone?" He replied. Siljanna paused as she heard the address roll off his tongue. How many times had he said that over the years, but directed at her father?

"We have a situation in Tivani. My father has been murdered. I know the culprit, a mage called Rylie Auren; but she isn't alone. My brother Harrison, a former warden is aiding her, and they have just eluded arrest. I am calling to request assistance in capturing them," she explained, her tone as firm and unrelenting as her mood. There was a long silence on his end of the line before Cameron replied.

"On my way," he said sharply, before hanging up.

Siljanna looked at the receiver in shock but placed it back on the handset feeling grateful. She wasn't sure how she expected the conversation to go but was relieved her father's reputation had warranted arguably the second most important person in Siranor to come to her aid. Just then, her radio crackled and Téa's voice was calling out to her.

"Commander Stone? Commander Stone! Please return to the tavern as soon as you can. We've found them," she called.

Telling herself there was no way Téa could've meant Harrison and Rylie, she hurried back towards the tavern to discover who they'd found.

Over the next few hours, the wardens managed to completely extinguish the fire and Morgan returned with the search party. He approached Siljanna but his disappointed expression told her everything she needed to know.

"I'm sorry Siljanna. We thoroughly investigated Harrison's loft, the smithy, and the academy; there is no sign of Rylie or your brother. His weapons and armour are missing, so they could have gone off the beaten track."

"Do you have any good news for me?" She asked, expecting not to like his reply.

"Only that Elijah Ashby and Samuel Fischer are coming to the guardhouse for questioning. They doubt they can help but are willing to try. Would you like me to begin questioning them?" Morgan asked, sounding doubtful but Siljanna was too distracted by the second name to answer his question straight away.

"Samuel Fischer? What is that—," she paused, stopping herself from saying something derogatory, "what is *he* doing here?"

"He boarded his horse at Elijah's stables and was there when I arrived. He claims he didn't see anyone, having just returned from the train station," Morgan explained.

"What about Elijah?" Siljanna asked.

"Elijah was at home but came when I asked. He and Harrison have become quite friendly over this past year so might have some useful insights," Morgan replied.

"Thank you, Morgan. You've done enough for tonight. Go, get some rest. I've just spoken with the Imperator's right hand, Cameron Weiss, and he is on his way so I may need you in the morning," Siljanna informed looking exhausted herself but having no intention of resting until the situation was dealt with.

Morgan gave her a polite nod before leaving. The thought of the Imperator's aide joining the investigation was frightening but at least Siljanna had believed his story. He just hoped that Elijah could now continue to point her in the wrong direction.

When Morgan told Elijah a highlighted version of the evening's events, Elijah wanted to help. He and Harrison had truly become friends over the last year and like Morgan, Elijah believed that both he and Rylie didn't deserve to be persecuted for crimes they didn't commit.

The woodland paths behind the smithy were very rural, with a variety of trees, mainly birch and pine scattered around the winding paths. Ferns and other greenery flourished between them with the only different spots of colour coming from the shoots of foxglove and patches of buttercups. The path itself was dotted with little stones and surfacing roots which Evie kept tripping over. Her feet ached but she tried her best not to complain. After walking for two hours, it had become too dark to continue so they stopped in a small opening to make a campfire.

Harrison encouraged Evie to help him collect the firewood and some kindling, stacking what they'd found neatly in a small pit. He was about to show her how to use the flint when he looked up at Rylie and realised she was trembling.

"Are you going to be okay if I light this?" He asked. "We need a campfire otherwise it'll get too cold while we rest."

Rylie felt cold but wasn't bothered by it and was shaking from fear, partially of the fire they needed but mostly the one within. It was only when she noticed Evie shivering, she knew Harrison was right. Swallowing her fear, Rylie nodded, confirming to Harrison he should light the fire. After a few attempts, the spark caught onto the kindling and soft flames danced over the logs. He encouraged them to eat something, but Rylie refused.

Before long, all of Evie's energy was drained. Wrapping a cloak tightly around herself, she curled up in a ball, used one of the bags as a pillow, and fell asleep. Sitting on a fallen log, Rylie looked over at her sister with a worried but loving expression. As Harrison came over, he draped his cloak over Evie as well, giving her an additional blanket and then sat down next to Rylie.

"How are you *really* doing?" He asked, concern written all over his face. He reached down and took her hand, a gesture that was so natural to them, but Rylie still flinched.

"I'm scared. I did know there was Ar'encal blood in my family, but now both Evie and I have powers that we have no idea how to control," she replied, trying to retract her hand but Harrison held on.

He looked at her, the golden flecks in his warm brown eyes highlighted by the fire. Placing his other hand behind her neck, he stroked her cheek with his thumb and she let herself relax into his touch.

"We'll work this out… together. Even if we have to circle the planet, we will find someone or something that will help both of you to control these powers. And until then, I *will* keep you safe," he promised softly, pausing as if wanting to say more but decided against it.

"Why Harrison? You'll lose everything to help us," she asked, biting her lip nervously.

"That's not true, you've been there for me more than anyone in my life, Rylie. I couldn't bear to lose you," he replied. Hearing his words, Rylie smiled softly and closed her eyes, shuffling down so she could rest her head on his shoulder.

He wanted to tell her how, earlier that day, Nate told him there wasn't anyone he'd trust more to look after them if something happened, but decided that mentioning her father would just make things worse. They wouldn't know for some time what became of either of her parents and could only hope that somehow they survived.

As the curls of Rylie's hair draped over his shoulder, he felt her grip his hand more tightly. She needed to rest but clearly couldn't get out of her own head so he reached over to the other knapsack and pulled out a book, knowing that although he hadn't intentionally put it there, he always had a book in each of his bags. Collecting it, he realised it was his favourite, the cursed warrior tale. He showed her the book and they both moved onto the floor so that they could lean back on the log.

Harrison put his arm around Rylie allowing her to curl into his side. She was slim enough that he could hold her and turn the pages without moving her. It was difficult to read by the fading light from the campfire but Harrison turned to the start and read almost from memory until he felt Rylie finally drop off to sleep.

As morning dawned, Harrison had barely slept, spending most of the evening watching the girls and being vigilant for any unusual sounds. Whether it was wildlife or wardens, he had to be prepared; but thankfully, the night had been uneventful. He woke Rylie and Evie early so that they could set off. The trail was still winding through the dense woodlands past Lake Ismay but Harrison had trekked through the area a couple of times and knew they should hit the main road to Yasras in a few hours.

As he led the way, Evie followed closely with her sister just behind. When he looked over his shoulder, he noticed Rylie warily placing her hand on a tree. It was clear she was still nervous about things spontaneously combusting at her touch, but each time it didn't, she seemed to calm. She ran her thumb over the bark of a pine tree, grateful to feel its rough texture on her skin. Her gaze followed the ivy growing upon it until she was looking up into the tree line. The view of the sky was obstructed but with the daylight back, it was much easier for them to keep going. The smell of the trees and the morning dew was invigorating, so the three of them pushed forward to Yasras.

It was mid-morning when Cameron Weiss arrived in Tivani. He travelled alone from the train station but when he reached the northern bridge, Siljanna was there to greet him. For the right hand of the Imperator, he looked younger and a lot more casual than she expected, wearing a white shirt, brown trousers and long leather boots. With a jacket slung over his shoulder and a short sword attached to his belt, it was almost unbelievable he was the second most powerful person in the Empire. His light brown hair was side-swept and he exuded confidence.

"Good morning Siljanna, thank you for coming to meet me," he said, shaking her hand.

"Thank you for coming so quickly," she replied.

"No problem. Please, lead the way to the guardhouse," Cameron requested. "You can fill me in on the situation on the way."

As they walked through the town square, Siljanna stopped in front of the tavern, now in complete ruin, and explained how she witnessed Rylie Auren set fire to the building using magic while her father, who was the victim of a bar fight with her brother lay incapacitated inside. Cameron took in the information but didn't react to the details. He was clearly assessing something but Siljanna couldn't tell if it was the situation or her personally.

They continued to the guardhouse as Siljanna detailed what they'd done to try and track down Harrison and Rylie throughout the night, advising the search of his loft and the academy left them with no leads. She only had one potential option to get information but her progress so far had been limited. Once seated in her office, Siljanna decided to get to the point.

"Mr Weiss, let me make myself clear. I need to find my brother and Rylie Auren. They must answer for what they've done; what they have taken from me. I will not rest until I avenge my father. What must I do to get the Empire's support?" She asked bluntly, folding her arms as she sat back in the sturdy desk chair.

"Commander Stone, I believe we can help each other. I heard much about you before travelling here but what I have seen and heard today has convinced me. I have a proposition and if you want the Imperator's help, you must come with me to Siranor, today," he said directly.

Cameron was difficult to read, but Siljanna couldn't resist the opportunity of having the Imperator's aid. No matter what it took, she was willing to make the sacrifice.

149

"I need a few hours to make some arrangements here, then I will meet you at the station," she replied firmly to reinforce her intent. Cameron smiled, giving her a slight bow as he went to exit her office.

"Two hours, then I go; my offer with me," he advised, departing swiftly. Once gone, she was about to radio for Morgan but he'd clearly been waiting, as before she could even reach the radio, he knocked and entered the room.

"So, what happened?" He asked, a dubious tone to his voice and checking the door twice before facing her.

"Morgan, I'm glad you're here," she began. "I have been presented with a time-sensitive opportunity to receive aid from the Imperator in the hunt for Rylie and Harrison, but it means I must travel to Siranor today. You will be acting Commander in my absence and I have no time for training so you'll be learning on the job. Understood?" She made no eye contact with him as she spoke, searching through her desk for something.

"Yes, of course, but what kind of aid?" Morgan asked. He hoped it sounded like an innocent enquiry, but was truly probing for more details. He couldn't warn Harrison but still wanted to know what his friend would be facing.

"I don't care, as long as it means I capture my brother and that murderous mage," Siljanna announced, her reply curt.

"Siljanna—" Morgan started but stopped himself.

"You don't believe they're responsible, do you? Just like you still don't believe that my mother was killed by a mage," Siljanna responded, finishing his sentence.

"No, I don't. There isn't enough evidence," he admitted but this time, it wasn't Morgan hesitating, but Siljanna cutting him off.

"My word isn't good enough for you?" She challenged, her eyes narrowing with suspicion.

"I didn't mean it like that," he explained, trying to defuse her irritation but instead took in a deep breath, preparing for her retaliation.

"At ease; I know he is… was, your best friend, but I also know what I saw," she said, ensuring she had Morgan's full attention. "There is no doubt in my mind. Rylie Auren, flames bursting from her hands, burnt down the Hawk Eye tavern with my father inside. Then, when I told Harrison, not only did he betray me by cuffing me to the railing, he confessed to subduing our father, leaving him defenceless. Then he walked away, choosing to protect the mage responsible."

Recounting the story, even so briefly, seemed to shake Siljanna's calm demeanour.

"Siljanna, I didn't mean to offend you," Morgan apologised, genuinely concerned for her. She seemed cold more than angry now, which was somehow worse. Visibly exhaling her frustrations, Siljanna continued.

"If you want more evidence, send my father's body to the institute in Siranor. He likely died of smoke inhalation, but if they can prove he was incapacitated from an injury and not just the drink, then perhaps you will accept the way things are. I know he had issues, I'm no fool, but it's not what killed him. He was murdered," she said adamantly.

"Fine, I will make the arrangements to have him taken to the institute and the findings sent to both of us. In the meantime, you can trust me to tend to everything here for as long as you need," Morgan assured.

"Good, now please advise the others of the situation, but send Téa in here too. I have one more task for her before I go," Siljanna instructed, picking up the file she'd been looking for.

As he walked out, Morgan headed to the break room, found Téa and told her to report to Siljanna's office. She made her way in as quickly as possible and made sure the door was securely closed behind her.

"Yes, Commander?" Téa enquired, quickly saluting as she stood to attention before Siljanna.

"Do you still have the suspects in custody?" She asked, flicking through the file.

"Indeed ma'am; as detailed in my report, they haven't been as forthcoming as we hoped," she said, sounding nervous. To begin with, Siljanna found Téa's anxiety annoying but she'd grown to like it. As her father proved, fear and respect came hand in hand.

"Arrange for them to be transferred to my custody in the capital and I'll deal with them there. Remember, no one, *especially* Morgan, can know they are still in my custody. Make it look like they have been sent for medical treatment," Siljanna emphasised sternly.

Téa nodded briskly and headed out of the room. She'd never forget how much Siljanna disliked hesitation after giving a direct order. Once she'd done all she could at the guardhouse, Siljanna made her way home to pack a travel bag.

As she walked through the front door, everything was just as she'd remembered; the cupboards open, liquor bottles on the floor and the house generally messy. She ignored it though, knowing she had no time or reason to clean and headed to the closet under the stairs where her father's old travel bag was stored. It felt only right to use it now.

Opening the door, she was confronted with a very different sight, however. The handcrafted axes from Harrison she'd put in there just yesterday. As she picked them up, she felt her eyes drawn to the words he'd so intricately engraved into the blade; '*Honour, Justice and Loyalty*,' shortly followed by the memory of Morgan's words, that Harrison had broken the oath they represented, and she snapped.

Taking the axes tightly in her grasp, she swung out, smashing the sideboard in the hallway. The violent act felt so exhilarating, she couldn't stop. She stalked through the house, axes in hand and began destroying everything in sight. After a few moments, she slung one of the axes as hard as she could towards the wall, lodging it there, and impaled the kitchen unit with the other. Panting, she looked at the damage and realised, she didn't care. Everything that made her once love her family home was gone, and she didn't want to stay there any longer than she had to.

She went to her room, removed her warden commander uniform, replacing it with her once and still favourite black armour, then took from the draw her favoured twin pistols and the chest straps she'd had designed to holster them. Returning to the closet, she found her father's old travel bag and filled it with everything else she would need for an extended time away. Even the possibility of not returning. After all, what did she have to return to?

Leaving the house and with all the arrangements she needed in place, Siljanna headed to the train station. She arrived just as the train pulled in, and Cameron Weiss was standing on the platform studying the watch on his wrist. He noticed her and looked back at his watch before strolling towards her.

"One hundred and nine minutes; you like to keep a guy waiting," he stated. She was fairly sure he was teasing but couldn't be completely sure.

"I just made good use of the time I had," she retorted.

"You're ready?" He asked, but Siljanna couldn't help feeling he didn't mean just to leave Tivani. She nodded and strode with purpose onto the train. Cameron smiled and then followed her off the platform. Soon after they were bound for Siranor.

Siljanna slept for most of the journey, exhausted from the events of the last two days until they neared the city.

"We're almost there," Cameron informed in a quiet tone, barely loud enough to wake her. "We'll go straight to the Imperial palace on arrival, for a private audience with Imperator Harlyn." The announcement made Siljanna focus but a thought clearly crossed her mind and Cameron noticed instantly. "Your suspects will be held in the prison in the meantime. The Imperator has ensured her private guards will collect and oversee them while we talk."

Siljanna looked at Cameron stunned. He must have learned about her transferring them while she slept but how had he already made arrangements to detain them? She rolled her eyes assuming Téa had been unable to provide a convincing transfer report but hoped it had only been picked up by Cameron, and not Morgan. As they disembarked the train, a car was waiting to take them to the palace.

Chapter Nine
Dark Intent

The drive was short but the roads and infrastructure of Siranor were like nothing Siljanna had ever seen before. Vast motorways and winding roads, tall buildings made of glass, concrete and stone. It felt like another world. They took an access road to reach the palace and it was the most impressive building of all. The ornate structure was white with a slight pinkish glow and all of the windows and doors were framed with gold. Statues embellished the rooftop and portrayed the gods; Ceris, goddess of the planet and Temu, the god of creation. Each statue was in a different pose, designed to emphasise the beauty, strength and power of each god.

The driver pulled over and opened the car door allowing Cameron to escort her inside. They passed through golden gates and across a beautiful courtyard before entering. Although impressed by the exterior, the interior took Siljanna's breath away. Her eyes were drawn straight to the sweeping marble staircase in the centre of the room until she noticed the person standing at the top, Imperator Harlyn Rainer.

"Good afternoon, you must be Commander Siljanna Stone. I have heard much about you," Imperator Harlyn greeted, her voice more formal and proper than Siljanna had remembered from hearing her address on the radio when she was first appointed.

Although Siljanna was only fourteen at the time, she still recalled her father speaking about the controversial selection of Harlyn Rainer as the new Imperator after the news of her father's death. Unlike in the Kingdom of Carlisse, ruled by a monarchy with each new ruler being the heir of the previous king or queen; the Imperator as ruler of the Siranor was voted in by the senior members of the council upon the death or resignation of the former Imperator.

Selecting the child of a prior leader was unheard of and combined with the fact Harlyn was just twenty-two at the time of her appointment, made it a memorable day when she addressed the nation. Since taking charge, she'd kept many of her father's initiatives in place, and appointed some of the best advisors to assist her, meaning the Empire stabilised rapidly under her rule.

Now, eight years later, Harlyn looked mature. Her straight ebony hair fell to her shoulders and was a stark contrast to her pale complexion and sky-blue eyes. There was something clinical about her expression which was emphasised by her high cheekbones and strong jawline. The biggest surprise, however, was her clothing. Siljanna expected a regal attire but Harlyn stood before her in a lab coat with a long black dress underneath and practical shoes.

Cameron indicated for Siljanna to wait at the base of the stairs as Harlyn approached them. When he gave a graceful bow, Siljanna copied.

"Welcome to the Imperial Palace," The Imperator said, perfectly polite.

"Thank you, your imperial majesty," Siljanna replied, still bowing before her.

"Please, call me Imperator Harlyn. Only my father enjoyed such a formal address. Join me in my study. Cameron has told me of your situation and I believe we can help each other, but this conversation should be held in private," she requested, leading the way.

After walking through several halls filled with impressive portraits and stunning artwork, they came to an intricately carved wooden door and entered a large study. Three of the walls were covered with bookshelves and there was a beautiful desk in the centre. Harlyn sat at the desk as Cameron pulled a chair out for Siljanna on the other side, and then stood quietly, arms folded by the door. Siljanna looked back at Cameron for a moment before turning to face the Imperator.

"Firstly, welcome to Siranor, Siljanna. I believe it's your first visit to our metropolis. Are you impressed with what you've seen so far?" Harlyn asked.

"Indeed; my father told many stories from his visits but nothing quite compares to seeing it with my own eyes. The institute has obviously accomplished much to create such a thriving city," Siljanna answered respectfully.

"Yes, and I am proud that despite being Imperator, I also retained my position as the head of the institute, which allows me to be at the forefront of some of our more crucial Encia studies," Harlyn replied, her expression as confident and proud as her tone.

"Encia studies? Not to sound ungrateful but if that's your focus, why did you want to meet me? I am no scientist," Siljanna interjected, looking perplexed.

"You are hunting a renegade mage are you not? Please, indulge me while I explain," Harlyn asked and with that Siljanna sat back in the chair, motioning with one hand for the Imperator to continue.

"Please go ahead," Siljanna said and once Harlyn was sure she had the young commander's full attention, she continued.

"Un-filtered Encia, as you know, is toxic to Humans and Terrans. The Ar'encal, however, and their descendants, including their half-human *'mage'* children, are immune to the disease we call the withering. I have made it my duty to find a way for all humans to become immune to the effects of Encia. For several years now, I have been studying the raw substance and we have uncovered a few resistant materials, but last year, some new evidence came into my possession and I believe I have created a substance that can truly absorb it," Harlyn began but paused when she noticed Siljanna not reacting as expected. She was used to her scientific peers being excited by her findings but Siljanna was clearly underwhelmed.

"That all sounds well and good, but why would this cause you to help me?" Siljanna asked, responding to the Imperator's hesitation.

"It's simple. I need to test this substance to see how it reacts to a mage. It is my hope that it will draw the magic from within them like it absorbs raw Encia. Once extracted, if that person is no longer able to wield magic, becoming fully human, they could be rehabilitated into society," she answered, her eyes relaxed and smile genuine, even though her speech felt rehearsed.

"A noble cause indeed, but the mage I seek and her accomplice are criminals. They do not deserve to be spared," Siljanna said, disgusted at the prospect.

"Oh, they won't be," Harlyn answered and for the first time, she wasn't polite or noble. She was just as Siljanna had remembered Joseph Rainer, the former Imperator to be; ruthless.

"I don't understand," Siljanna admitted quietly.

"They will face the charges before them but the mage, her sentence will include partaking in the Imperator's experiments," Cameron clarified, his presence behind her almost forgotten.

"I cannot test an unknown substance on law-abiding citizens, even volunteers, just in case there are dangerous side effects. But a fugitive mage who has committed murder, well now that's the perfect candidate," the Imperator added. The look on Harlyn's face was a combination of excitement and reservation. She was reading Siljanna for even the slightest reaction but decided to continue. "After my father passed, I kept the mage hunt initiative in place to appease certain members of the council. Now that I need a mage in my custody however, it has come to my attention that several years have passed since a hunter has brought a mage back alive."

"We can't rely on them," Cameron commented, glancing at Harlyn as if awaiting a signal.

"I can, however, rely on my personal wardens. They have received special training and under your leadership, I believe they could find the mage you seek and her accomplice. They would then face you and the repercussions of their crimes, aiding my research in the process," she concluded, making her intentions clear.

Siljanna couldn't deny the prospect was inviting. Having access to command the Imperator's personal wardens was a much greater assist than she had even dared hope for. Siljanna sat forward in the chair to show her interest had been piqued.

"You will allow me to command your personal guard, as long as I focus their efforts on locating Rylie Auren and my brother? In return, all I have to do is bring them back alive?" Siljanna checked.

"I only need Miss Auren alive. The fates of your brother and any other non-mage aiding her are entirely yours to decide," Harlyn answered without a hint of remorse.

"Then it would be my pleasure to accept your aid, Imperator Harlyn. Thank you for this opportunity," Siljanna replied graciously, extending her hand to the Imperator. Harlyn accepted the gesture before turning Siljanna's attention to the door.

"Then please let me introduce you to my private wardens, Juliette Lawrence and Dylan Rose," Harlyn said.

"Dylan?" Siljanna blurted out stunned. Hearing a familiar name was the last thing she expected but as she turned around to face the door, there he was, her old academy friend.

The years had been kind to Dylan but he had always been attractive. As he strode into the room, it was clear he'd retained his muscular build, which was highlighted by his close-fitting armour, but there was something about him that was darker than she remembered. His eyes were a deep shade of blue and his mousy brown hair was stylishly side-swept across his forehead and lightly spiked. The woman that walked in beside him was also notably attractive. Her black hair was cut in a short bob-style that circled her narrow face and rather than armour, she wore a provocative red dress that hugged every inch of her slim body. She draped herself over Dylan's shoulder as they stood before her while the Imperator summoned Cameron over for a private word.

"Good to see you again Siljanna," Dylan began, obviously aware he was about to meet her again.

"You too Dylan. You look… different," she remarked.

"As do you," he replied, being rather aloof.

"I have my reasons," she retorted, giving him as little insight into her situation as he gave her.

"Let's just say I do as well and move on, shall we? Juliette and I are eager to apprehend your fugitives, especially if it helps the Imperator with her quest for knowledge," he explained.

"Of course; I am pleased to already be familiar with the skills of my new allies," Siljanna replied.

"Believe me honey, we are all kinds of impressive," chimed Juliette as she fawned over Dylan, playing mindlessly with a strand of his hair. She stretched up onto her toes to whisper in his ear while continuing to eye up Siljanna. Dylan replied with a snort and a definitive 'No'. Whatever she'd asked, his response made Juliette smile and look towards the Imperator who returned her attention to them.

"So, when do we begin?" Dylan asked.

"Immediately," Imperator Harlyn replied. "Please escort Siljanna to the Imperial prison. She had some suspects transferred from Tivani and your first task can be to interrogate them. After that, you are to report to Siljanna. She and Cameron will keep me informed of your progress."

With that, Dylan, Juliette and Siljanna left the room and made their way towards the Imperial Prison. As they left, Cameron ensured the door was shut securely before turning to face Harlyn.

"Do you think she suspects?" Harlyn asked.

"Unlikely; you've given her exactly what she wants and a well-polished story. She should have no reason to doubt you, but even if she did, her quest for vengeance is overwhelming," Cameron answered, smiling at Harlyn.

He'd been her protector before she was appointed Imperator and knew politics were not her strength, so was genuinely impressed by her convincing performance.

"Good; Keep an eye on their progress for now, but make the preparations we discussed. Should anything go awry, it must be Siljanna that appears at fault," Harlyn replied mercilessly.

"Of course, good day my lady Imperator," Cameron replied, bowing gracefully as he too exited the study.

The driver that collected Siljanna and Cameron was still waiting outside by the palace gates. As Siljanna got back into the car, she looked over to see Dylan kickstart a motorcycle. He swung his leg over the saddle and Juliette placed herself behind, nudging up as closely as she could, wrapping her arms around his torso. Siljanna had to refrain from gagging at the constant public displays of affection. She told her driver their destination and they set off with the motorcycle trailing closely behind.

As they made their way, the driver, James, informed Siljanna he'd arranged an apartment for her and would continue to be her personal chauffeur for the duration of her time in the capital, at Mr Weiss' request. He also presented her with one of the newer technological advancements from the institute, a pager with a built-in radio for long-distance communication.

She couldn't help but wonder, *when did Cameron have the time to make all these arrangements? Did he have them in place before she accepted the Imperator's proposal?* She convinced herself it didn't matter. She was getting the help she wanted, and soon her hunt for Rylie and Harrison would truly begin.

As they arrived at the Imperial Prison, the building looked more like a courthouse than an actual prison. Certainly grander than the small stone room with five cells they had in Tivani. The entire building was white, made of limestone or marble and had a wide set of steps leading up from the road to the entrance. James told her the building was indeed a former courthouse but was now used by the Imperator's council for all matters of security. Basically, it was Cameron's domain, and the prison was located on the third basement level.

She imagined that this was where her father came every time he'd been summoned to the city and couldn't help but wonder how familiar she would soon become with the prominent structure. Getting out of the car, Siljanna made her way to the top of the steps and saw four large pillars before the doorway. Chiselled into each of them were different words; '*Discipline, Order, Justice* and *Integrity*'. As she read each one, she knew this would have been her father's favourite place, even if the rest of the city could immerse every sense or fantasy. This was the place where honourable men, like her father, went to protect the Empire and all its citizens.

As she stood taking in the building's facade, Dylan and Juliette arrived and escorted her inside. In the entryway, there was a large desk with a few receptionists, all taking calls or dealing with people, but they bypassed all of them and headed straight to the elevators. Juliette pressed the '*B3*'button, then looked back at Dylan biting her lip provocatively. The elevator jerked into life and they descended to the lower levels.

"Welcome to the shadow council Siljanna," Dylan smirked. "This is the secondary base for any of the covert trained wardens that come through the facility in Tulam, where Juliette and I both trained."

"Speak plainly Dylan," Juliette grumbled, still eyeing up Siljanna. "We are trained wardens but double up as mage hunters and, when required, assassins for the Imperator."

"Juliette, you're a warden too? I don't recall you being at the Tivani academy," Siljanna questioned, unwilling to believe Juliette had undergone the same training she had.

"My training was unorthodox," she replied. "In fact, it's thanks to your father I'm here. I was a medical student just finishing up my second year when your father heard of my unique proficiency. He provided me with the opportunity to transfer to Tulam a year earlier than usual so I could hone my craft," Juliette said with a devilish smile.

"So much for speaking plainly. What she means is that she's a poisons expert, while I prefer a more direct approach," Dylan announced and as he spoke, Siljanna realised he was turning a sharp dagger expertly in his hand.

"I picked up on that, thank you," Siljanna replied with sass. She didn't feel the need to validate her own abilities back to them. They answered to her after all.

The elevator churned to a stop and when the criss-cross iron doors slid open, Siljanna faced a darker, cold hallway, much more befitting a prison. As they headed deeper into the facility, she noticed an array of cells, an emergency infirmary and an interrogation room. She expected them to turn towards it but instead, they headed down to a lower level.

"Where are we going, I thought my suspects were being held in the interrogation room?" Siljanna asked.

"Oh, they're in a special room," Juliette replied, the wicked grin she'd worn earlier spreading across her face. They came to a heavy door that was locked securely. Dylan revealed the key and forced the door open, allowing them to enter.

"This is a soundproof interrogation room. Rather useful when more forceful measures are required. We felt it was fitting for your suspects," Dylan explained with a smirk. "They've been detained here since you arrived and we took the liberty of binding them, with only one causing a bit of a fuss."

Entering the room, Siljanna saw that just as Dylan had explained, her four suspects; Nate and Paige Auren, Elijah Ashby and Samuel Fischer were each bound to the walls and she felt herself smile inwardly. She'd been waiting for this opportunity for what felt like forever, even though it had only been a day.

As she examined each of them, she noticed Nate was slumped forward on his knees, unconscious and badly bruised. Clearly, he was the one that had *caused a fuss*. Paige had crumpled to the floor beside him sobbing, the chains preventing her from reaching her husband. Samuel was ranting and raving, demanding to be released. Once he recognised Siljanna though, he went silent and Elijah was slumped forward, the restraints seeming to hold him up. He looked as though he'd been sick.

When Paige lifted her head and realised Siljanna was there, she bolted up and came as close to her as the chains would allow.

"Siljanna! Please, there's been a terrible mistake, help us!" She begged.

"Why would I help you? I brought you here," Siljanna declared, shocking Paige enough that she retreated until her back was against the wall.

"But why Siljanna? Why would you do this to us? We have always been friends to you and your family!" Paige cried, shaking her head in disbelief.

"Because your daughter is a mage. She caused the fire that burned down your tavern, killing my father and then escaped my custody. You will help me and my associates to find her or face the consequences of being mage sympathisers," Siljanna said unequivocally.

"No, that's not possible! Evie could never—" Paige cried.

"Evie? Oh, so Evie's a mage too? I assumed she fled because she had nowhere else to go," Siljanna mused slyly. "No matter, I'm sure the Imperator will be more than happy to have two mages involved in the hunt instead of just one."

As the realisation that Siljanna was talking about Rylie set in, Paige straightened her back against the cold cell wall and stopped talking. Her eyes darted from Siljanna to Dylan and Juliette, who were standing close by. When Siljanna realised Paige seemed afraid of them and wasn't going to speak willingly, she decided to increase the torment, feeding just enough information to panic her.

"Your daughter Rylie is wanted for arson and murder, and my brother is wanted too, as her accomplice. I have an accord with the Imperator and full access to a network of mage hunters, as well as the Imperator's elite wardens, who I believe you are acquainted with. We will find her, but you can make your stay in the capital more comfortable if you give us the information we need. You are her mother. Tell me, where would Rylie go?" Siljanna interrogated, her tone dangerous.

As Siljanna fixed her gaze on Paige, she waited for a moment but Paige just shook her head ever so slightly, refusing to speak. Siljanna raised an eyebrow and was about to strike the other woman when Dylan placed a careful hand on her shoulder, drawing her attention away from her captives.

"Siljanna, let Juliette and I speak with the prisoners alone. After all, this is one of our *specialities*," Dylan requested, saying the final word in a truly sinister manner. Deciding that perhaps she didn't have the patience to get the information efficiently, Siljanna looked over to Juliette who was biting her lip again. "Just give us twenty minutes alone with them, we'll get them talking," he finished, once again encouraging Siljanna to leave.

Siljanna stopped at the door, looking back at the four prisoners, her green eyes scowling until she focused on Dylan. He was quite a bit taller than her and being so close, she had to look up to meet his gaze but made sure that although she was speaking to him, everyone in the room heard her.

"I want their location. Get it, by any means necessary," she instructed, stalking out of the room.

As Siljanna left, Juliette began clapping the tips of her fingers with excitement. She collected a satchel that was stashed in a nearby closet and pulled out several small vials.

"Ooh goody! Where shall we start?" She asked, looking almost giddy as she spoke to Dylan who was still standing by the door, flipping his dagger.

"You enjoy this part a little too much Juliette," he said, turning to face her.

"Don't get all high and mighty with me, Dylan Rose. I ensure you enjoy it too!" She answered back snidely.

He sniggered dismissively as she approached, encouraging him to trace his dagger softly over her body, outlining her alluring figure. She let his other hand glide over her hip before she walked away.

"See, you do love me," she teased, giving him a sultry look.

"No, I lust for you. There's a difference," he replied flatly as he moved towards Paige. Reaching her, Dylan could hear Paige's breaths become rapid as she mumbled a plea, begging him not to hurt any of them. In response, he slammed his fist against the wall by her face. "Now, Paige is it? You saw me beat your husband until he was unable to remain conscious, and my special friend repeatedly poison the blacksmith. How much more would you like to see before you tell us where your daughter is?" He threatened.

"Daughters," Juliette corrected, uncorking a small vial and pulling Elijah's beard until his mouth opened.

Paige looked over to Elijah, mouthing an apology as Juliette poured the unknown substance down his throat. He clamped his eyes shut as whatever it was caused him to spasm and urge. Juliette simply laughed and then turned her attention to Samuel. As she got closer, he couldn't resist pulling against his chains again.

"I *demand* you let me go! I have nothing to do with these people! I just stabled my bloody horse at Elijah's blacksmith," he protested, spitting the words in a flurry of panic and frustration. In his desperation, he spat on Juliette, and the face she gave him was a sinister mix of disgust and cruelty.

"Did you hear that Dylan? He can't help us," Juliette repeated, wiping the spit from her face as she glared at Samuel.

"Maybe we should let him go," Dylan replied. "But then again, that would make him a loose end."

"You know I hate loose ends," she said seductively.

"You should do something about that then," Dylan replied, his eyes fixed on Juliette like she was an addictive drug.

Clearly not pleased with his remark, Juliette sauntered over to Dylan and pulled him close. She raised a leg and wrapped it around his body making him pin her to the wall. Thrusting into him, she whispered in his ear.

"I want you to do it. You know your physicality arouses me," Juliette began, enthralling him. Waiting for his reaction, she nibbled his ear, like the thought of violence made her hungry.

"No," he finally replied, his response quiet but firm as he took one of her arms and pinned it above her head. Attempting to kiss her neck, she used her knee to push him away.

"I own you, Dylan Rose," she growled, her tone dark.

"You've never wanted anything this extreme before," Dylan replied, his resolve weakening.

"And yet such extremity wasn't a problem for you last year," she countered.

"I had to, you know that," he replied sombrely.

"And now you have to again. This is why our dynamic works," She said, her tone tantalising. "You wouldn't want to change that, would you?"

"No," he replied again, slower this time, looking at her with both temptation and contempt.

"So do as I command," she insisted, glancing below his belt, pulling him closer again just to touch him intimately. Her voice purred as she writhed sensually in his grasp.

Although the sight before her was mortifying, Paige couldn't draw her eyes away. The hunter, Juliette, wanted her partner to kill the young man next to Elijah... as a turn on! *Or was it a ploy to make her tell them about Rylie?* Either way, she couldn't bear to be responsible for an innocent person's death.

"Yasras! They might be in Yasras," Paige cried. "My family, we stayed at the inn recently. They might feel safe there."

Despite giving them what they needed, Juliette dismissed Paige with an evil grin, eyeing Samuel who was still pulling against his chains. Slipping out of Dylan's grasp, she gave him a look that portrayed her desire. As if unable to resist her any longer, Dylan approached Samuel at such speed it was almost hard to follow, pushing him into the wall with a force that sounded like it cracked his skull.

"That's it, Dylan, now!" Juliette beckoned and before any of them could say otherwise, Dylan buried his knife deep into Samuel's torso. The blade punctured his lung and Samuel doubled over in agony, coughing up blood while Paige screamed.

Instantly, Dylan returned to Juliette, thrusting her against the closet door. Bloody dagger in hand, he used the blade to cut the straps of her dress, the material draping down just enough to reveal her chest. Pulling him towards her again, Juliette allowed Dylan to ravish her body, groaning with pleasure as she looked over his shoulder to see Paige break down, covering her eyes as Samuel bled to death.

Slipping her hand to the doorknob, Juliette opened the closet and lured Dylan inside. Throwing her legs around his waist, she submitted her body to him, grinding her hips deeper with each advance. Everything Dylan did was savage but passionate, and Juliette enjoyed it.

They had obtained the information Siljanna wanted in less than ten minutes and she intended to relish every spare second they had. Although Dylan could do whatever he wanted with her body, Juliette knew she had his mind. In this state, she could coerce him into doing anything. Control over people, using desire to manipulate them, that was her addiction.

After twenty minutes, Juliette and Dylan exited the cell and returned to Siljanna. She noticed Juliette's torn dress and ruffled hair but didn't ask.

"They've gone to Yasras, likely hiding in the inn. We'll leave in the morning," Juliette said as she took Dylan by the hand, leading him towards the elevators.

Siljanna raised her eyebrows and shrugged. She watched as Juliette and Dylan got into the elevator and then pushed the iron door closed, so she couldn't follow as they ascended. She dismissed the rude gesture because they'd gotten the job done and didn't care how, or what they planned to do for the rest of the evening. She waited for the elevator to return and once back in the main lobby, Dylan and Juliette were nowhere to be seen, but her driver, James, was dutifully waiting for her.

She was about to greet him when she felt the pager in her pocket vibrate. It was odd having such technology, but Siljanna knew she'd get used to it. Retrieving the device, she learnt of an unheard voice message so headed to the reception desk and asked the lady there to help her. Being shown how to listen to the message, Siljanna pressed the device to her ear and heard the unmistakable voice of Cameron Weiss.

"Siljanna, Mr Rose informs me they have successfully identified a place to start the mage hunt and will be leaving tomorrow. I request you stay behind for a while. The Imperator believes your captives are withholding more information and your personal ties may prove useful for future questioning. I will meet you in the morning to discuss; good night."

With a disappointed grumble, Siljanna deposited the device back into her pocket. There was no point in arguing, so instead, she met her driver and instructed him to take her to her new apartment. When she entered the vehicle, however, she was surprised to see another familiar face sitting beside her.

"Hello, Siljanna. How long has it been?" Said the smooth, intelligent male voice.

"Charlie?" She exhaled, taken aback by his presence. Instinctively, she reached out and touched him but then recoiled. "It's been what, a year, maybe two?"

"Our graduation to be exact. Although I have written several times since," he replied, looking down at his hands as if recalling each unanswered communication. They'd left each other on a high that night but not spoken since, making the encounter now more than a little awkward.

"I'm sorry, a lot has happened, especially in the last year, I just... forgot," she stuttered, trying to explain. She wished she had a better excuse but found herself unable to lie to him.

"You forgot?" He repeated, shaking his head and closing his eyes. "We slept together Siljanna. I know it was a one-time thing but—"

As he faltered, she wished she'd lied but it was too late.

"Charlie, so much has happened, so much you don't know. The last thing I want right now is this," she moaned.

"Did it mean nothing to you? Maybe if you'd spoken to me at all in the last year, I would know what's wrong," he argued, looking back at her, his expression hurt. "I thought—"

"What Charlie, you thought what? That after one night we were meant to be. I'd expose my soul to you and be your one true love?" Siljanna replied, her remark so hurtful, he recoiled.

"I shouldn't have come," he said bluntly, turning to open the car door.

"Why did you come? I'm sure it wasn't just to rekindle our long faded night of passion," she asked, and the words came out so sarcastically that she was genuinely surprised when he turned to face her again.

"I foolishly came to see if you were all right. I didn't know what brought you here and wondered if there was anything I could do to help," he answered, trying to conceal the pain her words had caused.

She sighed, unable to take the wounded expression on his face and re-counted her tale briefly. He was clearly shocked, not just at the murder of her mother, and the recent fire which killed her father, but her blame and desire to capture Rylie and Harrison. She was in the middle of explaining how betrayed she felt by her brother when he stopped her.

"Siljanna just wait, you've jumped to so many conclusions. Did you even try to talk to Harrison or Rylie?" He questioned, his eyes searching hers for any hint of reasoning or compassion.

"Would you give the person who murdered your father the chance to defend themselves, or forgive anyone who helped them?" Siljanna argued.

"It's not as clear-cut as you are making it seem," he countered. "There are two sides to every story!"

"You sound just like Morgan. Listen I don't need either of you preaching to me. The Imperator and her right hand are supporting me, is that not enough for you?" She exclaimed but it was a rhetorical question. "If you came here to offer help, then maybe you can do something for me."

"What?" He asked cautiously.

"You're a warden at the institute, right? I sent my father's body here to be examined. Conduct the examination for me and I'm sure you'll find he was injured, unable to move when he died. That will prove Harrison's guilt and I don't need any further evidence of Rylie's crimes. I witnessed her causing the fire that killed him!" Siljanna spat adamantly.

Charlie looked deeply into her eyes, his own hazel ones searching for something. He placed a hand under her jaw and leant in, kissing her deeply. It was the last thing she expected but it sent her mind reeling. For a brief moment she was back at their graduation, the night one thing led to another, and they ended up sleeping together. Although she didn't push him away, she didn't kiss him back either and once their lips parted, he stared at her again, eyes filled with disappointment.

"I won't help you Siljanna. You're not the woman I fell in love with, and I cannot watch you go down this path. What we had, it was more than a drunken night, but anything you felt is clearly gone now," he announced. As his gaze pierced through her, he edged away, opening the car door. "I wish you no ill will Siljanna, but I beg of you, please don't do anything you'll regret."

And with that, Charlie was gone. Siljanna rested back in her seat and sighed. She thought of her current predicament but knew she couldn't stop now, not until Rylie and Harrison were made to pay for what they'd done. After her brief contemplation and resolving there was no turning back, she ordered James to take her home.

Chapter Ten
Safe Harbour

After a few hours of following the trail, Harrison, Rylie and Evie crossed a small stream to reach the edge of the woods. As the trees began to recede, they found themselves walking through an open field to reach the main road to Yasras. The sound of gulls squawking overhead proved they were close to the harbour town.

As the road descended, knowing that Yasras was at the base of a steep hill, Evie became excited. She grabbed Rylie by the hand and encouraged her to run, arms outstretched like wings down the hill. Rylie's hesitance was defeated by Evie's enthusiasm and the two girls were off. All Harrison could hear was giggling as the two of them made it to the first break in the hill. When he caught up, Evie pulled a serious face, expecting Harrison not to approve of her shenanigans but he just smirked, ruffling her incredibly long hair, causing her to groan in protest. At times, Evie acted much younger than she was but her innocence was refreshing.

They continued to follow the road as it snaked along the coastline and watched as waves broke against the large coastal rocks. They could just catch glimpses of Encia as the water crashed and receded. Before long, they were looking upon the welcoming sight of Yasras.

Although technically bigger, Yasras looked compact compared to Tivani due to its vast walls and the open ocean containing it. They could see the tall sails of merchant ships at the docks and clusters of small houses. As a traditional harbour town, most of the buildings were white-washed but with one obvious exception, the stone castle built upon a small rocky island in the harbour. It was connected to the town by a long stone bridge but otherwise looked impenetrable. Harrison presumed it was the Yasras naval facility, where fourth-year warden students trained and made a mental note to avoid it.

Reaching the end of the road, they approached the town entrance. The wardens on duty were idly chatting and only waved as the three of them walked past the checkpoint. Harrison silently thanked Morgan, assuming his friend had created a successful enough diversion that the wardens here were not aware of the situation yet. Hasting through the checkpoint, Rylie led the way to the Crown and Anchor inn.

It was one of the only buildings in town to have exterior exposed wooden beams, looking similar to the buildings in Tivani but, in keeping with the style of Yasras, they were painted pale blue while the rest of the exterior was white. The sign hanging over the main entrance showed a large fisherman's anchor with a small crown linked over one of the flukes. The words '*Proprietor: J & C. Marshall*' was written boldly underneath. Rylie and Evie rushed through the door to find their grandfather John standing at the reception desk. As soon as he saw them he opened his arms and the girls collided into his embrace.

"Girls, what are you doing here? I didn't know you were visiting again so soon. Where are your parents?" John asked, having no way of knowing just how hard answering those questions would be, or why Rylie and Evie both started sobbing. He looked in disbelief at each of them until finally glancing up and noticing Harrison.

John looked just like a typical, loving grandfather, or at least what Harrison assumed a normal one looked like, having never met his own. His thinning, grey hair was smartly combed and gave him a rather distinguished look while his rounded face and kind expression made him seem welcoming. Taking off his reading glasses revealed rich brown eyes, similar to Evie. Harrison stepped towards him, took off his gloves and shook the elderly man's hand.

"Sir, I'm Harrison Stone, a friend of the family. Something has happened and we need your help," he announced.

More than a little concerned, John led Harrison and the girls into a parlour, sitting them down and calling out to his wife, Cathryn. She was in the herb garden behind the parlour and came rushing in, at first excited to see the girls, until she saw them wiping away tears. Despite wearing jeans and a loosely fitted shirt, both of which were grubby from being in the garden, Cathryn looked incredibly similar to Paige. She was slightly shorter though and her hair was streaked with greys, highlighting her age.

They sat together in the parlour and John asked the girls to explain what was going on. Evie went very introverted, so Harrison looked towards Rylie, silently asking if she wanted him to explain but after clearing her throat, Rylie spoke. She told her grandparents all the events from the previous night, focussing on Sampson's condition and the significance of the day—the anniversary of Anora's death. She explained what caused the bar fight and that despite her father and Harrison's best efforts, Sampson ended up starting the fire. Cathryn gasped as she recalled the tale and Rylie only hesitated when it came to the part about why Siljanna, the commander of the wardens blamed her for the fire. Seeing the words get caught in her sister's throat, Evie spoke.

"Gran, Pop—how much do you know about our other grandparents, on dad's side?" She asked. As she did, John looked over to his wife and something seemed to register between them. He looked back towards his youngest grandchild and sat forward in the chair.

"When your parent's relationship became serious, your father was very honest with us. He told us his father was a mage and mother, an Ar'encal. Sadly they died towards the end of the war. Your grandmother and I could see how much your parents loved each other and once the mage hunts were announced, we all decided to keep his heritage a secret," John answered, looking ashamed they'd never mentioned it to the girls. "It was to protect them and of course, the two of you once you were born.

"Your mother told us that descendants can also become mages," Cathryn said quickly, looking at her grandchildren with worried eyes. "Your father never did but... have you girls become mages?"

Evie's lip started to wobble and in a desire to protect her sister, Rylie's words blurted out.

"I do; just me. I reached out for the burning door but instead of the heat scorching my skin, I... I don't know, it just didn't. Then when the warden commander saw my hands burning, she assumed I started the fire," Rylie stuttered, shaking her head to hold back the tears. "It's all a terrible mistake! Please believe us."

"Of course we believe you darling," Cathryn replied and without thinking, she leant over and hugged her granddaughters. Harrison let them have a moment before telling them the final piece of the puzzle.

"There is one more thing you both need to know. The warden commander, Siljanna, is my sister, and the man that started the fire, my father," he explained, his voice tinged with shame. "I've been estranged from them for the past year, longer in the case of my father but that doesn't change the fact that Siljanna will never stop hunting us. She's hated mages since our mother died and has always been blinded by her admiration of our father. If he died, she'll blame me."

"Young man, you've lived through so much hardship," John consoled, affectionately placing a hand on Harrison's shoulder.

"Please know, my priority is protecting Rylie and Evie. I'll do whatever it takes to make sure they're safe," Harrison declared.

"Such a dear boy!" Cathryn exclaimed.

"Thank you, son," John replied, shaking his hand.

Although he didn't expect the gesture, Harrison was grateful his honesty and integrity were rewarded. If he'd ever been so candid with his father, even before their feud, Sampson's reaction would have been anything but kind. It was the main reason why Harrison rarely spoke up in difficult situations. In his experience, words, even the right words didn't make a situation better; only more complicated.

For the next few minutes, John and Cathryn revealed everything they knew about Nate's parents. They knew very little about his mother, Emilia but Nate's father, Alistair had been a scholar and before the war, a royal advisor in Carlisse. John continued to say that when Nate had received a letter saying his parents had died, he refused to believe it; and all because he was convinced the letter was written in his father's hand.

John recalled how adamant Nate was. His father kept journals and according to Nate, the handwriting was identical. He went as far as making arrangements to return to Carlisse, with Paige set to go with him until another letter arrived insisting he stay away. It was written in a distinctly different hand and that's what it took for him to believe they'd really died.

The sun was just beginning to set when someone walking down from the rooms above caught everyone's attention and ceased their conversation.

"Hey Missus M, are you here?" the voice called out. Instantly, Cathryn jumped to her feet as John indicated for them to be quiet but not to worry, it was just one of their more chatty residents.

Cathryn shut the parlour door behind her but they could hear her speaking casually to the guest. They heard the pair's conversation become more animated before the guy trundled back towards his room. Within an instant, Cathryn was back in the parlour and looked panicked.

"We have a problem," she announced striding over to the radio in the parlour, switching it on. The news-readers' voice was placid but clear.

'Three fugitives wanted by the Tivani wardens are believed to be in Yasras. All residents are advised to be on the lookout for Rylie and Evie Auren, both suspected mages and their accomplice, Harrison

Stone. They are wanted in connection to a recent arson and murder in Tivani. Residents should take extreme caution and report sightings immediately to the local wardens. I repeat—' but before the announcement rolled over again, Cathryn switched off the radio and looked at her family.

"You won't be safe here for long. We have a shelter in the cellar that you can stay in tonight but we have to get you out of town," she implored, looking over to her husband and then back at her grandchildren.

Just then the parlour door handle began to turn and Harrison was up in an instant, drawing his sword and prepared to strike. As the door gently opened, a young man, not much older than Harrison, stepped through and both Cathryn and John breathed a sigh of relief.

"It's okay, it's just Zack, our resident," John said.

Zack waltzed in happily until he realised where Harrison was, and that he was armed. When he did, he jumped out of the way and feigned wiping his brow as if narrowly escaping a trap.

"Woah, take it easy there bud! I couldn't help but overhear your predicament and happen to know someone that can help... me!" Zack announced, with a grin that lit up his entire face.

Standing near Harrison, it was hard not to compare the two young men and how distinctly different they looked. Despite being similar in age, build and height, where Harrison was all warm tones, with soft brown hair and eyes, everything about Zack was bright. His skin was milky and his hair sandy blonde, styled in bold, messy spikes. His blue eyes were as vibrant as the sea in the harbour and brimming with eagerness. Not willing to trust him as easily, Harrison, still wielding his sword, stood in front of Rylie and Evie, ensuring he was between them and Zack.

"How much did you hear, and how exactly can you help us?" Harrison asked in a threatening tone. Zack raised his hands in submission but continued to smile.

"Some bodyguard you've got there ladies. Getting paid by the hour mate or just dedicated to the cause?" Zack jested but Harrison looked less than impressed.

"Answer quickly or I'll make you answer," Harrison replied, his tone serious.

"Okay, I get it, not the trusting sort," Zack quipped, his hands still raised despite starting to chuckle. "Honestly, ask Mr and Mrs M. I'm a mage sympathiser and in my spare time, help out mages that have gotten themselves in a pickle. Just like you and your friends."

"How exactly can you help?" Rylie asked, peeking out beside Harrison.

"You need to leave and I can get you passage on my employer's merchant ship bound for Revaine," Zack replied, glancing quickly at Rylie before returning his gaze back to Harrison's imposing blade.

"And why would you admit that? You have heard of the mage hunts, haven't you? Where mage sympathisers can be arrested just as easily as mages," Harrison questioned, his voice challenging. He couldn't bring himself to believe this guy was for real. "You have no idea who we are, why would you risk your life to help us?"

"Because I hate the war, and the mage hunts. I know it sounds crazy, but it's what I do. I grew up on the Eastern Continent and have seen the devastation caused by the mage hunts." As he said it, Zack's whole demeanour changed. "Rather than being the kind of guy that does nothing, I choose to help. So now the question is, do you *want* my help?"

Zack looked squarely at Harrison, and this time his charismatic smile was replaced with a steady look of sincerity. The room fell silent until finally, Cathryn spoke.

"You can trust him. We've known Zack for a while now. He's a good guy and really does help mages," she assured and shrugged as Harrison looked at her, still sceptical. "I can't have a mage descendant for a son-in-law and not be a sympathiser, right?"

Harrison let his gaze switch from Cathryn back to Zack and then to John who was nodding.

"It's true, Zack is like a smuggler. He's helped dozens of people with passage between the continents since we've known him," John added looking around the room, before resting his gaze on Zack. "Will you please help my granddaughters?"

"Of course, Mr M! As long as their muscle in the corner isn't going to chop my head off in the process," Zack jested, tilting his head towards Harrison with a grin. He figured Harrison wasn't going to hurt him but liked the idea of getting that confirmed.

"I'm not going to chop your head off... *yet*, but I am going with them. Can you arrange passage for me too?" Harrison asked.

At that moment, Rylie took his hand and squeezed. Zack noticed the silent gesture between them and smiled, his expression kind.

"You got it. Just give me a couple of hours to arrange some fake travel papers. The ship doesn't leave until morning so we'll need to hide out here for the night. I'd suggest getting stuck into a good meal and freshening up. The journey across the Ensen Sea isn't exactly a joyride," Zack advised, giving a flippant salute as he strode out of the inn towards the dock.

After he left, John headed to the kitchen to make a hearty dinner for everyone while the others each took the time to enjoy a shower. Cathryn set beds out for them in the cellar, just in case the wardens conducted a sweep of the guest rooms and also laid some strange-looking suits out for them. Harrison entered the cellar just as she was leaving and noticed the suits.

"What are those?" He asked.

"These suits are made from oilcloth. It's not perfect but the material is water resistant and the risk of Encia poisoning while crossing the sea is high. Being the main inn of a harbour town means I ensure we have plenty here for sale," she advised, looking at the suits briefly before continuing. "I know theoretically, Encia won't hurt

Rylie, and possibly Evie too but I'd hate to chance it. Besides, you'll need it and they'd look odd travelling without them."

"Thank you Cathryn," Harrison replied politely.

"Promise me you'll be careful, and look after my girls. I can see how much they trust you," she requested compassionately.

"I promise. I just wish I knew what to do once we get to Revaine," he admitted, the issue clearly concerning him.

"The best thing I can suggest is to search for anyone that knew Nate's father, Alistair Auren. Or perhaps, try to find his journals. He may have kept records in the royal library or left them with another mage sympathiser before he died," she suggested, and it was the best option they had. She was about to leave when Harrison felt compelled to express his sympathy.

"I'm sorry about Nate and Paige," he said and paused, registering her look of sorrow and then confusion.

"Why are you apologising?" She asked. "You have nothing to be sorry for."

"Nate is like a father to me, much better than my own at least. I wanted to go back and save him, Paige too, but I couldn't. Now, we have no idea what's happened to them. I should've done more to help," he mumbled, lowering his head.

"Please, don't apologise. All I feel is gratitude to you Harrison. You saved my granddaughters when you didn't have to. I also take some small comfort from that radio announcement," she replied and now it was Harrison's turn to look confused. She registered his reaction and continued. "The announcement said *'murder'* not *'murders'*. I can only hope that means Paige, Nate or hopefully both of them survived the fire."

As Cathryn departed, allowing herself to smile softly at her own hope, Harrison didn't have the heart to contest it could've just been simplified for the broadcast. They had no way of knowing the truth so what was the point in taking away what little hope they had?

As night fell, there was a loud banging on the main door. As suspected, the wardens had come to check the rooms in search of Harrison, Rylie and Evie. The cellar door was right by the main entrance, so they all stood with their ears pressed to the door in hopes of hearing what was going on. They could just make out John speaking to the wardens in a polite but firm tone and allowing them to inspect the property.

After a few moments, they could hear the wardens amble through the inn checking each room. Then they heard elevated voices and shouting. Fretting, Harrison reached for his sword and signalled for the girls to hide behind one of the containers in the corner of the room. He tentatively went back to the door, creaked it open and slipped outside. Creeping through the herb garden, he ducked under the parlour windows as he spotted John, Zack and two wardens. It was Zack doing all the shouting.

"Don't you sod's know how early we merchants have to get up in the morning? You know to travel the perilous seas and ensure each continent meets its trade agreements? No of course you don't, *but sure*, check my room for fugitives... *pricks.*"

The sarcasm and frustration in Zack's voice were tangible but when he spotted Harrison peering in through the window, he winked. The wardens had their backs turned to the window but saw the gesture and turned. Harrison ducked just in time.

"Did you just wink at someone?" One of them asked.

"Yes, the fugitive in the garden," Zack said initially and then noticed the wardens taking him seriously so quickly backtracked. "You really are morons. There's no one out there, I'm just tired and my eye twitched. Ever heard of sarcasm?" He blurted out, regaining the warden's attention. "Just get the search over with, so I can get back to sleep."

Zack flopped in one of the parlour chairs as the wardens grunted and headed towards his room. Harrison took the opportunity to dart back to the cellar and made sure Rylie and Evie knew it was only him as he entered. Realising she was terrified, he gave Evie a reassuring hug. Cathryn had set the beds up out of view from the main cellar door but Harrison quickly started stripping the bed sheets and piling them up on the beds.

"Make it look like piles of washing, just in case," he said in a hushed but hurried tone. They quickly piled all the sheets together to look like dirty laundry and then Harrison hid the girls, their bags and his weapons in a closet while he ducked under the bed, pulling one of the sheets down to cover him. A moment later he heard faint voices again.

The wardens were searching the herb garden and he knew they'd spot their hiding place. After what felt like a long silence, he heard the bolt on the cellar door move and John slowly but loudly opening the door. Noticing what they'd done with the sheets, he stepped aside letting the wardens look within.

"It's just where we keep the dirty linens until I can get them washed. You're welcome to take a look," he offered, managing not to sound too suspicious.

The wardens walked to the base of the stairs but to Harrison's relief, didn't look any further. One of them radioed that the inn was *all clear* while the other turned and thanked John for his co-operation. John apologised profusely for Zack's attitude, explaining the young man always got a little mouthy the night before sailing. The warden issued a warning for John to pass on to Zack but then said good night and left.

John began slowly closing the cellar doors again but quickly looked over his shoulder and gave a thumbs up, letting Harrison know the coast was clear. Breathing a sigh of relief and letting his head rest against the floor for an instant, Harrison crawled out from under the bed and opened the cupboard door for Rylie and Evie. It was a close call but they remained undetected so had to try and get some sleep. It would be the second night where Harrison didn't get much rest but even his body shut down for a few hours.

With no windows in the cellar, they had no idea it was dawn until Zack arrived. He entered flashing his winning smile and the fake travel papers he'd promised. He handed one to each of them and reminded them to put on the oilcloth suits. For the journey, Zack was wearing dark, baggy trousers which were tapered off by his russet brown boots and a thick matching belt. His charcoal vest top didn't conceal his oilcloth suit but the long black jacket he wore with its high collar protected most of his skin. His spiky blond hair seemed even more prominent than it had previously, but that wasn't the main thing Harrison noticed. His eyes were immediately drawn to the fact that Zack didn't have a weapon of any kind.

Even when he wasn't a warden, Harrison liked to at least have his sword equipped when travelling so how did a merchant moonlighting as a smuggler not have any weapons? He took a knife from his belt and offered it to Zack by the handle.

"Thanks, but no thanks. You don't want me handling anything capable of deadly force," Zack said, rejecting the blade.

"As long as you're sure. I never imagined meeting a smuggler that doesn't arm himself," Harrison replied, frowning slightly with confusion while returning the blade to its holster.

"What can I say, fighting has never been a skill of mine. I'm much better at sneaking. Don't worry, I've been doing this for months and I've not needed a weapon yet," Zack boasted with a grin.

"But last night, you sounded like you were ready to pick a fight with the wardens. If you're not a fighter, what was that all about?" Harrison asked curiously. If he was going to trust Zack with their lives, he needed to understand the guy better.

"Oh, that? It was all an act. Mr and Mrs M are nice people; sometimes a little too nice. I act like a jerk so that the wardens assume their politeness is to compensate for me, not because they are hiding something. If there is one thing I've learnt about wardens, it's that if everything seems too good to be true, they search even harder," Zack explained looking a little sheepish, acknowledging how he came across in those situations.

Both of them glanced towards Rylie and Evie to see how they were doing. Rylie was ready but Evie was still tying her bootlaces. Luckily both girls had left some stuff behind after their last visit and were able to wear better clothes for travelling. They also packed some spare items in the knapsacks, just in case. While they waited, Zack turned back to Harrison.

"You appear rather comfortable with that incredibly oversized sword and array of weapons on your belt. So, what are you, some kind of mercenary?" He asked, curious to learn the background of his new charges.

"Actually, I was a warden, until my father stripped me of the title last year. Then I became a blacksmith," Harrison answered, somewhat amazed he could summarise his life in such a short statement.

"That's awesome!" Zack announced, seeming genuinely impressed and gave Harrison a friendly punch to the shoulder. "You really are the ultimate bodyguard! Able to make a decent weapon and know how to use it. Why did you get removed from the wardens?"

"At least buy me dinner first," Harrison teased, Zack's candour making him laugh.

"Candlelight or are you more of a home-cooked meal kinda guy?" Zack replied jokingly. The way he acted was just like Morgan, and the familiarity made Harrison instinctively want to trust him.

After a few minutes, Rylie and Evie joined Zack and Harrison, both ready to go. They said emotional goodbyes to John and Cathryn as they headed for the docks, sticking to the back streets to avoid prying eyes. When they reached the dock, they followed Zack towards a stunning three-masted clipper vessel. The name engraved on the bow was the '*Pilgrim*' and Harrison couldn't help but hope it was a sign that although they weren't on a holy journey, they would find salvation along the way. A sailor was standing at the end of the boardwalk, collecting travel papers. Zack indicated for them to stop before getting too close.

"We need to minimise suspicion here. The three of you are being hunted by the wardens so I suggest we split up. Rylie, you come with me and Harrison, you and Evie follow behind in a few minutes," Zack instructed, gently placing his hand on Rylie's back as he ushered her forward.

Harrison couldn't help but smile as he noticed Rylie accepting Zack's touch without flinching. It was the closest she'd been to her normal self since triggering her abilities and he was pleased that having a focus seemed to help her keep calm. Harrison put his arm around Evie and ruffled her hair as they watched Zack and Rylie board. They let a few other passengers embark before heading towards the ship. Just before they made it out of the alley, someone grabbed Harrison from behind.

"Why are you wanted for murder?" Whispered a frantic but familiar voice. Noticing he'd been caught, Evie looked at Harrison, eyes filled with worry, but he signalled with a hand for her to remain calm.

"Hello Carter," Harrison replied.

"One year, one year of working with your sister and you snap?" Carter asked, continuing his barrage of questions.

"No, I promise it's a misunderstanding. Please, let us go," Harrison replied sincerely. He glanced over towards the ship and noticed most of the other passengers had boarded. They were running out of time.

"If I let you go, I'm risking my own neck, Harrison. I need more to go on than that," Carter insisted, looking at the ship and realising Harrison's plan.

"If you know any more, then you really will get in trouble. Please, I swear, I am not guilty of what Siljanna has accused me of," Harrison replied.

"Siljanna, she's launched the search? What about Commander Stone?" Carter asked, clearly startled.

"She is Commander Stone. Have I ever lied to you Carter, or been deceitful?" Harrison asked, trying to rapidly persuade his friend. He could see the thoughts ticking through Carter's mind, recalling their friendship.

"You were always honest, a good friend," he responded.

"Will you let me go?" Harrison asked again.

"Who's the little girl?" Carter responded suspiciously.

"This's Rylie's little sister, Evie. Siljanna has accused them both of being mages. She's hunting them for the events in Tivani and me because I chose to protect them," Harrison answered, hoping Carter would appreciate his honesty.

"This is insane!" Carter exclaimed. "Is Rylie on that ship too?"

"Yes… please I have to go," Harrison replied, his expression desperate as he reached out to his friend.

"I can't believe I'm saying this. Go," Carter replied, shaking his head in disbelief.

Harrison gripped his friend's shoulder firmly, expressing his gratitude as he and Evie rushed towards the boardwalk, showed their travel papers and found Zack and Rylie on the deck.

"What took so long?" Zack asked playfully as Evie hugged her sister.

"Long story," Harrison replied.

Chapter Eleven
Pilgrim

Aboard the Pilgrim, Harrison couldn't help but admire the ship. The main mast was about seventy feet tall and the sails upon it square, apart from the aft, which had angled sails rigged along the line of the keel. The rest of the rigging looked like a complicated system of ropes and cables which allowed the crew to traverse between the masts and the crow's nest high above.

Zack led them down to the cabins where the teakwood interior was pristine, and although small, the cabins were comfortable. He explained that including himself, there were twenty crew members and a further ten dedicated merchants that were regular sailors, so between them, they did most of the manual labour during the crossing. There were also two cooks, the senior officers and the captain but he assured them they wouldn't need to worry about exposure from any of them. Although a few of them were also involved in the mage smuggling, the majority were nomads and didn't care who was on board as long as they paid their fare.

It would take four days to cross the Ensen sea, or just under if the wind was on their side. When a crewman called all hands to deck, they knew it was time to depart. Zack darted to his station, only returning to the others when they were well underway. When he came back, he came with four flasks of hot soup.

"What's the plan when we arrive in Revaine? Have any of you been to the Eastern Continent before?" Zack asked.

"We need to try and find someone that knew Rylie's grandfather. Or at the very least, try and find his journals," Harrison answered, remembering Cathryn's suggestion.

"I wish he were alive," Evie said quietly. "He could've protected us."

"Hey... keen to replace me already?" Harrison countered, mocking her. "I thought you liked having me around?"

"Oh I do! I...I didn't mean," Evie stuttered, about to start apologising when she heard Harrison softly laughing. "Meanie!"

Sticking her tongue out at him, Evie pretended to be upset for a minute. The banter between them made Rylie smile as she took a gulp of soup.

"We've never been to the Eastern Continent before. It's going to be hard to know where to start. The only thing we know is that as a kid, Dad lived just outside Carlisse," she said, letting the soup warm her to the core.

"Maybe I can help with that. Once we arrive in Revaine, I was due to take a few days off. I could lead you to some friends that own a ranch on the outskirts of town. It's one of the only places between the harbour and Carlisse so they are pretty well connected. If anyone has heard of your grandfather, it'll be Drew and Elissa," Zack advised, blowing on his soup to cool it down.

"Thank you Zack, that's incredibly good of you. How can we ever repay your kindness?" Rylie asked. She felt a kindred spirit with Zack and wanted him to know they wouldn't take him for granted.

"Just promise if you find any other mages in trouble, that you'll help them too," he replied simply.

"Really, is that all?" Rylie asked to which Zack just smiled and nodded confidently.

"What's your story, Zack?" Harrison asked, genuinely curious what motivated such kindness to strangers when it came hand in hand with significant risk.

"I make a point not to talk too much about my past. There's little I'm proud of," he replied, not intending to say more. With all of them looking at him intently, however, he took a deep breath before continuing. "All you need to know is that my mum was a mage sympathiser but died when I was little. It was my fault, or so my brother told me every day until the day I left home. Everything I do to support the mages is to honour her memory."

His blue eyes went dark, like the deep ocean as he recalled the painful memory. Harrison placed a hand on his shoulder, sympathetic to his story.

"I was blamed for my mother's death too. She was killed last year by a merchant with the withering and my father, who was warden commander then, blamed me because I let the man into town. It took me a long time not to blame myself, and if there was anything I could do to make her proud, I'd do it. I'm glad that honouring your mother brought you to us just when we needed it," Harrison remarked.

"Does this mean you definitely won't be chopping my head off?" Zack asked, causing all of them to laugh.

"Nah, you're all right mate. But I might give you a haircut one of these days!" Harrison teased, looking at Zack's overzealous spiked hairstyle.

"Dude, not the hair!" He replied, guarding his head and causing them all to laugh again. They spent the rest of the day chatting and exploring the ship and it was probably the first time Rylie, Evie and Harrison had all felt relaxed since fleeing Tivani.

It was late morning before Siljanna received the call from Cameron saying he was on his way. The lack of action since Dylan and his obnoxious partner had gotten the lead yesterday left her in a foul mood. She checked the time and tried calling Dylan again but every call she'd made to him or Juliette went unanswered. After several rings, she hung up and decided to use the pager to send a message. Ordering them to make their way to Yasras immediately and investigate the town, starting with the Crown and Anchor inn, she emphasised that she wanted an update as soon as possible. Chucking the pager onto the sofa in her new apartment, taking her frustrations out on the little device, Siljanna calmed herself with a coffee on the balcony.

The apartment was small, with a lounge-kitchen-diner and a separate bedroom with an ensuite bathroom. It was similar in size to her old room at the academy but the similarities ended there. It also had a large balcony that looked out over the city. Despite telling her all about his time in Siranor, Siljanna had never pictured just how incredible the city would look based on her father's descriptions. She could see the Imperial palace and prison from where she stood and also in the distance a large building that looked to be completely made of glass, which she presumed was the famous science institute.

While taking in the view, her mind began to wander, and she thought of Charlie. The wardens that complete their training in Tivani always seemed to remain wardens, guarding the towns and cities they were posted to, while the ones that trained elsewhere often diversified into other roles. Téa was the only recruit Siljanna had met who finished her training in Siranor but decided to be a guard rather than a scientist or politician. It probably explained why Téa didn't have the same instincts as Siljanna or Morgan but always had something intelligent to say. It also felt like a complete waste of talent to Siljanna.

At least the wardens that finished in Tivani put their skills to good use as guards, although she was coming around to the Tulam facility too, which she'd discovered after meeting Dylan and Juliette was where they finished training students in covert operations allowing them to become mage hunters, spies, assassins and in exceptional cases, the personal wardens of the Imperator.

Although Siljanna knew the work of the scientists was important, she couldn't see the point of three years of physical and mental training as a warden just to become a scientist. Still, she couldn't stop thinking about Charlie and the things he'd said to her. Just as she was deep in thought, there was a loud knock. Snapping out of her reverie, she answered the door and let Cameron inside. He noticed the coffee in her hand and she felt obliged to offer him a cup.

"Before we start, I know you are probably frustrated that we want you to stay behind rather than travel to Yasras," he acknowledged.

"You're right, I am. Nothing is more important to me than catching my brother and Rylie Auren. What possible reason could there be for keeping me here?" She replied, releasing her anger.

"Your captives," he replied directly. "I went down to clean up the mess left behind by Dylan and Juliette's interrogation. Granted, they obtained a lead but it was, shall we say, in a rather distasteful way. The young man is dead and the blacksmith, well I've moved him into intensive care at the hospital."

"I didn't realise—," she began but then noticed Cameron was unfazed by the extreme measure. Siljanna had said *'by any means necessary'* and clearly this wasn't the first interrogation fatality Cameron had encountered. "How is Elijah?"

"Heavily drugged. He shouldn't remember the events of the last few days once he recovers. We'll take him back to Tivani once we can be sure he is of no threat to us," Cameron replied matter-of-factly.

Despite their tactics being *'distasteful,'* Dylan and Juliette had gotten the job done efficiently, without moral interference. Siljanna found herself quietly impressed.

"What about Nate and Paige?" Siljanna asked.

"The father is in pretty bad shape. Dylan did a number on him but he's awake. The mother is distressed and still not talking," Cameron replied.

Siljanna sat back in the chair, her expression contemplative. She would have been annoyed if either of the Auren's had been killed. If anyone could give them leverage over Rylie, it was her parents.

"Good, they aren't expendable, yet," Siljanna declared.

"I spoke with Imperator Harlyn and she feels that the parents must have more knowledge on mages and magic in general. With two mage children, Harlyn wants you to find out all you can from them while Dylan and Juliette search Yasras. We will join the search once we have confirmed a location for the fugitives but for now, knowing what we are up against is imperative," Cameron said convincingly and although still reluctant, Siljanna agreed.

"Okay, I will continue to interrogate them. What are you and the Imperator doing in the meantime?" She asked.

"I will coordinate a task force consisting of the best military recruits at my disposal should we need to leave Siranor with the Imperator and she is going to continue developing her *En-glycerol*, the substance that absorbs Encia," he advised.

"Is there anything else?" Siljanna asked.

"Yes, Imperator Harlyn wants you to discover which side of the Auren family are the Ar'encal descendants, break that parent and send them to her for testing. It's not as good as an established mage, but it's a start," he replied to which Siljanna nodded with a sinister grin.

After finishing their coffee, as if they'd spent the last few minutes talking about the weather, Cameron departed followed by Siljanna as she made her way back to the prison. Knowing that Nate was awake had given her an idea to get more information in a *slightly* less violent way.

Once at the prison, she took a moment to call the warden guardhouse in Tivani before heading to the lower levels. To her surprise, it was Téa that answered instead of Morgan.

"Téa, where's Morgan?" She enquired.

"He's been working solidly since you left. He needed to get some sleep but is still in the staff quarters at the guardhouse. Should I wake him?" Téa replied politely.

"No, just relay a message. I want the wardens to expand their search in the woodlands," she instructed.

"Of course ma'am, but why? I heard the fugitives were in Yasras," she asked.

"Do not question my orders Téa," Siljanna replied sternly. "They *may* be in Yasras, but the woodlands are vast and they could easily have travelled north and hidden in the Wutel canyon or headed to Hale. If there is even a small chance they've gone north, I won't let them slip through my fingers."

"Apologies ma'am, I will send the message immediately," Téa replied nervously, quickly hanging up the phone.

It would take them several days but if she wasn't leaving Siranor straight away, it was worth keeping the search area open. Once she knew where they were, nothing would stop Siljanna from getting her hands on her brother and Rylie.

The first day sailing on the Pilgrim had been exhilarating to Rylie. Every time she stood on the deck, feeling the breeze whip through her hair, it felt like flying. She often heard the crew say they'd never known the wind to propel the ship so vigorously and she wondered if it was because of her. Could the wind be reacting to her emotion? Luckily none of the crew seemed to care, in fact, the only time they approached her was because they were concerned she was too close to the railings.

The next few days went quickly and on the final night of the crossing, Rylie was back on the deck stargazing when Harrison found her. She was hugging herself in the chilly night air as he approached. Standing closely beside her, he placed a hand on her shoulder and matched her upward gaze.

"Mesmerising isn't it?" He asked.

"I never noticed before, but there is something so peaceful about the night sky," she replied, smiling at him.

Harrison recalled many nights at Elijah's blacksmith when looking up to the stars would fill him with peace and inspiration. He'd learnt most of the constellations and recognised the ones above them.

Pointing them out to her, he began to recall the names and related stories of the clearer formations. When he pointed out the Phoenix constellation and told Rylie the mythology of the firebird, her face lit up in a way he hadn't seen since the night of his graduation.

While she continued to gaze upwards, Harrison's eyes were drawn to Rylie. Strands from her fringe danced in the wind around her hypnotic eyes and all her features seemed to soften. It would have been so easy to cup her face in his hands and kiss her. As the thought rushed through his mind, she rested her head on his shoulder and yawned.

"Oh I'm sorry! I guess I better get some sleep," she said, covering her mouth in the process. "I heard the crew say we'll arrive in Revaine by mid-morning. See you for breakfast in the galley?"

"Yes, of course," he replied. "See you in the morning."

She held his hand as she walked away, stretching her arm and only letting go at the last possible moment. He watched as she went below deck towards the cabins. Once out of sight, he released a big sigh, looking up again at the stars. Spotting the Romansa constellation; the famed lovers of the cosmos, he couldn't help but say under his breath, *stop making it look so easy,* rolling his eyes at the mythical couple.

Shortly afterwards, Harrison headed below deck to the cabin he was sharing with Evie. Their travel papers stated they were brother and sister, so they had been playing the part ever since, although it came pretty naturally. As he entered the tiny cabin, Evie was on the top bunk and snuggled in a variety of blankets. She held one tightly and seemed to be talking in her sleep. He smiled at first, not thinking anything of it until Evie's eyes opened abruptly.

"Evie, are you okay?" He asked, noticing her cheeks were rosy as she placed her hand on her heart.

"Harrison, do you have feelings for my sister?" She asked, turning on the little bunk to face him.

"What, where did that come from?" He replied, shocked at the suddenness of her question.

"I think I just had a vision, or maybe a dream—," she began, her eyes searching his.

"What did you see?" He asked.

"For the first time in a long time, what I saw was good. It was you and Rylie kissing, or at least, I think it was. It's hard to tell sometimes but I could've sworn it was you," she explained as her sweet, chocolate-brown eyes glistened with hope. "Is it true, do you like Rylie?"

"Of course I like her," he began, trying to conceal the truth.

"No, Harrison! Do you really *like her*?" She clarified in such a teenage fashion.

Harrison smiled, still stunned but met Evie's gaze. He wanted to say yes, tell her that he did have feelings for Rylie but then the voices of the crew and the boat breaking through the waves reminded him of where they were, and more importantly why they were there.

They were on the run from his sister, who was hunting the girls for being mages and Rylie specifically, framing her for the fire at the tavern. He sighed and took Evie's hand in his own, using his other hand to place a finger against her lips, hushing her. She seemed to recognise from his expression that her suspicions were true but waited intently for his response.

"Can we keep this our little secret for now, please? I care very much for Rylie, but with everything going on, now isn't the time to tell her," he explained with a sad smile. Evie looked gutted and was about to protest when he stopped her by tapping the finger against her lips. She pouted until he moved his finger away.

"Fine," she groaned, crinkling her face in disappointment. "Just know that when the time is right, I think you would be perfect for each other. You'll have to spell it out for her though. She's totally oblivious to any subtle romantic gestures. I had to literally tell her when Bradley, the guy from the apothecary shop liked her. I'm only just thirteen and could tell but Rylie, totally clueless!"

"You should've skipped telling her about Bradley," Harrison teased. He never liked that guy.

"Yeah okay, I live and learn!" She replied, owning up to the fact that Bradley hadn't been ideal boyfriend material. She smiled again before snuggling back under the covers. Harrison couldn't resist tucking her in and ruffling her hair, knowing how much it wound her up, before crashing into the lower bunk. He turned the lantern knob, extinguishing the flame inside so the room went dark and closed his eyes.

"Hey Harrison?" Evie whispered, clearly wanting to get one last thought off her chest.

"Yeah?" He replied quietly.

"I love you... like an annoying big brother," she said and her words warmed him.

"I love you too Evie. Now get some sleep, otherwise we'll both struggle in the morning," he replied, smiling peacefully. He heard her breathing slow as she buried her head into the pillow and fell asleep. With her words still comforting him, Harrison soon drifted off also.

Meeting over breakfast, Zack chatted idly to the others until Revaine came into view over the horizon and he had to report to his station. Once the ship docked, they disembarked together and he led them through town, advising that the fastest way to meet his friends was by horse and carriage.

As they walked through the streets from the dock, it was clear to see Revaine was a stark contrast to Yasras. It was more like a slum than a town, with most of the buildings looking like they were pieced together with corrugated metal, plywood and tin. There were dozens of children, some as young as five or six, but most pre-teens, running around unsupervised.

"Why are there so many kids here? Where are their parents?" Rylie asked, watching the children as they ran by.

"It's been like this since before I first visited. The locals say that ten years ago, a large group of marauding mage hunters came into town and started pillaging the houses, taking out anyone that got in their way," Zack advised. He paused, hating the story but knowing it almost by heart. "They killed hundreds of residents, claiming they were mages or sympathisers and left several youngsters without their parents. And the ones that did survive, had no way of providing for themselves or the orphans."

"That's awful! Nothing like that ever happened in Tivani. I guess it was easy to forget about the mage hunts... until now," Rylie admitted, feeling terribly guilty for not even having heard of Revaine, let alone its recent history.

"It's been a year since I first visited and I've seen the people slowly rebuild, but it's hard for them. That's why the Pilgrim always stops here. The crew will buy whatever supplies we can from the locals. It's not much but the produce is good, and we pay a fair price," Zack added with a kind smile, feeling proud of the crew he worked with who tried to make things better here.

They were walking through what looked like a market, the streets packed with people bartering for food and other supplies when Zack stopped at a stall and seemed to make pleasant conversation with a vendor.

"Take a minute everyone, I just want to catch up with Daryl," Zack said when suddenly, a teenage boy bumped into him.

"Oh, sorry mister, I didn't see you there," the kid exclaimed, politely raising his hands in apology.

"Don't worry about it kid," Zack replied as he turned his attention back to the vendor. Rylie and Evie watched as the boy walked away and Harrison went further down the street, spotting a stall selling sword grips. Rylie nudged her little sister to get her attention.

"Hey Evie, can you see that, underneath Zack's collar?" She asked, pointing subtly towards a swirling black mark protruding into view. "It's some kind of tattoo. I noticed it when we were on the ship, but he wouldn't talk about it. Do you remember any other crew members having a mark like that?"

"No, there was one guy with a load of tattoos but nothing like that," she replied, hoping Zack wouldn't notice as she looked. "I wonder what it means."

As they pondered what the secrecy was all about, their conversation was interrupted by Zack cursing.

"Where's that punk kid? He stole my money pouch!" Zack shouted. Rylie and Evie both turned on a dime and tried to spot the boy from before. Scanning the vast crowd they found him just slinking behind Harrison.

"Harrison! Quick, grab that boy, he's a thief!" Rylie cried out and as she pointed, Harrison reacted like a bolt of lightning, grabbing the young boy by the scruff of his jacket. Zack came charging through the crowd with Rylie and Evie close behind.

"Give it back you little runt!" He shouted, pulling at the boy's jacket and searching his pockets. As Zack rooted through, he found the pouch with all his coin inside and glared. The young boy resisted, desperately trying to free himself of Harrison's grasp but wasn't strong enough.

"All right! You've got your money back, now let me go!" He yelled.

"What's your name kid, why are you stealing from us?" Harrison asked. Rylie could tell he'd been paying attention to Zack's story as he was making sure not to hurt the boy while restraining him, showing a significant amount of mercy compared to when they first met Zack.

"Why should I tell you? Just lemme go already!" The boy insisted, continuing to struggle.

"If you don't tell me your name and why you stole from my friend, I'm going to drag you around town until someone tells me who you are. So why not make it easier for the both of us?" Harrison warned, his tone nowhere near as threatening as it could be, but the boy had no doubt his captor would make good on his threat.

"Fine, whatever. My name is Alex Flynn. And I stole because well, I had to. My big sister hasn't had a decent meal in days and that guy looks like he can spare some change so... I dunno, I just helped myself," he answered, looking at the ground and shuffling his feet.

The rest of the group looked between themselves with varying looks of receding frustration, concern and sympathy. Harrison noticed Zack tuck the money pouch into a deeper pocket and then nodded, as if silently agreeing to an unspoken plan.

"Okay Alex, take us to your sister. We need to have a discussion with her," Harrison instructed as Alex groaned. It was an over-dramatised reaction but Harrison ignored it and encouraged the boy to march. "Come on, which way?"

"To the nursery; A plant nursery, not the other kind. My sister works there, helping to gather produce," Alex said, walking slowly towards the eastern side of town.

As they walked through the crowded streets, the heat was intense. It was much hotter in Revaine than on the Western Continent. Alex made two failed attempts at breaking free until they came up to a building that was covered with sprawling plants. There were also greenhouses and outdoor harvest patches with several people tending to the varying crops.

Harrison eventually let Alex go as a young woman rushed towards them. She reached Alex and grabbed him by the shoulders. Clearly his sister but although older, she was short, her teenage brother already the same height as her.

"Alex? What happened, what did you do?" She asked, her tone going from worried to warning. This obviously wasn't the first time her brother had gotten in trouble.

Alex turned his head away from her, his dark blonde hair flopping past his eyes but unable to disguise his guilt, so instead he decided to sulk. The young woman huffed at him before standing up and facing Zack who was staring at her.

"I am so sorry, whatever my brother took from you, I'll return or pay for," she promised, tucking a strand of her raven hair behind her ear.

Wearing a simple ecru-coloured dress that came down just below her knees, ankle boots and a cropped tan jacket, the young woman before them was petite, with very soft features and kind, hazel eyes. There were a few ground stains on the edges of her dress and most of her hair, apart from the fringe and a few strands were pulled away from her face by a beige bandana. Her golden brown skin tone combined with her thick, dark hair were all of a rich palette, but the actual look of her attire told a very different, modest story.

"My name is Lianna Flynn," she continued, extending her hand towards Zack who was mesmerised.

"You are the most beautiful person I have ever had the pleasure of meeting. Such an enchanting name," he mused, taking her hand. "Almost as beautiful as you are."

Harrison, Rylie and Evie all just stared at each other, wide-eyed and dumbfounded by Zack's reaction. Lianna quickly retracted her hand and gave Zack an awkward smile.

"Umm, thank you, I think," Lianna said, lightly scratching the back of her neck before stepping towards the others so she was addressing all of them and not just Zack. "Please, tell me what happened?"

Harrison and Evie were both still stripped of words after seeing Zack's initial reaction so Rylie explained the situation and the attempted robbery. As she recalled the events, Lianna notably cringed before turning back to her brother. Apart from hair colour, their features were identical.

"I can't believe you did that Alex! I told you, I'm fine. I should get paid at the end of the week and we can make do until then," she scolded. Alex mumbled an apology but was still sulking as Lianna turned back to the group. "Please, can I offer you some fresh fruit or vegetables from the garden? You look like travellers so it might be nice for the road."

Zack was still looking at her with ogling eyes and Evie finally cracked, laughing at him. That in turn made Rylie giggle.

"No honestly, we can't take free food from you if you're barely getting to eat yourself, but thank you. We should get going," Harrison answered. His reply was kind but had a sense of urgency that Lianna picked up on immediately.

"Are you all right, you seem anxious?" She asked.

"I'm fine. Honestly, don't concern yourself," he replied but frowned, not thinking he'd been that obvious.

Harrison strode over to Zack and gave him a shove, making him come to his senses. He still wore a goofy smile when he looked over at Lianna, but clearly had no intention of reprimanding her brother further so Harrison tried to get him to lead on. Lianna edged over towards Rylie and Evie and whispered to them under her breath.

"Is he always like that?" She asked, unable to ignore Zack's continued attention. "You know, goofy and love-struck? I find it pretty easy to tell how people are feeling but it's hard to imagine that guy's for real."

"I've never seen him this way before, but we only met a few days ago," Rylie explained, still giggling. "He's our guide."

"Your guide, really? I've never seen him in town before. Do you need help getting somewhere?" She asked, not being intrusive, just helpful, with an underlying curiosity.

Her question sparked a worried reaction from Evie and urgency for Rylie, remembering that they were on the run and needed to get to the ranch Zack had mentioned as soon as possible. Evie started to shift, fidgeting with concern.

"No, we should be fine, but thank you," Rylie answered.

"You don't need to be afraid of me," Lianna said, crouching down so that she was looking up at Evie. "I only want to help."

That was when Zack finally re-approached her, placing a hand on Lianna's shoulder. It made her jump but as she turned around, his gaze wasn't ogling, but serious. His bright blue eyes seeming to read her for a moment before speaking.

"Are you an empath?" He asked in a hushed tone. Now it was Lianna's turn to be shocked into silence. Alex rushed to her side and tried to push Zack away.

"Leave my sister alone! I can do much more than just pick pockets you know!" Alex shouted in as menacing a tone as he could. Despite the threat, Zack's gaze remained fixed on Lianna. Harrison stepped in, placing his hand on his blade, drawing Alex's attention to it.

"We don't want any trouble," he said firmly, hoping that noticing the huge blade would be enough to deter Alex's anger and make him calm himself. It seemed to work as Alex cowered a little but stood firm between Zack and his sister. Zack looked down at Alex and smiled before removing his jacket and revealing the mark on his collar bone.

"Does this mean anything to you?" He asked, technically speaking to Lianna but looking at both of them. The mark clearly did mean something to her as she reacted with a gasp. Alex looked up at her before flicking his gaze back to Zack. They were all expecting Lianna to speak but it wasn't, it was Alex.

"You're the mage smuggler?" He asked dubiously.

"That's what the rumours say. Either way, I mean you no harm. I just couldn't help but notice how you instantly picked up on each of our feelings and I wondered if maybe… *I'm the one that can help you?*" He said, his voice hushed but kind.

He looked over at Harrison who wore a wary expression. His hand still hovered near the handle of his blade, and he seemed ready to unsheathe it should the need arise. Surprisingly, Lianna started to cry, with gentle tears rolling down her cheeks and the reaction melted Zack's heart. Alex stepped aside as Zack carefully wiped her tears away.

"A face this beautiful should never cry," he muttered softly.

Upon hearing his words, Harrison couldn't help but remember the times he'd seen Rylie sad and felt exactly the same way.

"I can't help it. We've been trying to contact you for months," Lianna explained. She smiled and it was clear to see they were tears of relief. She took a step back from Zack and then placed her arm around Alex, showing themselves as a united pair.

"I'm sorry, I never got a message about you, otherwise I would've made contact sooner," Zack replied solemnly.

He glanced over to Rylie, Evie and Harrison as if trying to silently say he'd explain later. Lianna looked coy as she said what was clearly a rehearsed speech.

"We have no money and little to offer but must ask you for your assistance. People have become suspicious of my abilities and with such a great fear of mages in town, it isn't safe for us anymore. I'll pay you any way I can, but please will you take us somewhere safe?" She asked, looking at Zack with hopeful eyes.

"Of course, you can come with us. My friends are seeking a safe place for mages too, and I'm taking them to people that can hopefully help," he replied and then quickly glanced at the others, realising they might not be comfortable with the idea.

As if recalling his words from the ship, when he told them he helped mages to honour his mother and that they could repay him by helping other mages too, Harrison relaxed and nodded as Rylie left Evie's side to give Lianna a friendly hug.

"You're both welcome to come with us, no discussion needed. And no payment either, right Zack?" She said, knowing what his answer would be.

"Absolutely, although I'll take a donation in the form of a kiss," he replied flirtatiously.

"Let me give you an *'I owe you'* on that count," Lianna replied with a giggle, returning Rylie's embrace. "And for the record, you don't need to be worried," she said, looking at Rylie, startling her. The silvery grey of her eyes became more dominant as she tilted her head in confusion.

"What do you mean?" Rylie asked.

"I can't explain it, but I could tell you were worried about hugging me," she clarified. Rylie raised a hand to her mouth and stuttered a short laugh.

"Let's just say I can't always control my powers as well as you appear to," she replied.

"Control?" Lianna exclaimed a little louder than she intended. Hushing her voice back down she continued. "I barely have any control over this… gift. That's why we need to leave town. I'm so glad we found you when we did."

"At least you don't need to worry about burning down the neighbourhood as you leave," Rylie replied, trying to make a joke of their situation, but her heart wasn't in it and the comment came out flat. Lianna clearly didn't understand but led them towards her home to grab some things before they left town.

Chapter Twelve
Driftwood

Hearing the horrific tale of the town's past, Rylie expected to be confronted with heartbroken people as they continued to make their way through Revaine, but to her surprise, most of the townsfolk seemed cheerful. There was a real community spirit which had obviously grown in the aftermath of the tragedy. She could however also see why Lianna needed to leave.

Everyone seemed to know everyone, and a lot of the people they passed forced smiles towards Lianna and Alex, their underlying suspicion obvious. They passed a building that was clearly a shelter, with dozens of children playing outside. There was a make-shift soup kitchen in front, with people offering handouts to the needy. A young girl came running up from the kitchen to Lianna, smiling from ear to ear.

"Lianna, you're back! Have you brought some more pebbles for our mosaic?" She asked.

"Sorry Maisie, not today; Alex and I are going to be heading out of town for a while but I promise, when I'm back, my bag will be full of arts and crafts we can do together," Lianna replied with a sympathetic smile, feeling bad that she didn't intend to return any time soon.

"But I don't want you to go! Is it because of what my uncle said last week?" Maisie asked, looking worried.

"Don't blame yourself, Maisie, it's not because of you or your uncle, but Alex and I have to go for a little while. I'll come back one day though, just to see you!" She promised, giving the little girl a big hug.

Collecting her bag of belongings, Lianna waved goodbye and rejoined the group. Everyone but Alex was looking at her curiously and the attention made her nervous.

"You're confused, why?" She enquired.

"Do you live at this shelter?" Zack asked, shocked to see so many youths hanging around, clearly having little more than a sleeping bag and backpack of belongings to call their own.

"We had nowhere else to go. I also volunteer with the kids. That little girl I was chatting to, Maisie, she took a bit of a shining to me. She's kind and so artistic... I love spending time with her, but her uncle was the first person to suspect I had abilities," she said, her expression changing, becoming sad.

"Did he threaten you?" Zack asked with urgency.

"He didn't mean to, at least I don't think he did," Lianna replied while Alex scoffed.

"Why would he do that?" Rylie asked.

"Fear. It was about two years ago when he first confronted me. Alex and I have tried to keep to ourselves ever since but, it's hard in a town like this."

"How well does he know you?" Harrison added, suspecting there was a deeper level to the story that she wasn't expressing.

"When we lost our parents in the attack, I was twelve and Alex four so we could ask for help, but Maisie was just a baby so when her uncle brought her to the shelter, I spent a lot of time with them. For a long time, we were like extended family," Lianna explained.

"Yeah well, Daryl's a jerk, so I'm not going to miss him one bit!" Alex huffed, clearly defensive of his sister.

"Don't say that Alex, he's just scared," Lianna reprimanded. Alex responded by sulking as he had before while Zack recognised the name but focused on Lianna's compassion.

"I know Daryl, he is very afraid of the mage hunters but I never thought he'd turn on a friend, especially someone as kind as you Lianna. I've been in and out of town for six months, how have we never met?" Zack asked, still love-struck.

"Maybe we are destined to be star-crossed lovers," Lianna replied cheekily, but Zack didn't notice.

He was about to praise her again when their attention was taken by Evie's excited reaction. They'd made it to the path leading out of town and by the make-shift gate were the horse and carriages Zack mentioned. They were all tacked up and a sign offering rides stood prominently by a huddled group of drivers. Evie rushed straight to a palomino horse that was munching happily on some hay and started stroking it.

"I've never seen a gold horse before!" She exclaimed.

"We've got loads of different colours, my favourite is the chestnut, look, over here," Alex replied, showing Evie one of the other horses. After a moment of fussing the docile creatures, Evie came dashing back to the group.

"Can we *please* take a carriage ride to get to the ranch?" She begged, looking between Rylie, Harrison and Zack. Her eyes were glistening with hope but as they looked over to the sign asking for five silver pieces per journey, Harrison was about to say they couldn't afford it when Zack strode forward.

"Of course we can young lady. Which steed would you like escorting us? Oh wait, I know, what about our new friend?" He suggested, walking back towards the chestnut horse Alex had shown her. The horse had a big white stripe down its face, gentle eyes and huge ears. When Evie came up to it again, it gave her a little nudge with its muzzle.

"Oh yes, I love him!" She declared, stroking the horse and laughing as it licked her fingers, hoping for food.

"Ok everyone, jump into the carriage, I'll be right back," Zack said as he disappeared to speak with the driver.

Rylie chased after him to say they couldn't take his money, not after everything he was already doing for them but when she saw Zack shaking hands with the carriage driver, she assumed it was too late.

Climbing into the carriage, Rylie took a seat up front next to Evie when to all of their surprise, Zack hopped into the driver's seat and collected the reins. Rylie just about heard him whisper *'hello my old friend'* to the horse before looking over his shoulder and speaking to the group.

"Everyone present and accounted for?" He asked, checking they were all seated. "Good stuff, off we go!"

With a click of his tongue and a snap of the reins, the carriage lurched into life and they were trotting down the dirt path. The land on the outskirts of Revaine was beautifully open, with farmland spreading as far as the eye could see. There were several different types of crops growing and where they passed some larger hedges or small walls, they spotted some basic wooden boxes with produce inside and price lists pinned to the edge.

"We call them hedge-veg boxes," Lianna said to no one in particular. Rylie giggled at the concept but Harrison looked suspicious.

"Don't people just take what they want? There's no one there to make sure the produce is paid for," he questioned, unable to imagine any Imperial merchant being that trusting.

"I know it seems strange, but no. We had one of these outside the shelter. It's one of the best ways of making extra coin. People were always honest and paid whatever price was listed. In fact, we often found people overpaid," Lianna replied.

"That's crazy… or possibly genius, I'm not entirely sure," Harrison commented, shaking his head but smiling.

After about an hour on the road, Zack slowed the horse down and turned onto a long narrow path, under a large wooden archway with a hanging sign. There were a few apple trees scattered around and once on the trail, the horse seemed to know exactly where he was going, so Zack relaxed the reins and turned to face the others.

"Welcome to the Driftwood Ranch," Zack announced.

Once they passed the apple trees, the view down to the ranch was clear. Like the other farms they'd passed, the land around them was vast and there were a number of different crops growing in each of the fields, but the ranch also had dozens of horses and other livestock grazing in opposing fields and a charming, rustic ranch house at its centre. The path wound around the fields until Zack veered the carriage towards the main house and pulled the horse to a stop.

As the rest of them got out of the carriage, Zack began untacking the horse and led him to a trough of water. When he re-joined the others, he spotted their collective looks of surprise.

"What? I used to work here. That's why the driver let me take us, because for about two months this was my job," he explained cheerfully. "Cruise, our steed, was always my favourite. Dopiest thing this side of the Ensen."

"Oh I think I've met something dopier," Harrison quipped, winking at Zack.

"Haha, you're hilarious!" Zack replied sarcastically. Rylie came up beside Harrison and playfully slapped his arm but her expression told him she found his remark funny too.

"You can't say that!" She scolded mischievously and then whispered, '*out loud*' in Harrison's ear.

"What? It's true. His attempts at flirting with Lianna are painful. I never thought I'd see anything worse than Morgan talking to my mother, but now, I have!" He joked quietly back to her, still chuckling. Rylie covered her face with one hand but couldn't hide her smile.

"It was pretty bad," she smirked, and the two of them laughed between themselves as the group headed towards the ranch house.

Zack bounded up the steps to the house while signalling for the rest of them to hang back. The ranch itself was beautiful, with a strong stone foundation supporting the large wooden structure. There was a deck out front and a fire pit to the side with a short path leading down to a two-story barn. Knocking on the front door, Zack began to whistle, shifting his weight front and back playfully until a woman greeted him.

"Zack! I didn't know you were in the area! How have you been?" The woman exclaimed, giving him a welcoming hug. It was clear she'd just come from tending to the animals or repairing the farm equipment as the olive-green blouse she wore was splattered with oil stains and her worn-out jeans were mucky. Her coral hair was tied back in a plait and she wore a thick headband but several unruly strands managed to escape.

"It's so good to see you, Elissa!" Zack replied enthusiastically. "You're looking so tanned. Spending all your time with the horses these days?"

It was easy to tell Zack was in his element at the farm. It made Rylie wonder why he ever left.

"When I'm not fixing that blasted plough, yes. The horses miss you though, especially Cruise. He was fussy for days after you left us," Elissa said, her smile spreading across her face.

He was just about to introduce the group to her when something leapt at him from inside the ranch. It was a dog, a very excitable and fluffy, bearded collie. Evie had to cover her mouth to prevent another squeal as they watched Zack give the animal plenty of fuss, ruffling its fur and talking to it like a baby.

"Jasper! My ol' buddy. How ya doing boy-o? Have you been a good boy? I bet you've been a good boy, haven't you? Yeah!" He praised as the dog started frantically licking Zack's hands, trying to jump up and lick his face too. The dog's tail was wagging like crazy, showing just how happy he was to see him.

After another few seconds of fuss, Zack finally looked back at Elissa and introduced her to the group.

"I'd like to introduce you to some *special* friends of mine," he began, moving so that she could see the group.

"Well, hello," She greeted pleasantly before glancing back at Zack. "Are they *special* like my Drew or like you?"

"Oh, they are definitely *'Drew special* Elissa," he replied, "apart from *Mr Muscle* with the big sword and the little swindler boy behind him, they're the more normal variety of special friends I sometimes find."

"Well, if they're normal, they're not *special* like you," Elissa teased. Hearing his own words but enjoying that Elissa knew exactly what he meant, Zack only laughed.

"You know, if normal people heard us talk, they'd think we were the *special* ones!" Zack added.

"No doubt about that," Elissa chuckled in agreement before turning her attention to the others. "Welcome to Driftwood, my family ranch. There is no need for anyone to fear here, even mages. We would never turn away a friend of Zack's, special or otherwise. You are welcome to stay in the rooms above the barn if you need shelter for a few days."

"Thank you very much," Harrison expressed gratefully. Evie had already crouched down and focused all of her attention on Jasper the dog, as the rest of the group also thanked Elissa. Evie looked towards her with a big smile and mouthed a *'thank you*' in between licks. The dog had taken to her instantly.

"Jasper has incredibly good taste, so you, my dear, must be a lovely person," Elissa said, making Evie react coyly. "Is there anything I can do to help you settle in?"

"There is one thing," Rylie began, stepping forward cautiously. "Have you ever heard of a man called Alistair Auren? He was our grandfather and the only link we have to help us find a safe place to go."

"Alistair Auren? There's a name I haven't heard in a while. We knew Alistair. He sheltered here a few years ago when he had to flee Carlisse. I'm so sorry about your grandmother," Elissa replied.

"A few years ago?" Rylie questioned, clearly shocked and confused. "That can't be, he died before I was born."

"You should talk to my husband. Drew spent much more time with Alistair when he was here, maybe he can explain," Elissa suggested, obviously worried that she'd made a terrible mistake. "Get your things into the barn and come by the house when you're ready. I'll get some dinner cooking."

"Thanks Elissa," Zack replied before Rylie could ask more questions. "We'll see you and Drew at the house in a little while."

As they watched Elissa take Jasper back into the house, Rylie turned and glared at Zack.

"Why did you stop me from asking about my grandfather? If there's any chance he's alive, I have to know, we have to find him!" She insisted, her words flying out like an assault.

Harrison carefully placed a hand on her shoulder, making her shudder but the contact also made her pause. It was like his touch extinguished the fire within her like water would an actual flame. He waited for her to take a deep breath before speaking.

"If your grandfather is alive, this is going to be a shocking step for both you and Evie. It's best that we take it steady and listen to what Elissa and Drew have to say," Harrison replied, being the voice of reason.

"You're right," she admitted, looking over to her sister who was clearly shell-shocked. "I never imagined he'd be alive."

"We'll get to the bottom of this, together," Harrison said reassuringly, taking Rylie's hand and giving it a gentle squeeze.

"Dad received letters saying they'd died and suspected they were fake, I can't believe he was right," Rylie added, her mind whipping frantically to every time her parents had recalled a memory of her grandfather.

"Let's drop off our bags and go hear their story," Harrison suggested, putting an arm around Evie and giving them a sympathetic smile as they all headed to the barn.

There were three rooms above the barn with varying cot beds and sofas they could sleep on, as well as a little shower room above the horse stalls and a feeding store. Zack explained to them that Driftwood is a working ranch, so travellers could either pay for a room or work to earn their keep. He'd worked here for a few months until he met the captain of the Pilgrim, which is how he'd become good friends with both Elissa and Drew.

After taking time to clean up, the group returned to the ranch house. Rylie was particularly eager to get inside but Harrison kept her arm linked with his to keep her calm. As they sat down to dinner, they met Elissa's husband Drew, who took a seat at the top of the table. His dark hair and golden skin were akin to Lianna's and clearly a trait of people from Revaine. The only key difference was his eyes, which were crystal blue, just like Zack's.

"Welcome to our humble home," Drew greeted smiling at the group "and welcome back Zack. It's great to have you with us again."

"Thank you for having us, sir," Lianna said politely, as she tried to ignore the fact that Alex had dived straight for the food. They all took a moment to thank Drew and Elissa for their hospitality, but Drew could see the anxious looks on Evie and Rylie's faces. Elissa had told him that they wanted to know about Alistair and so he settled in to explain.

"So you must be Alistair's granddaughters, yes?" He asked kindly. "I can see a resemblance in both of you."

"Yes sir, my name is Rylie and this is my little sister Evie," she advised quietly, giving her sister's nose her usual affectionate pinch. She turned towards Elissa momentarily. "I'm sorry about my outburst earlier. It was just a little overwhelming to hear you met my grandfather."

"It's okay darling, I didn't realise what Alistair had done all those years ago, but Drew can explain," Elissa replied.

"Your grandfather came to us three years ago, seeking shelter as he and a few other mages had escaped Carlisse. Once King Grayson Brock took the throne, lives for mages in the kingdom were even worse than before," Drew began.

"Worse, how? I thought mages in the kingdom were slaves," Harrison asked, his warden studies kicking in.

"After the war, Alistair made an accord with the former king, protecting the known mages in the city so that although they had to be servants, they would be treated with some dignity. Once the king died, however, his son took over and life became almost unbearable for all the mages and Ar'encal in the kingdom. Grayson treats them as nothing more than property," Drew explained, recalling Alistair's story. To everyone's surprise, it was Evie who asked the first question.

"But why was our father misled into believing both our grandparents died? He received a letter instructing him not to return long before either of us were born," she enquired, her timid voice curious.

"It could've been to do with his accord with the former king. Either that, or he felt it was too dangerous for your father to return. It seems like an extreme measure, but if your father was safe, returning to Carlisse to be with his parents would have tied him to their fate," Drew said, giving her a reassuring smile.

"Do you know what happened when they fled the city?" Rylie asked, uncertain she wanted to know the answer.

"Alistair told me he orchestrated an explosion in the kingdom so that he and the gathered mages could escape, hoping people would presume they died in the blast. But things went wrong. Your grandmother, Emilia died during the chaos," Drew continued, which made Evie whimper and Jasper snuggle between her legs, trying to comfort her.

"How did Alistair and the other mages get here?" Harrison asked, wondering how Drew and Elissa got involved.

"There's an underground passage between the bakery in Carlisse and the barn out back," Drew admitted, glancing at Zack with a mildly embarrassed expression.

"You have a secret tunnel into Carlisse?" Zack blurted out, staring at Drew in disbelief, clearly shocked. "How did I not know this?"

"Well, it wouldn't be a very good secret if we told everyone that worked here!" Elissa chimed. "We presume it was built as a smuggler's tunnel but when we bought the ranch, we used it to provide goods to the baker. But when Caitlin went to work in the castle, we started using it to get messages to her as well."

"I'm sorry, who's Caitlin?" Rylie asked.

"Our daughter," Drew replied. "Her friend was chosen to be Grayson's bride just before he became king and Caitlin got work in the castle to support her, despite the dangers. You see, my daughter and I are both mages. Luckily, we can conceal our talents quite well."

"What abilities do you have?" Lianna asked, surprised she hadn't sensed anything.

"I'm a psionic mage, although not a particularly good one. If I honed my abilities, I should be able to move objects at will and control people's thoughts, but to date, the most I can do is levitate objects and sometimes coerce people to look in a different direction. The horses love my dancing carrot routine though!" He answered, making a joke out of his own diminished skills.

"And Caitlin is an illusionist. She can manipulate the area around her, distorting it so that onlookers see a different image to what is actually there," Elissa explained.

"I can't count the number of times she's tricked us into believing she was in her room studying when in fact she was in the barn playing with Jasper," Drew added with a smile.

"That's incredible!" Lianna gasped, clearly unfamiliar with all the distinct types of magic.

"What abilities do you have?" Drew asked the group.

Rylie and Harrison shared the responsibility of recounting their tale, speaking about both Rylie and Evie's powers, their escape and meeting Zack, Lianna and Alex. Lianna then took over and explained her predicament and why she and Alex joined them.

"Meeting Zack and the others when we did was a stroke of luck. Alex and I have lived in Revaine our entire lives but after our parents died in the attack ten years ago, life has been hard. We spent most of our time living in the shelter but before we even found that place, I triggered my abilities," Lianna said.

"She's an empath Drew," Zack explained, seeming to know their host would take an added interest in the revelation.

"I didn't know what I was. Only that there was so much sadness and pain in the town after the hunter's attack, such devastation, and I could feel all of it," Lianna added.

"One day, Lianna was weak and sweating so much, I thought she was going to die," Alex recalled, helping her to explain their story. "I was only four or five and didn't know what to do. I remember wanting to ease her fever so I collected some water from a nearby stream on the outskirts of town and made her drink. I didn't know about Encia back then or how toxic it is, but the water reduced her fever and that was all that mattered to me at the time."

"When Alex told me what he'd done, but I didn't come down with the withering, we realised I must've had some link to magic. Later on, I heard the term empath," she added, making Evie realise in a way she'd been lucky.

"That must've been terrifying!" Elissa exclaimed, placing a trembling hand over her mouth as she wondered if her own daughter would've survived in a similar situation.

"Our home had been destroyed by the mage hunters too and I knew we couldn't survive on the streets; it was luck that the shelter was established, and we were able to stay there for so many years," Lianna continued with a shallow smile.

"We would've been happy there too if it wasn't for that jerk Daryl," Alex butted in, but Lianna hushed him.

"I found it hard with both my parent's support and living in the safety of our home, I can't imagine surviving in your shoes," Evie confessed, causing Lianna to gently squeeze her hand.

"Did Daryl endanger you in any way? If he did, I will break my no weapons rule when I next see him," Zack asserted angrily, making Alex give him a big toothy grin.

"Daryl did nothing wrong," Lianna insisted, emphasising each word and glaring at both Zack and Alex. "He's about five years older than me, but his brother was also killed in the attack and left behind his baby girl Maisie. In the early days we—" she hesitated, knowing how much Alex hated the next part but carried on regardless. "We were close."

"He was just using you, Lianna," Alex huffed. "He didn't want to raise Maisie and used her to get close to you, until he suspected you were a mage."

"Why was he so scared?" Rylie asked.

"He's terrified of death. Fearing the hunters was one thing, but he blames mages for their existence, and indirectly for the attack itself. I tried to hide my abilities from everyone but I cared for Daryl so my empathic powers flourished uncontrollably around him. When I sensed he was falling in love with me, I had to pull away. I couldn't live a lie and he'd never accept me as a mage," Lianna revealed, wiping away a tear before it escaped down her cheek.

"Well, I for one am glad. You are perfect just the way you are Lianna, and shouldn't have to hide any part of yourself," Zack declared, dreamily gazing at her again. She rolled her eyes and finished her story.

"Ironically, once I broke up with him, he became cold and started to notice my abilities anyway. Rumours soon spread that I was different and I knew it was him. I began to work at the nursery instead, minimising my time around the shelter, but after a while, we were basically living on the streets to avoid him," she concluded, looking at her hands as if ashamed.

"Oh Lianna, I'm so sorry," Rylie sighed, taking the other girl's hand and giving her an affectionate squeeze.

"Thank you," she replied, returning the gesture.

"Although Lianna tried, she'd never admit what she earned wasn't enough to support both of us, so I started working the streets. At first, it was just odd jobs around town but then, I started pick-pocketing too," Alex said coyly, as if admitting it made him nervous.

"As much as I didn't approve of Alex's newfound money-making tactic, it was from working the streets and picking up gossip that we heard about the mage smuggler. A guy with a strange tattoo on his neck that would help mages find safety. I'd been trying to make contact and then, well, Alex unintentionally brought you to me!" Lianna recalled with a smile.

"Best coincidence of my life," Zack replied, causing Lianna to grumble a polite laugh.

"Yes dear," she mumbled, her comment dripping with ridicule. It made Harrison burst out a laugh, almost choking on the water he was drinking.

As the group finished dinner, Zack and Alex offered to help Elissa clear the plates while Drew spoke to Harrison and Rylie.

"I'm afraid I can't tell you where Alistair has gone but wherever he is, it'll be somewhere safe for mages. You should try the royal archives at the castle and see if you can find his old apprentice. Before King Grayson took over, he was the overseer of the archives and may have left a clue to guide other mages looking to escape the kingdom," he suggested, giving them a small ray of hope.

"It's a good place to start," Rylie said, filled with anxious energy. "Thank you, Drew, what you've told us could really help."

"Can we ask one more favour?" Harrison added, recalling the underground passage he'd mentioned earlier.

"The passage? Sure, you can use it... but I have one request," Drew replied. "Will you check in on Caitlin? She hasn't responded to any of our letters in weeks and Elissa and I are very worried. I hate to put a further burden on you kids but it would mean the world to us."

"Of course we'll ask after her," Harrison replied as Elissa, Zack and Alex returned from the kitchen.

"Don't think that means you don't have to earn your keep for tonight," Elissa reminded with a cheeky grin. "Zack, would you mind cleaning out the stables and finding a few other odd jobs for your friends?"

"Of course not, come on everyone! We've got a barn to clean and animals to feed," he replied joyfully.

Evie leapt straight to her feet with enthusiasm as they all headed out the front door and agreed on jobs for the day. Evie and Alex offered to take Jasper for a walk while Lianna said she'd prepare their living quarters. Harrison wanted to familiarise himself with the surroundings so offered to check the fences which left Zack and Rylie to groom the horses and clean the stalls.

As they set to work, Rylie watched as Zack fussed over Cruise, the horse that brought them from Revaine. He tied the horse outside its stall to brush him down while Rylie combed his mane. She loved his big ears and the wonky white stripe that ran from his forelock down to his muzzle.

"This place is amazing Zack, why did you ever leave?" Rylie asked.

"Ever since I left home three years ago, I've never stayed in one place for too long. I guess I'm a nomad. When you don't stay, you can't disappoint people. This way, I use what skills I have to help, but without the pressure," Zack replied, focussing on brushing rather than looking back at Rylie.

"You think you're a disappointment, Zack? Harrison dropped everything to be there for me and Evie, and I'll always love him for that, but you; you stepped up without even knowing who we were, and you're still helping us even though you don't have to! That makes you a good person in my book," she emphasised honestly, making Zack look up at her and smile gratefully.

They finished grooming Cruise, cleaned out his stall and put him inside before moving on to the next horse.

Standing ankle-deep in dirty shavings, Rylie noticed Zack looking to the rooms above, knowing Lianna was up there and couldn't resist speaking boldly.

"Come on, fess up. Do you like Lianna or are you just a really terrible flirt?" She asked with a smirk, fairly sure she already knew the answer.

"I am *not* a terrible flirt!" He proclaimed, offended yet bemused. "But yeah, I can't stop thinking about Lianna. I think I'm in love."

"Why come on so strong then? Can't you see your approach is *not* working? Even in the short time I've known you, I can tell you're usually good at reading people," Rylie replied, her tone playful but her smile genuine.

"My brain literally turns to mush around her. Is it that bad? My flirting I mean," he asked, his cheeks flushing to a near crimson colour.

"Yeah, it's pretty bad; awful actually," Rylie confirmed, failing to hold back a giggle.

"She's an empath though, surely she knows my feelings are genuine. I'm not trying to deceive her," Zack reasoned, looking from the ceiling to Rylie and back again. "In fact, I've never felt this way before. Please, tell me she knows that."

"I think she's overwhelmed by what she's hearing, so even with her powers she can't sense your underlying feelings. If you want a girl's advice, tone it back a notch... or ten. Let her like you before hoping she'll love you," Rylie advised, her voice still playful. Zack could tell she felt for him, but her kindness was interrupted when she flicked some horse hay at him.

"Hey!" He grumbled, dodging the flying food.

"Then again, I get dating tips from a thirteen-year-old! Maybe she's really into you and the sarcastic quips are her way of showing it,"

Rylie replied, laughing as he retaliated by throwing another clump of hay in her direction.

Carried away by play fighting, they barely finished their task before Evie, Alex and Harrison returned. Evie released Jasper from the lead who promptly trotted up the stairs and barked happily at the door. Lianna opened up and gave the dog a pat as he passed, watching as he lolled over to his bed in the corner, spun a few times and flopped down. The others all followed the dog upstairs and headed into the barn loft.

Lianna had made a wonderful job of making the place feel cosy. She'd made cushions by stuffing some old feed sacks with straw and found enough blankets for all of them. She'd also refilled their water bottles, prepared snacks and repaired a tear in one of Evie's tops. Although she'd been with them for just a day, she'd already become the carer of the group.

"Wow, thank you, Lianna! You didn't have to do this," Evie said, holding up the top in delight.

"After ten years of patching up Alex's clothes from all the bumps and scrapes he's gotten into, fixing that little tear was no trouble at all," she replied, her eyes glistening happily.

"Hey, come on! Don't make me sound like a total troublemaker," Alex mumbled defensively.

"Says the pick-pocket," Zack teased.

"Come now children, don't make me use this," Harrison interjected, drawing his sword and flashing its sharp edge.

"You don't really use that thing… do you?" Alex asked sceptically. "It's just a scare tactic, right?"

"Not at all! This blade has had my back since I was seventeen. It's like a natural extension to my arm, and I've trained extensively for years to make sure when I need to use it, I do so with deadly force," he replied, winking at the younger boy.

"That is *so* cool!" Alex replied, his eyes glinting as he looked at Harrison and his broadsword in a totally new light. "Can you teach me how to wield a sword? I want to learn to fight!"

As Alex became clearly overexcited at the prospect, Harrison smiled, glancing at Lianna who was grimacing and shaking her head.

"One day buddy, but first, you have to prove you have a warrior's heart," Harrison said encouragingly whilst slyly nodding at Lianna.

"How will I know when I've done that?" Alex asked, desperately wanting to start training.

"When you do, I'll start training you, and that's how you'll know," Harrison replied. "For now, I think it's time we get some rest. Drew said he'll let us through the passage just before dawn. Hopefully, that way the streets in Carlisse will be quiet when we arrive."

With Alex far too excited at the prospect of becoming a warrior, he didn't get much sleep, but the others took what time they had to rest before the early morning start.

Chapter Thirteen
Departure

Pressing the elevator button, going down to the Imperial prison for the fourth day, Siljanna felt a deep frustration building within her. She tried interrogating Nate, Paige still being mute since witnessing Samuel's death, but he was stubborn and would not yield. She wanted him to admit that Harrison injured her father and left him to die when the fire started but Nate adamantly proclaimed Harrison's innocence. He kept spewing the same lies as Harrison, saying Sampson attacked them but she knew better.

Imperator Harlyn had offered to personally examine her father's body and confirmed he'd suffered a serious head injury before dying from smoke inhalation, and that was all the proof Siljanna needed to know Harrison was as much to blame as Rylie for his death. Descending to level B3, she resigned herself to the fact that it didn't matter, as long as she made them pay for what they'd done to her father, but that didn't stop her wanting the satisfaction of a confession.

Dylan and Juliette had arrived in Yasras and found nothing. The innkeepers recognised the sketch of Rylie but were convincing when they said they hadn't seen her in months. They had been complicit to a number of security checks by the wardens and allowed Dylan and Juliette to stay free of charge while they investigated the rest of town, giving Siljanna little reason to doubt them. She did doubt them but after being betrayed by two of the people she trusted most so recently, trust didn't come easily for her now. She ordered Dylan and Juliette to stay within striking distance of the harbour until she could find a way to break Nate. A physical beating wouldn't work, Dylan had already done that, and threats had done little to faze him either. But every man has a weakness, and she had a good idea what to do next.

As the elevator doors opened, Siljanna made her way through the dank corridors to the dungeon cell where Nate and Paige were still being held. She barged through the door, letting it slam behind her.

"Let's crack on with this, shall we?" She announced as Nate and Paige both stood up, grasping each other's hands. She'd loosened their chains before leaving the night before hoping that taking away that little bit of comfort would add to today's tactic.

She yanked on the central chain which forced their hands and arms apart and then a second chain that pulled Paige's restraints even tighter. Siljanna strode over to Paige and placed her hands around her throat, pressing fiercely.

"What are you doing Siljanna? Stop this!" Nate begged, watching as his wife who was already weak both mentally and physically, desperately struggle.

"I'll stop when you tell me what I need to know! How much do you know about magic, what's your link to mages and where's Rylie?!" Siljanna demanded. She was shouting by the time she finished and with each word, her grip around Paige's throat became tighter. Gasping, Paige's breaths became short as she did all she could to get oxygen into her lungs.

"No please, stop! Don't hurt her, hurt me!" Nate shouted, his face panic-stricken.

"I only need one of you, so why don't I just finish Paige off first, and then you'll get your wish," Siljanna threatened, turning all her attention and rage towards Paige as she continued to squeeze. Paige started shaking, her hands banging against the wall as her skin went red.

"I'll tell you! Leave her be and I'll tell you," Nate said, defeated. Siljanna loosened her grip and smiled a dreadful, sinister smile. *Every man has a weakness* she thought to herself, and for Nate, it was his love for Paige.

"Talk... now," Siljanna insisted, releasing her grip and letting Paige drop to the floor, clutching her throat as she tried to breathe freely.

Nate sunk his head down, wishing his heritage would kick in, that he could trigger some kind of abilities to help them get out of this mess, but nothing happened. He was left with only one choice that would keep Paige alive, and so he spoke.

"I am the descendant of the Ar'encal," he admitted. He then went on to tell Siljanna of his parents, his life in Carlisse, his travels all the way to meeting Paige and staying with her in Yasras during the war. Unlike Paige, he didn't think to cover the fact that her parents were the innkeepers and Siljanna connected the dots.

"Thank you for your co-operation," she replied, as menacingly as she could. She headed over to the small ledge in the corner of the room and picked up a syringe. Tapping it lightly, making sure the fluid inside ran freely, she walked back towards Paige.

"What is that? You promised you wouldn't hurt her!" Nate cried, pulling as hard as he could on the chains.

"I also promised my father he would see me become a worthy successor. Sometimes, it's just not possible to keep promises," she replied, thrusting the needle into Paige's neck. Whatever the fluid was, Paige gasped as it coursed through her.

"Nate—" she whimpered before passing out.

Siljanna unchained her and called in one of the guards to collect Paige's motionless body.

"Take the prisoner away. She's no use to me anymore," Siljanna ordered, making sure to glance over and assess Nate's reaction. He was both distraught and livid, pulling frantically against his chains. He pulled so hard that the skin around his wrists broke and she could see blood seeping down his arms.

"What have you done?" He cried as Siljanna walked out the door, just behind the guard carrying Paige. She heard Nate scream her name; it was a guttural noise and only made her smile deeper. His cry was completely cut off once the door slammed back into place, proving the room was truly soundproof.

Heading back towards the elevator, she felt proud of herself. The Imperator wanted to know where the magic came from in the Auren bloodline, and it was from Nate. If that display of force didn't trigger his abilities, nothing would, but either way, Harlyn had a new test subject, and Siljanna had a new lead.

Once back in the main lobby, Siljanna took out her pager and messaged Dylan.

'Interrogate the innkeepers again. They are Auren's grandparents!' She wrote.

'Understood' was all he replied with, but she knew the job would get done. It was unlikely they'd need to use the same level of force as they had against Nate and Paige, but if Siljanna was honest with herself, she didn't care. Rylie had taken her father away and she was willing to take away all of Rylie's family in return.

Her next job was to call Cameron. Using one of the desk phones, she dialled his number and placed the phone to her ear. It only took a few rings before he answered.

"Calling with good news?" He asked.

"I broke him. Nate has the Ar'encal bloodline and if he's going to trigger any magical abilities, it'll happen now. If Harlyn still wants to experiment on him, collect him soon," she replied, and Cameron could hear her smile.

"Well done, I'll make the arrangements. He'll be taken to the institute. What about the woman?" He asked.

"I injected her with the same substance you gave Elijah, only a greater dose," Siljanna confirmed.

"Good, I'll ensure she's kept in the hospital for observation. Just in case we need her again," Cameron said clinically. "That reminds me, the blacksmith is going to be released today. He seems to have bought the cover story we told him. He'll be returned to his smithy but with a warden guard on-site at all times."

"Have you spoken to Morgan? He's the interim commander in Tivani," she asked. Morgan liked Elijah and she couldn't risk him catching on to what they'd done.

"I have, only I told him the blacksmith fell severely ill in the city and has been in hospital for the last few days. Morgan didn't question the series of events and was just eager to look after the man upon his return," Cameron advised to Siljanna's relief. "Is there anything else you need?"

"Would it be possible to make an accord with King Grayson of Carlisse? I have reason to believe it's worth investigating the city for my fugitives and more information on magic too. Scholars there may have retained more information than we realised after the war, which could help the Imperator," she explained.

"Consider it done and keep me posted," Cameron said before the click down the line told her he'd hung up. She was about to leave when the pager screen lit up again and she saw the message from Dylan.

'Innkeeper lady was soft. She admitted both Harrison and Rylie stayed at the inn before boarding a ship bound for the Eastern Continent. Orders?' He wrote.

'Leave the innkeepers and get passage over to the Eastern Continent. Cameron is arranging an accord with the Carlisse King. Head there on arrival.' She replied. She wasn't expecting a reply but the pager pinged again.

'Spoilsport—J.'

The message was from Juliette who had probably wanted to inflict more harm on the innkeepers before departing. At first, Siljanna wasn't going to reply, Juliette's thirst for debilitating people was sadistic but useful, but then reminded herself that they answered to her and shouldn't be allowed to act so flippantly.

'Follow orders or I will find someone that will.' She sent back, tapping the pager impatiently, waiting for their response. Finally, a message popped back.

'I'll keep her in check—D.'

With that, Siljanna returned to her apartment. It was a waiting game now. The passage to Carlisse would take Dylan and Juliette at least four days and she had to wait for a confirmed location before the Imperator would let her pursue.

As Dylan closed his pager and dropped it on the table, he glared over at Juliette who'd flung herself on the bed, giggling. She slowly started to undress in front of him but her wiles failed to seduce him.

"Get dressed," he demanded. "We have to arrange passage across the Ensen Sea and get to Carlisse."

"It can wait an hour, maybe two," she replied seductively, letting her dress fall to the floor, revealing herself in just lacy underwear and high-heeled boots. As she approached him with the intent of wrapping herself around him, Dylan resisted, pushing her away.

"Do you ever take anything seriously? Is this all just a sick game to you?" He asked, his tone challenging.

"Everything is a game you idiot, and I intend to enjoy playing every minute. Now get your ass over here or I will make you regret it," Juliette threatened, using her body like a calling card.

Dylan stared at her, taking in the outline of her long legs and slender body, before meeting her eyes. They were cold and calculating and whatever heat her body exuded was extinguished by the look on her face. He recalled why they were even together, the series of events and regretful actions he'd taken that bound him to her, but her attitude angered him enough that for the first time, he didn't submit.

"I'd like to see you try," he replied, turning his back on her and walking out of the room. She shouted various profanities but he didn't care, he had a job to do and could distract himself with the task at hand.

Drew was up early and in the barn when Evie came down from the loft. She couldn't help but giggle when she saw him levitating carrots in front of each of the horses while filling up their water buckets. His dark brown hair was almost black and draped over his eyes while he worked. In comfortable-looking jeans and a scruffy shirt, Drew looked like he was ready to work the fields when he spotted her and the others, apart from Zack, who hadn't woken yet.

"Good morning everyone, I hope you slept well. Where's Zack, will he be joining you?" He asked.

"He's sleeping so heavily and being honest, he's done so much for us already, we couldn't ask him to come along again. He's got to be back at the Pilgrim tomorrow, otherwise he'll lose his job," Harrison said, clearly hesitant.

"I think you should wait for him. I got the distinct impression last night he wants to continue helping you," Drew suggested with a smile as he continued to torment the horses with the levitating carrots. He let them take the odd nibble and Cruise was whinnying softly, trying to consume the rest of the vegetable, his lips smacking the air every time he missed. Rylie couldn't help but look at the loveable, dopey horse and think of Zack. It was like they were kindred spirits.

"Drew's right, we should wait and ask him. If nothing else, we shouldn't leave without saying goodbye," she conceded.

The rest of them agreed and Evie was thrilled to have another few minutes that she could play with Jasper. She went outside the barn to find the dog and Alex quickly joined her.

"Budding romance there, or is it just me?" Lianna asked, linking her arm with Rylie, an exuberant chime to her tone. Rylie couldn't help but giggle, thinking of her conversation with Zack the night before. Lianna could pick up the subtlest of signs between Alex and

Evie and yet she couldn't or didn't believe the affection coming from Zack.

"Maybe!" Rylie replied fondly, grateful to see Evie happy again. She hadn't mentioned any bad nightmares, headaches or visions since the night they fled Tivani and it was so good to see her able to be like a normal teenager, even temporarily.

As she, Lianna and Harrison headed outside, the sun was still rising but they could tell it was going to be a dreary day. The clouds overhead were dark, heavy with rain that could fall at any minute. Rylie's abilities made the elements react to her but at times, she also felt like she was reacting to the elements.

It was strange to think that despite how little people knew about Encia, the one thing everyone knew was that unlike the sea and rivers, rainwater was harmless. It was rather easy to see Encia, especially in the dark as the essence was luminescent, but when the water evaporated, the Encia would remain in the ground, like salt, so rainwater was pure.

It was how the earliest known civilisations were able to survive, collecting rainwater for drinking until the Terran paragon, Lokhum and the team of engineers working with him created the Encia filters, allowing other water sources to be purified for consumption too. In general, water was calming to Rylie but somehow the impending rain combined with the chill in the air made her feel troubled. She glanced over and saw Harrison fixing his giant broadsword to his back and checking the knapsacks Lianna had prepared when all of a sudden they heard frantic steps from inside.

"Don't go! Wait for me!" Zack yelled, running through the barn doors, clattering into some buckets as he did, just about managing to jump instead of falling over them. He reached Harrison, Rylie and Lianna and doubled over breathing heavily.

"Good morning!" Rylie said with a grin.

"I thought… you'd left… without me," he panted. He hadn't run far so it was just the urgency that caused him to lose his breath.

"We weren't sure if we should ask you to carry on with us Zack," Harrison admitted, turning and walking towards him. He patted him firmly on the back but it was a friendly gesture. "You've already done so much for us, are you sure you want to come along to Carlisse too?"

"It could take us time to find someone who knew my grandfather, his journals or some other clue to his whereabouts. You said you only had a couple of days off and well, we didn't want you to get in trouble," Rylie added, a look of worry on her face but secretly hopeful he would continue with them.

There was something about having Zack along that gave her confidence. He'd travelled extensively and had many contacts in the kingdom so it was like literally having a guide for a friend, one that also knew and supported them despite the ongoing mage hunts. He stopped panting, looked up and smiled.

"I'm coming," Zack replied with conviction.

"We don't know what we'll face in Carlisse. It could be dangerous," Harrison added.

"Are you kidding, I laugh in the face of danger," he teased, striking a strong pose, flexing his biceps and faking a bold laugh.

"Sure you do!" Harrison mocked.

"Okay, so maybe I don't, but you've all become my friends and I want to make sure you find a safe place. You don't mind me tagging along, do you?" He asked curiously.

"Of course not!" Rylie replied instantly. She walked over to hug him and even Lianna smiled gratefully.

"Come on, let's get Evie and Alex. Drew said it was better to get into the kingdom early while there aren't as many guards doing the rounds," Harrison reminded as Lianna and Rylie headed off to get their siblings.

Once together again, Drew led them down a set of rickety wooden stairs to a padlocked door which he opened with a heavy brass key.

"Follow this path to get underneath the city walls. It'll take you a few hours but it's worth it to avoid the guards. Carlisse is a rather medieval town compared to what you may have seen or heard about Siranor but their defences are still impressive," he warned. "Try not to draw attention to yourselves or confront the guards unless you have to."

"We won't, not unless we absolutely have to. How will we contact your daughter when we get there?" Harrison asked.

"Once you reach the end of the path, you will see a trap door above you. It opens into the baker's storage shed on the western edge of town. Head out a few at a time, a big group coming out of that small store will look suspicious," Drew instructed and Harrison nodded, paying close attention to every word. "Opposite the baker is a laundry house. Ask inside for Caitlin and say that we sent you. One of the ladies should fetch her."

"Thank you Drew, and please thank Elissa for us too," Lianna expressed, not accustomed to this much generosity.

"We'll add you to the list of people that we have no way of truly repaying," Rylie added.

"It's been our pleasure to help. Oh and one last thing; when you meet Caitlin, tell her you came via the bakery. She'll understand that means you're mages," Drew said with a smile. "Now get going. I won't say goodbye, just see you soon. You are all welcome back here any time."

The underground passageway was dimly lit but there were signs it had once been regularly used. Thick spider webs decorated the ceiling and a layer of dust could be seen on the crates, but the floor itself had signs of footprints. As they walked through the tunnel, Rylie increased her pace until she was walking alongside Harrison, nudging him to get his attention.

"Is it just me or does this tunnel remind you of the halls in the academy?" She asked humorously.

"I was literally just thinking that!" He replied. It made Rylie smile as they recalled their shared memories of the academy.

"If Tutor Anderson is standing around the next corner though, we've taken a wrong turn somewhere," Harrison joked making Rylie laugh again, and the sound warmed his heart. He reached out and took her hand and just like before any of this happened, she let him, squeezing back affectionately.

"A lot has changed since our days at the academy, huh?" Rylie asked, but it was more of a statement than a question.

"Yeah, but one thing that will never change; is us," Harrison replied, making Rylie turn to face him, her expression filled with gratitude but also sorrow.

"I never said it before, but I'm really sorry how things turned out with Siljanna. You've already lost so much and now, you've lost her too; because of me," she apologised.

"It's not your fault," he replied, surprised at how the conversation turned. "I don't blame you for any of this."

"I couldn't do this without you, Harrison. You've been by my side through everything and your support means so much to me," she admitted, holding his hand just a little tighter. When she released his hand, he put an arm around her, pulling her sideways into him so that he could kiss her forehead.

"I wouldn't be anywhere else," he promised and she relaxed her head into his shoulder.

Seeing and feeling the connection between them, Lianna pulled back until she was next to Evie, tapping her on the shoulder and speaking in a hushed voice.

"Are those two—?" Her question was implied.

"Sadly, not!" Evie groaned in a quietly frustrated tone.

"Why? I can feel such a sense of love between them," Lianna questioned, looking shocked.

"Because my sister is oblivious and Harrison claims he doesn't want to put any more pressure on her, but I think he's scared about ruining their friendship," Evie replied, sharing her suspicions.

"It's funny, I can usually feel the difference between a loving friendship and friends in love but the sense I get from them is… fuzzy," Lianna explained. "Maybe it's because Rylie really can't tell he feels that way."

"If Rylie knew how he felt, I'm sure she'd feel the same. I had a vision not long ago and it was the first good vision I can remember. It was of them kissing!" Evie said, covering her mouth before her voice got too loud.

She glanced over to ensure Harrison and Rylie hadn't heard her, but Zack and Alex who weren't far behind, came up to join the conversation.

"Who's kissing who?" Zack asked in an over-emphasised whisper.

"And why are we whispering?" Alex added, matching Zack's curiosity and tone.

"We're talking about those two!" Lianna explained, slyly pointing at Harrison and Rylie.

"Oh you mean the fact he's clearly in love and she's totally clueless?" Zack asked and the wide-eyed looks from the others made him smile wryly.

"What?" He said, shrugging.

"How do you know that?" Evie asked.

"Well, Harrison is about as easy to read as the books in his knapsack; and Rylie, she just doesn't see his advances because they're such close friends," Zack replied. To him, the situation was obvious. He was mildly surprised this was the first time it'd been mentioned.

"I had no idea you were so observant," Lianna remarked.

"There's a lot about me you don't know my dear," Zack responded flirtatiously. Lianna grimaced, having no way of knowing just how truthful he was being at that moment.

"But does Rylie love him too? I can sense strong feelings between them, but I just can't tell if hers are love or just a deep friendship," Lianna asked, more invested than she initially realised. She'd only known these people for just over a day and yet already cared for all of them.

"I think so. The way she spoke about him to me on the Pilgrim, and the way they are together... all I can say is if I felt that way about someone, I'd speak up," Zack answered, looking at Lianna. "True love should not be kept in silence."

"But sometimes silence is a good thing," Lianna hastily retorted, breaking away and walking ahead of him. Evie and Alex laughed as Zack gave her a look of longing, even though she was barely six feet away. Still chuckling, Alex jogged a few paces to catch up with his sister.

"That guy just doesn't take a hint, huh sis?" He remarked.

"It's so tiring! Don't get me wrong, he's a nice guy and I'm so glad we found him but he clearly only wants one thing and well, I'm just not that kind of person," Lianna began, almost forgetting she was talking to her teenage brother.

"Yuck!" He exclaimed as she covered her mouth and giggled.

"My thoughts exactly!" She replied as they continued walking down the dim passageway.

When they finally reached the end of the passage, the area became so cramped that Harrison and Zack had to crouch. They found the trap door in the lowered ceiling and Harrison unlatched it, vaulting himself up and then aided the others to clamber through. Just as Drew said, they were in the baker's storage shed which was brimming with bags of flour, sugar and other ingredients. Looking out the window, they could see it was still morning and across the road, Harrison located the laundry house.

"Zack, have you been to Carlisse before?" Harrison asked.

"Once, but only for a couple of weeks," Zack replied. "I don't know the city inside out, but know my way around if that's what you mean."

"I propose that Lianna and I head into the laundry house and make contact with Caitlin, while the rest of you remain nearby," Harrison suggested to everyone's surprise. "Zack, is there somewhere nearby we can easily re-group if things go wrong? We may need to get back here in a hurry."

"If I recall, there's a small park just down the street. It wouldn't take more than a few minutes to get back here if we needed to," Zack confirmed.

"But why are you and Lianna going into the laundry house alone?" Alex questioned, looking at Harrison suspiciously. "I don't want to leave my sister."

"It'll only be for a short time, Alex. Two people walking into a laundry house doesn't look strange, but a group of six... that's not normal," Harrison explained, reassuring him. "Lianna, with your abilities, you might be able to tell if anyone in there is feeling on edge or lying to us, and if anything does go wrong, I can handle any guards they send and give you all time to escape."

"But why are we planning for things to go wrong? Drew wouldn't send us into a trap!" Evie asked, confused and slightly distressed by the plan for escape. "I thought the whole idea was to get into the castle, not run away."

"I'm sorry Evie, I didn't mean to frighten you," Harrison comforted. "I'm just preparing for the worst-case scenario. Hopefully, everything will be fine."

"Come on, let's go find that park," Rylie said, extending her hand to her sister and encouraging both her and Alex to follow.

Evie reluctantly nodded and the three of them left the storage shed first. Zack slipped out next, circling the bakery so it looked like he'd gone the other way, leaving Harrison and Lianna to exit last and head into the laundry house.

Chapter Fourteen
The Apprentice

As they walked inside the laundry house, Harrison and Lianna were both hit by the heat from the steam. Dozens of people were huddled over large wooden tubs filled with heated water, cleaning vast piles of linen and other clothing. They headed over to an older woman who looked like the supervisor and Lianna introduced herself.

"Excuse me? Hello, my name is Lianna. I'm looking for Caitlin Mason. We are family friends visiting for the week and her parents told us we could find her here," she said.

The woman studied Lianna and then shifted her gaze to Harrison, her eyes curious when she noticed his sword.

"What's the sword for?" She asked, her grungy hair tied back in a bun and her skin pink from the heat. Harrison stepped forward and politely shook her hand.

"I'm a travelling smithy. This sword is one of the better examples of the wares I craft. I was hoping to pop into the market after we see Caitlin," he explained. The lady took a moment to consider his response but eventually was satisfied.

"Caitlin is working full-time in the castle as the queen's chambermaid. It's not as easy as it used to be for her to step away but I'll send a message. Go conduct your business in the market and she'll find you there. She can't exactly miss that sword," the supervisor remarked, struggling to tear her eyes away from the bulky blade.

"Thank you, ma'am," Harrison replied before ushering Lianna back outside. The cool air was welcoming and Harrison couldn't imagine being stuck in that room all day, every day.

Heading to the park, they found Rylie and the others. After briefly updating them on what'd just happened, they perused the market in two groups, just to ensure they didn't raise any suspicion while they waited for Caitlin. An hour had passed when Harrison was tapped firmly on the shoulder.

"Excuse me, man with the big sword," said a friendly female voice. "Hello! I'm Caitlin Mason. I hear you've come to see me."

Harrison turned abruptly towards the voice. The sight before him was the spitting image of Elissa, only younger and with even more vibrant red hair. Her kind, curious smile, dimpled slender face and sea-green eyes made her look incredibly welcoming, just like Rylie. She was wearing a humble dress, not too dissimilar from Lianna's, but embroidered with the emblem of the kingdom, indicating she worked for the royal family.

"Hello!" Harrison stammered which made Caitlin laugh gently, her stance relaxed, with one foot turned in as she twisted on the spot. She leant forward playfully, pretending to examine Harrison.

"The message told me to look for a giant sword and ask for Lianna... but you don't look like a 'Lianna' to me," she said pleasantly. At that moment, Lianna moved next to Harrison and extended her hand.

"Hi, I'm Lianna and this is my friend Harrison. We stayed at your family's ranch last night and your parents asked if we could find you. They said it's been a while since you wrote to them, and I think they're getting concerned," she explained.

"Oh of course! They must be so worried. I've been so busy at the castle lately, spending all my time helping the queen. Thank you for reminding me, I'll make sure to write to them as soon as possible. Was there anything else?" Caitlin asked.

By this point, Harrison had regained his composure and also reached out to shake Caitlin's hand.

"Sorry, I'm not used to being caught off guard; and yes, we are hoping you might be able to help us," he began.

Realising they were chatting to Caitlin, the others joined Lianna and Harrison and introduced themselves too.

"It's good to meet you," Rylie greeted warmly

"My friends and I came here *via the bakery*," Zack added, pausing to make sure she picked up on the hidden meaning.

"It's always worth stopping in there. Jonah's pastries taste simply *magical*, don't they?" She replied with a wink. "But I digress, you said there might be a way I can help you?"

"We're looking for a man called Alistair Auren. He used to work at the castle archives a few years ago," Harrison advised.

"Hmm I don't remember anyone called Alistair but I'm terrible with names," Caitlin admitted.

"Can you help us get inside? Someone might remember him," Rylie asked.

"The best person to ask is my friend, Spencer. He's worked in the royal library for five years. The archives are in the same building so I'm sure he'll have worked with the guy you're looking for," Caitlin replied enthusiastically, her smile kind.

"That would be fantastic," Rylie exclaimed, looking towards Evie briefly before carrying on. "Our father's family were originally from Carlisse, and well, Alistair is our grandfather. We've travelled here to hopefully meet him and learn about our family history."

"I'm sure Spencer will be able to help you. There haven't been many different faces at the library in the last few years," Caitlin said cheerfully. "If you're ready, follow me. We can get into the castle through the servant's entrance, and I'll take you to the library on my rounds."

Making their way through the walled city, they couldn't help but take in its beauty. The limestone walls were high, at least twenty feet tall and reinforced by a dozen guard towers and fortifications. Caitlin picked up a heavy bag of laundry and lugged it over her shoulder, obviously making use of being summoned to the laundry house earlier. Harrison offered to take it but she told him not to worry, she was used to the weight.

Passing through a large wooden portcullis with metal spiked edges, the group looked up at the sweeping path that was dotted with trees to lay their eyes upon the royal castle, which was built on the summit of the hill. The resplendent building was literally shimmering in the sunlight. The royal wing was notably fancier, with intricate carvings adorning the exterior walls and every entrance guarded by warriors in colourful uniforms. On the other side of the castle were plainer buildings and as she led the group towards them, she pointed out the one on the very end.

"That's the royal library, it's a public building so we shouldn't get stopped by the guards on the way," she said confidently. "Spencer should be there for another hour at least. Oh and for those of you that are mages, don't worry about hiding your abilities from him. Like me, Spencer is a mage. A healer to be precise!"

Rylie, Evie and Lianna were all surprised at the open revelation but took the opportunity to tell her they were the mages in the group and what their abilities were, to the best of their knowledge at least.

"So the girls have all the power!" Caitlin added, her tone jovial. She noticed their concern that she wasn't even attempting to be subtle and tried to reassure them. "Sorry, I'm so used to being open about my abilities but it must come across strange to you."

"A little bit," Rylie admitted.

"Aren't you afraid of hunters or being forced into slavery?" Evie asked.

"I'm already an unpaid servant, what else can they do to me?" Caitlin replied flippantly.

"To be honest, it's refreshing to meet a mage that isn't afraid," Zack commented, and Rylie agreed. She'd love to not be afraid of her powers or be in their current predicament.

"I've always been rather forthright but Spencer was the one that helped me control my powers. He had a mentor for a couple of years and although I never met him, the lessons he gave Spencer have really helped us both. I also work directly for the queen, she is a friend and true mage sympathiser which helps," Caitlin explained.

"The queen is a mage sympathiser?" Harrison asked, genuinely surprised. He understood they were friends but just hadn't expected the queen to support all mages.

"Yes, but that's a long story for another time," Caitlin replied as they approached the servant's entrance.

As she opened the gate and ushered them through, they passed a beautiful garden with a traditional well in the centre and a variety of plants growing around the walls. Rylie looked around, taking in the beauty of the garden and recognised many of the plants and herbs from her medical training.

"This garden is incredible!" Rylie uttered, her tone astonished as she turned on the spot, looking all around her.

"It's one of my favourite places in the castle," Caitlin confirmed, dropping the bag of laundry she was carrying by a wooden side door. "And the best part... it has direct access to the library. Come on, we're nearly there."

She skipped past the group to the other side of the garden and opened another gate. There was a narrow staircase that led upwards and into the building. They reached the top of the stairs and Zack grabbed the door, holding it open for the rest of them. He bowed gracefully as Lianna passed, treating her as if she were royalty but all he received in return was a look of indignation.

Once inside, all they could see were vast bookshelves. They hugged every wall and each had sliding ladders to allow avid readers the chance to reach the top shelves. It dwarfed the library at the academy which until that point, Harrison had always thought was extensive. The windows were adorned with rich, forest-green drapes and pulled back with golden rope ties which made the whole room feel decadent. Beneath them, they could see a large oak table and seated at it was a man, reading sombrely. He was wearing a dark suit that matched his equally dark, roughly cut hair. With a spring in her step, Caitlin sped down the stairs to greet him.

"Hey Spencer, it's me!" She announced with a friendly wave. He looked up as she approached and gave her a faint smile but looked emotionally drained. "I've got some friends with me too. Come on, say hello everyone."

Encouraging Harrison and the others to follow her downstairs, they each greeted Spencer while Caitlin explained they were searching for someone he might know. She had to excuse herself before long, saying she had more chores to do before the queen returned to her chamber.

Spencer invited each of them to take a seat at the table and asked them who they were looking for. As they recounted their tale again, the details getting more concise each time, Rylie focused on their link to Alistair Auren. As soon as she admitted they were related, the look on Spencer's face changed, his dark green eyes sparkling with interest.

"You're Alistair Auren's grandchildren?" He asked.

"So, you do know our grandfather?" Rylie replied.

"He was my mentor. You see, I came to work at the castle because a friend of mine is in a horrendous situation. It was my desire to help her that triggered my abilities as a healer. My friend is still severely sick and I'm not strong enough to save her, but I can help ease her pain thanks to Alistair's teachings," he explained rather humbly. He seemed to hesitate every time he said the word '*friend*' as if he was hiding something.

"When did you meet him?" Rylie asked curiously.

"When I started working here. I confided in Alistair and he and his wife, Emilia helped me to enhance my powers. Sadly, they needed to flee before I could grow strong enough to save my friend," Spencer admitted.

"So our grandfather really is alive!" Evie exclaimed, her voice filled with hope.

"There is one other thing we don't understand though. Our father received letters saying they both died just after the war," Rylie said, trying to keep calm as she spoke. "Why did he lie and keep our family apart all this time?"

"Ah, of course, his 'great sin' as he called it," Spencer recalled and prepared to tell them what he knew. "After the war, things were bad for mages in Carlisse and Alistair went from being a scholar and royal advisor to a servant for the former king. They had an accord but Alistair felt it was best that his son stayed away, or risk being forced into servitude too. He felt guilty about it every day, but believed it was in his son's best interest to lie."

Spencer paused for a moment, noticing the look on both Rylie's and Evie's faces. Lianna hugged Evie while Harrison and Zack each comforted Rylie.

"What happened next?" Alex asked, sitting on the edge of his seat even though he knew Alistair had left and survived.

"Because she was Ar'encal, Emilia was mostly confined to her quarters but Alistair worked here and took me under his wing. He went out of his way to help me," Spencer continued, remembering his mentor fondly.

"So why did they leave Carlisse?" Rylie asked.

"When the former king died and his son, Grayson took the throne, they decided to flee. King Grayson is a cruel and malicious man, with one true desire; Possession. If it isn't his by birth right, Grayson Brock intends to claim and exploit whatever he believes should be his," Spencer explained.

"That's awful!" Lianna gasped, sensing the underlying hatred Spencer held towards the king, but knowing instantly that it was justified. Although it was clear Spencer loathed the king; his expression was filled with sorrow.

"Your grandfather knew the mages would be slaves under his rule so he arranged for as many as he could to flee. They planned to use an explosion as a diversion but something went wrong and not everyone made it out," Spencer continued his tone grave. "That's when Emilia died."

"But if they offered you a chance to escape, why are you still here?" Zack asked confused.

"I couldn't leave my friend! She is bound to this castle and for as long as she is here, I have to stay by her side," Spencer answered without any doubt or hesitation.

"Wow, such an honest response," Lianna whispered, almost swooning. "You'd live a life of servitude to a tyrant, just to help your friend?"

"Absolutely! For as long as she needs me, I will stay by her side. No matter the risk to my own life," Spencer replied, his faint smile returning.

"How incredibly brave!" Lianna mused, edging closer to him.

"Or stupid!" Zack muttered under his breath, leaning towards Harrison and Alex. Hearing Spencer's story made Harrison glance over at Rylie and she met his eyes gratefully. They both knew they'd done the same for each other.

"Spencer, do you have any idea where our grandfather might've gone?" Rylie asked. "We've spoken to Caitlin's parents and although they aided him, he never told them where he was planning to go."

"Sadly I don't, but knowing I'd never leave the castle without my friend, he gave me all of his old journals. Would you like to read them?" He asked and the resounding '*yes*' from everyone in the room told him to retrieve the books quickly.

He returned with a trolley filled with at least thirty leather-bound journals, some slender while others were thick.

"Wow, that is a lot of reading!" Zack said, whistling at the sizeable stack.

"Here you go, all of Alistair Auren's journals. I've read through most of them over the years and they've taught me a lot; your grandfather had incredible insight into the world of magic and Ar'encal lore," Spencer explained. "I hope they help you too."

"It's going to take us a while to get through all of that," Rylie announced, supporting Zack's initial reaction.

"We better get to work!" Harrison remarked, thankful he was a quick reader.

"I'll help," Spencer offered. "I can't recall a specific place but I might be able to help narrow down the search."

Hours passed by as the group read through the pages of Alistair's journals. Rylie and Evie kept sharing things they found that mentioned their father or told them more about their grandfather, who seemed to be a good man. They also found insightful entries that related to all of their powers and Harrison found pages dedicated to the pact he'd made with the former king. He'd had the best of intentions at the time, but sadly his actions put the mages on the path of enslavement they now faced. Another hour passed and the group knew they couldn't stay much longer.

"Spencer, thank you so much for all your help today, we really appreciate it. Can we return tomorrow and continue reading?" Rylie asked.

Just as she spoke, Caitlin came charging back through the library doors. Her naturally happy nature was stripped away by pure panic.

"Spencer, you have to come right now! It's Nadia," she cried, her voice rasping. Immediately, Spencer dropped everything and rushed out the door.

They'd spent almost all day with him and he'd never mentioned his friend's name but they all safely assumed that Nadia was the reason he wouldn't leave the castle.

As they watched him leave, Caitlin pressed her back against the wall and sank to the floor, staring up at the ceiling. After a moment, she looked back at the group.

"I'm sorry about that, I know you needed him but the queen's in terrible shape. She needs Spencer's healing," Caitlin explained, a tear rolling down her cheek.

"The queen?" The entire group gasped in tandem.

"Spencer's friend, the one he stays to protect is the queen?" Lianna asked as she and all the others put the pieces together.

"She's the reason we both stay. Nadia is our dearest friend and being married to that tyrant bastard is far from the princess stories you hear in fairy tales," Caitlin replied, her tone changing from despair to anger.

"I've had my fair share of dealing with cruelty from a person that is supposed to love you," Harrison sympathised, referring to his father. "Is there anything we can do to help?"

"I wish there was," Caitlin replied. She noticed the setting sun outside and it seemed to make her beat herself up even more. "She was with the king for four hours today. I can't believe I left her alone with him for all that time!"

"What does he do to her?" Evie asked sincerely.

"It's not my story to tell," she said, returning to her feet. "I presume you all need a place to stay for the evening? Wait here and I will ask the queen for a royal invitation that will allow you to stay in the guest rooms."

"Thank you, Caitlin, but if the queen's unwell—," Rylie began but Zack cut her off.

"That would be wonderful," he thanked and then whispered to Rylie they should just be grateful for the gesture.

When Caitlin returned, they noticed bloodstains on her dress, but no-one probed her for details.

"Follow me. The queen has granted three guest rooms for you to share for the night. I'll take you there," Caitlin offered, forcing a smile as some guards patrolled the hall outside. They all stood motionless until the guards continued down the hall.

"Thank you," Harrison said, breathing a sigh of relief.

"Before you go, the queen has asked to meet you all. She is in no state for visitors tonight and will likely still need Spencer tomorrow, but please make the time to meet her. You can leave the journals in Spencer's office and return here after the meeting, if that's okay," Caitlin asked.

"Of course, no problem at all," Lianna replied, "we'd be honoured to meet the queen."

Caitlin helped them gather up the journals and hide them in Spencer's office before leading them to the guest rooms. Harrison and Zack shared a room so that Rylie and Lianna could share with their siblings.

"I'll see you all in the morning," Caitlin announced, and they all said goodnight as she speedily walked back, presumably in the direction of the queen's room.

Harrison and Zack headed into their room and as soon as he spotted the comfy mattress and plush pillows, Zack crashed down onto the bed, kicking off his boots. He crossed his arms behind his head and rested into the soft supporting structure. Harrison laughed as he sat on the neighbouring bed and also removed his boots. He was tired but more so than anything, wanted a shower.

As he rubbed his neck and felt the grime, he submitted and headed into the small bathroom. To his disappointment, the technology in Carlisse was rudimentary, even compared to Tivani so although there was a shower, it was a manually filled tank and the water was released using a pulley. It wasn't ideal but he wasn't about to complain. After a brief, cold shower, he returned to the bedroom to rest. Zack was still flopped on the bed, looking as though he'd fallen asleep.

"Are you ever going to tell her?" Zack asked, his eyes closed but tone friendly.

"Hey, I didn't think you were awake; tell who, what exactly?" Harrison replied.

"Rylie, obviously! And how you feel?" He clarified, assuming that had been apparent. Harrison groaned, rolling his eyes as he laid back on the bed, staring dutifully at the ceiling.

"Did Evie tell you?" Harrison asked.

"She didn't need to. Noticing things like that is sort of my speciality. Used to drive my father crazy," Zack replied with a chuckle.

"You don't speak about your family much. Or why you left your home. Feel like indulging me?" Harrison hinted, trying to change the subject.

"Nope, pick another subject," Zack said in a humorous but finite way.

"Well, now I'm even more curious. Come on, just tell me why you won't talk about it and I'll leave it alone," Harrison pried, hoping that Zack would take the bait.

Sitting up and taking off his jacket, Zack pulled down his shirt. Harrison rolled over on the bed and frowned, curiously.

"You see this?" Zack enquired, pointing to the tattoo on his collar bone. It was a symbol like nothing Harrison had ever seen.

"What is it?" He asked.

"It's more than just a tattoo. It's a rune, and it literally prevents me from talking about where I come from, unless the person I'm speaking to already knows of it," Zack answered.

"Oh, I just figured you had a bad relationship with your family," Harrison admitted, surprised by the revelation.

"Well, that's true too," Zack replied with a laugh. "One day, hopefully, I'll get to tell you all about my screwed-up life."

"We can compare notes, I reckon I'll give you a run for your money!" Harrison joked and at that moment, chatting with Zack reminded him of Morgan again. As much as he missed his friend dearly, he enjoyed the familiarity and was glad to have befriended Zack.

"But anyway, you may be an elite fighter but you can't dodge my question forever. When are you going to tell Rylie how you feel?" Zack asked again, more insistently.

"It was brought to my attention that I can't dodge for shit," Harrison replied with a smile, rolling onto his back again. "I just don't know how to say it, and even if I did, now isn't exactly the right time. I'd want the moment to be special."

"Now that I get. Well, the wanting it to be special part. Being open with feelings comes easy to me, but waiting for the right moment, I've learned that's important too. Just look at my failed attempts with Lianna," Zack confessed, mocking himself but revealing he really had low self-esteem.

"I was wondering if you knew how badly you tanked with her. I mean, even my friend Morgan would've done better!" Harrison teased, laughing internally at the memories.

"Do you think Lianna even likes me?" Zack asked, preparing himself not to like the answer.

"She likes you, you're just coming on too strong. Back off a bit and who knows. Ironically, it sounds like we need to take a page out of each other's books!" Harrison advised, making Zack laugh. "How about we focus on getting somewhere safe first, then, we can make further attempts at romance."

"No promises, but I'll try," Zack chimed with a wink. "She can't resist my charms forever, right?"

"I'm not even going to dignify that with a response," Harrison quipped.

"Night bud," Zack said, wriggling under the soft sheets until he was comfortable. "Better get some beauty sleep, we are meeting royalty in the morning!"

Chapter Fifteen
Sacrifices

Caitlin rapping on the door woke both Harrison and Zack, alerting them to the fact it was morning. They quickly dressed and met up with her and the rest of the group in the hall. Caitlin looked ragged but still managed to give them a hearty smile.

"Good morning everyone, ready to meet Queen Nadia?" She asked.

"A little nervous but yes, we're ready," Lianna said, looking at her dress which was so similar to Caitlin's uniform, she could've easily been mistaken for a servant. Rylie linked arms with Lianna and gave her a smile, reading her concern as if she were the empath.

"Don't worry, this isn't a formal audience. When Spencer and I told Nadia about you, she wanted to meet you, as a show of support. Come on, this way," Caitlin replied.

Heading down the hallway, the decor became more opulent as they neared the queen's chamber. Once at her door, Caitlin led them inside and they were all surprised to see Spencer asleep on the couch in the front room. His dark hair was dishevelled and his black suit, the same one he wore yesterday, was untucked and spattered with dry blood. He sat bolt upright as they entered as if preparing to explain his presence but calmed once he realised who it was.

"Sorry, did we startle you, Spencer?" Caitlin asked innocently. Lianna took one glance at him and felt his exhaustion. It was such a strong sensation that it turned her own legs to jelly.

She staggered a little and Spencer got up, catching and drawing her over to the couch to sit beside him.

"Are you okay?" He asked.

"I should be asking you that question. You feel exhausted. I don't think I've ever sensed anyone so drained before," she exclaimed, placing her hand gently on his thigh, as a sign of compassion.

"Of course, I almost forgot, you're an empath," he replied, shutting his eyes briefly and allowing her to comfort him. "I read about empaths in Alistair's journals. His wife Emilia had no limitations on her powers but had strong empathic tendencies too. Please, don't worry about me. Queen Nadia had a particularly bad visit with the king yesterday and it just took all my energy to heal her. I'll be fine."

"What happened?" Rylie asked, walking towards Spencer and Lianna, crouching next to them by the couch, equally concerned.

"That's a story better explained by me," said a voice from behind a veiled archway.

As Nadia came into view, they were all startled by her appearance. She was an icy beauty with tender features and pale blonde hair, which was tied up loosely in a clip. Her fair skin and blue eyes were somehow dull and emphasised she'd recently been unwell. Her satin robes draped across her shoulders all the way to the floor so they couldn't see her feet.

"Your majesty," Harrison greeted, giving a courtly bow that Zack and Alex copied while Evie attempted to curtsy.

"Oh please, there is no need for formality. I am a queen in title only, for I have no true power in or outside these walls. You may all call me Nadia," she replied, gracefully placing her hand on the wall.

At first, Harrison thought it was just an elegant gesture but then he realised she was using the wall to support herself. Caitlin rushed over and placed her arm around Nadia's waist so that the queen could use her body as a support instead.

"What happened to you both?" Lianna asked not meaning to sound blunt but feeling almost faint from the combination of both Spencer and Nadia's exhaustion coupled with Caitlin's worry. Nadia invited them all to come through to her bedchamber and take a seat. The bedroom was huge and filled with several chairs, a dressing table and couches but still not quite enough seats for everyone. Zack sat on the floor while Nadia rested on the edge of her bed; a grand four-poster with more satin drapes.

"I'm sure Caitlin or Spencer have already told you that my husband, King Grayson is not a kind man. He has done many abhorrent things, and the way he treats me is one of them. I had the displeasure of telling him yesterday that I am still without child," she explained, setting her shoulders back as she gripped the fabric on her bed as tightly as her weak fingers could.

"The king wants Nadia to produce an heir and often beats her when he discovers otherwise," Spencer added.

"He then insisted that we consummate repeatedly so that I will produce him with the child he demands," she continued, her words shocking the entire group, leaving them speechless.

"It was after Nadia returned from being with the king that Caitlin called me from the library. I've been here all night healing her," Spencer concluded, making Lianna turn towards him, her heart melting at his kindness.

"I don't understand, you're married, doesn't he love you?" Alex asked. Being a young man raised by his elder sister, although somewhat of a troublemaker, he had grown to respect women, and could never imagine being so cruel.

"Our marriage is a farce, my dear boy," Nadia said with a look of pure contempt as she thought of her husband. "He insisted that I was betrothed to him seven years ago, purely because he was attracted to me. My parents were relatively poor and accepted the offer, hoping it would lead to a better life for all of us. They had no way of knowing how wrong they'd be."

"Nadia tried to run and that was when I met her," Caitlin added with a gentle smile.

"She and her family offered me shelter at the Driftwood ranch for a few weeks but Grayson found and captured me, forcing me to return. We were wed early the following year and life has been a struggle ever since," Nadia added and then glanced over at Spencer.

"Nadia and I were friends growing up, so when Caitlin found and told me of her betrothal, I knew I had to do something," Spencer explained, mustering the strength to stand beside her. As he reached Nadia, she stroked the back of her hand down his cheek, resting it on his shoulder. "That was when Caitlin and I applied to work at the castle. We didn't want Nadia to face Grayson's evil alone."

"Before we were married, Grayson's cruelty was purely verbal but after his parents died and he took the throne, the surge of power encouraged him to take more liberties. He became aggressive, and that was when the beatings started," Nadia continued. "I fell into a vicious depression and one day decided I couldn't take it anymore. I drank Encia, determined to end my suffering."

"You drank Encia intentionally?" Lianna cried.

"So you're a mage?" Alex asked, innocently jumping to the most obvious conclusion.

"No, I'm not a mage," Nadia replied.

"Then how are you still alive?" Rylie asked, covering her mouth afterwards, not meaning to speak so candidly to a queen.

"I have the withering," she explained. Her announcement made them all look at her a little more closely, and the signs were there. Dark circles stained her eyes, her fingertips were discoloured and the dullness to her eyes and skin made sense.

"When I realised what she'd done, my healing abilities triggered," Spencer announced, "and I've been healing her every day since, to keep the withering from claiming her life."

Hearing his words made Lianna shed a tear. She had never been so touched by a story in her life. Here was a man that had given up everything to support his friend, no matter the cost. His humble, caring nature was the single most attractive quality she'd ever seen in a person, although she was magnetised to his physical appearance as well. Lianna could tell underneath his suit was a slender but sturdy build. She ached to gently wipe the strands of dark hair away from his face, to provide him with the comfort and stability he deserved. Her reverie was cut short by Alex speaking up again.

"I don't mean to sound rude but, why?" He asked. "Why save her? She made the choice to end her suffering, who are you to decide that she must live this way?"

"It wasn't Spencer's fault," Nadia interjected. "You see, when Grayson discovered what I'd done, he captured my parents and threw them in the dungeon, threatening to kill them unless I produce him an heir."

"That's awful!" Evie exclaimed.

"I know my parents forced me to live this life, but I still love them and cannot leave them to suffer. I must produce Grayson with an heir. Once I do, he's promised to let my parents go," Nadia finished, her lip trembling as she spoke. "But my condition has caused... complications."

"No—" Lianna whispered, her tears gushing as she felt a great emptiness from Nadia. She rushed from the couch over to the queen and silently asked to place her hand on her belly, knowing where the tale was going. She turned to the group, saying what the queen could not.

"I don't understand," Alex whispered towards Evie.

"Stillborn," Lianna stuttered breathing heavily as Nadia closed her eyes, transferring her weight from Caitlin to Spencer, who held her with one hand while extending the other to Lianna in silent thanks.

"Every time Nadia is with child, it dies. I cannot say for certain, but I believe each baby suffers from the withering as she does, but cannot survive the affliction," Spencer explained, his breathing laboured and distraught as he confirmed the worst.

"The king is always so cruel when Nadia tells him she's lost a baby. And to top it all off, we suspect him of several other atrocities over the years too." Caitlin added.

"He regularly sleeps with other women, that's no secret," Spencer began and then paused, checking with Nadia if it was okay for him to continue. Nadia nodded so he finished. "We also believe he somehow arranged for his parents to be assassinated just so he could take the throne."

"You're serious? I don't think I could've ever imagined a person so heartless and cruel," Rylie replied, wiping away a tear. She almost felt bad crying, she hadn't lived through the torment.

Nadia took a deep breath and locked eyes with Spencer, clearly dependent on him for both physical and mental strength. He nodded towards her as she gathered herself and supported her own weight once more.

"It has been a bitter pill to take but although I wanted to meet you, and show what little support I can give, I also wanted to ask a favour of you," Nadia said, making each member of the group look to one another in wonder.

"We'll help if we can," Harrison replied.

"Caitlin and Spencer have told me of your quest to find Alistair Auren. I remember Alistair, not just from working in the library with Spencer, but before that, when he was a royal advisor. He had so much knowledge on magic and Encia," Nadia began, looking at each of them. "If you find him, will you tell him of my plight? If anyone will know of a cure for the withering, I truly believe it's him."

"Of course." It was Zack that spoke first but they all agreed. "No one should have to live as you are. If we find Alistair, we'll ask him if there is any way to cure you of this condition."

"That does require us to find him first," Alex interjected, sounding despondent.

"We will," Harrison declared with conviction. "There has to be a clue in his journals. Queen Nadia, is it all right for us to continue using the library and guest rooms until we find some kind of clue?"

"Yes, certainly, although you will need a cover story for the King's guard," Nadia explained. "I know it's an awful thought but the most effective option is to say you are mage hunters. All the guards know that Grayson wants to capture and enslave more mages, so if they think you are tracking them, you'll likely be left in peace."

"Then that's what we'll do, thank you," Zack replied and although the idea of posing as mage hunters was off-putting, keeping a low profile was vital at this point.

Five days passed and the group had spent countless hours rigorously combing through each page of Alistair's journals, looking for any clue to where he might've gone. In several journals, he mentioned the forests south of Lorvale and the town of Iliria, where he stayed during the years he was able to study the Ar'encal. It was also where he met his wife Emilia, the grandmother Rylie and Evie would never meet. Finally, while reading a passage about her, Rylie gasped as she found a mention of a place she'd never heard of before.

"Have any of you heard of a place called Arencia?" She asked, looking around the room.

"Are you sure it's a place?" Harrison questioned, standing behind her, looking over her shoulder at the journal page.

"I think so. He's referring to spending time with our grandmother and it being her *'true home'*. He also says how its location *'deceives unseeing eyes'*. I mean, it could be a house, but it definitely sounds more like a place," she responded.

"Hang on, *'deceives unseeing eyes,'* is that what you just said?" Alex asked. Rylie looked up and nodded, tilting her head curiously. "He uses the exact same phrase here but referring to illusion magic."

Alex turned the journal, tapping the passage he was reading so the others could see it too.

"That can't be a coincidence," Zack emphasised.

"Why don't we ask Caitlin?" Harrison suggested. "Didn't Drew say that she's an illusion mage?"

"I'll get her!" Alex called, keen to do anything other than continue reading.

"I'll go with you," Lianna offered. "We'll be right back."

After a few minutes, they returned with Caitlin shortly behind them. They asked her about illusion magic and if she could shed any light on the phrase.

"Well, the point of illusion magic is deception. I've not been properly trained but the images I produce are pretty convincing. They fade if I get too far away though or if someone touches the image but if the mage casting was powerful enough, the illusion could be a more stable deception," she explained.

"Do you think a whole place could be concealed?" Rylie asked, wondering if that could be why none of them had ever heard of Arencia before.

"Theoretically. Do you think that's how the Ar'encal have hidden for all this time?" Caitlin asked curiously.

"It could be. It could also be where our grandfather is," Rylie replied, anticipation building.

"But how will any of us see through such a powerful illusion?" Evie asked, stating the obvious issue they faced.

"Well, my dad always used to say that he struggled to see through my illusions at first, but then he found a trick," Caitlin advised, giggling as she remembered the times she'd been scolded for disobeying him. "He never told me what it was but sneaking out became much harder once he sussed it out!"

"I think the best thing we can do now is head back to the ranch and speak to Drew. He might be willing to share his secret with us, it's for a good cause after all!" Evie enthused.

"We can take some of the journals with us too, but if nothing else leaps out, after speaking with Drew, I suggest we head for Iliria. I know the town well and it seems to be the next best place to continue the search," Zack suggested, looking to each member of the group to make sure they agreed. Everyone seemed to nod except for Lianna.

"I can't leave," she said abruptly, drawing everyone's attention, especially her brother.

"What do you mean, you can't leave?" Alex asked, looking at her in disbelief.

"We can't stay here Lianna, it's not safe, and we've promised the queen. We are more help to her, Spencer and Caitlin by going," Zack added, also shocked by her announcement.

"You can go, but I can't. I won't leave them to face such cruelty alone," she argued, looking down at the ground but keeping her tone firm.

"Zack's right Lianna, we can help them more by finding Rylie's grandfather. Alistair might lead us to a cure for the withering, that's what Queen Nadia really needs," Harrison countered, trying to convince her.

"No, I'm staying. I can pose as another chambermaid—" Lianna began but Rylie cut her off.

"We can't just leave you and Alex here! You'll be in even greater danger than you were in Revaine," she exclaimed, desperate for Lianna to continue with them.

"I said no!" Lianna cried out, refusing to look at any of her companions. "I can't leave him."

"Him?" Zack and Rylie repeated in unison while the others were speechless. They all realised, although her intentions were pure, Spencer was the real reason she wanted to stay. She'd fallen for him and that realisation was crushing to Zack.

Looking towards their friend, knowing his feelings for Lianna were genuine, Harrison and Rylie felt such sympathy for Zack. But all he could do was stare; waiting to see if Lianna would look up at him, feel his heartache and know that deep down his feelings were true.

But she didn't. Alex marched over to his sister and shook her shoulders, forcing her to look at him.

"We can't stay here Lianna. I won't! We agreed that if we ever had the chance to go somewhere safe, we'd take it and stick together, no matter what. You promised—" he yelled, glaring at her as the argumentative words stuck in his throat.

"I'm sorry Alex, my mind's made up," she replied.

"Well, mine isn't! You can't make me stay here," Alex protested, throwing his arms wildly in the air.

"Alex please, I need to be here for Spencer. I can support him, care for him in a way no one else can," she begged.

Alex just turned away from her and folded his arms. He was leaving, no matter what she said. Suddenly Caitlin approached Lianna and gripped her arm.

"Come with me," she insisted. "The rest of you, please gather your things. We'll meet you by the servant's entrance shortly."

As Caitlin dragged Lianna up the stairs and out of the library, they wound up back in the garden. Her grip on Lianna's arm was vice-like as she forced her to sit down on one of the benches by the well. Pacing before her for a moment, Caitlin finally turned and spoke.

"You don't love him," she announced with conviction. "You may think you do, but you don't. Your abilities are making you confuse empathy with true emotion."

"You're wrong!" Lianna interjected stubbornly.

"I'm not. For years, I told myself I was in love... with Nadia, but that wasn't true either," Caitlin shouted back.

"I know empathy. I *am* empathy! The way I feel about Spencer is more than that. Maybe what you felt for Nadia was real too. If you gave up, you never knew for sure," Lianna argued, yearning for Caitlin to believe her.

"He loves her... Spencer loves Nadia!" Caitlin blurted out, stopping Lianna in her tracks. "He'll never love you because he always has and always will love her."

"That can't be! He called her a '*friend*'. Why would he say that if he loves her?" Lianna protested, desperation filling her voice.

"Because they are doomed to love but never have each other. They desperately try to convince themselves they are only friends. That's the saddest part!" Caitlin admitted but realised it wasn't going to be enough to convince Lianna.

"No, it can't be true," she wailed. "You're wrong."

"He's loved her since they were children, Lianna. Her feelings came later, but it's been years for her too. Spencer knows that if he ever acted upon his feelings, the king would kill him; and that would ensure Nadia's death," Caitlin explained, knowing that her words would break Lianna's heart.

"But why? Maybe in time, he'll see—," Lianna whimpered, trying to give herself hope.

"Lianna, please don't," Caitlin begged. "Their relationship won't break. Every day, Nadia pays for trying to take her own life, and every day Spencer tries to heal her suffering. I know he prays that somehow, someday she will be free from the king's clutches, that is why he endures. He's waiting, hoping that in the future, they can be together."

Lianna released some ragged breaths, trying to keep herself from crying as Caitlin held her hand, squeezing affectionately.

"I've always dreamt of meeting someone like Spencer. Someone with a kind heart, who loves unconditionally. Of course, the one I fall for is already in love with another, typical!" She muttered, trying to laugh but failing to convince either herself or Caitlin that she found any of it funny.

"It sucks, right? I remember when I first met Nadia. Before she became queen. We spent weeks hiding from the royal guards around the ranch and I spent every single night dreaming of being with her," Caitlin said, softly smiling. "She means the world to me, but after I saw her with Spencer, I knew their connection was special. Although it took me a long time to admit it."

"Do I have to admit it?" Lianna asked.

"Not out loud, but let me save you the heartache of denial. Move on while you can, you'll be glad you did," Caitlin suggested, her voice turning from sympathetic to spirited as she attempted to cheer Lianna up. "At least you can blame your empathic abilities! Maybe what you felt was the love between them and it imprinted on you somehow."

"I wish that made me feel better," Lianna replied, now feeling stupid and heartbroken.

"But do you see why you should leave? By staying with your group, you could find what you truly deserve, a safe place to live and learn how to control your abilities. When you do, if you still love Spencer, you can come back and throw it in my face. Ideally with a cure for the withering too… okay?" Caitlin teased, finally getting Lianna to smile.

"I'll try," she replied and told herself that if she still felt strongly about Spencer after leaving, she would do exactly that.

After watching Caitlin drag Lianna out of the library, Alex stormed off in a huff towards the guest rooms to collect his things. Evie followed quickly behind, calling after him. They'd spent a fair amount of time together over the past few days and it was clear Evie was worried about him. Zack continued to stare at the spot where Lianna had been, the dismay on his face apparent.

"Are you okay?" Rylie asked, placing her hand on Zack's shoulder. He softly shook his head as he spoke.

"I thought it was because she didn't know me or didn't believe in love at first sight, but she's willing to risk it for him; for Spencer," he murmured, not looking at Rylie but allowing his hand to reach out and touch hers. "She doesn't know him either and yet, he's enough."

"Zack… I'm sure it's not that simple," Harrison consoled, unsure if there was anything he could say to support his friend.

"It's fine, he's a good man. She deserves a good man. I guess it's better I found out now, right? Better than getting my hopes up any higher," he replied, sounding dejected.

"You're a good man too, Zack. Just because it didn't work out with Lianna, doesn't mean you won't find the person that's right for you. Don't give up," Rylie encouraged, her words making Zack look away from where Lianna had stood towards his friends.

"Thank you, both of you. Now let's grab our things and get back to the ranch. We can re-supply and head onward to Iliria tomorrow, while still searching for that other place, Ancreia," he began.

"Arencia," Rylie said correcting him with a chuckle.

"Yeah, that place," he agreed, forcing a smile.

They joined Alex and Evie in the guest rooms and just overheard him saying he was packing Lianna's bag and would drag her with them if he had to. When he spotted Zack and the others, Alex stopped protesting but smiled after Harrison gave him a reassuring look, as if to say he agreed with his idea. Once they'd collected their things, they made their way towards the servant's entrance and as promised, Caitlin and Lianna were there. Rylie walked over to Lianna hastily and placed her hands on the other girl's shoulders.

"Please tell me you've changed your mind?" She asked.

"I have. Caitlin helped me realise you are all right, I should go. The best thing we can do is help find a cure for the withering," Lianna replied.

Rylie hugged her friend but was quickly barged out of the way by Alex, who came rushing over to his sister, his relief at knowing she was remaining with them palpable.

"Don't you dare think about leaving me again, you hear? I won't be so forgiving next time!" He grumbled, trying to sound threatening but was clearly just relieved.

"I promise Alex, and I'm sorry," she apologised, wrapping both of her arms around her brother. Seeing the love between them, Rylie hugged Evie and gave her nose a quick pinch as she always did.

"What was that for?" She moaned, rubbing her nose gently but enjoying the embrace.

"I forget sometimes how important you are to me. You're not allowed to leave me either, got it?" Rylie insisted with an honest smile. Evie gleamed back at her sister, giving her a firm nod.

"Are you sure we can't persuade you to join us, Caitlin?" Lianna asked. "I understand Spencer can't leave, but you can."

"I'm okay, honestly. My place is here, but please give this letter to my parents, so they know I'm fine," she replied.

"You got it," Zack said, taking the letter and tucking it into his jacket pocket. He leaned in and gave Caitlin a hug. It was a little awkward but she accepted the gesture. "I know we've only known you guys for a few days, but I worked with your parents for a while beforehand. This letter will mean a lot to them."

"Thank you, and be safe, all of you," Caitlin instructed, opening the gate and letting them pass. She waved as they headed down the path back towards the walled city and the underground passage.

As they approached the inner gate and its imposing portcullis, Harrison abruptly stopped as he witnessed a shocking but familiar sight. A royal guard unit was acting as an escort to two people, dressed very differently from the guards. Although he only partially recognised the woman, he knew the man instantly. It was his former academy friend Dylan Rose, and Dylan recognised him in return.

"The fugitives!" Dylan shouted, pointing at them.

His companion laughed, a shrill, high-pitched noise that exuded excitement. She had no weapon but Dylan pulled out a dagger and all the guards were armed. Harrison drew his broadsword and urgently looked over at Zack.

"Go! Get them out of here!" He shouted, quickly returning his gaze to Dylan and the other guards.

The guards charged, most of them wielding pikes or other lengthy blades but Harrison was able to parry each strike. It had been over a year since he'd fought a real adversary but muscle memory kicked in and his body reacted exactly how he needed it to. Taking the opportunity, Zack hurried the others down a side street, forcing them to escape.

"Rylie, we have to go!" Zack shouted, pulling her arm ferociously as she resisted.

"We can't leave him!" She cried.

"He'll be okay... he can fight them off but not if he's worried about us," Zack insisted, pulling even harder.

She screamed, her hands erupting into flames but Zack didn't back away. He reached up with one hand, pressing against the mark on his neck as if he'd just been stung but continued to pull until she had no choice but to follow him.

Harrison continued parrying blows, ensuring to stand between the attacking guards and his friends until they were gone. The woman who Harrison was wracking his mind to recognise tried to rush past him in pursuit, but he blocked her path, knocking her to the floor.

"How dare you!" She hissed, scrambling backwards until she was behind Dylan again. Dylan just looked at her and rolled his eyes, grabbing her by the arm and dragging her out of the way.

Then looking down at the dagger in his hand and seeming to compare it to Harrison's broadsword, he swiftly decided he didn't have the right tools for this particular encounter. He gave a submissive smile at his old friend before retreating up the path to the castle. Dylan's companion glared at him, watching as he walked away and then looked back at the royal guards, screaming for them to attack, but they were too slow.

"My turn," Harrison growled through gritted teeth, exploding into battle.

Chapter Sixteen
Seeking an Illusion

Watching the conflict, Juliette was amazed at the ferocity of each blow from Harrison Stone. The royal guards that'd been escorting her and Dylan were well-armed and in a united formation, but he overwhelmed them with a single, spiralling blow. The motion knocked many of them to the ground, and the guards that remained on their feet were also defeated when they attempted to retaliate.

Harrison was cleaving his way through them when Juliette realised he was aiming for her. With no weapon apart from her satchel of poisons, she had little choice but to dash up the path and try to catch up with Dylan. She turned back to see more guards approach from behind and Harrison's attention was taken from pursuing her to defending against the new arrivals.

Finally catching up to Dylan, Juliette used all her body weight to push him into one of the cherry trees adorning the path.

"You bastard, you left me!" She shouted, aiming to slap him across the face. He grabbed her wrist mid-swing and held it tightly, so much so that it hurt. They'd always been rough with each other, but he'd never been like this.

"Don't you dare," he snarled.

"Why did you leave? We could've taken him!" She snapped.

"No... we couldn't. We are inadequately armed and unprepared. You don't know Harrison Stone as I do. We trained together for three years and he was easily the most gifted swordsman I've ever seen.

The only person more threatening was and probably still is his sister," Dylan replied. He felt her still trying to strike him, so increased his grip around her wrist.

"You're hurting me," she protested in a firm but quiet voice. She tried to pull her arm free but involuntarily began shaking before he finally released her.

"Stop trying to hit me," he insisted firmly, knowing her intention was to retaliate as soon as he let go.

She stepped back, quickly glancing to make sure Harrison hadn't pursued them before looking back at Dylan.

"You've changed Dylan. Your desire for me was insatiable once, but now all you do is treat me with contempt," she accused, her tone cold.

"Perhaps I've learnt over these past few days who you truly are Juliette," he said bluntly, pushing himself away from the tree.

"What's that supposed to mean?" She replied, her brow furrowed into a furious scowl.

"You're tactless, impulsive and although effective with your poisons, in an actual battle, you're nothing more than a liability," he growled, each word cutting like a knife.

"How dare you? You might be a better fighter but if I wanted to, I could take you down and you'd never see it coming," she threatened, her tone acidic. Dylan turned sharply and thrust himself menacingly into her face.

"Do it then," he challenged. "Better to be dead than bound to you."

In that moment, while his eyes were locked on hers, she kissed him, secretly reaching into her pouch. As he pushed her away, Juliette uncapped the vial and launched it towards him. Raising an arm to protect his face and swerving, so only a few droplets of the substance hit him, he noticed his leather bracer beginning to dissolve. He ripped it off and threw it to the ground between them in disbelief.

"That was just a warning," she spat.

"Forget it. You've turned me into a person I don't even like Juliette, and I refuse to continue this way. You're on your own now. Good luck completing this mission without me," he declared, abandoning her and the last few years of his life.

"You can't just leave!" She shouted.

"Watch me," Dylan replied, marching out of sight.

Juliette screamed and found herself praying that Harrison was still there and might attack Dylan on sight. After watching him go, Juliette stomped into the castle grounds. More guards were there and opened the gate as she used the long-range radio to contact Siljanna.

"Status report," she said by way of greeting.

"Dylan is a deserter. We came across the fugitives in Carlisse and without cause, he left. We could've captured them here and now but instead they escaped," she wailed.

Siljanna was clearly about to reply, matching Juliette's frustration when there was a shuffling and Cameron became the dominant voice on the other end.

"That is disappointing," he commented calmly, and there was a long pause before he spoke again. All Juliette could hear in the background was Siljanna throwing out profanities. "I will issue a warrant for Dylan's arrest but in the meantime Juliette, your mission remains. You've positively identified the fugitives so meet with King Grayson and establish a foothold for us in Carlisse. Once you are confident we can encroach the city without raising suspicion, the Imperator and I will make our way to the Eastern Continent with Siljanna and the remaining prisoners."

"Fine," Juliette replied, killing the radio.

She waited for a few minutes in a grand courtyard until King Grayson followed by his entourage descended the stairs from the keep.

"Good day, Juliette Lawrence I presume?" He greeted, sauntering towards her and extending his hand.

She looked at him to assess his demeanour and could immediately tell he was full of himself. His exuberant ruby red garb was adorned with gold and large jewels, his appearance screaming *entitled*. His baldness made the crown placed upon his head stand out but his other features were rather unimpressive.

"Your majesty, it's an honour," she purred, bowing deeply to ensure her cleavage was fully exposed. His eyes were drawn straight to her bosom and she knew he was the type of man she could control without even having to try.

"I heard there were two of you coming, should I expect further company as appealing as you?" King Grayson asked.

"It is just I... my associate has abandoned our pursuit," Juliette explained.

"No matter, I just wish the Imperator's advisor had mentioned the aid he was sending was such a ravishing beauty," King Grayson replied, eyeing her every curve, each one flaunted by her tight-fitting dress. Juliette took the opportunity to giggle playfully, taking the king's hand.

"His majesty is a flatterer," she answered, batting her eyelashes and intentionally dropping her satchel. "Oops, clumsy me!"

She bent over from the waist so that the king was confronted with another provocative view as she collected the bag. She made sure to linger before facing him again.

"I believe we are going to get along, Miss Lawrence. Please, come with me, I will show you to your quarters while you remain in my kingdom," he asserted, leading her into the castle.

Zack slammed the door at the end of the underground passage behind him and forced Rylie and the others into the barn. Rylie was still protesting, wanting to go back for Harrison, her skin blistering hot as fire danced around her hands.

"Rylie, you have to calm down. Harrison can handle himself with those goons," Zack insisted, trying to stop her from fretting but she was hysterical.

"We have to go back for him, please!" She cried.

Hearing the disturbance, Drew and Elissa came rushing in from the fields and noticed Rylie's condition immediately.

"What happened?" Elissa asked, desperately flicking her glance between them until she noticed Harrison wasn't there.

"The hunters chasing Rylie and Harrison caught up with us in Carlisse. We had to run but Harrison stayed behind, giving us a chance to escape," Zack explained, his gaze still fixed on Rylie.

"He'll be okay Rylie, I just know it!" Alex assured, absolutely certain of Harrison's abilities although he'd never seen him in action before.

"I'm sorry, my mind is all over the place. Please stay away from me, I don't want to accidentally hurt any of you," she replied, striding away and making them all hesitate. It was Lianna that approached Rylie in the end but didn't touch her.

"You won't Rylie. How about we try and get some rest?" she suggested as it began raining outside.

"I'll head back to the passage and keep an eye out for Harrison," Drew offered, and Elissa quickly joined him. "You kids get some rest."

Time passed but Rylie felt every minute like a strain on her heart. She'd collapsed onto the floor next to a stack of hay bales, the literal fire diminishing but she still didn't want any of her friends or Evie to come too close. Only Jasper dared trot over and after sniffing her shoes, curled up next to her legs and rested his head on Rylie's lap. Looking up at her with wide, sympathetic eyes, Jasper's affection provided a comforting distraction. As she stroked him absent-mindedly, Jasper yawned, enjoying the repetitive massage. When Zack believed Rylie had calmed down, he edged over, crouching beside her.

"He's coming back Rylie," he told her confidently.

Rylie nodded but kept her eyes closed. Then Zack glanced over at Evie and saw her squeezing her eyes tightly shut while Alex had a friendly hand on her shoulder.

"What's the matter, Evie?" Alex asked.

"I want to have a vision. These things have plagued me for most of my life but the minute I want one, I can't see anything but the backs of my eyelids!" She declared, clearly frustrated.

"It doesn't work like that," Lianna said, trying desperately to sound kind but her words came out irritable, picking up Evie's energy. "I can't force myself when to feel or not feel the emotions of the people around me."

Breathing through the bombardment of feelings running through her mind, Lianna turned her back on Evie.

"That's not fair Lianna, you're presuming that just because you can't do more, that Evie can't. She's not hurting anyone by trying," Zack replied harshly, taking everyone by surprise.

"I'm sorry, I didn't think," Lianna stuttered, his tone making her feel anxious.

"No, you didn't," Zack replied, cutting her off but then stopped himself, hearing how mean he sounded and sighed. "I'm sorry, that was unjust. We are all worried so please, just let Evie try."

The group fell into silence and continued to wait, to hope. They could hear the rain as it spattered on the gambrel roof above them and dripped onto the ground outside, forming puddles by the door and on the path leading up to the ranch house. It was difficult to tell how long they'd waited as the rain clouds made the sky darker than it should be. There was no clock in the barn either, but none of them were willing to leave, wanting to be as close to the passage door as they could.

A while later, they saw the door to the passageway push open and Elissa stepped out. Rylie was straight on her feet, to Jasper's disappointment, and hung onto the edge of the barn door, waiting to see who came out next. It was Drew but he wasn't alone. There was an arm slung over his shoulder and as he hauled the person out into view, Rylie found herself hurtling towards them. She didn't even think, she just moved.

The rain seeped into her clothes, soaking her but she didn't care. It was Harrison. When she reached him, she flung her arms around him, embracing as tightly as she could. He staggered backwards as she collided into him but once he'd secured his footing, wrapped his arms around her, matching her embrace.

"You're okay!" She exclaimed, breathing a heavy sigh of relief. As she did, the rain seemed to ease. He held her until her grip loosened and she stepped back, wiping tears from her eyes.

"I'm okay," he confirmed.

"Don't ever do that to me again!" She demanded, a smile breaking through as she scolded him. He laughed, but the reaction made him wince.

"Don't make me laugh," he pleaded, reaching for his side.

"You're hurt?" Rylie asked, worry overpowering her thoughts once again.

"What, this? It's nothing. One of the guards got in a good jab but I'll be fine," he countered, placing one hand on his sternum and offering the other to Rylie who took it without hesitation.

When Harrison looked up towards the barn, he could see the others gathered in the doorway and with Rylie in tow, dripping from head to toe, he headed towards them. As soon he was inside, Evie wrapped her arms around him, giving him a big cuddle. Lianna and Alex were next, and finally, Zack came forward, his confidence rewarded. He intended to shake Harrison's hand but ended up hugging him too.

Altogether, they headed into the ranch house and Harrison allowed Rylie to tend to his wound. As they all sat around the large table that they'd shared dinner on less than a week ago, Zack reached into his pocket, pulled out Caitlin's letter and gave it to Elissa. She held it close to her heart, thanking him as Drew bought in a tray of drinks and towels for them to dry off with.

"What happened with the guards, how did you escape?" Zack asked as Harrison placed his shirt and armour back on.

"The guards were poorly trained but numerous. I could subdue them but after two patrols attacked, I had to slip out of sight," Harrison explained.

"What about that strange-looking pair?" Alex added.

"One of them was a warden, Dylan Rose. Do you remember him, Rylie?" Harrison asked.

"Of course! I barely recognised him," she admitted. "Did he fight you?"

"No, in fact, he seemed to turn his back on his partner and leave the city," Harrison advised, recalling how frustrated his former friend looked as he departed. "I don't believe he's a threat to us anymore."

"What about the girl?" Zack probed, worried about the abandoned partner.

"Another former acquaintance. Sadly one I'm not so keen on. Her name is Juliette Lawrence," Harrison confirmed, having recalled who she was on the walk back through the underground passage.

"Juliette, from my med class?" Rylie questioned.

"Yes, although she disappeared from the course and is apparently now a warden. I can't even imagine how," Harrison said, pressing his fingers into his forehead, trying to comprehend how and why she would be working with Dylan. "She made it to the castle though, so we can't risk returning. The king will certainly be aware of us by now."

"Great," Zack muttered sarcastically. That meant the royal guards would be looking for them, as well as Siljanna, Juliette and any other hunters from Siranor.

"I made sure to take several diversions before entering the passageway. No one followed me," Harrison advised but was clearly still concerned.

"So the low-profile thing didn't exactly go to plan," Drew teased, trying to make light of the situation. Alex chuckled but quickly muffled his reaction when no one else laughed.

"No, but we have a new goal, finding Arencia. With any luck, we'll find Rylie's grandfather and it'll be a safe place where the girls can learn to control their abilities," Harrison replied, bringing their focus back to the task at hand.

"Arencia? I've never heard of a place called Arencia before," Elissa admitted curiously.

"That's the thing; we have reason to believe it's a sanctuary for mages, but it's concealed from the outside world by an illusion of some kind," Rylie explained.

"Drew, when we told Caitlin about this, she mentioned that you'd learnt how to see through her illusions. Can you tell us how? The magic protecting this place is probably going to be incredibly strong but if we know what to look for, we've got a chance," Harrison added, and the entire group looked at Drew as he considered how to respond.

"The best way I can describe it is that the area around the illusion seems to shimmer. Like the edges are fluid somehow. The centre of the illusion is always strong and difficult to see through, but it was the little details around the edge, where it met reality that would give it away. I'm sorry, it's not much, but I hope that helps," he advised, looking to each of them before finally resting his gaze on Zack. "Do you have somewhere to start looking, are you going to continue guiding them?"

"I'm staying with them for now and if no one has any objections, I say we start in Iliria. I know the town well and it was mentioned in Alistair's journals a few times," Zack suggested.

While all the others nodded in agreement, Rylie's mind was stuck on how Zack had said '*for now*'. The prospect of him leaving made her anxious, but then she told herself his aid was never meant to be permanent and other mages might need him more than them.

"Rest here for the night," Elissa offered, taking away their empty cups and wet towels. "You can depart fresh in the morning. It's a long journey to Iliria, but we can lend you some of the horses as far as Lorvale. We have contacts there that can return them and it'll shave a day off your travels."

"Thank you," Zack replied, "for everything."

At first light, the group met in the stables. Zack was already tacking up Cruise, lovingly stroking him as he placed a rope bridle, riding sheet and leather saddle on his back. Rylie headed over to the next stall where a coloured horse, with blotches of black, brown and white fur was nibbling on some hay.

"What's this guy called?" She asked, walking over and stroking the horse, offering him a carrot she'd stashed in her pocket. The horse seemed extremely grateful that the vegetable didn't float away.

"That's Drew's horse, Paint," Zack replied.

"Imaginative!" Rylie giggled.

"His other horse, the palomino, it's called Goldie!" Zack chuckled.

"How original!" Rylie teased. "Well, hello Paint, I hope you don't mind giving us a lift to Lorvale," she said and the horse just continued munching, unfazed as she began tacking him up.

"Paint is a cool customer, just like Cruise," he advised, finishing up and moving over to another horse named Bandit. Rylie offered to help and they were almost done when Harrison and Alex entered the barn carrying their original knapsacks and saddlebags filled with extra supplies.

"This should be more than enough to keep us going. I'm hungry just thinking about chowing down on all this stuff," Alex admitted, smiling as Harrison playfully snatched the bag to make sure he didn't try and steal anything.

"Don't even think about it!" Harrison teased.

Once Lianna and Evie joined them, the group said their final goodbyes to Elissa and Drew and began their journey south, first to Lorvale and then onwards to Iliria.

Her view as the sun rose had not been what Juliette expected when she'd arrived in Carlisse the day before. Barely covered by the silk sheets around her and straddled over King Grayson's chest was much better than she'd even dared contemplate. The king had an enviable sexual appetite and having lost Dylan, she found his attention satisfying. It had taken very little to get him to act on her advances but she was surprised when he'd suggested playing with bindings. He hadn't intended to be the submissive but that was how the situation played out. As she sat over him, Juliette played with the restraints tying Grayson to the bedpost before standing up, letting the sheets fall to her feet as she walked away from him.

"Leaving so soon?" He asked unmoving but testing the strength of the restraints. "And here I thought you were enjoying my company."

"I do my lord, but there are other things I enjoy too," she mused seductively, reaching down to her satchel and walking over to a small dressing table on the far side of the room. There was a queen somewhere as indicated by the bottles of perfume on the table but Grayson obviously didn't care about monogamy.

"Show me," he requested, sitting up as much as he could, watching as she picked up one of the perfume bottles and tipped its contents onto the floor. "You know that stuff is worth a small fortune, right?"

"What I can make is worth even more," she replied, taking the empty bottle and a selection of vials from her satchel. Crouched at the bottom of the bed, with only a thin sheet obscuring her view, Juliette began mixing the solutions together. As she added the last ingredient, she quickly corked the bottle and the new liquid began to hiss.

"What is that?" King Grayson demanded, feeling more threatened than he had a second ago.

Juliette gave the bottle another gentle shake and watched for a second. The part of the bottle not filled with liquid quickly filled with a gas that had a slight green tint to it. With a sinister smile, Juliette stood up and stepped back onto the bed, walking over Grayson and placing herself back on top of him.

"This is an acid compound. If thrown, on contact the glass will break, and the liquid will begin to disintegrate any light material. It works wonders on leather... cloth, anything soft really," she whispered, pausing only to eye up Grayson's already naked body. He calmed slightly, seeing her mischievous look and seemed confident that he wasn't her intended target.

"Well, clearly that isn't needed in my case," he suggested.

"I would never use anything like this on you, my lord," she replied, trying to sound innocent. "As well as the detrimental side-effects of the liquid, contact with the vapours would be even more dangerous. The unfortunate soul would find their eyes, nose and throat severely swollen, or worse," she advised, carefully placing the poisonous bottle on the bedside table.

While she was distracted, Grayson managed to wriggle his hands free of the bindings and once sure she'd placed the threatening bottle down, he grabbed her around the waist and pulled her beneath him.

"You are both dangerous and alluring, Juliette Lawrence. As fascinating as your concoctions are, can we resume our prior activities?" He requested, without giving her a chance to respond. Instead, he kissed her deeply until she groaned with pleasure.

After another few hours of their '*prior activities*,' Grayson had fallen asleep leaving Juliette free to grab her pager and send an update to Siljanna. She still found it bizarre that the kingdom had so few technological advancements, but there was something quaint about the resulting way of life. And luckily, her device still worked.

Pager in hand, she started typing a detailed message to Siljanna, writing about her '*advancements*' in Carlisse and the '*bond*' she'd developed with the king as instructed, but, upon reading her own words, she heard Dylan in her head and deleted everything, opting to send a short, simple message instead.

'*Situation in Carlisse is under control. Ready for Imperial arrival. Mission update? —J*'

She waited several minutes until the pager pinged indicating a reply. Grayson stirred at the noise but didn't wake so she clicked on the message to read it.

'Imperial entourage inbound. Remain in Carlisse and keep up relations until we arrive—Siljanna.'

She smiled at the context of the message. She was more than happy to keep up relations, figuratively and literally.

Closing her pager, Siljanna dropped onto the sofa in her apartment and smiled. When she discovered Dylan had abandoned the search, she'd been livid, still desperate to find Harrison and Rylie, but later that day, Cameron took her to see Imperator Harlyn and they informed her of their simple but effective plan. Rather than chasing her prey, they would lure them to her.

Politics had never been of interest to Siljanna, but tactics had, and when Imperator Harlyn made it clear that her father Joseph, the previous Imperator, had once envisioned overthrowing the outdated monarchy ruling Carlisse and spreading the Empire to the Eastern Continent, she wasn't interested until Harlyn explained how securing Carlisse presented another opportunity.

The Imperator's experiments on Nate Auren had resulted in nothing, and the man hadn't displayed any magical abilities despite being forced to consume Encia and En-glycerol, so he and Paige served little use to them, other than bait. If they could control Carlisse, they could set a trap using Rylie's parents to lure her, Harrison and anyone else supporting them back to the city, where Siljanna could finally capture them. The only thing Siljanna didn't like about the plan was that it was unfamiliar territory. There was a chance things could go wrong, but she decided it was worth the risk.

Picking up the phone, Siljanna dialled Cameron's number in order to update him on the situation.

"Any news?" He asked as soon as he answered.

"Juliette has secured Carlisse. We can infiltrate the city under the guise of friendship and once in command, we can set the trap as discussed," she replied.

"Good, I'll update Imperator Harlyn. Transport has already been arranged on the Imperial warship so we will arrive in Carlisse in about six days. Be ready, your patience will soon be rewarded Siljanna," he said confidently.

After finishing their call, Siljanna caught a glimpse of her reflection in a mirror. For the first time, she could see elements of her father in the image staring back at her. It wasn't just the colour of her hair but the way she held herself. Without meaning to, she'd embodied his strength and hardened herself to the harsh reality of what justice meant; arresting her brother and childhood friend, sentencing Rylie to a fate worse than death. As she locked eyes with her reflection, she admitted that deep down she wanted Rylie to suffer, but reminded herself there was no forgiving Harrison's betrayal either. She was ready to do whatever it took to avenge her father.

The ride to Lorvale had been untroubled and went faster than they'd expected. Handing the horses over to the other stable hand working for Drew and Elissa, the group set off on foot to Iliria. The landscape around them was heavy with woodland, with all the houses and shops scattered amongst the trees except for a small cluster in the centre of town. As they pressed on, the woods became denser, but the path they were on headed south, running adjacent to a powerful river. The water rushed ferociously, splashing up whenever it hit the rocks.

"We can follow this river all the way to Iliria. Just be careful not to fall in, the water is rich with Encia as well as being obviously turbulent," Zack advised, aiming the comment specifically at Harrison and Alex as they looked towards the water with worried expressions.

"How long will it take to reach Iliria?" Harrison asked, making sure to watch his step.

"About three hours; the path is pretty flat and will take us around the woods. It's safer to go around than through because of the grizzly bears. They're cute, unless you're between them and a meal! It's a nice area to hike too... when you aren't being hunted by both human nations and mage hunters that is!" Zack muttered.

"That's not funny!" Lianna remarked.

"I wasn't trying to be funny, just factual," Zack replied sharply. Rylie and Harrison looked at each other, both knowing the reason for Zack's attitude but feeling bad that even with her abilities, Lianna didn't understand.

When Harrison heard a noise from behind, Zack extended his stride to stand beside him. As Harrison turned, his hand reaching up to the handle of his blade, ready to strike, they were relieved to see it was just a fox sneaking through the bushes. Relaxing, he turned and saw Alex staring at him.

"Umm Harrison, have I shown a warrior's heart yet? I really want to learn to fight, just like you!" Alex asked, eyeing up the blade. He grabbed a long stick, attempting to hold it like he'd seen Harrison wield the sword and took some practice swings, making Lianna giggle. She nodded subtly to Harrison.

"Answer me one question; why do you want to fight?" Harrison asked.

"To protect my sister, and all of you; my friends. And because you look so cool!" Alex replied, his enthusiasm sincere.

"Good answer, protecting the people you love is one of the best motivations. Okay, Alex, I'll train you... when we find Arencia okay? Once we're safe, I'll teach you everything I know. We might start with something a little smaller though," he suggested, breaking the stick so that it was about the length of a standard sword and easier for Alex to wield.

"I want to learn too," Rylie announced surprisingly. "Leaving you the way we had to in Carlisse was the worst thing I've had to live through since the fire. If we are ever in that position again, I need to be able to make a stand."

Harrison barely masked his surprise and found himself concerned, impressed and proud she wanted to learn to defend herself. He also thought that combat training could give her skills that would help control her powers too, even just the breathing techniques.

"Okay, I'll teach both of you, anyone else?" Harrison asked curiously.

"No thank you!" Lianna said definitively. "Feeling pain is bad enough, let alone causing it!"

"I'd rather not either," Evie replied sweetly.

"Zack, what about you?" Harrison enquired.

"I'm good. Like I told you before, I'm much better at sneaking than stabbing. The last time I held a sword, let's just say the practice dummy was still standing but I wasn't," he admitted with a grin.

Chapter Seventeen
Arencia

After three hours walking, they spotted a sign for Iliria but Zack veered them off the main path to continue along the river, which had gotten larger and stronger as they went. When they finally came to the end of the road, before them was a stunning crescent waterfall. Surprisingly, there was nothing to safeguard people on the path from the cascading water, which descended at least two thousand feet before hitting the rock pool below. Before Zack even had a chance to explain, Alex charged forward towards the edge.

"This is it. Can't you see?" He proclaimed, waving his arms at the area around him. Lianna was instantly panicked by her brother's proximity to the edge and the Encia infused water.

"Alex, get away from there!" She cried.

"I'm serious, this is it!" He repeated, pointing at what he could see were the edges of the illusion. He turned to look at each of them and was stunned by their dubious expressions. Even Lianna didn't look as though she believed him. Alex decided the only thing he could do to convince them was defy the illusion.

He turned and ran as quickly as he could, hearing the terrified shouts of his sister and Evie as he went. They all watched as he vanished into the scene before them. He didn't jump or fall but simply vanished. Startled, Lianna fell to her knees in silence and Rylie rushed over to support her friend. It was Evie who cautiously approached the edge, raising her hand and reaching out to where they'd seen Alex disappear. As she did, her hand vanished from view. A moment later, she was pulled forward and disappeared as well.

"Don't panic, they're okay," Zack said confidently.

"Is this really it, the illusion protecting Arencia?" Harrison asked, turning to look directly at Zack. He couldn't nod or speak but his eyes told them the answer was '*yes*'. Looking at him dubiously, Lianna scrambled back to her feet and glared at Zack. *He let her panic, and for what?* She was about to hurl herself towards him but seeing Lianna's anger, Rylie held her back.

"Why didn't you tell us? All this time, you knew about this place!" She screamed.

"It's hard to explain," Zack began reluctantly.

"Why?" Lianna shouted, her rage building.

"He couldn't tell us," Harrison interjected, standing between Lianna and Zack. "That mark on his neck, the tattoo you thought was just the symbol of the mage smuggler, it's more than just an ordinary tattoo. It forces him to remain silent about this place until we discovered it for ourselves."

Harrison's brief explanation sedated Lianna slightly as she turned her gaze back to what still looked like the sheer drop of a waterfall.

"So this is Arencia?" Rylie asked, looking at Zack and then across to the area where both Alex and Evie had vanished.

"Cross that threshold and you'll know for sure," Zack replied in a reserved tone.

"Are you coming with us?" Rylie asked.

"No, I can't return. I don't belong there anymore," he answered, looking sadly at each of them. "It has been my honour to help you get this far."

As he finished speaking, Lianna relaxed, showing Rylie she no longer needed restraining. After releasing her, Lianna walked towards Zack, studying him intently.

"I don't believe that Zack. This place means more than you're letting on. It's fear stopping you," she accused. It was the first time he'd tried to conceal something from her and in turn, it was the first time she was able to clearly read him.

"Please Zack, don't leave us now. We want you to stay, all of us," Rylie pleaded, trying to soften Lianna's point.

"This was your home, wasn't it Zack?" Harrison asked, remembering their conversation back in Carlisse. "Whatever happened here, it's in the past. You've changed, become a better person. Don't run, stay and help us not just survive, but make things better for all mages like Caitlin and Spencer."

Harrison hoped that Zack, who had become a good friend, would stick to his morals and continue to support them, even if it meant facing his past. Zack looked towards each of them and then dropped his head, laughing softly.

"You drive a hard bargain," he replied, looking up with a smile. "Let's go."

As they each passed through the threshold of the illusion, the image around them transformed. What had looked like the edge of the path and a sheer drop became a thin balcony overlooking the falls. Alex and Evie were standing together smiling nervously as behind them, stood a guard in a uniform Harrison had never seen or even read of before. The young guard approached them, his hand readied above his blade, but he didn't draw.

"Zack?" The guard announced, sounding surprised and displeased.

"Hello brother," Zack replied.

Announcing the person before them as his brother made every member of the group study the man in more detail. He did have the same graceful features and striking blue eyes as Zack, but his hair was a darker shade of blonde and styled in a volumised, blowout look. When he smiled though, there was no denying they were related.

"How long has it been, two years?" The brother muttered, any gladness to be reunited with Zack clearly absent.

"Three," Zack replied curtly. He took a deep breath and returned his attention to the group. "Everyone, this is my brother, Noah. He is one of the Aegis Guard, the protectors of Arencia."

"Why have you come?" Noah questioned, not looking at anyone in particular but his gaze paused on Harrison, taking in the distinct warrior vibe he exuded. Rylie stepped forward and joined Evie as Alex retreated so that he was next to Lianna.

"I am Rylie Auren and this is my sister, Evie. We are mages, being hunted by the Siranor Empire. We seek shelter and… our grandfather. Does a man called Alistair Auren live here?" She asked, her voice filled with caution.

"We have been on a strenuous journey, luckily finding help, and friends along the way," Harrison added, drawing Noah's attention not just to himself, but Lianna and Alex too.

"We all seek refuge, a place that'll be safe for mages and our families," Lianna concluded, reaching for Alex's hand.

"May we stay, please? We have nowhere else to go," Evie asked, beseeching Noah, hoping he was kind like his brother.

Noah took another moment, looking with great suspicion at Harrison and Zack before speaking.

"It's not for me to decide whether you can stay, but mages and mage sympathisers are welcome here. Please follow me, I'll take you to see Maia Uriel, the leader of this place. If she agrees to let you stay, you can see your grandfather," Noah replied.

"You mean he really is here?" Rylie gasped her tone hushed in suspense. Noah nodded and she and Evie shared an expression of joy. Placing her hand over her heart, Rylie let out a sigh of relief. For the first time in a long time, she felt they could be truly safe.

Noah noticed her expression and walked towards Rylie, reaching his hand out and placing it on hers. She was shocked at the gesture for a moment but allowed his hand to rest there while his other hand gently touched the base of her chin, tilting her head so that her eyes looked directly into his.

"You have the same enchanting eyes, like the mist emanating from these falls," he mused, his words direct and honest, just as Zack had been when admiring Lianna, but less forceful. It made Rylie blush as she carefully shied away, breaking their contact.

A faint spark crackled between them but only Evie seemed to react to it. She glared at Noah and then turned to look back at Harrison who was standing uncomfortably, watching every move Noah made. *Was he just going to let this random guy flirt with Rylie? Why didn't he step in?* Then she remembered he still hadn't told Rylie how he felt, so couldn't create a scene now. They'd worked too hard and travelled too far to find this place, he wouldn't jeopardise their safety over a flirtatious advance, as much as Evie wished he would.

Noah led them towards the end of the balcony and they noticed a platform that lowered into a crystal frame, running adjacent to the mighty falls. As the mist and spray hit the crystal, the light refracted around them in a rainbow of colours. As they descended, they could see Arencia. The city had been built on ledges within the falls and out across the lake below them. The water seemed to naturally veer away from each of the buildings, but they all presumed it was magic rather than nature at work.

Each ledge was connected by a series of pale wood and crystal bridges, and although every building was unique, they shared the same elegant architecture, with sweeping roofs, lightly pointed at the edges and intricate detailing. None of the group had ever imagined such a beautiful place and the fact it remained hidden from the rest of the world almost seemed unfair.

Stepping off the platform, they continued to follow Noah as he led them to the largest building in the city, its pointed spire reaching high above the other buildings.

"Where are we going?" Harrison asked quietly.

"That's the pavilion, it's where the Ar'encal and mages hold important meetings and celebrations, that sort of thing. Don't worry,

Noah *is* taking us to see Maia, her study is above the pavilion," Zack replied.

"There's a tense history between you and your brother, right?" Harrison asked, recalling his avoidance of the subject.

"He hates me and is part of the reason I left this place. Despite his charm, be wary of Noah. He's not as kind as he likes people to believe. I'll tell you the whole story another time," Zack replied quietly as Noah stopped in the archway of the pavilion, indicating for all of them to ascend the winding staircase.

The detail on the exterior of the building was matched, if not outdone by the interior design. The wooden beams, so pale as to be almost white retained their tree-like features, curving and arcing in slender branches to hold up the heavy roof. Verdant green plants wound their way through the gaps in the framework, bringing the walls to life.

On the upper floor, they walked down a thin hallway and through another beautifully carved arch until they saw a woman standing beside a delicate wooden desk. She wore a dark green, shoulder-less dress and lace shawl which draped from a choker around her throat to her waist. The dress was fitted tightly to her upper body by a frontal corset, the trimmings actual moss and flowers. Adorned with tiny clear crystals, the remainder of the dress fell gracefully from her waist to the floor. Her dark hair was short, falling barely to her shoulders and feathered in such a way that her features, especially the ridges on her nose and elongated ears were highlighted.

They'd all imagined what the Ar'encal might look like but the one thing that took them all by surprise was how young she appeared. Although Ar'encal aged differently to humans, the woman before them looked barely eighteen. As Noah approached, he bowed in a deep, exaggerated fashion.

"My lady—," he announced in a courtly manner.

"Do not start that nonsense again Noah," she replied, giving him a look of indifference. He laughed, which made the woman smile before turning her attention to the group.

"Maia Uriel, let me introduce Rylie and Evie Auren, Lianna and Alex Flynn, and their guard, Harrison Stone. And of course, you'll remember my brother, Zack," he said, speaking Zack's name with distaste.

"Welcome. I can tell you've all had quite the journey to get here. Are you well?" She asked, and despite her appearance, her voice was mature. She may have looked young but in her case, appearances were deceiving. Rylie stepped forward and spoke on behalf of the group.

"We are much better for being here, thank you. My sister, Harrison and I have travelled extensively to find this place. We are being hunted by the Siranor mage hunters and the wardens, led by Harrison's sister, all for crimes we did not commit," she explained as Harrison came to her side.

"Along the way, we were fortunate enough to meet Zack, who has been pivotal to our survival. All he asked for in return was that we aid any other mages we met, which is how Lianna and her brother Alex came to join us," he added, looking towards them to see their grateful expressions.

"Zack helped us not only escape the people hunting us but also to search for our grandfather," Rylie continued, explaining as concisely as she could. "His name is Alistair Auren, and it was finding his journals in Carlisse that led us here. We are hoping he might be able to help us. We have a scarce understanding of our powers, and he is the only link to our Ar'encal heritage."

"You're Alistair's grandchildren?" Maia asked, her expression a mix of suspicion and wonder.

"We are. We'd been told our entire lives he passed away but found out just recently that he's alive," Rylie explained, confirming that part of their almost unbelievable tale.

"He always wondered if he had grandchildren," Maia mused, smiling softly. "He'll be so pleased to meet you."

"Can we meet him?" Evie asked, shying behind her big sister but youthfully hopeful. "We don't know what happened to our parents so, he might be all the family we have left."

"Oh you poor child, of course. Noah, please fetch Alistair. In the meantime, I would like to hear your whole story from the beginning, if I may," Maia requested, offering for all of them to be seated in the open-air study.

They'd almost finished re-telling their tale when they heard footsteps clattering up the stairs. Before long, a man was standing in the archway to the study, panting. His grey hair tousled from running, as was the long robe he wore over his smart, vested shirt and pin-striped trousers. As he searched the room, his gaze landed on Evie and Rylie and he seemed to melt with joy. He was immediately recognisable to them and Harrison too as he looked just like Nate, only older.

Both of the girls stood up when they saw Alistair but neither was able to speak. Finally, Evie ran towards her grandfather and gave him a hug. Rylie approached more slowly, wearing a coy, but uncertain smile. Alistair just raised his hand, cupping her face. She relaxed into his touch and he smiled, the expression heartfelt and pure.

"I cannot believe this. When I woke up this morning, I never dreamed this day would end with meeting my granddaughters," Alistair exclaimed, kissing Evie's head.

He listened as they finished explaining what they'd each been through to get to this point. When they spoke about meeting Caitlin, Queen Nadia and Spencer; Lianna went very quiet. Rylie was the one who finally mentioned Nadia's request about a cure for the withering, directing the question to her grandfather.

"She desperately needs a cure, is there such a thing?" She asked.

"I'm sorry, it's something I've been working on for years, but I haven't discovered a cure. We can prevent the withering, with runes like the one Zack has, and at one point, we discovered a compound that can absorb Encia, but never a way to extract it from a person already suffering," he explained, filling each of them with a great sense of sadness. Unable to bear disappointing them and wanting to do what he could for the tortured queen, he quickly added, "I will keep trying though."

Once they finished recounting the last details of their journey, Lianna looked towards Maia, sensing the woman's empathy.

"May we stay? I know my brother and Harrison are not mages, but we all really need a sanctuary. Somewhere that we can truly be safe," she asked.

"Of course you can stay. We are a community here, so you will all have to earn your keep, but this can be your home, if you want it to be," Maia replied. "Alistair and I can also help each of you to harness your abilities, if you are willing to learn."

"I'm particularly well-positioned to help you Evie... and in a way, Lianna too," Alistair added, quickly garnering their attention.

"You are?" Evie asked excitedly.

"I used to get visions, just like you sweetheart, but with Maia's help and the other Ar'encal, I've learnt, not only to have more control over those visions but to conjure them at will," he advised. "And my wife, before she passed, had a strong empathic connection. She showed me several techniques to channel it."

"That's incredible!" Lianna exclaimed happily. She and Alex had a safe place to live and Alistair was able to help her understand her powers.

For a moment, Lianna thought it was everything she ever wanted, and then remembered Spencer. She wished he could've been there, safely with her but then recalled why he wasn't. Because Queen Nadia needed him, would always need him, and because Spencer loved Nadia, not her.

Seeing her expression change, Alistair wondered if he'd said something wrong and tried to reassure her of his knowledge.

"Maia and her people have been kind to me over the years. Now, I can pay that knowledge forward. Emilia, my wife taught me many things about her empathic gifts before she died. I am confident I can help you," he confirmed, earning another tight embrace from his youngest granddaughter and a smile from Lianna, who snapped herself out of her thoughts and into the present.

Rylie shifted in her seat, not wanting to interrupt but had to ask about her own predicament.

"Can you tell me anything about my abilities? They have been difficult to control and at times, dangerous. What can I do to ensure I don't hurt anyone?" She asked, running her fingers through her hair nervously as her gaze shifted between Maia and Alistair.

"You'll train with me Rylie," Maia said immediately. "Elemental powers can be tough but I'll show you techniques to control your emotions, which in turn will help you to control the elements."

"Thank you," she declared, genuinely relieved.

"All magic is tied to our emotions. The greater control you have of your emotional state, the stronger you will become, but practice goes a long way too. Anyway, you've all had quite the journey. We can begin training tomorrow," Maia suggested. "I'll have Noah escort you to the lower city where we have some vacant houses and can offer you one to share."

They thanked both Alistair and Maia again before Noah returned and led them to the lower city as promised. They crossed several of the bridges they'd seen earlier but as they headed away from the magnificent falls, the water beneath them quickly calmed, giving the entire area a feeling of tranquillity.

Walking along a raised dock, they came to an area filled with small houses built on wooden stilts, all with similar architecture to the other buildings in the city, just on a smaller scale. Noah indicated one of the homes and opened the door, encouraging them all to head inside. As the group passed, he stopped Rylie, gently pulling her aside.

"Rylie, I just want you to know that now your home is here, the Aegis Guard... I will protect you, against anything," he vowed, standing close to her, moving his hand so that his little finger could stroke hers. She felt the gesture and shied away coyly, but he was not deterred.

"I already have a bodyguard," she remarked with a smile.

"Maybe I can be more than just a bodyguard then," he replied, taking her hand in his. She smiled again but frequently looked away, unsure how to react to his advances. No guy, especially one as handsome as Noah had ever been this directly flirtatious with her, so she wasn't sure if he was truly interested or just an extrovert.

"Maybe," she whispered, showing her uncertain curiosity.

He leaned in closer, pressing her body gently against the outside wall of the house until his face was next to her ear. His warm breath tickled her skin as he whispered.

"I'm sure I can find another reason to be close to you," he said, loving how she giggled when he spoke. "Go out with me."

"Really?" She asked, her eyes locking onto his.

"Yes. I'll send a note with a place and time," he answered, kissing her lightly on the cheek before slowly walking away. She smiled when he looked back from halfway down the walkway, taking in the sight of her like something truly wondrous.

Watching through the window, Evie couldn't believe what she was seeing. Noah was not only flirting with Rylie, but she was reciprocating. She felt her heart breaking, knowing how Harrison felt and why he'd held back. She had to do something. She couldn't pinpoint why, but she didn't trust Noah and the last thing she wanted was for Rylie to pick him over Harrison. With everyone exploring their new home, she marched over to Harrison and pulled him into the hall, away from the others.

"You have to tell her now Harrison! Otherwise, it'll be too late," Evie insisted urgently.

"What? Evie, slow down, what are you talking about?" He asked, startled by her demeanour.

"Rylie! You have to tell her how you feel, now! Zack's brother is making a move and if she doesn't know how you feel, she could fall for him," Evie replied frantically.

Harrison looked towards Rylie as she walked in with a look on her face that said she had a secret, one that made her smile from within. He shook his head in dismay, realising Evie had a point and returned his attention to her.

"Evie, I don't even know if she'll feel the same way about me. If she's attracted to Noah, I shouldn't stand in the way," he submitted, trying to convince himself it was the right thing to do. He failed to convince himself but Evie's reaction suggested she believed him.

"Do you even really love her?" She challenged. "How can you? You're not even trying!"

"Evie, enough! I know you mean well but this isn't helping," Harrison protested, speaking more firmly than he intended. She recoiled, giving him a genuinely wounded look so he softened his tone. "I care about Rylie, you know that, but our friendship is precious to me. I'm not going to risk it unless I feel there is more between us— a spark."

She huffed but nodded, remembering the literal spark she'd seen between Rylie and Noah.

"I'm sorry Harrison, I just really want to see you both together, like in my vision," she replied.

She was such a timid girl so speaking to him in this way was really out of character. He pulled her in for a quick hug and stroked her hair.

"Perhaps it was Noah in your vision," he suggested.

"No! Don't say that, it was you, I know it was you," she replied, shaking her head and closing her eyes tightly.

"Well let's hope you're right. Everything will turn out the way it's meant to Evie, and no matter what, I'll always be there for you and Rylie," he promised.

"I know… I just want you and Rylie to be happy, and I know you would be if you were together. But I won't meddle, I promise," she replied, shuffling into the other room and leaving Harrison to his growing melancholy.

Chapter Eighteen
Essence

Their first week in Arencia passed quickly with Rylie training with Maia and Lianna and Evie with Alistair. Zack also had an emotional reunion with his father, Lucas and showed both Harrison and Alex around the guardian's compound. They had an impressive array of facilities including training grounds, an armoury and a smithy.

As captain of the guard, Lucas couldn't have been more different from Harrison's father. He was softly spoken and kind when he'd met them but as the week went on, he'd also shown how strong and agile he was. It was easy to see why he'd been chosen to lead the Aegis Guard and train new recruits. With the same blue eyes as both of his sons, but much darker, short brown hair and a full, neat beard covering his prominent jaw, he managed to look both approachable and robust.

Harrison was heading back to the compound after receiving a request from Lucas to display his skills. He wanted to see if Harrison would be a good fit to serve the Aegis Guard. Harrison's mind reeled back to his days in the academy and the trials he'd once faced. He hoped anything they required wouldn't be as challenging. When he arrived, Zack and Alex were already there.

"Hey Harrison! Good luck today, I can't wait to see you in action," Alex told him supportively, his eyes glinting.

Alex had really come to idolise Harrison, or possibly just his sword but Harrison was glad the young man had stopped thieving since he and Lianna started travelling with them. Harrison had started giving him a few lessons in hand-to-hand and sword combat and it was seeing them train that encouraged Lucas to give Harrison the opportunity to join the guard.

"We've come for moral support," Zack added, smiling in a mischievous fashion.

"Why are you so happy?" Harrison asked.

"I know what your test is," he replied enigmatically. His smile spread from ear to ear and Harrison knew that whatever it was, Zack was eager to watch.

They made their way into the training grounds and found Lucas, a few other guards and Noah waiting in the main field. Noah was dressed in training armour and wielding a sturdy wooden staff. Harrison dropped his head in a subtle nod, smiling. He knew instantly that he was going to be asked to duel Noah.

"Good morning Harrison," Lucas greeted, as he reached the group of gathered guards, "thank you for accepting this challenge. I've seen glimpses of your battle prowess, and as such, I am fairly confident you won't need much training to be worthy of joining the Aegis Guard, but it is customary to prove your worth against one of our top fighters."

As Lucas tipped his head towards Noah, indicating the challenge, Harrison nodded politely, the way he used to for his tutors.

"I am ready to face whoever you see fit," Harrison responded, even though he already knew what Lucas was going to say.

"Noah is one of our most gifted fighters, something I am immensely proud of, not just as a father, but as captain. Best him in one-on-one combat and you will prove your worth," he replied, confirming Harrison's suspicion.

Knowing Zack had a difficult history with his brother and that Noah had been flirting with Rylie every chance he had, Harrison decided he was going to let himself enjoy this. He received a similar staff to Noah and turned to see his over-confident opponent smile. Adopting his battle stance, Harrison watched as Noah sauntered towards him and without waiting for his father to announce they could begin, lashed out with the staff. Harrison blocked the shot easily and remained still while Noah began trying to rattle him.

"Come on, attack me," he taunted. "You're supposed to be some big-shot warden. An Imperial super-soldier. You don't seem all that super to me."

Noah was arrogant but the other guards around them laughed and joined his taunting. Harrison refused to rise to the bait and waited for Noah's next attack, which came seconds after he finished speaking. He was the most predictable opponent Harrison thought he'd ever faced, and couldn't help but be quite concerned that he was one of the best fighters the Aegis Guard had. Noah started posturing, showing off to his friends, and when his guard was down, Harrison attacked.

Using a series of short blows, he knocked Noah off balance and followed with a heavy upward swing of the staff. Harrison's blows collided with Noah's torso and sent him crashing to the floor. As he walked up to him, kicking the staff out of Noah's reach, Harrison used his own staff to pin him down.

"Do you submit?" He asked, a wicked smile forming in the corner of his mouth. He heard all the guards gasp but then start to laugh, especially Zack. None of them, aside from Zack, were expecting Harrison to find it that easy. Noah raised his hands in defeat and once Harrison relaxed his staff, Noah scrambled to his feet in horror.

"I've been waiting to see that my entire life!" Zack declared, launching himself towards Harrison, giving him a congratulatory hug. "What did I tell you, this guy is the real deal!"

Clearly impressed, Lucas came over to Harrison and extended his hand, which Harrison took, shaking firmly.

"Noah underestimated you, and he's needed an ego check for some time," Lucas confessed. "Zack also tells me that along with your skill with a blade, you are trained in smithing too, is that true?"

"It is, after I was made to leave the wardens, I became a smith in my hometown for about a year. I focused mainly on crafting weapons but I can forge armour too," Harrison replied, not to brag but also not selling himself short.

"With your skills, I'd be mad not to ask you to join our ranks. All I need to know is if you'll accept the Arencian rune?" Lucas questioned, looking intently at Harrison.

Zack had told him as much as he could about the rune since they arrived in the city and with everything in mind, Harrison had no doubt that he wanted to accept the mark.

"I will," he replied, giving Lucas another reason to smile.

"I won't lie, accepting the mark hurts, but, if you can bear the pain, the benefits are worthwhile. The rune will protect you from Encia, and therefore the withering. You will also become resistant to magic," Lucas continued.

"I will bear the pain happily if it means I can serve the Aegis Guard and protect my friends," Harrison replied, glancing at Zack who placed a hand to his own rune without thinking.

"The rune will also prevent you from speaking of this place to anyone that doesn't know of its existence. It's a defence mechanism in case any member of the Aegis Guard gets captured by mage hunters, or worse. Lucas checked, giving Harrison one final chance to decline.

"Yes," Harrison replied with conviction.

Lucas patted him firmly on the shoulder and confirmed he'd advise Maia. She'd send for him when it was time to receive the rune. As Lucas and the other guards left, Alex and Zack stayed, continuing to enjoy Harrison's swift victory over Noah.

"Mate, you have to teach me how you did that! I sparred against Noah for years and was never able to defeat him, let alone in under two minutes," Zack exclaimed, still laughing.

He and Alex grabbed the staffs on the floor and started playfully sparring with each other. Alex made overzealous noises that were probably meant to sound like battle grunts while Zack darted around him easily. Harrison couldn't help but notice how light on his feet Zack was and grew curious.

"Hey Alex, chuck that here for a minute," he instructed, indicating towards the staff. Alex threw it over and Harrison took up his battle stance again. "Come on Zack, show me what you've got."

"Hey woah, I was just playing, I don't want to spar against you," he placated, instantly dropping the staff and shaking his head vigorously.

"You're incredibly agile, you know that? I bet I could train you; we just need to focus on your strengths," Harrison offered and could tell Zack was intrigued.

"I don't have any strengths, that's the problem," Zack replied, picking up the staff and leaning on it like a cane, almost falling when it toppled over.

"I beg to differ. Okay, so swords and by the looks of it, staffs are not your thing, but have you ever tried ranged combat, like throwing knives or archery?" Harrison asked.

"Well, no... I guess I haven't. I spent years here, training with my father and brother but it was always with swords or other close combat weapons, whatever Noah liked. Noah was always able to get the better of me and even if I got close to defeating him, all he had to do was mention my mother and it'd throw me off," Zack admitted as if only realising now that he'd never had the chance to try different types of weapons or that his brother used under-handed tactics to defeat him.

"What happened to your mother? Why does your brother have such a hold over you?" Alex asked.

Sometimes it took the bluntness of a teenager to ask the questions that would otherwise go unsaid. Zack sighed but smiled, almost impressed by how forthright Alex was.

"It happened when we were kids. I was four and Noah seven. Although we were raised here in Arencia, we spent a lot of time in the woodlands around Iliria. It was where my parents had lived before the war and Noah liked playing there—" Zack began then paused, the memory still painful. "It was eighteen years ago in the height of the mage hunts. My mum, Cara, had taken us to Iliria for a day out while my father was travelling to Lorvale, he was just a merchant back then."

"The woods we travelled through to get here?" Alex checked.

"The very same; Noah and I were playing when a group of mage hunters spotted us. They recognised my mother as a mage sympathiser and attacked," Zack continued, taking a deep breath.

"You don't have to say anymore, Zack," Harrison began but Zack stopped him.

"No, it'll be good for me to tell someone that hasn't heard Noah's angle first. When the hunters came for us, Noah told me to run but I couldn't keep up. The hunters almost caught me but my mother sacrificed herself so they wouldn't. Hunters get their bounty for an arrest or a kill, so my unarmed mother didn't stand a chance. She fought just long enough for us to get away but the last thing Noah claims he saw was one of the hunters plunging a sword into her chest."

"Zack—," Harrison stammered but genuinely didn't know what to say to his friend.

"For years afterwards I ran, whether it was around these training grounds, to and from the pavilion, even inside the house. If I could run, I would. I wanted to make sure I'd never be too slow again, but my father's devastation was heart-breaking, and Noah never forgave me. Three years ago, I just couldn't take the guilt anymore. I was a terrible fighter and a disappointment to the Aegis Guard and so I left. I guess it just felt natural, running away," he explained.

"You can't blame yourself for what happened!" And to Zack's surprise, it was Alex who'd spoken up.

"But it was my fault," Zack replied but Alex just shook his head.

"I was four when my parents were killed too, and there is nothing I could've done to stop the men responsible. You were a kid, just like me. The only people to blame for your mother's death are those wretched hunters; and if you want my opinion, your brother is a jerk for blaming you."

"What he said!" Harrison added chuckling, while Zack was left speechless, his jaw gaping. Finally, he laughed.

"Well, there's no arguing with that," Zack chuckled.

"I bet with a trainer like Harrison, you'd thrash your brother in combat!" Alex exclaimed.

"All right then, let's give combat training another shot. Where should we start?" Zack asked.

Harrison walked over towards the armoury and came out with a bow slung over his shoulder and a handful of throwing knives. He gave the blades to Zack and then dragged over a nearby training dummy, scribbling a big 'X' on the centre before standing behind Zack and indicating the target.

"So this time, the training dummy might stay standing, but he won't feel well if he does!" Harrison jested, remembering what Zack had said when he first offered him a blade.

"We'll see about that," Zack replied, still uncertain.

Harrison made sure Zack, who was right-handed, stood relaxed but straight, with the correct foot forward. He showed him how to hold the blade by the tip, keeping his thumb on top and fingers back, to ensure it wouldn't affect the trajectory of the blade. They were standing about six feet away from the dummy and using moderate force, Zack propelled the blade forward and it sunk deep into the dummy, just above the target. The shock on his face was hilarious.

"There you go, first shot and you almost nailed it!" Harrison cheered, lightly slapping his friend on the back.

"That was amazing! Teach me, teach me!" Alex burst out and the three of them spent the next few hours training with the throwing knives and bows. Alex was good but Zack excelled instantly, especially with archery. When they decided to call it a day, he didn't want to return the bow to the armoury.

"I think I'll hang onto this. I've never felt an affinity with a weapon before, but this feels right," he admitted, caressing the wooden recurve bow.

"If today has proven anything, it's that you are far from the man that left this place three years ago. You should never think of yourself as too slow or a failure again," Harrison confirmed, receiving a grateful nod from his friend.

"Can I keep this one?" Alex asked, turning over a butterfly knife in his hands. Harrison quickly went to take the blade, imagining Lianna's reaction if Alex returned with fewer fingers than he'd started the day with.

"Not quite yet," Harrison said quickly. "You're getting good, and I like your enthusiasm but let's have a few more training sessions before you keep a blade, okay."

"Fine," Alex grumbled, allowing Harrison to place the blade back in the armoury. When Harrison returned, Alex spoke again. "Can we go find Evie and the others? They were having a lesson with Maia this afternoon and I'd like to see how they're getting on."

"Sounds good, do you know where?" Harrison asked.

"Evie mentioned they'd be near the lake by the falls, I'm not sure where though," he replied.

"She probably meant Lake Baliten, it's not far from the falls and often used by the mages for training. Come on, I can take you there," Zack advised, as they strode off towards the lake.

When they arrived, they approached quietly as Rylie, Lianna and Evie were all sitting cross-legged with their eyes closed, listening to Maia who walked slowly between them. It was as if she had them in a meditative trance while she spoke. Alistair was also close by, watching the session.

"Encia is the essence of the planet. Just as blood flows through our bodies, Encia flows through the water of the planet," Maia began, her words slow and calm. "If you believe in the mythology of the Gods;

Temu—God of creation, was the first to walk upon our planet but Ceris—Goddess of life is the planet itself. She guarded the world and helped it flourish and grow. Over time, Temu and Ceris fell in love and together they had seven children. Each were gifted with particular abilities."

"What's going on?" Alex whispered.

"Maia is teaching them Ar'encal lore. It was never my favourite subject but was always good when I needed a nap," Zack replied jokingly. Alistair gave him a stern nudge, willing him and the others to remain quiet as they continued to listen.

"First came Viritus, the blessed one. God of healing and protection. As firstborn, he was believed to have the purest soul. With healing powers so immense, he could bring a person back from the brink of death. Then came Rowana, the trickster and goddess of illusion. Her gifts taught us that sometimes deceiving one's enemy can be just as effective as defeating them. The third child was Nera, goddess of shadow. A great calamity was said to have afflicted the planet when she was born, cursing her. As she grew, she hid in the shadows and could bend negative energies and dark magic to her will."

"A calamity?" Alex whispered quizzically.

"Like a disaster," Zack answered, causing Alex to ponder what could've happened while Maia continued her lecture.

"Next was Piral, the God of precognition. He received visions of the world and how it would one day become and used that foresight to steer the gods to make better decisions."

Maia paused, noticing a faint smile on Evie's face. The condition she had always thought of as a sickness was, in Maia's tale, used for a good and noble purpose.

"It's probably one of the most underrated abilities but control over precognition can lead to incredible knowledge," Alistair whispered to the guys, although he was somewhat biased.

"But what about the seizures Evie has? That doesn't feel like a blessing," Harrison remarked.

"It's only because she was afraid, fighting off the images. Once she learns to accept them, she won't feel pain. It'll be easier once she understands that the images are not a foregone conclusion too. If she can analyse it properly, she can make decisions that could alter the outcome," Alistair explained.

"The fifth child of the gods was Syris, the psionic master. Able to utilise telekinesis, read minds and sway thoughts, his connection to the mind immeasurable. The sixth child was Luna, goddess of channelling and empathy, the most understanding and kind of all of the children. Her gifts not only sensed how others felt but allowed her to take away the pain and suffering from those in turmoil," Maia continued, glancing softly at Lianna.

"I wish the girls could've met my wife. Emilia was so in-tune with her empathic abilities. So much so she could ease negative feelings like fear or sorrow at will," Alistair said, still in a hushed tone as he continued to listen.

"Finally, came Talia, goddess of the elements. Although the youngest child, her power was one of the greatest, having control over every element on the planet and able to conjure them at will," Maia explained and noticed the resolve in Rylie's expression. "Now, open your eyes."

As they did, the girls found symbols representing each of the gods marked into the ground around them.

"I wish we'd been able to learn all of this in the outside world. The Uprising took so much from us, more than we ever knew," Lianna whispered, her tone sad while the others marvelled at the mythological symbols.

"The Uprising was a dark time in the history of our world, but it happened," Alistair agreed, stepping forward to join the group. "But you are here now and can learn how to truly control and even develop your abilities. All you need do is focus and trust in both Maia and I to guide you."

"What happened to the gods?" Evie asked. "How did all the races come to be?"

"If you believe the myth, Temu and Ceris grew apart and Temu decided to create more children in his own vision. This gave birth to both the Human and Terran races. Appalled by Temu's actions, Ceris prayed for a way to prove that her children, the first of the Ar'encal, were the true descendants of the planet. In an attempt to please her mother, Nera made Encia toxic to Temu's other children," Maia explained.

"She granted her mother's wish by making the water a death sentence for Temu's created children, that seems rather harsh don't you think?" Evie questioned, shocked that the child of a god could be so spiteful.

"It's Nera's story that makes shadow magic so widely feared, even among the Ar'encal. We avoid using it for it feels... tainted," Maia added.

Having grown up with the religious story of the God Temu, creator and saviour of humanity who was seduced and tricked by the wicked goddess Ceris, each member of the group accepted that if there was any truth to the legend, the Ar'encal likely had the most plausible version. Harrison had never believed in the religious fables and instead thought it was equally possible for a more scientific explanation but chose not to express that opinion in his current company.

"It is because of these tales we believe that when the humans and Ar'encal rekindled and cross-race children were born, these children were also unharmed by Encia because they shared the connection to Ceris and the planet," Alistair concluded, looking lovingly towards his grand-daughters.

"What about people who don't trigger abilities but have Ar'encal heritage?" Lianna asked. "Our parents died years ago, so I have no way of knowing where our link comes from, but I know Encia doesn't harm me. My concern however is for Alex. He's never triggered abilities, so we've always been cautious but as he'll share that same bloodline as me, does that mean Encia won't harm him?"

"Is there any chance you aren't biologically related?" Alistair asked, and if looks could kill, he wouldn't have survived Lianna's answering glare. Alex was the one that stepped forward first, seeing where this line of questioning would end up.

"We were too young to ever know. As you can tell, we strongly doubt it, but there is always a chance. I won't touch Encia, just in case," he promised, garnering the respect of both Alistair and Maia while calming Lianna.

"That is an admirable approach young man," Maia said, smiling at Alex. "Continue training with Harrison and the Aegis Guard and one day I believe you'll be worthy. When you are, we'll bestow upon you the Arencian rune. If you have Ar'encal blood, the rune will not take to your skin but if you don't, you'll receive it and be safe either way."

"Thank you, I will continue training as hard as I can," he replied with a smile, stepping back to allow Maia to continue her lesson.

She turned back to the girls and invited them all to stand and they edged closer to the lake as she continued.

"Because of our connection to Encia, not only does the essence not harm us but consuming pure Encia can strengthen us. There is a delicate balance, but in time we'll learn what each of your limits are and can use the essence to help grow your talents," Maia advised as she pulled out three vials from a hidden pocket in her dress, passing one to each of them.

"Is this pure Encia?" Rylie asked.

"Yes, there is a natural spring deep within the forest south of here. When you are ready, come to me with your vial. The added power from even this small amount of pure Encia will allow us to test your abilities," Maia advised.

"May I try now?" Rylie asked to everyone's surprise.

"Are you sure? There is no hurry," Maia replied.

"I'm sure. Please, can I try?" She asked again. Maia nodded and encouraged Rylie to drink the contents of the vial. Harrison gave her a look of concern, but her eyes told him she was ready. She popped open the lid and drank the contents before facing Maia.

"That's good Rylie; remember, keep your breathing steady as we continue. As your trigger ability was fire, it will be the hardest for you to control, so let's focus on manipulating water," Maia suggested and as she spoke, she swivelled and walked from the path *over* the lake.

As her feet touched the surface, the water rippled but she didn't sink. She stopped a few feet from the edge, looking back and encouraging Rylie to step forward. Taking a deep breath, Rylie cautiously made her way to the water's edge and placed her foot on the surface. At first, her foot slipped in as it normally would. She tried again, her concentration visible and on her second attempt, the water held her weight. She stepped forward, causing tiny ripples, but was able to walk across the surface to join Maia.

"Look at that!" Alistair expressed proudly, putting his hands on Evie's shoulders. She turned, looking up at him with the most heart-warming smile.

"That's good Rylie," Maia began. "Now, focus on the water. It may be strong enough to hold our weight, but it is also fluid. Take your hand and try to move the water around you."

As Maia said the words, she flicked her own fingers and the water reacted, rising and falling with the motion of her fingertips. Rylie looked towards her own hands and tried. At first, there was no reaction, but as she moved her hands with more conviction, the water shifted, following her fingers. As she raised her hands higher, the water rose, droplets trailing in the gentle breeze. Before long, she was moving gracefully over the surface, each step creating ripples and every rotation of her hands and body causing the water to arc around her as if the water was dancing.

As Harrison looked on, he felt his heart hammering in his chest. Rylie looked so beautiful, her smile as the water obeyed her whim was joyous and her eyes sparkled. Maia joined Rylie, the two of them almost sparring, creating vivid shapes with the water, all whilst floating upon it. Maia began to turn rapidly on the spot and as Rylie copied, the water beneath them began to rotate, lifting them higher until they were several feet in the air. As they walked slowly on the elevated water, Maia commanded it to form a bridge, returning them safely back onto dry land.

"You are incredibly gifted Rylie," she congratulated.

"I had no idea I could do that!" Rylie exclaimed.

"I'd be willing to bet you can do that and much more. We'll keep training but be proud of yourself today," Maia replied, her expression reminiscent of the tutors from the Warden Academy on the day Harrison and his friend's graduated.

When she turned towards the group, Rylie was bombarded by Evie and Lianna who both rushed over, hugging tightly and congratulating her. It was an incredible feat that left Harrison in awe. Rylie glanced in his direction, and he gave her an elated smile so that she knew he was overjoyed for her too. He'd always known it, but that display proved just how incredible she was.

Chapter Nineteen
Accused

Siljanna had never travelled over water before and spent most of the journey to the Eastern Continent in her cabin, trying not to be sick. She didn't even want to think of what it must be like for her prisoners who were kept in the brig on the lowest level, feeling every wave as it crashed into the side of the ship. She'd been relieved when they arrived in Revaine and a royal guard unit was waiting to escort them to Carlisse, allowing them to bypass the slum city quickly.

As they travelled by carriage through the vast farmland, Siljanna sent a message to Juliette. For the Imperator's plan to work they needed the king and queen out of the way, but emphasised they should not be killed. That could start a different, but equally devastating war. A few moments later, Juliette simply replied with *'consider it done'* and Siljanna was content to not know how but just that she would accomplish the task.

When Juliette closed her pager, she smiled to herself after reading the details of her next task. She'd enjoyed playing with King Grayson up to this point, but he was a particularly nasty piece of work. While bedding her, the king was also sleeping with one of his servants and demanded the queen visit him in order to conceive his heir. His relationship with the queen was clearly strenuous but regardless, she'd been brought to his chambers every other day and was due to visit again today.

Every time she did, her maid brought wine and that was the perfect target for one of Juliette's favourite concoctions. The same one she'd used on the blacksmith they'd tortured back in Siranor, but a less potent mixture, just in case the king had a delicate constitution. She mixed the toxins together and made her way towards the king's bedchamber. On the way, she spotted the maid, Caitlin, just like clockwork, pouring the wine into crystal goblets on the table outside. Juliette collided into her, making her knock over one of the goblets and it smashed on the floor.

"I am *so* sorry, I didn't see you there," she said, over-exaggerating her words, which Caitlin picked up on and knew she wasn't sorry.

"Of course you didn't," Caitlin replied, disinterested. She crouched down to pick up the broken pieces and while she wasn't looking, Juliette slipped the solution into the remaining goblet and hid the empty vial back in her satchel.

Just as she did, Queen Nadia came around the corner and spotted her chambermaid crouched over the broken glass.

"Caitlin, what happened?" She asked.

"Miss Juliette didn't notice my presence and bumped into me. I knocked over the goblet in the process, sorry my lady," Caitlin explained, giving the queen due respect whilst in public.

"Don't worry about it. Grayson is the one who insists on drinking during our... meetings. Just deliver his drink, I'll be in shortly," Nadia responded.

As Caitlin took the tainted glass into the king's chamber, Nadia turned to address Juliette.

"I don't trust you," she announced, scowling.

"You shouldn't your majesty. I have been sleeping with your husband," Juliette replied, smiling menacingly.

"There is no accounting for taste," the queen replied as she turned and reluctantly headed into the king's bedchamber.

As Juliette walked away, she whistled a lively tune to herself. She'd expected that to be harder. At the end of the corridor, she found a lounger with a great view over the city and made herself comfortable. She wouldn't have to wait long.

Less than an hour later, Caitlin marched passed Juliette again and knocked softly on the bedroom door. The queen exited looking worse for wear, as she usually did and with Caitlin's help, headed back to her room. Once out of sight, Juliette hopped up and made her way to the bedchamber. She also knocked but didn't wait for a response, walking in as she'd done on several occasions, already lowering the straps of her dress. She pretended to be shocked when she laid eyes on the king. He'd turned pale and was sweating profusely as he lay in bed.

"My liege, you look unwell. May I comfort you?" She asked, continuing to saunter forward.

"Juliette, I am in no state to see you this afternoon. Please leave," Grayson mumbled, trying to swallow back something that clearly tasted unpleasant.

"Of course, if that is truly what you wish," she replied. She went to leave but then Grayson doubled over, grabbing his stomach. A second later he reached over to the side of the bed and threw up. Juliette smiled to herself before turning back, putting on the best look of concern she could fake and went rushing to his side.

"Grayson, what's happened to you?" She asked, trying to make her voice match her false look of concern. Grayson tried to sit up but was sick again. All he was able to do was point towards the wine goblet on the bedside table. Juliette rushed over, making sure to avoid the parts of the floor covered with vomit and picked up the glass. She waited until she knew Grayson was watching and then ran her little finger along the edge and licked a droplet from within.

"Sire, I believe you've been poisoned!" She announced in a startled manner. "Who brought you this wine?"

The look on Grayson's face was furious as he snatched the goblet from Juliette's hand.

"The queen's maid always brings my wine," he advised snarling. "If that wench poisoned me out of some misguided loyalty to my wife, she will lose her head."

"Is it not more likely the queen commanded it? In the short time I have been here, even I've noticed her disdain towards you," Juliette suggested, stirring the situation the way she'd intended. Grayson was about to say something but then stopped, having to hold back a further convulsion of sickness before he could speak.

"Did the queen hire you to do this?" He asked bluntly.

"My lord, how could you say such a thing?" Juliette asked, feigning a hurt expression.

"You have demonstrated a unique talent in this field, how could I not?" He answered, sweat dripping down his forehead as his body started to tremble. Juliette doubted that the sweet act would work on the king so quickly decided to change tack.

"If I may be so bold, had the queen enlisted my service for this particular task; you'd already be dead my lord," she confirmed, and that answer seemed to convince him.

"Please forgive my accusation. Whatever this poison is has affected my judgement as well as my body," he replied, trying to earn her forgiveness.

"Of course, no need to apologise," she said graciously, reaching for his hand. "What the queen didn't anticipate however is that by having me on your side, I can ensure you survive this Grayson. I call myself a poisons expert because I also know how to counter the effects too. Once I find out what's been used, I can create an antidote. In the meantime, you should not let the queen's treachery go unpunished."

"Believe me, I won't! Fetch my guards. I have a priority arrest order to deliver," he replied furiously.

Arriving back in the queen's room, Caitlin helped Nadia to the nearest chair and called for Spencer. Grayson hadn't been as forceful this time but she was still in pain, and it was always made worse by the withering.

"I'm so sorry Nadia," Caitlin declared, hating the fact she endured this treatment every other day.

"It's not your fault Caitlin. I am just so grateful to both of you for staying with me. I would die without you," Nadia replied, her head hanging low from exhaustion. "I just wish I could bring a child to term. The sad thing is, I genuinely believe Grayson wouldn't touch me if I were with child."

"Would you really want to bring *his* child into the world?" Caitlin asked, knowing it was a cruel question but found herself needing to know.

"If I had any choice, I would leave him in a heartbeat. But my parents' lives depend on me producing an heir. I also have to believe that just because Grayson is a cruel man, that doesn't mean our child would be. I could raise the child better, to be good. Or at least, I could try," she replied, placing a hand just below her stomach, feeling the empty space that had almost brought them a child several times now.

"Let's focus on getting you healed for now Nadia, please. Until I can find a way to prevent the withering from killing your unborn child, the last thing you want is to be pregnant again," Spencer explained as he entered the room, gently running his hands over her body, healing the fresh bruises.

The number of times Spencer had run his hands over her body was like an added layer of torture. How he longed to place his hands upon her skin, not to heal but to show her what true passion felt like. She deserved to know that a man's touch could be soft, loving and pleasurable, but they both knew if he did, and the king found out, he would be killed. While he continued to heal her, Caitlin stepped out to fetch them a pot of tea. She knew she could leave Nadia safely in Spencer's care and sometimes seeing the bruises was too much for her to bear.

Walking towards the kitchen, she had to quickly get out of the way of four guards that were marching towards the queen's chamber.

Suspicious, she followed, staying out of sight as they approached Nadia's door.

"Queen Nadia, we command that you open this door," the guard called out. A few seconds later, wearing only a skimpy nightdress, Nadia pulled open the door and faced the guards.

"What is the meaning of this? I have served the king today and now I need my rest," she answered defiantly, trying to close the door again.

"If you think we are going to believe your lies, you are gravely mistaken," the first guard said before the second barged into the room and cuffed her.

"Queen Nadia, you are under arrest for the attempted murder of our noble king, Grayson Brock," he announced. "You can 'rest' in the castle dungeon."

"What? No!" Nadia gasped and tried to resist. As she did, the guard wrenched her by the arm and pulled her out into the hallway. Seeing the disturbance, Spencer came rushing to the door and challenged the arresting officer.

"You cannot take her, she's exhausted and wounded, she needs care," he proclaimed.

"She should have thought about that before poisoning the king," the guard countered, dismissing Spencer's protests.

In a fit of desperation, Spencer lashed out and struck the guard detaining Nadia, only to get arrested himself. He caught a glimpse of Caitlin and called out to her.

"Caitlin, run!" He shouted.

Realising she had no choice, Caitlin darted down the hall but Spencer's cry alerted the guards to her presence and she found herself pursued by the two guards that weren't holding Nadia and Spencer. She did the only thing she could and created an illusion of herself running in the direction of the servant's quarters when instead she turned and ran towards the library, knowing she could escape using the path from the upper level into the garden.

The guards fell for it and in the time it took for her illusion to fade away, she escaped, fleeing through the garden and towards the underground passage by the baker's shop. She knew her only hope was to find Harrison and the others and prayed that somehow, they could help her save Nadia and Spencer.

As they disembarked the carriage in the courtyard outside the Carlisse castle, Siljanna, Imperator Harlyn and Cameron were greeted by Juliette, who walked out of the castle with a smug look on her face. Just as she met them, she turned so they could see Queen Nadia and another man under arrest, being taken to the dungeon by the royal guards.

"The king is otherwise indisposed," Juliette advised, looking at each of them to see if they were curious. To her pleasure, they clearly were. "Quite the scandal if I do say so myself. The queen attempted to poison the king! He is terribly unwell but luckily, I was able to identify the poison and have given his majesty a suitable antidote. He should be back on his feet in a week or so."

"Well done Miss Lawrence," Harlyn expressed, speaking up first. "Your services in this endeavour have been pivotal."

"Thank you, Imperator Harlyn. Now if you don't mind, I must return to the king, to keep up appearances," Juliette replied, giving a slight bow as she departed.

"I think that is the first time she has truly impressed me," Siljanna admitted, still shocked at the efficient manner that Juliette had accomplished what they needed of her.

"She said she was *all kinds of impressive,*' didn't she?" Cameron replied, asking the rhetorical question whilst also trying to mask his surprise at the swift turn of events.

Turning his attention back to the present, Cameron instructed the soldiers that had accompanied them to follow the royal guards and take Nate and Paige to the dungeon. It was clear they were going to have fairly free rein of the castle so it was time for them to prepare the trap. They had the bait so just needed a way to let their prey know as much.

The next morning was cool in Arencia, and Harrison hoped it was the chill making him shiver but admitted it was partially nerves too. Maia had summoned him to the pavilion to receive the Arencian rune and be formally initiated into the Aegis Guard. He'd been told that accepting the rune was painful but aside from that, was excited to be a guardian again. In a strange way, it felt like coming full circle, back to his days as a warden.

Rylie had wanted to be there for the ritual, but Zack explained it was a rite of passage and had become a tradition that only the warrior, Lucas and Maia be present at the time. Reaching the top of the steps to the pavilion, Harrison made his way inside and saw Lucas and Maia, both standing in ceremonial grabs at the far side of the room.

"Good morning Harrison, are you ready?" Lucas asked as Harrison approached them.

"I am Captain Harper," Harrison confirmed, hoping the formality sounded as respectful as he'd intended. Lucas smiled and came towards him with an odd-looking crest. Upon examination, Harrison recognised the design as the same mark on Zack's neck.

"This is the sigil of the Aegis Guard. It represents our service, as protectors of the Ar'encal and mages here," Lucas began, explaining the intricate design. Harrison took another look at the crest, appreciating its beauty as a craftsman.

"It's so elegant," Harrison whispered under his breath.

"When you are ready, please place the sigil against your collarbone, between your throat and your heart," Lucas instructed, indicating exactly where by revealing his own rune. Harrison matched the placement as Maia came towards him.

"With this sacred rune, I bestow upon you, Harrison Stone, the gift of the Ar'encal, in return for your servitude to the Aegis Guard. Long may you protect us as this rune will protect you," she announced, speaking clearly as she touched the sigil.

As she did, he felt a burning. He withstood the pain as the power coursing through him seared his skin. He imagined this was what branding felt like but clenched his fists and gritted his teeth, willing himself to endure. A few moments later, the burning stopped and Maia removed the sigil from his skin.

"It is done," she confirmed, touching him gently on the shoulder. Her fingers glided across the rune and with a cool, soothing sensation, the pain faded away.

"The pain, it's gone," Harrison exhaled, having never been healed by magic before.

"You only need endure the creation of the rune," Maia said kindly. "There is nothing in the rules that prevents me from healing you afterwards. How do you feel?"

"Much better, thank you," he replied, turning to a nearby mirror to see the rune upon his skin.

"There will be a gathering here tomorrow, to celebrate your initiation, but until then, the day is yours. I believe your enthusiastic young friend Alex and my son are hoping you'll give them another combat lesson," Lucas advised with a chuckle. "At the rate they are learning, I should send the rest of my guards to you for additional training."

"I'm happy to train the other guards anytime. Although I doubt your eldest son would be too pleased," Harrison remarked, making Lucas laugh in a short, loud burst.

"You're probably right there," he replied.

"I believe there is someone else looking for training from you today too," Maia added, piquing his curiosity. "After her impressive display yesterday, I gave Rylie a day to rest but I believe she intends to spend her time with you and the other boys learning how to defend herself."

Her words reminded Harrison that Rylie had indeed asked him to train her too so he excused himself and headed over to the training grounds. It wasn't that early when he arrived so was surprised to find that Alex and Zack weren't there, but Rylie was. She was standing just outside the armoury holding two stiletto knives, looking curiously at each of them. He headed towards her and when she realised he was there, she looked up and smiled.

"Hey you! Is it official, do you have the rune?" She asked inquisitively. As he got closer, he pulled back the top of his armour just enough to show the upper edge of the rune.

"It's official, you're looking at the newest member of the Aegis Guard," he replied, feeling just as pleased as he sounded. "It all feels a bit surreal."

"I'm sure it does, but you'll find your feet in no time," she encouraged. She knew that although he'd found ways to enjoy life as a smith, in truth, he was happiest during his time at the academy and the early days of being a warden. Being a guardian was his calling and within the Aegis Guard, he had the chance to be that person again. "May I have the first training session with the new recruit?"

"Of course! Do you like the feel of those knives? It's a difficult talent to master, dual wielding, but I've seen you do some pretty incredible things lately and I'm sure you could learn this too," Harrison replied, making her grin.

"I'd like to try," she confirmed, gripping the knives more firmly.

"All right then, let's get started," he enthused, looking forward to sharing his skills with her.

They spent the first hour practising a good battle stance, something that would feel natural to her but also keep her well-guarded. Harrison had always preferred two-handed weapons but had studied dual wielding in his first year at the academy. Remembering Tutor Taylor who was particularly well-versed in knife combat, he tried to recall and instruct Rylie in a way that'd make

Taylor proud. When he felt confident she'd grasped the basics, he collected his sword and encouraged her to spar.

"You need to get a feel for them, take a few practice swings at me. See how it feels when the blades come into contact with another weapon, the recoil and most importantly, learn how to recover," he suggested but with a playful look on his face. He wanted her to strike first.

"You want me to attack you, seriously?" She asked.

"Don't worry, I'll go easy on you!" He replied, winking. He saw her expression change, a confident smile spreading across her face. She was going to accept the challenge.

Adopting the stance they had been practising, she raised the blade in her dominant hand while keeping the second blade low, protecting her body should he attempt to retaliate. Harrison nodded and she cautiously made the first blow, connecting the blade with his sword. He could tell the intensity of the recoil had been more than she was expecting but her determination won out as she spun and returned to the starting stance.

"And again," he said, encouraging her to keep trying. "Try to string a few strikes together, I can take it."

"All right, you asked for it," she replied boldly.

As they continued training, she gained familiarity quickly, and with her confidence came speed. Before long, they were properly sparring and Harrison had to concentrate to block her advances. They manoeuvred around the training grounds, making use of the space when Zack and Alex arrived. Once they noticed Rylie training with Harrison, they rushed over to cheer her on. Hearing the commotion, Noah also made his way into the training grounds but stayed out of sight. After his embarrassing defeat at Harrison's hand, Noah had zero interest in being friends but he was drawn to watch Rylie.

"Rylie, you're awesome!" Alex shouted, jumping at the side-lines as he watched Harrison block attack after attack.

"I had no idea you had it in you!" Zack followed up, also cheering. Rylie didn't risk looking but enjoyed their energetic encouragement. Harrison gave her another wicked smile, enticing her to keep coming at him, and so she did.

With a flurry of strikes, her blades clattered over and over against his sword, the metal humming as they sparred. The moment she saw an opening, Rylie shifted her weight and changed the direction of her assault. Obviously not expecting it, Harrison quickly moved his sword to block again and as their blades collided, he automatically pushed back as he would've when training with Morgan or Siljanna and the motion sent Rylie toppling to the floor. Harrison rushed over to apologise until he noticed she was laughing. Knowing she was okay, Harrison shook his head, then laughed too.

"You made me work for that one," he admitted, offering her a hand to get back to her feet.

"And yet I'm the one lying in the dirt," she replied with a chuckle, grabbing his hand and allowing him to haul her up. His aid was stronger than she expected and as she got back to her feet, she stumbled forward and into his arms.

They continued to laugh but more softly, standing closer than they had in a long time. She regained her balance by placing both hands against his chest and he also steadied her by gently holding her shoulders. She was just about to step away but instead, touched his new rune with her fingertips while Harrison lightly brushed a few strands of her hair away. Their eyes met, and they looked at each other warmly.

Harrison wondered if maybe this was it, his time to finally tell her how he felt, but then remembered they had an audience. He allowed Rylie to step away but as she did, she gently ran her hand down his arm, their fingers catching for a second. When their hands parted, Harrison felt it, a spark. It wasn't subtle either, but a literal spark. His rune burned slightly, absorbing the magic but when he looked to see if Rylie had felt it too, it was too late. She'd already turned away, collecting her knives.

The other person that noticed the spark between them, however, was Noah. With his dislike for Harrison growing, Noah decided that this was too perfect an opportunity to take revenge. Harrison had made a fool of him at the battle test but now, Noah knew how to get back at him.

Returning her daggers to the armoury, Rylie said goodbye to her friends.

"Well, I better get going. Evie and Lianna have been training with Alistair—" she advised, then paused, smiling as she corrected herself, "my grandfather today. He was going to focus on helping Lianna channel her empathy and give Evie some techniques that could trigger more specific visions."

"Did Evie mention our narrow escape from Carlisse by any chance?" Harrison asked, already knowing the answer.

"How did you guess?" Rylie responded playfully.

"Maybe I've got pre-cognition too, or secretly psionic and read your mind," he replied making her laugh.

"You wish soldier boy! Stick to your shiny sword and I'll try round two in a few days. By then I might've learnt how to throw fireballs so watch out!" She teased, winking at him.

As Rylie left the training grounds, Harrison caught a glimpse of someone hiding behind the infirmary. He couldn't be sure but his gut told him it was Noah. Whatever he was there for was none of Harrison's concern, so he returned his attention to Zack and Alex.

"Who's my next victim?" He asked, slashing the air a few times with his sword to show that despite the hours of training with Rylie, he was still full of energy. In fact, those final moments with her had only energised him further.

"Come on then hot shot, let's do some target practice," Zack challenged retrieving bows for all of them. They lined up by the targets and after letting loose a few shots, Zack landed a perfect shot in the centre of the yellow bullseye.

"You did it, Zack!" Harrison applauded. "You know you're going to have to do that every time from now on, right?"

"You're hilarious," Zack replied sarcastically but with a huge smile. He was clearly proud of himself. "I think I'm going to leave that arrow there, just for a bit. I want to enjoy this moment."

"Come on, I'll treat you to a glass of water to celebrate!" Harrison jested.

"No, we can't stop now, I want to hit the bullseye too!" Alex protested.

"Keep your elbow up and I reckon you'll be striking yellow in no time," Harrison advised, causing the young man to re-focus and release a series of shots.

Leaving him to continue practising, Harrison and Zack strolled over to the water fountain by the infirmary. Harrison couldn't help but look over to where Noah was skulking earlier. Collecting the water in two glasses as he'd promised, Harrison handed one to Zack and took the chance to chat while they drank.

"I saw your brother around here earlier," he began, the feeling in his gut telling him Noah was up to no good.

"Probably marking his territory," Zack replied. "He must hate the fact that I'm back and the way you beat him during my father's test too."

"How long do you think he'll hold a grudge for that?" Harrison asked, raising a curious eyebrow.

"Noah is the undisputed champion of holding grudges. I'd say at least the next twenty years but you could be in for a life sentence," Zack answered, taking a swig of water.

"Fantastic!" Harrison replied, rolling his eyes. In truth, he didn't care. Noah hadn't done anything to earn his friendship or respect. "It's a good thing I've got the good brother on my side."

"It was him you know, Noah. He convinced me I wasn't good enough to be an Aegis Guard and told me I should leave Arencia. My father never noticed the way he spoke to me, Noah was always his protege."

"I know that feeling," Harrison confessed, opening up too. "I could've single-handedly defeated an army but it was always my sister's accomplishments our father relished. But Siljanna was kind, unlike your brother."

"Your sister, the one hunting us, is kind?" Zack questioned.

"I know it's hard to believe, but yes. Any relationship with my father was tough, to say the least, and I can't say I'm sad he's gone but growing up, Siljanna was always good to me," Harrison admitted. "We were close until my father's stubbornness and violent tendencies pulled us apart. The people in Tivani are safer now that he's dead."

"By violent tendencies, you mean arson," Zack commented, getting a subtle smile from Harrison in response.

"I just wish Siljanna believed that," Harrison began. "All of this could have been avoided if she'd just listened and believed that as much as she loved him, our father was to blame for the fire, not Rylie."

"But then if you'd never been on the run, you may have never found this place, and the girls might never have had this chance to learn about their powers or meet their grandfather. Plus, you'd never have met me! Surely that would've been the biggest travesty," Zack replied playfully, making Harrison laugh, almost coughing up his water.

"One day, I have to introduce you to my friend Morgan. You guys are like two peas in a pod," Harrison chuckled.

"Sounds like a fab guy! I'll hold you to that," Zack replied, "and in the meantime, just forget about Noah. He's always been a difficult person to like."

"So, he's a jerk?" Harrison asked, smirking.

"Yeah, Alex summed him up pretty perfectly," Zack replied cheerfully. "Unfortunately, he's a jerk with charisma, a nice haircut and a superiority complex. Everyone in town has always idolised him so he's never needed to be likeable. Well, until you came along."

"Happy to be of assistance," Harrison chimed. "Even your father seemed pleased I knocked him down a peg or two."

"Yeah, that was great!" Zack said with delight, casting his mind back and replaying the memory in his head. "The only thing I would say, seriously—" and as Zack spoke, his tone changed, becoming stern, "don't let him get too close to the girls. He'd betray any of us in a heartbeat if it gave him some kind of advantage."

"That could be a problem," Harrison replied.

"Why?" Zack asked, instantly concerned.

"Because he's already expressed an interest in Rylie, and she might return his feelings," Harrison answered, his eyes shifting to the floor nervously.

"Oh no, you've got to shoot that down and soon!" Zack replied, looking urgently at Harrison. "Seriously man, do not let Rylie fall for my brother. He's a charmer but unlike me, he'll take what he wants, no matter who gets hurt in the process."

"It's okay, I want to tell Rylie how I feel. I felt a spark today, a real spark so I think she may have feelings for me too," he replied, and Zack's reaction was ecstatic.

"Really? That's great! When are you going to tell her? Tonight, please say you will speak to her tonight," Zack begged, his words coming out at an unprecedented speed.

"I was thinking maybe at the gathering tomorrow. It feels like that would be the right moment," Harrison advised, watching as Zack clapped with joy. Harrison laughed and outright called Zack a child but he clearly didn't care.

Finishing their drinks, Harrison and Zack headed back over to Alex who was shouting for them, wanting to show off his improved aim.

Chapter Twenty
United

Having seen the affectionate display between Harrison and Rylie, Noah slipped away from the training grounds unnoticed to formulate a plan. Already attracted to Rylie and planning the date he'd promised, all he had to do was speed up his efforts for maximum impact against Harrison. He was confident Rylie was interested in him and whether Harrison's feelings for her were just growing or deep-set, losing her now would teach Harrison not to underestimate him.

Writing a poetic note, he invited Rylie to meet him in the forest at dusk, putting the letter in a bottle with a map marking the spot and a rose on her doorstep. He was confident she wouldn't resist his romantic gesture but stayed nearby until she returned home, to make sure she found it. Reacting just as he'd predicted, he watched Rylie dash inside before sauntering off to get ready. He was determined to sweep Rylie off her feet.

After collecting everything he wanted to set up a little picnic, Noah dressed in his best shirt and favourite dark jeans before setting off to the secluded location he'd marked on the map. When the sun started to set he lit the candles that adorned the pathway and scattered rose petals, knowing Rylie would shortly arrive. When she did, Noah forgot for a moment that their date was part of his greater plan to antagonise Harrison, because he was mesmerised by Rylie's appearance.

Unlike earlier in the day when she had her hair tied back and wore comfortable training gear, Rylie was now dressed in a dark purple asymmetric dress, embellished with a slight lace detail around the neckline and straps. Her gentle curls rolled over her shoulders, the orange light from the fading sun highlighting the lighter stands in her hair. Walking towards him, impressed by the candle-lit pathway, she looked amused and he realised his mouth was gaping.

"You look stunning," he said by way of a greeting.

He stepped to the side, revealing the picnic spread and invited her to sit. He didn't know what she liked to drink but had bought wine, and she gracefully accepted when he poured her a glass.

"This is wonderful Noah," she commented, clinking his glass. "You didn't need to do so much just for me."

"But I wanted to," he asserted. "I want to know you better Rylie, more intimately."

She took an intentional sip of the wine after hearing the word *intimately* but her smile told him she was intrigued.

"But why me?" She asked. "Surely there are a number of women interested in you from Arencia."

"Isn't it obvious? Your beauty is undeniable and your powers incredible. How your heart has not been won by another remains the biggest mystery," he answered flirtatiously, edging closer to her so that their thighs were lightly touching.

Feeling speechless and softly worrying her lip, Rylie reached over to the fruit basket he'd laid out. Taking in every curve of her body as she moved, each one flattered by the style of her dress, Noah decided not to bother with small talk. As she reached for the fruit, Noah wrapped his arm around her waist, rolling her onto the blanket until he was hovering above her. She gasped as he leaned in, passionately kissing her. She went rigid under his touch, stunned at how forward he was but didn't stop him. He moved his lips down, kissing her neck and then looked up into her eyes. She was hypnotised and he used the opportunity to press himself against her as their lips connected again.

As she relaxed into his kiss, he felt a heat. At first, it was only slight but after a second, her skin and lips felt as if they were on fire. The sensation seared his lips and as it did, he felt his rune ache and his body reacted. Violently pushing her away, Noah launched himself to his feet.

"You burned me!" He shouted, touching his lip and glaring as if she'd attacked him.

"I'm sorry, my powers are linked to my emotions—" she stammered, her eyes apologetic and desperately trying to explain it wasn't intentional.

"I don't want to hear it," he snarled, his ego bruised as the realisation sank in that if he didn't have his rune, she could've injured him. "If this is how you treat people who are attracted to you, it's no wonder you're alone."

"Noah, please," Rylie winced, covering her face with shame.

"This was supposed to be fun, playing with you, taking you away from him," he hissed, the initial attraction he'd felt evaporating as he looked down at her. He was always attracted to powerful women, but Rylie wasn't powerful, she was an unstable force. That wasn't good enough for him.

"What?" She exclaimed, mortified. "This was just some sort of conquest to you?"

"And what if it was?" He replied audaciously.

"I can't believe this," she whispered, stupefied.

"And I can't believe you! After what you just did, I'm going to make sure everyone knows it's too dangerous to touch you," he replied, looking at her as if she were dirt.

It was a totally unjustified reaction, but it hit Rylie hard. As the anxiety she'd felt when first triggering her powers surfaced, she glared at Noah, almost unable to comprehend how quickly things had turned. Flames began to flicker between her fingers which had only happened when she was overwhelmed before, but now, she was angry. She felt herself about to burst but at the same time, didn't want to prove his point. Instead, she picked up the glass of wine and threw it in his face. Momentarily blinded by the liquid, Noah grumbled and swore. He cleared his eyes but when he looked back, Rylie was gone.

Kicking the basket of fruit at his feet, Noah screamed, releasing all his frustrations. After stomping around the picnic area for a few minutes, he skulked back home. He'd almost made it when he decided to about-face and head to the training grounds. He was in the mood for a fight.

Marching across the main field, Noah was pleased to see that Harrison and Zack were still there. Although convinced he could take them both on, Noah settled on the idea of challenging Zack. Defeating him always made him feel superior. Picking up a sword, he hurled it at the training dummy next to Zack.

"What the...!" Zack exclaimed as he reactively jumped out of the way. "Noah, what's your problem?"

Reaching his brother, Noah threw a wild punch but Zack easily dodged it, causing Noah to lose his footing. Harrison capitalised with a strong push, knocking Noah to the floor to defend his friend. He landed with a crunch but kept his attention on his brother.

"Afraid to fight your own battles brother?" He spat.

"Not anymore, but I have no reason to fight you," Zack responded. Noah pulled himself back to his feet and continued to glare at his brother.

"Well, I have enough reasons for both of us. Let's settle this, one-on-one. Unless you can't face me without your new protector," he replied snidely.

Harrison reached out to Zack, stopping him.

"Zack, he's just trying to rile you. You don't have to fight," Harrison insisted, not wanting Zack to succumb to Noah's taunts.

"Thank you, Harrison, but I do," Zack replied, turning back to face Noah who was rolling his shoulders, preparing to attack. "I need to end this once and for all, by myself."

Harrison nodded, stepping back to allow Zack to face his brother alone. Realising that Zack was going to accept his challenge, Noah gritted his teeth, clenched his fists and took a swing. Zack was able to dodge again but this time, Noah kept his balance and turned sharply, following up his first strike with another and another, missing Zack each time. He was quicker than Noah remembered but speed alone wouldn't save him.

On his next attempt, he feigned with his dominant hand and as Zack evaded, he moved straight into Noah's intended strike with his off-hand. The blow winded him and gave Noah the chance to strike him hard. Zack tumbled to the floor but before Noah could continue his assault, Zack kicked out, catching him in the shin so that Noah fell to the floor beside him.

"What's gotten into you, Noah? This is madness!" Zack yelled in between heavy breaths. They rolled away from each other, getting back to their knees as Noah replied.

"What's mad is that you brought these people here, to my city!" He shouted wildly. "You were not welcome here, but not only did you return, you bring a soldier to ruin my reputation and that unstable bitch of a mage too! Rylie just lost control and burnt me, she should be taken away from this place and left for the mage hunters."

Hearing that a guardian of mages would even suggest such a thing, let alone that the intended target was Rylie, enraged Harrison. He reacted immediately, unable to stand back. Grabbing Noah by the shirt, he pulled him to his feet and slammed him against the armoury wall.

"Talk, Now! What happened between you and Rylie? Where is she?" Harrison demanded, his voice seething.

"Like I'd tell you. I don't care what happens to her. I'm doing the world a favour leaving her lost in the woods," Noah replied, spitting as he answered.

As he took in Noah's response, Harrison erupted. He began mercilessly hitting Noah over and over, only pausing when Zack pulled them apart. Harrison tried to get around his friend to attack again, as did Noah who wanted to retaliate, but Zack remained between them.

"Harrison stop, he's not worth it! It's more important to find Rylie," he cried, keeping his arms outstretched to prevent both of them from lashing out again.

"You'll never find her. She buggered off into the forest, and good riddance I say," Noah retorted, wiping blood from the corner of his mouth. At that, Zack turned and shoved his brother against the wall.

"Can you stop being a jerk for one minute?" He asked but already knew the answer. "Just leave us be Noah. Go lick your wounds and get over yourself. Our feud is over and I won't tolerate you threatening me or my friends again."

"You can't stop me," Noah replied which resulted in Zack hitting him squarely in the face. He fell to the ground with a loud thud.

"Actually, I can Noah. You are the weak one brother, and if you make me, I will stop you," Zack asserted. "Now, where's Rylie?"

Noah frowned, refusing to speak after being defeated again.

"He's not going to tell us anything is he?" Harrison asked, his rage replaced by worry. "I need to find Rylie."

"Forget him, he's pitying himself too much to care about anything other than his ego," Zack replied. "Let's find the others, maybe they can help."

Rushing from the training ground to their overwater home, Harrison and Zack ran through the front door to see Evie, Lianna and Alex just settling down to have some dinner.

"Do any of you know where Rylie is?" Harrison asked desperately. Evie looked a combination of sad and angry at the question so Lianna replied.

"Oh, you didn't know? She's got a date tonight with Noah! They're out in the forest, hopefully having a great time," she informed, but when she saw the distressed look on both their faces, Lianna's expression turned to mirror their concern. "What's happened?"

"Something went wrong. We just had a run-in with Noah at the training grounds. Rylie is somewhere in the forest, alone. Noah said she lost control of her powers, burnt him and fled," Zack explained. "He's almost certainly exaggerated things but regardless, she could need help."

Taken aback by his explanation, Lianna gasped as she rushed to her feet, shortly followed by Evie and Alex.

"What can we do?" Lianna asked.

"Is there anything you can do to help me find her? Sense her in any way or see her in a vision?" Harrison asked, obviously desperate to find out if she was okay. Evie and Lianna looked at each other and nodded. They held hands as Evie took out her vial of Encia and drank.

"What's she doing?" Alex asked, startled.

"Alistair taught us a technique this afternoon. If she concentrates all her energy on Rylie, she might be able to force a vision of where she is. By keeping a close contact, I can help her to keep calm and focus so that she controls the vision and not the other way round," Lianna explained.

Evie shut her eyes and shook slightly, the Encia surging her power, but a tight squeeze from Lianna seemed to help. Her eyes were moving behind her closed lids, just like a person dreaming, when she spoke.

"I can see her. She's alone, sitting somewhere in the forest. There's a waterfall, not the main one around the city but something smaller, running down into an enclosed lake. There's a large tree in the centre and some kind of white lanterns around her," Evie explained, trying to detail everything she could see.

"That sounds like Maiden Falls. It runs just off Lake Baliten, maybe ten minutes down the path. I could take you there," Zack offered. He paused just as Evie dropped to her knees, Lianna and Alex rushing to her side.

"You guys go, we'll look after Evie," Lianna suggested.

"No! Let me go alone, please. *I* need to find her," Harrison insisted and before Zack had a chance to reply, he was gone. Zack let his friend go alone, knowing that just like facing up to his brother, this was something Harrison needed to do by himself.

It was dark by the time Harrison passed Lake Baliten, the Encia in the water luminous in a way he'd never seen before, sparkling like stars underneath the surface. The pathway around the lake was visible thanks to a few crystallised lanterns and the moonlight, where it peaked through the heavy tree line. As the path descended, he found himself beside the singular fall that Evie mentioned and before him was an enclosed lake with a large tree at its centre, just as she'd described.

The water was rich in Encia and combined with the glowing crystal lanterns, the whole area was illuminated almost more than it would have been during the day. The tree in the centre spiralled upwards, its bark thick and sturdy, as if it had been there for hundreds if not thousands of years. It was faintly glowing, like it had fused with the Encia in the water below. The hanging branches were filled with verdant leaves that just skimmed the surface. Taking his gaze away from the tree, he scanned the shoreline and found Rylie.

With a sigh of relief, he jogged towards her. She was sitting on the floor holding her legs, facing away from him, also taking in the magnificent sight of the lake and its surrounding flora. As he neared, she heard his footsteps and turned.

"Rylie, are you okay?" He asked, pausing before he got too close. He had expected her to be upset but her expression told him otherwise.

"I'm fine. Sorry if you were worried," she replied, her voice quiet but with a hint of frustration.

"Of course I was worried, we all were! What happened? Noah said you lost control—" he asked, crouching beside her.

"I didn't! I—," she stuttered, sinking her head down and looking away from him. "Noah kissed me tonight, and I let him. I let myself *feel* and of course, without controlling my emotions, my powers reacted. I thought it was only the slightest warmth but apparently not. He freaked out, accused me of burning him and threatened me."

As her anger rose, he could see her visibly trying to stop the flames from igniting in her hands.

"Did he hurt you?" Harrison queried, and the care in his voice made Rylie face him.

"Not really. He pushed me down, but I'll be all right. I'm just so angry; at him, and at myself! He'd made it clear he liked me but I've never been so bold with a person I barely know. Not only that, but I told myself he would understand, having lived with mages his entire life, but of course, he didn't," she muttered quickly.

"I don't care about Noah, only you!" Harrison replied.

"Surely he knows magic is tied to emotions and that a first kiss would be emotional. Plus, he has a protection rune!" She ranted, her hands holding onto her legs tightly. "Harrison, I swear, I didn't lose control, I just wanted to let myself connect with someone I thought could love me."

She stopped herself then as if silently scolding herself. As she went to turn away, Harrison stood and reached his hand out. He stayed close so that she had to look up at him. As her gaze travelled from his hand to his eyes, she tilted her head quizzically.

"Dance with me?" He asked.

"What? You've never offered to dance with me," she remarked, recalling the night at his academy graduation.

"Maybe I've changed," he replied with a smile.

Seeing his expression, she reached up and took his hand cautiously. As soon as they touched, a spark flickered between them. There was no denying it. She searched his warm brown eyes, trying to understand. His expression was confident, in stark contrast to her own. The blue flecks in her otherwise cool grey irises were brightened by the Encia shining around them as she looked questioningly at him.

As she gave him her hand, he pulled her intentionally into his arms, raising his left arm and wrapping his right around her, resting it just below her shoulder blade. She immediately relaxed, the stance being so natural to her. Like her father had once told him, she was born to dance.

With their eyes still locked, he moved forward, quietly humming the waltz tune her mother had played time and time again in the tavern. She followed with an easy grace, only letting her head turn away because it was the correct way to dance. They glided along the shoreline and as they did, she closed her eyes, every worry and negative thought in her mind evaporating.

Glancing to the side, Harrison saw the ripples of water moving towards her, reacting to her positivity. He decided to prove once and for all that she could let go and still control her abilities. Decisively, he stepped off the edge of the path and onto the lake, the surface of the water supporting them just as it had in Rylie's training session. She hadn't noticed where they were but Harrison was elated and continued to dance in the moonlight, the Encia glistening at their feet.

"See Rylie, you can do anything," he said lovingly as they glided to a stop. At that moment she realised where they were, looked around and down to the water beneath her feet. Just as she did, the once firm surface of the water liquified and they went crashing beneath the surface.

The water was only deep enough to reach Rylie's elbow so after being initially submerged, they could both stand but were both completely soaked. Once they realised as much, Rylie burst out laughing. Harrison smiled and could resist no longer. He reached forward with both hands, cupping her face and kissed her. The kiss was filled with desire and longing but short, as he pulled away anxiously. Her eyes remained closed as she reached up and touched her lips.

"That was—" Harrison tried to speak but lost his breath.

"A kiss... at least, I think it was, it's all a bit of a blur," she murmured, her tone hushed and eyes fluttering open to look at him. He smiled, laughing under his breath as their eyes locked.

"Shall I clarify for you?" He asked but he didn't let her reply, sliding one hand down her neck so that her face tilted towards his as he kissed her again. This time, the kiss was long and tender, any anxiety he had washed away.

He felt the warmth rising from her, but it wasn't a burn, it was like drinking hot tea when you were freezing and thirsty. He wanted more, and she did too, so their kiss deepened. She wound her arms around his neck and they pulled each other close, gravitating together.

Harrison's rune began to ache from resisting the Encia around him and the magic within her, but he barely felt it. All his senses were attuned to one thing, Rylie. When their lips finally parted, she grazed her hand down his cheek, her fingers lingering on his jawline, close to his lips.

"How long have you wanted to do that?" She asked, with a slightly wicked tone.

"Longer than I should admit," he replied, his cheeky grin enhancing his already delighted expression. Her mouth gaped but the smile behind it was clear. She was about to say something else but splashed him instead. He laughed, wiping the water from his face.

"Oh, it's on now Auren!" He called out and they began play-fighting in the water, only stopping when Rylie noticed his rune burning so she forced him to get out of the lake.

"Let's go home," she whispered softly.

He couldn't resist kissing her again before taking her hand as they headed back to Arencia.

When they walked through the front door of their home, Harrison and Rylie were greeted by the anxious faces of all their friends. The first thing the group noticed was that both of them were soaking wet and gave a combination of concerned and confused expressions.

"So I have good news," Harrison announced with a cheeky smile, alerting Evie and Lianna. "The rune works!"

"Is that all?" Evie probed. Laughing at their deflated reaction, Harrison continued.

"Oh, and I finally told Rylie how I feel," he added, grinning.

That announcement had the desired effect and made the group notice that Rylie and Harrison were holding hands, looking at each other lovingly. It was all the confirmation Evie and Lianna needed, flying off their chairs to hug them, Evie going straight for Harrison and Lianna to Rylie.

"It's about time!" Evie exclaimed as she embraced him.

"Your vision was spot on kiddo, and believe me, it was worth the wait," he replied, messing her hair affectionately.

Evie and Lianna swapped over to give more hugs as Alex and Zack joined them, also thrilled. That night, they all slept more peacefully than they had in weeks, waking up the next day feeling truly rested.

The following day was Harrison's celebration gathering and everything leading up to it went smoothly. Harrison didn't want a big affair and so when it came time to enjoy the party, they dressed comfortably and headed to the pavilion. It had been decorated slightly but it was the smiling faces of Maia, Lucas and several of the other Aegis Guards, Ar'encal and mages that Harrison noticed first. Walking in with Rylie on his arm and his friends around him just made the whole night perfect. Noah even turned up but kept to himself and left as soon as he realised that Harrison and Rylie had become an item. Seeing him reminded Rylie of his threat, however, and she quickly headed over to speak with Maia.

"Maia, can we talk for a moment?" She asked.

"Of course Rylie, although I think I already know what this is about," Maia replied.

"Has Noah spoken to you?" She queried, worrying at her lip, her fingers clasped together.

"He has, but you have nothing to worry about. Noah has a tendency for exaggerating but I want you to know that even if you did lose control, my goal is to help mages, not turn them away or endanger them. Your place here is not at risk," she confirmed, her words making Rylie visibly relax.

"Oh thank you, that is such a relief," she replied.

"You have nothing to thank me for. Now go, enjoy the party with your friends, and don't worry about Noah," Maia added cheerfully. "He's been sheltered most of his life and isn't used to adversity, but I believe he'll come around."

"I hope you're right," Rylie said, smiling shyly before turning back to re-join Harrison and the others.

The rest of the night was filled with merriment. When Harrison took to the floor with Rylie, they danced to both quick and slow songs, their faces filled with joy. Alex and Evie stood on the side-lines, giggling at Alistair's *dad dancing* with Maia, while the others chatted idly.

Noticing she was alone, Zack headed over to Lianna with a glass of wine.

"Can I offer you a drink?" He enquired nervously.

"No cold shoulder or over-zealous romantic gesture?" She asked, teasing him.

"I deserve that," he replied, sitting down and handing the drink over to her. She accepted it and took a sip.

"I'm happy for them," she mused, looking towards Harrison and Rylie.

"Me too," he said honestly. "I wanted to tell you… I'm sorry. I know I came on a bit strong when we first met."

"A bit?" She giggled, looking back at him with raised eyebrows.

"Okay, a lot too strong, but I really did like you. I know now that I went about it the wrong way *and* it would take a blind man not to see you have feelings for Spencer," he replied, pausing to smile as she grimaced at the statement.

"I did lose my mind a little over Spencer," she began but he hushed her.

"Shhh, I need to say this. I'm sorry for reacting the way I did and treating you so coldly. Can we be friends?" He asked and she could feel how genuine his question was.

"Of course we can," she replied without hesitation. "If it makes you feel any better, I don't think things are going to work out between me and Spencer."

"Am I allowed to be happy about that or will it ruin our newfound friendship?" He asked playfully.

"It might ruin things a little," she replied, looking at him out of the corner of her eye.

"Well, in that case, I'll say what a good friend should and tell you not to give up hope. You never know what will happen and he'd have to be pretty damn stupid not to love someone like you," Zack comforted, placing his hand on her shoulder.

"Thanks, that means a lot," she replied, gratefully leaning into his touch.

"And if he doesn't come to his senses, I can always shoot him for you. Turns out, I'm a pretty good shot!" He jested.

"No! No shooting anyone on my behalf, especially Spencer," she insisted, unable to stop herself from laughing. The gesture was innocent, and she appreciated it but Zack still made a big show of groaning at her answer before reaching over to the bottle of wine to top them both up.

"To not shooting Spencer!" He toasted, as they clinked glasses and enjoyed the rest of the evening from the side-lines.

The next morning, everyone woke up late and even Maia left an announcement on the pavilion noticeboard that classes would start later in the afternoon. Zack was the first to stir among the group and decided that after reconciling with his father, standing up to his brother and patching things up with Lianna, there was only one more thing he needed to do to get over the ghosts of his past. He needed to go back to the Ilirian woods where his mother had died and forgive himself for what happened that day.

He made his way into the kitchen to prepare a knapsack, in case he was out longer than expected and left a note for the others. He was just about to leave when Lianna came out of her bedroom and spotted him.

"Where are you going?" She asked curiously.

"I'm heading to Iliria, just for a few hours. There's something I need to do," he replied. Her continued look of confusion told him to explain. "Meeting all of you in the last few weeks has given me something I've never had before; real friends and the chance to live the life I was meant to. Because of all of you, I have the courage to return to my past once more. I need to forgive myself for what happened the day my mother died."

"Let me come with you," Lianna offered to his surprise. She could sense this was important to him.

"Really? I don't want to be a burden," he began.

"It's no burden, this is what friends do," she replied and her expression told him not to argue. He smiled gratefully as she packed a few extra things and they headed towards the crescent falls.

After ascending to the top, he led her from the platform, diverting through the town they'd missed on the way in, to the area of woods where he and Noah used to play as children. He remembered the path well, the route ingrained into his memory and quickly found the spot he was looking for.

"Was this the place?" Lianna asked, feeling his anxiety.

"Yeah… Noah and I were over by those trees and the hunters attacked from the West. I fell about here, unable to keep up and my mum got between me and the hunters just there," he explained, pointing to the place where she died. He was trying to recall the event without giving away how much the memory hurt, then remembered he was with an empath.

Lianna walked over to him and gave him a compassionate hug. Although a lot shorter than Zack, it didn't matter and she held him tightly, allowing him to bury his head into her shoulder.

"You were four years old Zack, there is no way it was your fault," Lianna said comforting him. "Your mother would have never wanted you to beat yourself up all these years. Try to forgive yourself."

"Thank you, Lianna, you're right. My mother wouldn't have wanted me to blame myself. I just hope that if she can see me now, she's proud of the man I've become," he mumbled with uncertainty, stepping away from her embrace.

"She is Zack," Lianna replied whole-heartedly.

They stayed for a while and Zack told Lianna what he could remember of his mother. They were just about to leave when the sound of desperate panting and heavy footsteps caught their attention. Looking towards the noise, they were stunned to see Caitlin emerge from further down the woodland path. She skidded to a halt when she realised it was them.

"It's you! I can't believe it, I found you," she cried.

"Caitlin? What's going on, why are you here?" Zack asked, both worried and puzzled by her sudden appearance.

"There was an attempt on the king's life; Nadia and Spencer have been blamed and arrested! Please, I need you and the others to help me save them," she begged.

The three of them rushed back to Arencia and with Lianna there, not bound by the secrecy of the rune, they were able to lead Caitlin straight through the fall's illusion and into the city. Caitlin was clearly in awe of the magic sustaining the illusion and the beauty of the city but they didn't have time to give her a tour.

Striding purposefully, they made their way to the pavilion and found Maia who was in her study with Lucas and Alistair. Zack quickly got their attention and introduced Caitlin. She and Alistair vaguely recognised each other and while she told them what had happened in Carlisse over the last few days, Lianna rushed to the house to fetch the other members of the group. When they arrived, Caitlin filled them in too and then looked desperately around the group, begging for their help.

"Without you, there is no way I'll be able to get Spencer and Nadia out of there. The king will hang them for treason once he's well enough, unless that awful female hunter helps him concoct an even worse punishment," Caitlin pleaded, worrying her bottom lip.

"Juliette, the hunter from the Empire is still in Carlisse?" Harrison questioned urgently.

"Yes, she's been there since the day you all left. And she's not alone anymore. When I got out of the city using the tunnel to my parent's ranch, they told me they'd seen an Imperial entourage on the road. The Imperator was there with her right hand, a blonde woman and a handful of guards," she explained.

"Do you think that's Siljanna?" Rylie asked, looking at Harrison after Caitlin mentioned the *'blonde woman'.*

"I'd bet my life on it. I should've guessed she'd seek allies in Siranor. With my father's old contacts, she must've gone straight to the top," Harrison replied.

"I don't care who's there or against us, we have to help Spencer and the queen," Lianna pressured, her tone as desperate as Caitlin's. "We'd never have found this place without their help, and I cannot leave them to die at the hands of that horrid king."

"King Grayson truly is an evil man," Maia interjected, her calm but firm tone getting everyone's attention. "Whatever punishment he derives will be cruel, a fate I wouldn't wish on anyone, least of all Alistair's former aide and the queen."

"Thank you!" Caitlin replied but her relief was short-lived as Maia raised her hand indicating she hadn't finished.

"That being said, I cannot risk the lives of my people or this place being discovered. I can permit a small group of guards to assist you but—" she paused, looking around each member of the group before her, "consider this, is it truly wise to attempt this rescue?"

Caitlin dropped her head in despair. She had nowhere else to turn and truly feared that she'd be leaving Arencia empty-handed.

"I'll go," Zack announced. Hearing his words, Lianna looked at him stunned and then threw her arms around him in thanks while Harrison looked at Rylie, reading her resolve and spoke up too.

"Count us in," he confirmed, causing the grateful smiles from both Caitlin and Lianna to widen.

"Then it's decided," Lucas asserted. "I will arrange and lead a small group of Aegis Guards to escort you. We can help infiltrate the city, find your friends and with any luck, escape undetected. If luck isn't on our side, we should have the force and experience to fight our way out."

"I want to come too!" Alex proclaimed, but harmoniously all his guardians refused.

"You can't Alex!" Lianna commanded.

"Why not?" He whined rebelliously.

"Your enthusiasm is great Alex, honestly," Harrison began. He really was proud of how far Alex had come in training but knew he had to persuade the young man to stay behind. "If the stealth mission goes awry, I would feel much better knowing an able fighter remains here. Can you do that for me?"

Initially, Alex shook his head, he knew what Harrison was trying to do, but eventually groaned and nodded.

"I'll stay back too," Evie advised quietly. "As much as I want to help, I'd just get in the way."

Rylie reached over and squeezed her little sister. She didn't have to say it but Evie knew that Rylie would feel much better knowing she was safe in Arencia. Evie and Alex stood together with Alistair behind them, indicating he would stay too.

"Although I can't risk my people, I can risk myself," Maia announced, surprising them again. "I will accompany you. My mystic talents could prove vital to your success. Besides, the last thing I want is to lose my guard captain and most recent recruit."

Caitlin looked up at each of them, tears rolling down her face as she found herself speechless. Lianna embraced her and uttered the words she was longing to hear.

"We'll save them, both of them," Lianna said with conviction, embracing Caitlin who clung to her words.

"Thank you all so much," she replied.

"Just give me some time to gather volunteers from the guard and get everyone protective gear, then we'll make our way to Carlisse," Lucas instructed, and as he did, the group dispersed, gathering what they needed to not only travel but to fight.

Chapter Twenty-One
Aegis Alliance

Nadia couldn't stop herself from shivering on the cold dungeon floor. When the guards had taken them, she'd still been in the skimpy nightdress that Grayson insisted she wore for their rendezvous, and it had been two nights since they'd been thrown in the dank cell. The only thing keeping her going was Spencer. He'd taken off his suit jacket, wrapping it around her at first but when he realised she was still cold, had cradled her body with his.

She knew he loved her and had for many years, but always told herself they could never be together as Grayson would likely kill him, or both of them if he found out. But now, lying on the floor in his arms, she didn't care. They were both going to face their own mortality soon anyway.

"I love you, Spencer," she whispered, unsure if he was even awake. There was a long silence and then he turned her gently so that she was lying on her back facing him.

"Tell me I didn't just dream that," he asked, staring longingly into her eyes. He watched her chest rise and fall, her pale skin flushing as she reached her hand up to caress his face.

"I love you," she repeated, pulling him towards her so she could kiss him. His lips were soft and gentle on hers but he kept his hands away. He'd already seen her naked dozens of times, having to heal the various bruises and cuts left on her skin by Grayson, but every time,

Spencer waited, only touching her when she allowed it. He would never take advantage or harm her.

She took one of his hands and placed it over her heart, allowing him to touch her for no other reason than desire. His gaze went to the hand she held and with it, he traced the outline of her chest. When he reached her slender waist, he stopped and she felt his hand shaking. When she looked at his face again, his eyes were closed as he breathed heavily.

"I've wished for this, for the longest time. To show you what true love is, how it should feel," he murmured.

"Show me now," she whispered, raising her body so that every part of her that could, was touching him. Despite her encouragement, he was still frozen, searching her eyes, and questioning if this moment was real.

To convince him, she opened the buttons of his shirt, slowly moving her hand down to his belt, stroking his chest along the way. He wasn't able to resist the intimacy of her touch for long and eventually, kissed her. After the first, he kissed her again and again; on the lips, down her neck and then lower, over her chest all the way to her belly button. Her body reacted to each kiss, lavishing his every passionate touch as she mumbled sweet nothings in his ear. After years of longing, Spencer was finally able to be with Nadia.

Warm for the first time in days, they fell asleep in each other's arms and remained that way until the guards came bursting in a few hours later.

"Get up, *your majesty*," called one of the guards, saying her title as sarcastically as he could.

"What do you want from her?!" Spencer hissed, protectively placing Nadia behind him.

"It's time to face the music. King Grayson is still recovering from the poison you slipped into his wine but has instructed us to ensure that the first thing he sees when he gets out of bed, is your execution," the guard announced.

Nadia buried her head into Spencer's shoulder, silently telling him she was going to submit, believing the situation hopeless.

"You can't take her!" Spencer exclaimed, desperately trying to think of a way to save her.

"And why not?" The guard asked callously.

"Queen Nadia is with child!" Spencer shouted, the words coming out before he thought them through. "So unless you want to be the one to tell the king you killed his unborn child, I suggest you leave her be."

Both guards fell silent as they looked at the queen. She too was speechless so Spencer tried to convince them further.

"How can you be sure?" The second guard enquired.

"You know who I am?" Spencer questioned.

"You're the mage servant from the royal library," replied the first guard.

"Indeed, I am a servant, but my magic is that of a healer. It is the reason King Grayson permits me to stay by the queen's side. I keep her healthy and can tell when she is with child. I am telling you now, the queen is pregnant," he insisted, his tone stern. The guards both nodded, turning towards the exit.

"We will inform the king," the first guard replied, departing the room. Before the second was able to leave, Nadia spoke up.

"Now that I am with child, can I see my parents? The dungeons are vast and I have not seen them since being here," she pleaded.

"That is not for me to decide. We will inform the king of your condition and follow his command on what to do with you next," he replied, shutting the dungeon door behind him.

After the guard was gone, Nadia released a whimper and collapsed, her knees turning to jelly beneath her. Spencer turned just in time to catch her.

"Spencer, how are we ever going to sustain this lie? He won't let my parents go until I deliver a child! I want to save them, but I just don't think I can carry on. I never want that monster to touch me again, not now that I have you," she admitted, allowing him to hold her upright. He kissed her again and, while gazing deeply into her eyes, spoke with conviction.

"Caitlin could help us maintain the ruse, at least until we come up with another plan," he affirmed, his voice filled with determination. Suddenly, Nadia looked at him with a clarity he hadn't expected.

"What if you were the father," she suggested, her hands shaking as she spoke. "You say that mages are immune to Encia, perhaps if I were pregnant with your child, the baby would survive!"

As he registered her words, he wanted nothing more than to agree, to be with her and give her the chance to have a child she could bring to term, which in turn would save her life and her parents, but doubt plagued him.

"Nadia, if the king ever found out, he'd kill you and the baby. I wouldn't survive that," Spencer confessed.

"But what if he doesn't find out? I've lived a half-life, my entire life Spencer. I would rather risk it all now for the chance to have just a fleeting life with you. Grant me that much," she pleaded, her tone desperate, begging for him to accept; and he did.

Lucas, Maia and a group of three Aegis Guards, including Noah were at the top of the crescent falls' platform when Caitlin and Lianna arrived, with Harrison, Rylie and Zack not far behind. As Caitlin looked at each member of the group, she truly believed that between them, they would find a way to save Spencer and Nadia, as long as it wasn't already too late. She was letting that thought worry her mind when Lucas approached.

"Our regiment is ready young lady. Some of our best warriors have volunteered for this mission. If there is any chance, we will rescue your friends," Lucas advised, attempting to comfort her.

"Thank you," she replied sincerely. "But we do have one problem. There is no way a group of armed soldiers can use the tunnel from my parent's ranch to Jonah's bakery without getting noticed."

"I had an idea about that," Zack said, stepping forward to address the group. "When we were last in Carlisse, we had *a lot* of reading to do but in one of the journals, Mr Auren detailed some other smuggler tunnels that he was using to help mages escape, as well as the one from Driftwood. One of them is on the northern edge of the city. It's larger, forming part of the sewer system and would take us much closer to the castle. It's our best option."

"Can you lead us to it, Zack?" His father asked.

"I believe so, the journals were very descriptive," he replied, shooting a smile at Rylie as they both silently thanked Alistair's flair for literature.

"Excellent work Zack," Maia added, and everyone looked decidedly pleased, except for Noah who scowled in silence.

Harrison noticed his expression and wondered why he was even there but figured Lucas or Maia had insisted. With his hubris so damaged, there was little chance he'd be a helpful addition to the team.

It took the whole day to reach the Northern edge of Carlisse and locate the tunnel Zack had spoken of. They were a fair way back from the city walls but directly behind the main keep and concealed by thick woodlands, which was an added bonus. As Lucas and the other guards set to work removing a grate that was blocking the tunnel; Zack, Maia and Lianna spoke to Caitlin to find out how to get inside the castle. With everyone busy and only Noah glaring at them with disdain, Harrison took the chance to pull Rylie aside.

"Rylie, can I talk to you for a moment?" He asked.

"Yes, of course, is everything okay?" She enquired, answering his question with a question. He nodded, keeping hold of her hand while checking her new gear.

Each of the warriors wore the Aegis Guard uniform apart from Zack and Harrison, who stayed in their armoured travelling clothes. Maia had also wanted to make sure that she, Rylie and Lianna had protective wear so asked Harrison to help improve the training garments they had, which he'd happily done.

He thought the sight of Rylie the night they danced on the lake would have been the most beautiful she'd ever look, but every time he'd seen her since, he found something even more stunning. Before him now, in the armour he'd helped to enhance, her hair tied back in her signature half-plaited ponytail and the twin daggers she'd trained with linked through her belt, she exuded a fierce beauty. He pulled her towards him and kissed her, almost forgetting what it was he wanted to say. She melted into him, completely receptive to his touch before gently pulling away.

"You know, that's not talking," she teased, her eyes glinting in the fading light.

"Some things can be said without words," he replied, matching her tone. She thought that was all he wanted and went to re-join Lianna but after a gentle tug, Harrison kept her close.

"I know I said before things between us would never change, but they have Rylie," he began, fixing his gaze on her hand.

"Harrison, I care for you. You know that right? I want us to have a future together, but if you're having doubts," she interrupted hastily, looking at him with concern. She tried to search his expression for what it was he truly wanted to say.

"I have no doubts… there's just so much I want to say to you—" he stammered, wishing he could express himself better.

"I'm here Harrison, I will always be here, with you. Take all the time you need," she replied and he visibly relaxed.

"So you are. It just seems too good to be true," he admitted, kissing her softly. She made a show of blowing out a long breath after his kiss, the air turning into an icy mist, making him smile.

"Shall we finish this conversation later?" She asked, her tone as light and warm as the air that surrounded them.

"I want you to have this," he began, reaching into his pocket and pulling out an odd-looking coin.

"What is it?" She asked inquisitively.

"It's the first thing I ever smelted back in my academy days, when I discovered I was good at smithing. It's not much but it's become somewhat of a lucky charm for me ever since. I want you to have it," he explained, holding out the coin to her.

She grasped his hand with the coin within for a moment, kissed his cheek and then took it gladly.

"I'll keep it close to my heart," she promised, placing it in the chest pocket of her shirt. "But I have nothing for you."

"I have all I need right here," he replied, kissing her again, more deeply this time.

During their conversation, Harrison and Rylie forgot Noah was watching them from his solitary perch. His blood boiled as he realised their relationship was more meaningful than he first thought. He couldn't help but feel that once again, Harrison had been victorious over him. With no one paying him any attention, Noah slipped away from the group vowing that Harrison would get his comeuppance, if it was the last thing he ever did.

Leaving his comrades and the rest of the group, Noah made his way around the walls to the main gatehouse, aiming to alert the royal guards of the insurgent force approaching from the North. Zack was the first to notice he'd disappeared.

"Hey, where's Noah?" He asked.

"No idea," Harrison replied.

"Maybe he's scouting the woods," Lucas suggested, automatically defending his eldest son.

"Maybe, but why didn't he tell anyone?" Zack queried, raising everyone's suspicions.

"There's bad blood between you, right?" Caitlin asked, aiming the question at Zack but was surprised when both he and Harrison confirmed the hostility.

"Do you think he would betray us?" Lianna asked, looking towards Lucas and Maia who had vouched for him.

"He can be bitter, but I don't believe he'd endanger us," Lucas replied, but his tone wasn't convincing.

"We can't assume that Lucas," Maia said, her voice firm. "Over the last few days, he's had to swallow a lot of pride. He may be scouting, but if he's abandoned our cause and intends to betray us, we need to get in and out fast."

Quickly agreeing not to wait for Noah as the other guards finished removing the grate, the group pressed on. Wading through the sewage tunnel was far from pleasant but before long, they found an established path and stairwell that took them into the lower level of the castle. Lucas was leading the group with Maia close behind until they approached a door to what sounded like a kitchen and he indicated for the group to stop. They heard a guard unit pass, talking loudly as they did.

"We must alert the king. Intruders are attempting to gain entry through the northern sewage tunnel!" Called the guard. It confirmed their worst fears about Noah and that they had to hurry if they were going to save Nadia and Spencer.

Once they heard the guard unit disperse, Lucas called Caitlin forward and asked her to enter the next room first. If other servants or workers were in there, they wouldn't be concerned by Caitlin's arrival. She carefully pushed through the kitchen door, checked the room and then waved the others inside.

"This is the secondary kitchen," she explained once the group were all together. "It's rarely used unless the king is hosting a banquet but that won't happen while he's unwell. From here, there are two paths to the dungeon. The first is through the keep but it'll likely be heavily guarded now. The other route is through the main dining hall. It should be empty at this time of day but we should still be cautious."

"What about security in the dungeon? Anything to worry about?" Lucas asked.

"Usually only two guards at the door. One of them will be the key-holder so we mustn't let either of them get away. Each cell has a unique lock so we'll need those keys," she replied.

"Fine, then I suggest that Caitlin, you lead me, Lianna and Zack to the dungeon. I'll secure the entrance while Zack obtains the keys and you girls can free your friends. Maia, stay close in case we need your magic," Lucas commanded and she agreed.

"Rylie and I will secure the route through the dining hall," Harrison offered, also supporting the plan.

"Good, I will instruct the other guards to keep this exit clear. If this area is compromised, there will be no escaping for any of us," Lucas concluded, heading over to the remaining guards to give them their orders.

With the plan in place, the group headed out. Once they pushed through the heavy doors into the dining hall, they came against a sight they foolishly hadn't even considered. Standing high above them on four separate balconies overlooking the grand room were Siljanna, Juliette, Cameron and Imperator Harlyn.

"Well, look at that, there are rats in this castle," Imperator Harlyn announced, looking down at them with a sickening grin. "Are these the people you've been hunting Siljanna?"

"Yes, that's my brother and the mage, Rylie Auren; my father's killers," she answered, gritting her teeth as she did.

"We didn't even need to spring our trap," Cameron added, mirroring the Imperator's expression. "And look at that, not just mages, they've brought an Ar'encal with them too."

"We are here for the queen and her aide, nothing more. If you intend to fight us, you will regret it," Maia threatened, displaying a show of force by using her psionic abilities to launch a pike from a nearby suit of armour into the wall above Juliette.

"You'll pay for that!" Juliette yelled, dodging the projectile. As she shouted and flailed, they could see she was holding a key and what looked like a spherical glass bottle. Harrison and Lucas drew their weapons, standing in front of the group, protecting them while Rylie took out her daggers and Zack drew his bow, aiming at the Imperator.

"I wouldn't do that spiky," Siljanna shouted towards Zack. "Not if Rylie ever wants to see her parents again."

"What did you say?" Rylie called out in shock, her eyes wide as she clenched the knife handles. All this time, she believed her parent's died in the tavern fire.

"Your parents, I have them in custody," Siljanna growled, her eyes piercing as she looked at Rylie. "They've been my prisoners since you fled Tivani. They're a little worse for wear but alive. Unlike how you left my father!"

"Don't forget to mention they're here in the dungeon," Cameron added in a cocky tone.

"Let them go!" Rylie screamed, flames travelling from her fingers down the blades.

"Make me," Siljanna argued, holding up another key just like the one in Juliette's possession before moving out of sight.

As soon as Siljanna was gone, Rylie was too, sprinting off down the path underneath the balcony she'd been on. Harrison quickly chased after her as well, leaving the rest of the group to deal with the others. Assuming the keys they'd flaunted were to the cells in the dungeon, Lucas shouted instructions for Zack and Lianna to go after Juliette while he and Maia tracked down Imperator Harlyn and Cameron, who had disappeared. Caitlin had also vanished without a trace or possibly created an illusion to mask where she hid.

Looking up towards Juliette, Lianna and Zack saw her turn sharply on her heels and head in the opposite direction to Siljanna. Zack didn't like the idea of splitting up but they had little choice. Lianna ran down the hall with Zack jogging briskly behind until they emerged in a small lounge area, once again with a balcony above them. Juliette was there, holding up the glass object they'd seen before but now, she'd tied the key to it.

"You want to free your friends? Here, catch!" She shouted, hurling the object towards Lianna.

"Lianna, look out!" Zack cried, pushing her out the way as the bottle smashed on the floor at his feet. The key tied around the top went skidding across the floor towards Lianna, but her attention was drawn straight back to Zack.

Whatever had been inside that bottle began to dissolve his leather boots but it was the vapours that caused the real damage. As she looked up at him from the floor, Lianna could feel the intense agony coursing through him. Shaking from the searing pain that made his every breath burn and blood stream from his eyes, Zack fell to his knees. In seconds, his throat had swollen so severely he couldn't scream, but Lianna did it for him.

The sound she made was blood-curdling and hearing her, Maia and Lucas came charging into the room. They initially headed towards Lianna, believing her to be the one in pain, but with tears streaming down her face, they saw her clawing across the floor to Zack's side, and once they noticed him, Maia and Lucas rushed to his aid. Lucas pulled him away from the burning liquid on the floor as Maia crashed to her knees and began healing him.

She focused all her attention on his throat to ensure he could breathe and then on the rest of his face. Lianna had made it to his side and was shaking ferociously, scared but desperate to touch him, needing to know if he was okay. Thankfully, he'd passed out so Lianna no longer felt his pain but when Maia took her hands away without a word, Lianna looked to the other woman, desperately questioning.

"Is he... please tell me he's okay!" Lianna begged, her voice trembling.

"He'll survive," Maia replied, allowing Lucas and Lianna to breathe sighs of relief. "I restored his airways in time but—"

"But what?" Lianna questioned.

"I fear the damage to his eyes could be permanent. He may be blind," Maia stammered between heavy breaths. As she registered

Maia's words, Lianna gasped, falling back and covering her mouth with her still shaking hands while Lucas hung his head, cradling his unconscious son.

Leaving them to process their grief, Maia stepped away and grabbed the key that was lying on the floor. As she did, Caitlin and the other Aegis Guards emerged. Two of the guards collected Zack and promised their captain they would carry him to safety. Watching them take him away, Lianna felt her heart literally torn in two directions, part of her wanting to rescue Spencer and the other, to remain with Zack. She chose to trust the Aegis Guards and joined Caitlin and Maia as they headed down into the dungeon to find Spencer and Nadia.

Lucas remained at the door, also longing to go with his son but knowing he needed to keep the area clear for the others. Maia handed the key over to Caitlin and as she rushed down the stairs, she was elated when she saw both Nadia and Spencer in the cell nearest to the door.

"Caitlin! How did you get here?" Spencer exclaimed, rushing to reach the bars as soon as he saw her.

"I escaped just after you were arrested and got help from Lianna and the others. They're here now, and we're going to get you out!" She replied, slotting the key into the padlock on their door. It turned with a loud click and as soon as the mechanism was released, Caitlin threw it on the floor and flung the door open.

As she did, Lianna arrived and when she spotted Spencer, with his arm wrapped around Nadia, she could feel that something had changed between them, their relationship somehow deeper. When he looked up and saw her, he smiled.

"You came for us, thank you," he said, having no clue what had been sacrificed to do so. She couldn't speak of it now and just tried to return his smile. They were about to leave when a quiet voice from within the dungeon called to them.

"Wait! Don't leave us here," a fragile female voice cried.

"Please, can you let us out?" added an exhausted male voice.

Caitlin focused on getting Spencer and Nadia out while Lianna and Maia cautiously stepped deeper into the dungeon to find out where the voices had come from. Finding another couple, huddled together, badly beaten and shaking in a cell, Lianna approached the bars.

"Oh my, what happened to you?" She asked, their fear and pain resonating within her.

"We've been prisoners of a woman called Siljanna Stone for weeks now. She took us from our home and tortured us, all in an attempt to find our daughters and her brother who she blames for crimes they didn't commit," the man said, his voice strained although he was desperately trying to remain strong.

"We have to escape, Siljanna plans to use us as bait to capture them. Please, will you help us?" The woman asked and Lianna recognised that the people before her had to be Rylie's parents.

She reached over, grabbed the key and tried it on their padlock, but it didn't work. It was just as Caitlin had said, each of the cells had unique locks.

"I'm sorry, the key doesn't work," Lianna began to say and thinking that she was going to leave them, Paige crumbled into her husband's arms and began to cry.

"We don't need a key," Maia growled clearly having seen enough cruelty, using her psionic abilities to twist the metal bars wide enough so they could escape.

"Thank you, thank you so much," Paige mewled as she and Nate slipped out of the cell.

"Wait, are you Paige and Nate Auren?" Lianna asked, making them stop in their tracks and face their liberators.

"Who are you, how do you know our names?" Nate asked suspiciously.

"My name is Lianna Flynn, I am friends with both of your daughters, Rylie and Evie; Harrison too. Most of us are here in the castle, helping our friends escape. If you come with us, I can reunite you," she answered and the fear she'd previously sensed from them was quickly replaced by hope.

"You can take us to our girls?" Paige asked, her voice brimming with hope although some anxiety remained.

"Yes, but please, we must hurry! When we parted ways, Rylie and Harrison were chasing after Siljanna. She has the key to your cell, which they think we still need," she replied as they all ran up the stairs and out of the dungeon.

When they were back in the lounge area; Caitlin, Lucas, Spencer and Nadia were urging the rest of them to get moving. Realising they were intending to go, Nate took Paige by the hand and told her he couldn't leave until he found Rylie and Harrison. As much as she clearly didn't want to leave her husband, Paige reluctantly let the others lead her away.

As they headed back towards the kitchen to re-join the Aegis Guards, Maia offered to join Nate as he searched for Rylie and Harrison. She could see the family resemblance to Alistair instantly but knew she shouldn't mention that now as he currently thought his father was dead. Taking that in while escaping captivity and trying to find his daughter would be too much for anyone to process. Suddenly, they heard a loud, thunderous crack and ran as quickly as they could towards it.

Having dashed down the hall after Siljanna, Rylie could hear the other girl's footsteps for what felt like an eternity, but couldn't see her. She had to get that key and free her parents at any cost. She arrived at a crossing of four corridors, and it was only the sound of footsteps above, that made her veer right. The corridor was long and narrow so she sprinted, looking back just before she reached the end to see Harrison distantly behind her. She decided she couldn't wait and pushed through the door at the end of the hall which opened out to a small courtyard.

The area was adorned with several arches and stairways that all reached up onto the castle walls. Rylie scanned the area until her vision landed on Siljanna, striding purposefully down the stairs on the far side. Before Rylie could do anything, she felt someone grab her from behind, knocking the daggers from her hands and restraining her tightly with solid iron cuffs. She urgently pulled against the restraints but to no avail. As she looked over her shoulder, she discovered she was being held by the Imperator's right hand, Cameron Weiss. Throwing her gaze back at Siljanna, Rylie realised she'd drawn a gun and was aiming it directly at her chest.

"Siljanna, no! Remember our arrangement," Cameron shouted but Siljanna continued as if she couldn't hear him.

Her body was reacting to her deepest desire for revenge. With her eyes fixated on Rylie, she looked to her enemy's hands and saw the flames once again flickering around her fingertips. Her mind recoiled, back to the night of the tavern fire and her father's death. Shaking her head, refusing to let reason stop her, she knew what she had to do and pulled the trigger.

The bullet whistled through the air and found a target, but not the one Siljanna had intended. Harrison had arrived just in time and stepped between his sister and Rylie, intercepting the shot. The bullet pierced through his chest, knocking him off his feet and sending him crashing to the floor.

"*No!*" Rylie screamed, looking at Harrison who laid motionless on the floor. Her scream ripped through her throat and as she shook, the ground beneath them began to tremble. There was a loud crack of thunder as a bolt of lightning struck the area behind her, sparks exploding in every direction as it hit Cameron and he collapsed to the floor, dead. As Rylie tore her eyes away from Harrison, a single tear rolled down her cheek and froze mid-descent, shattering as it hit the floor.

Focussing on Siljanna, her rage and devastation overwhelming, the flames that had originally just been around her fingers spread.

The heat was so intense that it melted the iron restraints binding her and coiled up her skin, engulfing her entire body. The curls of her warm brown hair began to burn, the tips literally becoming flames, and her cool, peaceful eyes burned like an intense heat. In mere seconds, she had embodied the element of fire.

Siljanna's eyes darted from Harrison to Rylie as the realisation of what she'd done sunk in. She dropped her gun and staggered back a few steps, looking at Rylie but seeing none of the scared girl she'd torn away from the burning tavern door just a few weeks ago. Instead, before her was quite possibly the most terrifying thing Siljanna had ever witnessed.

Refusing to succumb to cowardice, Siljanna raised her chin high, prepared to join the rest of her family in death when suddenly she was grabbed and pulled into the room behind her, just as Rylie launched a fireball. Siljanna tumbled backwards as the stranger that saved her bolted the door, hurried her down the corridor and through another door, sealing it as well. They heard Rylie scream, the noise visceral, as she crashed against the first barricade.

"Who are you?" Siljanna demanded of the stranger.

"My name's Noah Harper but more importantly, that *thing* after you is called an aeon. If you want to live, follow me. When we are out of imminent danger, I can tell you more," he explained, directing her up a narrow set of stairs onto the upper level and back towards the dining hall.

When Maia and Nate arrived at the courtyard, they saw the blackened marks on the floor from the lightning strike and the corpse of Cameron Weiss, his skin singed from the force that struck him. Next, they just caught a glimpse of who Maia knew was Rylie, every inch of her covered with flames, but before she could do anything, Rylie kicked down the door before her and disappeared. That was when she heard yet another cry.

"Harrison!" Nate shouted, skidding to the floor beside him. Maia, having some empathic powers, could feel that Nate cared for Harrison like a son and followed his gaze to see the bullet wound. He was still bleeding, but that was a good thing because it meant he was still alive. Nate immediately applied pressure to the wound but when Maia darted over, she placed her hands above his and immediately allowed healing energy to emanate from her, through Nate's hands and down to Harrison.

Nate couldn't help but stare at the Ar'encal who he'd met just minutes ago and realised that if she saved Harrison's life, he would already owe her two debts of gratitude that could never be repaid. After a tense few moments, Harrison's eyes fluttered open and he groaned, rolling onto his side. He tried to stand but was clearly still weakened from the impact and staggered. Nate caught him and allowed Harrison to lean against him. When he realised it was Nate supporting him, Harrison's knees gave way from shock.

"Nate?" He asked dubiously, unable to believe what his eyes were seeing. "You're alive!"

Nate slipped his arm under Harrison's, taking his full weight, while Maia reached down and collected his sword. It was almost as big as her but she carried it with grace.

"I am, Paige too! Your friends saved us," Nate advised, still grateful to the other group.

"What happened?" Harrison asked, looking around and seeing the devastation in the courtyard.

"It's Rylie," Maia announced, causing both Nate and Harrison to look at her. "She's become an elemental aeon. I'm sorry, there is nothing I can do for her now, we have to get away from this place but I promise I will explain everything when we get to safety."

Realising that Maia was referring to the embodiment of fire they'd seen a moment ago, Nate was the first to react.

"That was my daughter? That was Rylie?" He asked, his tone equally shocked and terrified.

"We can't just leave her Maia, what if Siljanna gets to her?" Harrison demanded, trying to hold himself up rather than leaning on Nate.

"It's not Rylie you need to worry about, but your sister. She is the one in danger now. Please, we must go," Maia replied urgently. Having never heard her speak in such a grave tone, Harrison reluctantly agreed and Nate trusted his judgement.

The three of them made their way as quickly as they could to the others. Although Maia's healing had gone a long way, Harrison still needed aid. As they reached the dining hall once more, the sight before them was again not what they'd expected.

Lucas and the other Aegis Guards had found and cornered Imperator Harlyn. She was standing with her hands raised in surrender, her intelligent eyes searching for any of her own soldiers. Nate instinctively wanted to beat her senseless for allowing Siljanna to torture him and his wife, but Harrison stopped him in favour of getting information from her.

"You aided my sister in her hunt for us, why?" Harrison demanded. The Imperator looked at him in disgust, earning nothing but a blade thrust towards her throat.

"Answer the question, or lose your ability to answer," Lucas threatened. Although she hadn't been the one to injure his son, she'd been complicit.

"Power, why else? I needed a mage brought to me alive and this seemed like the perfect opportunity to get one," she hissed, shifting her gaze from Lucas to Nate and finally landing on Harrison as she spoke.

Above them, on the same balcony as before, Siljanna and Noah were crouched below the parapet, trying to sneak away before Rylie could find them. Witnessing Harlyn trapped and speaking about her, Siljanna hesitated. Noah tried to force her to continue but when she saw Harrison alive, she refused; standing to take in the sight of him and enjoy a moment of relief. Noah waved a frustrated hand gesture before abandoning her.

"So much for being my saviour," she muttered under her breath as she continued to eavesdrop on the scene below.

"How would getting a mage bring you power?" Nate asked, stupefied. After everything he and his wife had endured, he found himself needing to know that answer.

"Over the last year, I enhanced an Encia absorbing substance and I wanted to test it on a true mage, rather than just a useless descendant. If it works as intended, the Empire could finally weaponise magic, proving once and for all our dominance by destroying the Ar'encal and overthrowing this feudal kingdom," she declared, and he found the answer only provoked him further, but Nate wasn't the only one.

Hearing her words, Maia pushed passed the others and punched the Imperator as hard as she could, causing Harlyn to crash into the wall.

"It's that kind of thinking that started the Uprising! Forcing my race and our supporters into hiding for the last twenty-five years isn't enough for you? You really have such hatred for us and our connection to the planet that you intend to eradicate us?" Maia screamed.

"Yes," the Imperator replied directly, staring at Maia while wiping the blood from her lip.

"But why us?" Harrison asked again. "Why help Siljanna in her vendetta? Surely you knew there was a risk she'd try to kill Rylie. To me, you've lost more than you gained, as your right-hand lies dead outside."

Hearing of Cameron's death threw Imperator Harlyn, but only for a moment.

"Call it poetic justice. You see, my breakthrough discovery came from my uncle, whose body your father kindly delivered to me... after he killed your mother," she said sadistically, enjoying her captor's reaction.

"How can that be?" Harrison demanded furiously.

The only person in the room feeling it equally was Siljanna, who remained tucked out of sight, her relief at learning Harrison lived quickly destroyed by the realisation she'd been played for a fool.

"It's all rather simple when you have all the pieces of the puzzle," Harlyn added venomously. "My uncle, Dr Elias Rainer had been forced to flee Siranor after the council accused him of murdering my father. We'd been working for years at the institute, mainly on Encia related projects but when he was forced to leave, we couldn't finish our vital work."

Imperator Harlyn paused, smiling snidely when she knew everyone in the room was listening to her with intent.

"What does that have to do with my mother's death?" Harrison growled, losing his patience.

"My uncle had several theories which he tried to test outside the city but without our technology, he succumbed to the withering. In what little time he had left, he wrote his best theories down and was trying to get those notes to me. As a wanted man, the only way he was getting into Siranor was in a body bag. To ensure his death would not be in vain and his body sent to me at the institute, he had to commit a heinous crime as close to the capital as possible. Your mother was just in the wrong place at the right time," she explained, and as the words sunk in, Harrison's eyes went wide with disbelief.

His brain raced back to that night; recalling his struggle to reach his mother, Morgan trying to talk her captor down and his father standing beside the scene, frozen.

"Is that why my father didn't take him down?" Harrison asked. "Because he knew it was Dr Rainer holding my mother and felt obligated to take him back to Siranor alive?"

"Possibly, but if that was his desire, he was destined to fail and sealed your mother's fate. My uncle was willing to do whatever it took to reach me, and he did. His notes and a letter explaining everything were tucked in his cloak and proved invaluable to me; well worth sacrificing one pointless woman."

"How dare you!" Harrison yelled, lunging towards the Imperator. "She was my *mother*!"

"And he was *my father*! At least I believe he was," the Imperator barked back, breathing heavily despite the blade still held precariously close to her throat. "When I caught word of your sister's plight, hunting down a renegade mage that murdered her father, it was the ideal situation."

Taking in everything the Imperator said, Siljanna slumped against the parapet, tears rolling down her face. Harrison and Morgan had been right the whole time, her hatred of mages was unjustified. Dr Elias Rainer, a man with the withering killed her mother, and her father really hadn't stopped it. She was just about to continue her retreat when Imperator Harlyn began laughing hysterically.

"What haven't you told us?" Harrison demanded.

"I guess there is no point in hiding the truth. I may have *adjusted* your father's autopsy results to further drive your sister's hatred," Imperator Harlyn boasted. "He was intoxicated but had no paralyzing injuries. Siljanna was so blinded by loyalty to him that I knew, if she thought you contributed to his death, she'd ignore the facts and relentlessly hunt you down."

"You're a monster," Harrison exclaimed.

"If we'd accounted for your allies today, believe me, you would've learnt just how monstrous I can be," she replied maliciously.

Hearing the truth drove Siljanna into a murderous rage. She had felt betrayed by her brother and Rylie every day since the tavern fire, and everything she'd done since was to make them pay for that. Now, it turned out, she'd actually been betrayed by her new allies, and that was too much to bear. She was about to stand and raise her gun but then realised she'd dropped it after shooting Harrison while watching

Rylie become whatever she was now, an aeon as her cowardly saviour had phrased it.

At that moment, Rylie came crashing through the door behind Siljanna, forcing her to vault over the parapet, dropping to the room below. When Harrison saw her, she sprinted towards the corridor closest to where they'd cornered Harlyn and made it apparent to the Imperator that she wasn't going to help her.

"Siljanna, you traitor!" The Imperator cried, not realising she'd overheard everything, but Siljanna couldn't have cared less. She hoped Harlyn died for her lies.

Just as Siljanna made it into the corridor, Rylie hurled another fireball, the flames igniting some nearby solution. The liquids combusted and resulted in a small but loud explosion that startled Lucas and the other guards enough for Imperator Harlyn to escape.

No one pursued her however as all of their gazes were fixated on Rylie as she charged across the balcony continuing her pursuit of Siljanna until she was out of sight again. Every bone in Harrison's body wanted to go after her but Maia prevented him.

"I told you, we cannot help her yet. We must go!" Maia commanded sternly. With little other choice and still sore from the gunshot wound, Harrison and the others retreated to the sewer exit in the kitchen.

When Harrison saw Zack unconscious on the floor by the exit, his eyes were drawn to Lianna sobbing beside him. He looked urgently to everyone in the room, his eyes questioning.

"It was the mage hunter," Lucas said, answering his unspoken question. "We need to get him home, now."

The return journey to Iliria took longer than before, with the Aegis Guards having crafted a makeshift stretcher for Zack but carrying him made them all walk slower. When they arrived in town, they rested at the inn and picked up a few supplies for the onward trek to Arencia.

Hearing their plan to continue on, Spencer announced that he and Nadia were going to stay in Iliria with the intention of returning to

Carlisse once aeon Rylie was gone. With Nadia's help, he explained to everyone, but mainly Caitlin the ruse they'd devised.

"How can you think you'll be safe there?" Maia asked, baffled by the announcement, the plan and more than a little annoyed because they'd sacrificed so much to get them out of the city in the first place.

"We won't return straight away and are both truly grateful for your aid, but if we don't return and continue this ruse, Nadia won't be able to save her parents," Spencer explained.

"With Rylie in pursuit of Siljanna, she'll have to escape the city and with all her support gone, the Imperator will likely depart soon too," Nadia added.

"It's unlikely given what just happened that Juliette will stay in Carlisse either so in theory, it's going to be the best place for us to be," Spencer finished, hoping the others understood. It was clear Caitlin was going to take some persuading but they believed they would get her support.

As Harrison and the rest of the group continued preparing to return to Arencia, Spencer approached Lianna.

"Lianna, I just wanted to thank you again. I don't know how I can truly express my gratitude," Spencer began, trying to get her attention. She remained glued to Zack's side and barely even looked at Spencer when he spoke. "I know you must've been the one to persuade the others to help Caitlin save us."

"It wasn't me, it was Zack," she murmured, softly running her hand through the spikes of his hair.

"I'm truly sorry about what happened to him. Is there anything I can do?" He asked, his remorse sincere.

"If Maia cannot heal him, then I doubt you can," she replied, her voice cold. He recoiled, making her recognise how harsh she'd come across. "I didn't mean to sound like that. I'm sorry, thank you for offering."

"Please, thank him for us when he wakes. I hope he recovers and that his sight is somehow restored," Spencer concluded, wanting to say more but deciding to leave her be.

Lianna watched as he returned to Nadia and kissed her softly. She felt her heart wrench, not with longing, but regret. Caitlin had been right, Spencer would always love Nadia; Lianna could see that now. When she felt a squeeze on her hand, her mind was immediately drawn back to Zack.

"Lianna?" He whispered, his voice shaky. "Lianna, is that you? I can't see you. I can't see anything."

"It's me, Zack. I'm here," she replied, breathing short, sharp breaths as she tried to hold back more tears. "You've been hurt so don't try to open your eyes, okay."

"Are you crying, Lianna?" He asked, genuinely worried by her ragged breathing. "Why are you sad?"

His question made her troubled breathing even harder as she wanted to laugh and cry.

"Here you lay, wounded and possibly blind… and you're worried about me?!" She questioned in total disbelief.

"Yeah, I am," he replied, squeezing her hand again.

"Zack, I'm crying because what happened to you should've happened to me. I was the reckless one and you pushed me out the way. All the pain you felt, the wounds you have, it's all my fault!" She cried.

As the words escaped her, she buried her head into his chest, the tears falling again. After a moment, she felt him raise an arm and gently wrap it around her, allowing her to cry into him.

"I'd do it again in a heartbeat," he whispered. After he spoke, she shot up to look at him, the redness around his eyes still incredibly prominent.

"Why would you say that?" She exclaimed. "Why would you even think that?"

"I would never want someone I love to go through this... never," he replied, and she knew he meant it.

For the first time, she could feel how genuine a person he was, and how true his love for her had been. Lost for words, she clutched onto his hand and instructed him to rest. They would soon return to Arencia.

Epilogue

Evie woke with a feeling of dread. She'd dozed off waiting for the others to return but during her slumber, had the same vision she'd experienced on the night her home burnt down; a vision of skin burning. She shook it off and walked to the pavilion meeting her grandfather and Alex along the way. When they spotted the platform from the falls receding, her concerns were distracted as they rushed to greet the others.

Evie's first sight was almost unbelievable, it was her parents. With tears flooding down her face, she ran to them, momentarily overjoyed. Then she saw Harrison, clearly wounded but trying not to make a fuss and Zack, being stretchered in behind him. She wanted to ask what happened but Lianna and the Aegis Guards took Zack straight to the infirmary.

Shaking his head and looking quickly between Evie and his sister, Alex made the split decision to follow Lianna and after having a quiet word with Maia, Lucas left too. Alistair cautiously approached when he saw his son for the first time in nearly twenty-five years. Nate, who until that moment had no idea his father was alive, recognised him instantly and faced the awkward reunion. Alistair introduced himself to Paige in a true, gentlemanly fashion until both he and Evie realised that Rylie was nowhere to be seen. They turned to Harrison to ask, but Maia stepped forward to explain what had happened in Carlisse.

After detailing Noah's betrayal, the Imperator's ambush and the attacks on both Zack and Harrison; Rylie's transformation, their escape and the revelation of Queen Nadia and Spencer's plan, Evie was left in silent shock. When Maia mentioned the term *aeon*, Alistair's reaction made Harrison seek a proper explanation.

"What does that mean? You keep referring to Rylie as an aeon but what is an aeon?" Harrison asked, his tone both worried and impatient.

"Until now, I considered it a myth. In the eighty-nine years of my life, I've never seen an Ar'encal or mage transform," she began, looking to the walls of the pavilion which were engraved with drawings of their deities.

"Eighty-nine?" Paige whispered, not the only one momentarily distracted by her actual age but quickly refocused as Maia continued.

"It was believed by our ancestors that the year a child was born, would indicate what their greatest mystical talent would be. Similarly, when the half-race children came to be, it was thought that those mage children, if they triggered the ability of the deity whose year they were born in, would be... special," Maia explained, pausing to look at each of Rylie's loved ones.

"That's an understatement Maia and you know it," Alistair accused, looking to his peer and encouraging her to speak openly.

"Fine, the truth is those children, both Ar'encal and mage were believed to have the potential to embody the power of their birth god. I've never seen it myself but those who attained such abilities were called *aeons*. Can I safely assume Rylie was born twenty-one years ago?" She asked.

"Yes, Rylie is twenty-one," Paige answered, instinctively.

"Then, by our calendar, she was born in 336-Talia, the year of the elemental goddess, and she is an elemental mage. I believe her combined grief and rage at what she thought was your death Harrison, has turned Rylie into a fire aeon," Maia concluded.

"Is there a way to fix this, to get my daughter back?" Nate asked, his gaze darting between Maia and Alistair.

"There is, but it will not be easy," Maia answered. "We'll have to create a suppression rune, similar to the one we bestow upon the Aegis Guard but on something that we can place easily upon Rylie. Then, if we can let her see that Harrison is alive, her parents too, I believe she can regain control of her body and mind."

As she finished speaking, she could see the solid looks of resolve on each of their faces, especially Harrison.

"Just tell me what is required and I will create something that can bear the suppression rune. Whatever it takes, I'm getting Rylie back," Harrison insisted, his voice filled with determination. Maia smiled, feeling an even deeper respect for him.

"Even if you can create the suppression rune, how will we find Rylie? Where is she going?" Paige asked.

"I can't tell you where, but I can tell you who. Rylie will be going after Siljanna," Harrison advised, taking in a deep breath at the thought of confronting his sister again.

"Do you think she survived? Escaped Carlisse?" Nate asked, unsure that such a feat was possible.

"The biggest mistake we could make is to underestimate my sister. She escaped, I know it," Harrison replied.

After dashing past them in the dining hall and evading the explosive blast, Siljanna had escaped and fled Carlisse, heading North-west until she reached the town of Beyasil. She'd heard of a small port there and planned to barter travel on a ship back to the Western continent. She told herself putting a large body of water between herself and the fiery being Rylie had become was the most sensible course of action, but also knew she needed help.

Her first thought was to return to Siranor and hope that she could appeal to Charlie but quickly ruled that out. By abandoning Imperator Harlyn, albeit for good reason, whether she'd survived or not meant any reception in the capital would not be a welcome one.

Her next thought was Juliette, but she ruled her out too. She was a manipulator, not the type of person you entrusted with your life. Deep down she knew who she really wanted—her brother, Harrison. Maybe it wasn't too late to reconcile her grievous mistakes and unite with him. The only way she could think to reach him however was by returning to Tivani and speaking to Morgan. If there was anyone outside of his current allies Harrison would contact, it was him. As she made her way cautiously through the small seaside town, another familiar face found her, Dylan Rose.

Imperator Harlyn stared at the ground before her, having evaded imminent death and found herself hiding in the royal wing of the Carlisse castle. The view from the windows looked out over the city and to her shock, she saw Siljanna escape. The flaming creature that had caused the explosion in the dining hall soon stalked down the same path, clearly in pursuit, but although Harlyn enjoyed the fact that Siljanna's treachery came at a price, she wasn't prepared to assume the fiery being would kill her. An enemy of Harlyn's was an enemy of the Empire and she intended to use her position of power to eliminate her enemies. And not just Siljanna, but all of them; the Ar'encal, the mages, their guardians and anyone else who stood in her way.

As she made her way through the castle, she marched towards the king's bedchamber. He refused to see her so she shouted through his door that she was returning to Siranor and that his support would be expected in the events to come. A few hours later, she'd made the preparations for passage back to Yasras and sent word to Juliette so that she would know where to go if she wished to remain loyal.

As she departed the city with her guards, Harlyn was surprised to be stopped at the gate, not by any member of the royal guard, but by a solitary man wearing a uniform that looked identical to the ones worn by the men that threatened her. She was about to order her guards to attack when he raised his hands in surrender and announced that he just wanted to talk.

"Speak; once I hear what you have to say, I will decide if you will live past this encounter," Harlyn called out, indicating for the guards to raise their weapons.

"My name is Noah Harper. I was part of the group that supports Harrison Stone. *Was*," he emphasised and paused. When she didn't command the guards to attack, he continued. "I turned my back on those people and want to help you defeat them."

"Why would you do that?" She asked curiously.

"I have an innate desire to see certain members of that group suffer, and siding with you will allow me to achieve that," he announced boldly.

"An alliance then, for now," Harlyn offered with no intention of trusting him, but certain she could use him.

"What's your first move?" Noah asked, joining her in the carriage.

"A reckoning!" Harlyn replied, with deadly intent.

Ingram Content Group UK Ltd.
Milton Keynes UK
UKHW020833140723
425125UK00008B/301